"CONTACTS!" Fitz screamed.

He swung his MK11 up just as one of the creatures grabbed the marine next to him on the dock. The monster plucked his head off with the ease of a man popping the tail off a shrimp. The sound of the man's skull disconnecting from his spine made Fitz's stomach roll. He angled his MK11 up, chambered a round, and shot the monster in the right eye, blowing out the back of its head over the water.

Rico grabbed Fitz and pulled him away from the ramp as two more of the beasts emerged, their claws gripping the top gate of the landing craft. Their talons shrieked over the metal as they pulled themselves up.

"Move!" Rico screamed. "Get back to the MATV!"

Fitz fired off two more rounds as soon as a pair of bulbous eyes emerged over the side of the ramp. One of the creatures opened its mouth and sucked down a round that exited through the armor lining its neck. The second juvenile jerked to the left an instant too late, and Fitz shot it in the skull. Chunks of armor and flesh peppered his helmet.

"On the Two-Forties!" he yelled, waving to the other vehicles. He pushed his mini-mic to his lips and opened the channel to Team Ghost. "Dohi, get on the big gun!"

Marines emerged from their MATVs and climbed into the turrets, swerving the automatic weapons into position. Within seconds the whine of 7.62-millimeter rounds sounded, echoing in the enclosed space. They streaked in all directions, smashing through armored plates and sending juveniles spinning down to watery graves.

EXTINCTION AFTERMATH

The Extinction Cycle
Book Six

NICHOLAS SANSBURY SMITH

www.orbitbooks.net

Copyright © 2016 by Nicholas Sansbury Smith
Excerpt from *Extinction War* copyright © 2017 by
Nicholas Sansbury Smith
Excerpt from *Six Wakes* copyright © 2017 by Mary Lafferty

Author photograph by Maria Diaz
Cover design by Lisa Marie Pompilio
Cover art by Blake Morrow
Cover copyright © 2017 by Hachette Book Group, Inc.

Orbit
Hachette Book Group
1290 Avenue of the Americas
New York, NY 10104
orbitbooks.net

Originally self-published in 2016
Published in ebook by Orbit in February 2017
First Mass Market Edition: October 2017

Orbit is an imprint of Hachette Book Group.
The Orbit name and logo are trademarks of Little, Brown Book Group Limited.

The publisher is not responsible for websites (or their content) that are not owned by the publisher.

The Hachette Speakers Bureau provides a wide range of authors for speaking events. To find out more, go to www.hachettespeakersbureau.com or call (866) 376-6591.

ISBNs: 978-0-316-55820-4 (mass market), 978-0-316-55818-1 (ebook)

Printed in the United States of America

OPM

10 9 8 7 6 5 4 3 2 1

For Jeni Rico

You left this world way too early, but your smile and memory will always live on. Team Ghost salutes you, "Sergeant."

We shall defend our island, whatever the cost may be, we shall fight on the beaches, we shall fight on the landing grounds, we shall fight in the fields and in the streets, we shall fight in the hills; we shall never surrender.

—*Winston Churchill*

Prologue

A tidal wave of darkness washed over the cobblestone streets of Rome. Sergeant Piero Angaran and Lieutenant Antonio LoMaglio watched the wall of black swallow up steeples and rooftops, rising over the skyline, inching closer to the bridge where they stood.

Piero lowered his Beretta ARX160 assault rifle as the crimson yolk of the sun retreated below the horizon. Piero and Antonio retreated, too. And they were running out of time to get back to their shelter.

Tossing back his head, Piero swallowed his last two stimulants and chased them down with a swig of wine from his hydration pack. For the first time in his life, he longed for water instead of wine. But clean water, like everything else in Rome, was in short supply.

"Come on," Antonio insisted. There was panic in his voice, unusual for a man who usually laughed and cracked jokes.

Antonio flipped his night-vision goggles over his eyes and waved Piero forward. They ran side by side across the historic bridge spanning the Tiber.

Rome had been sacked before over the centuries, but she had always risen from the ashes of conquest. The Gauls, Visigoths, Normans, and even the troops of the

Holy Roman Emperor Charles V had tried to bring her down. But now demons had accomplished what humans couldn't. The unholy beasts controlled Rome, and there were only two men left to defend the ancient city.

Piero and Antonio were the last remaining members of their unit, part of the Fourth Alpini Parachutist Regiment. They had fought together in Afghanistan against the Taliban and in Iraq against Al-Qaeda, surviving in wilderness and desert against overwhelming forces. But it had only taken a single night for the juvenile Varianti to slaughter their brothers.

Their mission to take back the city had failed. Everyone was dead. Now, two weeks later, Piero and Antonio were running on fumes. They were exhausted, starving, and injured. Today they'd made a rookie mistake by not returning to their shelter before the sun went down. The juveniles were most active at night.

Despite having his friend and team leader by his side, Piero had never felt more lonely or helpless in his life. They had discovered only a handful of survivors trapped in the city. The last of those had been killed three days prior, ripped to shreds by a juvenile Varianti that had tracked them to their bunker.

Piero blinked away the memory and dragged a tattered sleeve across his forehead. He would need to reapply more repellent later when they got back. The German-made liquid worked like bug spray, but it was composed of chemicals that smelled much worse. The smell was the least of his worries. Neither of the men had showered for weeks, not since they had parachuted into the city. They still wore the same green fatigues, though they looked more like rags pulled from a garbage bin now.

Antonio held up a hand and took a knee in a single motion. He centered his ARX160 on a statue of three muscular men dressed in robes. Piero mimicked the lieutenant's action, pressing the scope of his rifle to his NVGs. Nothing moved in the green-hued view. He raked his weapon from left to right, dividing his line of sight into thirds and checking each one for motion. The crosshairs fell on a body lying facedown. Bones protruded out of the corpse's shirt where a Varianti had pulled out the lungs like the Viking blood eagle ritual.

Satisfied the area was free of contacts, Antonio waved them forward.

The two continued across the bridge, the Tiber flowing strongly beneath them. Water churned across the red hull of an overturned speedboat. Piero examined a park on their right that overflowed with vegetation left unchecked. Vines crawled up the stone façade of an adjacent building. It hadn't taken long for the grass and weeds to reclaim parts of Rome. Nature had gone on without humanity.

The next street took them through an open market with dozens of restaurants and stores. Bodies stripped clean of flesh littered the ground amongst upturned tables and tattered umbrellas. Glass had piled under shattered windows. In every storefront Piero passed he saw faces—the faces of people who had once dined and shopped inside. When he was a child, his parents had taken him and his sister to Rome every summer. He would stuff himself with Carbonara while his parents ate seafood risotto and shared a bottle of Pinot Noir. Afterward, they would gorge themselves on gelato from a little shop near Trevi Fountain.

When in Rome, do as the Romans do.

He had always liked that quote. Before the hemorrhage virus had changed everything seven months ago, going with the flow had been an easy thing to do in Italy. Now it meant dying.

Rome was the hardest hit of the Italian cities. And Italy was one of the hardest hit countries in Europe. They had deployed both bioweapons the Americans had designed to kill the Varianti, but by then it had been much too late. Over ninety-nine percent of the population was dead.

Passing the shattered ruins of a bakery, Piero cringed at the sound of his growling belly. The rumble was loud enough for Antonio—and any nearby Varianti—to hear. Neither of them had eaten a solid meal in days, and raiding the abandoned buildings for food was increasingly dangerous. They never knew where the juveniles dwelled.

For several seconds they stood there in silence, listening. A jeweled sky and half-moon cast enough light over the city that Piero flipped his NVGs up. Antonio did the same.

In the glow of the natural light, Piero studied his friend's face. They were both thirty-five and could have passed for twins with their matching filthy beards and dark brown hair. Despite the tension, Antonio still managed to smile. If there had been a comedian in their unit, it was the lieutenant. He'd always known how to lighten the mood with a joke.

"What you lookin' at? I got something on my face?"

"A *mameluke*," Piero fired back. It was the term his grandpa had used on him as a kid when he did something foolish or stupid, and Piero had used it on his friends ever since.

Their smiles quickly faded at the sound of a distant howl, a reminder that monsters were out there, hunting.

The men exchanged a nod. Antonio shouldered his rifle and moved into the shadows cast by a nearby church. Piero followed close behind into a courtyard that had been home to a daily farmers market. The stands were still there, but the fresh produce had long since rotted away.

In the center of the space was a fountain with a statue of a Roman soldier pointing east. His armor was stained white with bird droppings. Piero and Antonio swept their rifles over the courtyard. They were almost back to their shelter, and in Piero's pocket he carried more than just the melted chocolate bars he had scavenged. He had the radio parts that would allow them to communicate with Command. He wasn't sure which he was looking forward to more.

The thought of the chocolate made his stomach rumble again. But it was another sound that quickened his heart rate.

Antonio froze, hearing it in the exact same moment.

At first it reminded Piero of the river rapids, but it quickly transformed into what sounded like a waterfall.

What the hell is that?

Piero moved his finger from the outside of the trigger guard to the trigger itself. He scanned the streets for any sign of juveniles, but the sound wasn't coming from the roads or buildings. It was coming from the sky.

All at once, hundreds—no, *thousands*—of birds took flight. Their black wings were so thick they blocked out the moon, like a blanket of darkness rippling overhead.

Piero's pounding heart slammed against his chest. He'd witnessed something like this the first night they had parachuted into the city. The night they had awakened a nest of juveniles from their lair.

Antonio glanced back at Piero.

"Run," he whispered.

Piero tucked his helmet down and took off after his only friend left in the world. Their shelter was two blocks away, in a maintenance tunnel built into the ancient wall running along the Tiber. Instead of taking the route along the river, Antonio had opted for a shortcut. That shortcut had taken them back into the city. They must have ventured too near one of the underground lairs.

The cobblestone streets began to rattle under their boots, but this was no earthquake. The trembling ground reminded Piero of the bull runs in Spain. The exhilaration of running from a herd of bulls amongst hundreds of other people was almost unrivaled—until he experienced being chased by a herd of juveniles the size of baby rhinos.

He hugged his rifle against his chest. Sweat dripped into his eyes, but he ignored the burn and the urge to wipe them clear. Motion along the rooftops to the east flashed in his blurred vision.

Antonio pointed to a trio of row houses. Several small juveniles had climbed the exterior of the center build-ing. They perched on the rooftop terrace and sniffed the night with bulbous noses covered in warts. It took them only seconds to locate him with reptilian eyes the size of espresso saucers. The clank of their armored plates echoed as they scattered to report the news of fresh meat.

Those monsters were just the recon unit—runts of the litter, about half the size of their older brothers and sisters. But they were just as fast, if not faster, and their armor just as thick.

Piero struggled to get air as he ran. Antonio was a hundred feet ahead. He had always been faster, but usu-ally he waited for Piero.

Not tonight—not when they were about to be torn apart by hundreds of very hungry Varianti.

Antonio took a left at the next corner, but he halted a few strides in.

It was a dead end.

The cloud of birds flapped over the streets, casting a shadow on the two men. Piero turned and ran the way they had come, slipping on a puddle. He crashed to the ground but instantly felt Antonio's hands helping him up.

"Come on!" Antonio yelled.

With his legs under him again, Piero ran with his friend back into the open market. They made for a side street to the west that led to the French Embassy. Side by side now, the two soldiers ran down a narrow alleyway that opened onto a wide street outside the embassy. The French flag still hung from a pole overhead.

Piero had never really liked fighting alongside the French, but he would have been happy to accept their help now. Hell, he would have got down on one knee to welcome them.

The shaking of the ground intensified, and a flower-pot fell from the sill of a nearby building, shattering on the cobblestones.

"Hurry!" Antonio yelled. He bolted down a narrow street to the right of the embassy. The shops here were smaller, mostly owned by local artists. Piero had salvaged some wine from one of them a few days earlier, the same wine now in his hydration pack.

They were almost back to their shelter. The alley emptied onto a road, and after that only a bridge lay between them and safety. Antonio halted next to a tree, shouldered his rifle, and scoped the bridge ahead. Then he waved his hand at Piero. As they moved into the road, birds filled the sky above them. Wet droppings rained down, hitting Piero's hand and his face, but he didn't care. Shit he could wipe off.

He made the mistake of looking over his shoulder when he reached the bridge, nearly stumbling at the sight of a herd of juveniles galloping to the south. For a moment, their armored bodies moved as one, like a tank barreling down the road.

All at once, dozens of yellow eyes seemed to lock onto him.

His heart nearly burst from his chest.

Antonio yanked his final repellent grenade from his vest. He bit off the pin, tossed it into the street, and then took off running.

The hiss of the canister was hard to hear over the stampeding monsters and the piercing howls that sounded as they hit the wall of smoke. The gas was supposed to disorient the creatures, but they didn't cease their pursuit. The high-pitched noises rose until they hurt Piero's ears so badly he had to cup his hands over them.

Ahead, Antonio was doing the same thing. He dropped to his knees, screaming in pain. Piero clenched his jaw and pulled his friend back to his feet. They dragged each other across the final stretch of bridge. The ladder to their hideout was less than a hundred feet away—but the monsters had already reached the other side.

This was it. They either fought and died on this bridge, or they died running like cowards. Piero shouldered his rifle and aimed it at the wall of monsters, but Antonio slapped it to the side.

"Come on!" he ordered. Climbing onto the right ledge of the bridge, he pulled himself onto the railing and looked down. It was a twenty-foot drop, and the current was fast here. The juveniles could swim much better than their Varianti parents.

Piero climbed up next to him, and for a single second they both stared at the advancing beasts. Fifty curved heads speared the air, and two hundred pairs of claws shattered bricks that had endured centuries of abuse from wagons and vehicles.

Grabbing Piero's arm, Antonio pulled him over the side. They dropped into the water with their knees bent, like they had been trained to do. The impact rattled Piero's senses and a rock grazed his leg, pain racing up his bones. As soon as he surfaced, Piero heard the splash of monsters jumping off the bridge at the other end.

Antonio swam with the current toward the shore. It had taken Piero a moment, but now he understood what his squad leader was doing. He had decided to jump instead of make a run for the ladder because it would take them out of view for a few seconds. It was their only chance to get to their hideout without being spotted.

Coughing, Piero spat out water and swam after his friend. Antonio may have been faster on land, but Piero was quicker in the water. He quickly swam ahead. Stroke, breath. Stroke. Stroke, breath. He reached the ledge a few moments later, grabbed it, and pulled himself up. There was a bike trail between the wall and the shore. The door leading to the maintenance tunnel was just under the bridge.

When Piero turned to offer his hand to Antonio, he faltered at the sight of curved heads and ridged backs of the monsters cutting through the water. Dozens of them were swimming across the Tiber, quickly gaining on Antonio, who made the mistake of pausing to look at the beasts, treading water for a few precious seconds before kicking away. By the time he started swimming again, the current had already swept him ten feet farther down shore. Piero ran down the path, eyes flitting from his friend to the beasts, and then to the birds still choking the sky. The *whoosh* of wings caught his ear. But the noise wasn't a culmination of the thousands of flapping wings. This was from a single pair...

Piero stumbled backward as the curtain of wings parted, making way for a massive creature that swooped through the sky like a demon from hell. A spiked tail whipped back and forth behind the abomination.

"My God in heaven," Piero muttered.

The beast cut through the air with wings that had a span of at least twelve feet. A misshapen face with a long horn for a nose and roving eyes gazed down at its brethren in the water. It opened bulging sucker lips and let out a piercing hiss.

The sound seized the air from Piero's lungs. He had heard it in the night, waking him from his fitful sleep.

He could see the door leading to the hideout. If he ran, maybe he could escape down the tunnel and make it out the other side.

"Piero!" Antonio screamed between strokes. "Piero, help me!"

Piero considered abandoning his friend for a second before running to the water's edge. Just as Piero gripped his friend's hand, something jerked Antonio back into the water. His helmet vanished under the surface in a rush of bubbles.

The winged abomination dived at them, wings buffeting Piero. He fell on his ass and scooted backward, staring up in awe.

"Help!" Antonio yelled as he resurfaced.

Pushing himself to his feet, Piero shouldered his wet rifle and scanned the water for a target. Antonio was already gone, pulled under the surface again.

Piero paced at the edge of the river, eyes flitting from the sky to the water. The winged juvenile had vanished in the darkness, but he could still hear the sound of its wings.

"Piero!" Antonio screamed. He'd reemerged again ten feet to the right, gasping for air. "Help me!"

Before Piero had covered half the distance to his friend, the abomination from the sky swooped down and grabbed Antonio's head with a pair of talon-tipped feet. It yanked him from the water, away from the grasp of its hungry brothers and sisters.

The pale, armored body of a seven-foot-long juvenile shot out of the water, reaching for Antonio's feet. It grabbed his right leg and pulled, even as the winged juvenile rose into the air.

Piero watched in horror as the two juveniles pulled in opposite directions. Antonio screamed in agony. There was only one thing he could do now. A moment before Antonio was ripped in half, Piero put a bullet in his brother's brain.

Antonio had always said he intended to die with a smile on his face. He wasn't smiling now, his expression a bloody mask of horror. Half his body was being pulled into the sky while the other half was being yanked under the water.

Sickened, Piero stepped back, tripped over an abandoned bicycle, and dropped his rifle. He tried to feel something, but there was only numbness. He gasped for air and tried to make himself move, realizing that he would be next if he didn't. The open maintenance door was only a short jog away. He darted through and locked it behind him. Placing his back against the rusted metal, he closed his eyes, trying desperately to breathe, to block out what had just happened.

What he had just done.

No, he thought. *This can't be happening.*

Darkness shrouded him, close and suffocating. There was water in his lungs still. He tried not to cough, but he couldn't hold back. He choked, bent over, and spat water onto the ground. Gagging, he threw up what little food had been in his stomach.

He wiped his mouth with one hand and reached up for his NVGs with the other. His fingers scraped against his helmet. The goggles were gone, lost in the Tiber. At least his rifle had NVG optics.

Piero cursed under his breath.

In the chaos, he had forgotten the rifle outside.

Alone, unarmed, and in complete darkness, Sergeant Piero Angaran shuffled down the tunnel. He held up his hands and felt for the damp wall to guide him. A second later, something hit the metal door behind him.

He ran then, ran with his eyes closed and hands out in front of him, not caring if he fell. The door rattled, then was hit by another thud, which broke it off its hinges. Moonlight flowed into the maintenance passage, and silhouetted in the eerie light was the form of a great winged beast.

1

A summer breeze rustled Master Sergeant Joe Fitzpatrick's shaggy red hair as he crossed the deck of the USS *Iwo Jima*. The *Wasp*-class amphibious assault ship cut through the rough waters of the English Channel, paving the way for the USS *Mesa Verde* and the USS *Ashland*. Together, the three amphibious vessels made up what was left of the Twenty-Fourth Marine Expeditionary Unit. The Arleigh Burke–class guided-missile destroyer, the USS *Forrest Sherman*, was hours away from joining the MEU.

Fitz touched the handle of the hatchet he kept in a sheath on his duty belt. It wasn't regulation, but he kept it to honor the bravest woman he'd ever known. All the losses over the past seven months had weighed heavily on him during the lonely ocean journey, making for long days and restless nights. Without Captain Reed Beckham and Master Sergeant Parker Horn by his side, he felt more alone than he had in a very long time.

He thought about the friends and brothers he'd never see again: Sergeant Jose Garcia, Staff Sergeant Jay Chow, Staff Sergeant Alex Riley, Lieutenant Colonel Ray Jensen, and so many others. But the one he missed most was Meg Pratt. She had been like the sister he'd never had.

Stroking the handle of her favorite weapon helped ease some of the loss. Part of her still remained with him, even if it was just wood and steel.

He approached the warning line on the edge of the deck and peered up at a red sunset that looked like a gunshot. He smoothed down his uniform, fresh from a supply locker on the *Iwo*. His hair whipped in a gust of wind. It was far too long. His black carbon blades and black fatigues weren't regulation either, but he no longer had a commanding officer breathing down his neck about little things like polished boots or facial hair.

Now that Fitz was the new noncommissioned officer in charge of Team Ghost, he operated mostly independently of the other soldiers. He reached down to scratch his second-in-command behind the ears. Apollo sniffed at the salty breeze, his ears perked as if ready and waiting for orders.

Those orders would have to wait.

They were still an hour away from making landfall in France. Over seventy years ago, the Allied Forces had stormed the beaches of Normandy during Operation Overlord to take back the country from the Nazis. Now Fitz and his team were about to repeat history to take France back from the Variants.

He was ready to do that legacy proud. More than ready. After a nearly three-month hiatus, the Twenty-Fourth MEU was going to join the fight for Europe. President Jan Ringgold and Vice President George Johnson had answered the call from the new European Unified Forces, only to have their help delayed due to bureaucratic red tape and military commanders who decided not to follow orders. They had insisted that the United States Armed Forces needed to prioritize their own country's safety. Their argument sounded a lot like what Colonel Zach Wood had said before Fitz blew his head off.

America wasn't safe by any means, but rebuilding was under way. The Variants had been almost completely wiped out, and the juveniles were on the run. But the rest of the world wasn't so lucky. Rumors of new types of Variants were popping up all over—creatures with monstrous mutations.

Team Ghost had spent nearly two months with the Twenty-Fourth MEU, helping with recovery efforts along the Eastern Seaboard of the United States. The next three weeks were spent clearing the Pacific of derelict ships and raiding navy destroyers whose crews, infected with the hemorrhage virus, had managed to escape the deployment of the bioweapons designed to bring them down. Fitz had lost several new friends on those missions. He had no doubt he would lose more in France.

Like they had so many times before, the marines were prepared to fight evil wherever it emerged. Only this time, the marines were fighting at a fraction of their original forces. Only five percent of the Marine Corps was left. The Twenty-Fourth MEU consisted of around two thousand men and women. Many of them were volunteers that Vice President Johnson had requested to help rebuild the shattered ranks of the American military. Hundreds of the new faces were already gathered on the deck, helping load M1A1 Abrams Tanks, LAV-25s, Humvees, Assault Breacher Vehicles, MTVR heavy trucks, and Fitz's new ride, an all-terrain version of the heavily armed MRAP vehicle, the MATV, which took a crew of six plus an additional twelve in the back.

The precombat sounds sent a phantom chill up the legs Fitz didn't have, and adrenaline emptied into his bloodstream. He spat over the railing.

A full moon rose over the bloody horizon. For a split second he saw the silhouette of what looked like a dragon moving across the moon. He had seen a lot of monsters, but he knew that was impossible. Regardless, he still reached up, rubbed at his eyes, and focused on the moon. The silhouette was gone.

He turned to check on the *Mesa Verde* and the *Ashland*, still trailing the *Iwo Jima*. Final mission briefings were under way on the decks of the other ships. Armament specialists were carefully loading weapons systems while pilots checked their instruments. Everyone had a duty.

A trio of Black Hawks passed overhead. The choppers soared toward the rising moon, buzzing away like bugs toward a floodlight. He pushed his earpiece in and listened to the radio chatter. It was difficult to hear over the clank of machinery and raised voices of combat troops on the deck behind him, but he could vaguely make out the transmissions.

"Command, Rogue One...Echo Four and Echo Five report Variants on the shore. Adults in the vicinity."

"Come again, Rogue One. Didn't get your last. Confirm...*adults*? EUF said the area was clear."

"Copy that, Command. You heard right. EUF must have been wrong. Echo Four and Echo Five confirm Variants on the ground. We got ourselves an adult problem."

A hand on Fitz's arm startled him. Sergeant Jeni Rico flicked a blue-tipped lock of hair from her face and smiled, dimples deepening in her cheeks.

"Fitzie, you hear that shit?" she asked. "Sounds like the French didn't do a very good job of bug spraying. Kryptonite must not have been deployed everywhere."

Fitz sighed and bent down again to stroke Apollo's soft fur, catching a glimpse of the brace still on Rico's injured leg. She was lucky she wasn't in a cast.

Apollo whined, amber eyes searching Fitz's face. He knew something was up with all the activity on the deck.

"It's okay, boy," Fitz reassured him. He stroked the dog's head gently. Fitz guessed it wasn't fear making the dog uneasy. He probably missed Beckham and Kate. Fitz had promised them the Twenty-Fourth MEU wouldn't be gone this long, and Beckham had reluctantly allowed Apollo to come to keep Fitz safe.

That was three months ago.

Fitz sighed and stood. He missed his friends too, and being so far away from Plum Island made him feel anxious. How could he protect them if he wasn't there?

"You're not going to say anything about my new hair color?" Rico asked.

Fitz shook his head like he hadn't noticed. "Is it different?"

She twisted a blue strand. "It's not blue anymore."

He examined her from the corner of his eye. She was cute, smart, and fun, but he'd only ever had time for one relationship—the Marine Corps. Rico might have been flirting, but Fitz wouldn't know how to flirt back if he tried.

Rico changed the subject with a frustrated huff. "How fucking hard is it to replicate Kate's bug killer?" She chewed her gum furiously as she spoke, one hand on her hip. "I mean, all they had to do was launch that shit into the air and sit back in lawn chairs and watch."

Fitz managed a nod. He wasn't sure exactly what to expect in France. No one was. The EUF had finally taken a section of Paris back, but intel was hard to come by. General Vaughn Nixon, the man in charge of the invasion, had planned Operation Beachhead without much to go on. Not long after the final briefing, Colonel Roger Bradley, the commander of the Twenty-Fourth MEU, had pulled Fitz and the other leaders into a meeting and dropped a bombshell. Fitz still hadn't figured out a way to tell Team Ghost.

"Fitzie, you listenin' to me?"

"I told you not to call me that," Fitz snapped.

Rico stopped chewing and glanced down at the deck.

"I'm sorry. I'm just sick of waiting to get off this damn ship. Clearing derelict vessels and performing recovery operations is boring as hell," Fitz said.

A pair of Ospreys took off and climbed into the sky, engines zooming louder than a fleet of riding lawn mowers.

"You'll get to fight soon enough," Rico said. She pulled the strap of her sawed-off shotgun tighter around her shoulder.

More Black Hawks joined the Ospreys on the horizon.

"Shit, we really got an adult problem, don't we?" Rico muttered.

"It's not the adults I'm worried about. It's their offspring. They've had longer to evolve over here. And the Variant adults have had time to breed longer, too."

He eyed the vehicle assigned to his squad. The two-inch tan armor of the MATV was designed to protect the occupants from IEDs, but he wasn't sure how it would hold up against the juvenile toxins.

Rico scowled. "I hope Captain Davis is having better luck back in the States."

Fitz raised his brows, thinking of the woman who had helped take back the USS *George Washington* from the deranged officer who'd attempted a mutiny. Lieutenant Colonel Marsha Kramer had been convinced that a nuclear solution was their only option to defeat the Variants. If it weren't for Davis, Fitz would have been nothing more than a pile of ash on the concrete in DC. The Captain had caught a couple of bullets in the process, but from what he had heard, Davis was already back in action on the *GW*.

"I'm sure she's doing just fine," Fitz said. He forced his

gaze away from the horizon and jerked his chin toward their ride. "Let's round up the new team, shall we?"

Rico nodded and blew a bubble. They crossed the deck together and put their gear down next to the MATV. Staff Sergeant Blake Tanaka, Specialist Yas Dohi, and Sergeant Hugh Stevenson were already loading the troop hold at the back of the truck.

"Gentlemen," Fitz said as he approached.

All three men spun around and fell into a line. Fitz scrutinized them each in turn, just like Beckham had taught him to do. He started with Tanaka, who was fumbling with an iPod. The soldier hailed from New York and had a hint of a Brooklyn accent. A head shorter than everyone else, Tanaka made up for his lack of height with the build of an Olympic wrestler. He was in his early thirties, about the same age as Fitz.

"Those better not get in the way," Fitz said when he saw the long blade of a Katana, as well as its short-bladed companion Wakizashi, strapped to Tanaka's back under his slung M4.

"These have been in my family for generations. My grandfather killed with these blades during World War Two, and my family would be honored if I kill Variants with them during World War Three. I understand they're not regulation, sir, but neither is that." Tanaka's eyes dropped to Fitz's hatchet.

Fitz shrugged. "Hey, if you can kill Variants with them, by all means, bring them. But you use your primary weapon unless we're down to hand-to-hand combat. Got it?"

"Sir, yes, sir."

Stevenson laughed and unslung his M249 SAW for everyone to see while he stepped behind Tanaka to look at the swords. "Good luck with that," Stevenson said with a chuckle. "I'll be using my baby girl, Lilly, while you use those toothpicks to poke the armored juveniles."

"What did you say?" Tanaka pulled his earbuds out of his iPod, the music so loud that Fitz caught a drip of a Lil' Troy song he hadn't heard in years. "You want to try and clean your teeth with one of these?"

Stevenson stepped in front of Tanaka and glared at the smaller man. The music continued to blare from Tanaka's earbuds and he pulled off a glove to shut off the device.

"Why do you listen to that crap?" Stevenson asked. He shook his head and folded his muscular arms across his chest.

"Crap? This shit is gold!" Tanaka straightened his back. "What the hell is your problem, man?"

"Cut the horseshit," Fitz said. He stepped between the two men—his first opportunity to lead, and an important one, considering they were preparing for battle.

"Sorry, sir," Tanaka said.

Stevenson came to parade rest when Fitz shot him a glare. The youngest member of the new team had grown up in Texas and played college football, like Big Horn. Stevenson wasn't quite as big, but his chest muscles bulged under the black armored pads he had added to his gear. He'd spent most of the voyage to Europe doing yoga and reading the comic books he had dragged halfway across the world.

To Stevenson's right was the oldest member of Team Ghost: forty-five-year-old Specialist Yas Dohi, which he'd told Fitz meant "rock" in Navajo. He was a quiet man, with dark black hair and a silver goatee, but Fitz got the feeling that he'd seen a lot in his time. His sharp brown eyes didn't miss much, and he was the best poker player Fitz had ever met. His weapon of choice was an

M4 with an M203 grenade-launcher attachment. He also carried a combat Tomahawk.

Fitz scanned his team a final time, just like Beckham had always done, to see if they were frosty. All three men were transfers from other Special Forces units. Stevenson was a machine gunner from a Marine Recon unit, while Tanaka and Dohi were both Navy SEALs specializing in tracking, recon, and amphibious insertion. Their service ranks had transferred with them when they were assigned to Team Ghost.

It was slightly unorthodox to mix SEALs and marines, but with the military still in disarray it wasn't unusual to have a new fire team consist of soldiers from different branches. It also wasn't unusual for soldiers to carry custom weapons such as swords or the hatchet hanging from Fitz's belt. He had even seen a guy carrying a baseball bat on a mission to take back a container ship.

Up ahead, a jagged coastline emerged, silhouetted in the moonlight. Mist drifted across the water, and Fitz remembered the steamy heads of Variants cresting the ocean back at Plum Island when he was in his old guard tower. The sight emptied another rush of adrenaline into his system. He shivered in the cool night air, wondering if this was how his grandfather had felt before he'd stormed the beaches with tens of thousands of other men to take the coast back from the Nazis.

"Listen up," Fitz said. "First off, you all need to stop calling me 'sir.' Fitz, Fitzpatrick, or even 'brother' works."

His team nodded back and he continued. "Operation Beachhead starts in a few hours. We hit the beaches after the tanks clear a path. Then we work our way inland to help build the FOB. We make contact with the EUF and wait for orders. Any questions?"

Rico raised her hand. "Fitzie ... ?"

Fitz glared at her, watching her dimples fold into a frown. Sometimes she reminded him a lot of Riley. Her humor was usually welcome, but she still had to learn when to joke and when to be serious.

"I mean Fitz, sorry," Rico said. "Where are the EUF?"

"Yeah," Stevenson added, putting his hand over his eyes like a visor as he looked at the cliffs. "I don't see any white uniforms out there."

This was the moment he'd been dreading. Fitz took a deep breath and said, "They aren't coming."

Every member of Team Ghost focused on him.

"What?" Stevenson asked, his mouth hanging open.

"Colonel Bradley briefed us an hour ago and said the EUF can't risk sending us any forces. They were assaulted last night by an army of juveniles and are hunkered down in Paris. They are barely hanging on to their base. They are surrounded in all directions, and it's our job to clear a path to them."

"And save their asses?" Stevenson said.

"That's what we're here for," Fitz said sternly.

Dohi pulled a piece of licorice root from his pocket and wedged it between his teeth, chomping on it slowly. Everything he did was slow and discreet. Fitz could never get a read on him, which is what made him so good at poker.

Rico stopped chewing her gum at the news.

"They aren't fucking coming ..." Stevenson mumbled.

"No, they aren't, but that doesn't change our mission," Fitz said. "And I know we haven't worked together very long, but we're all experienced at fighting Variants. We will learn to fight together."

Standing as straight as possible, Fitz let out a breath and nodded at each member of his new team. They needed more than reassurance right now. They needed to know they were part of something bigger than themselves.

He reached into his pocket and pulled out the extra Delta Force Team Ghost patches Beckham had given him the day Fitz had boarded a ship with Apollo three months ago.

"This is it," Fitz said. "The moment we've been waiting months for. Welcome to Team Ghost."

One by one, he handed out the patches. Afterward, he stood next to his team and looked out over the cliffs. His grandfather had made it home from World War II, but many of his brothers hadn't. Fitz had experienced similar losses during the War on Terror and now the war with the Variants. He thought of his friends, both alive and dead, and straightened his helmet. He was going to make them proud.

"We're with you, sir," Tanaka said.

"I guess we'll do this shit on our own," Stevenson said with a shrug. He pulled an arm across his chest to stretch. "I've got your back, sir."

"Me too," Rico said while flashing a contagious smile.

Dohi nodded reassuringly.

Apollo looked up and wagged his tail.

"For Europe," Fitz said, his voice deep and confident. "For humanity."

The second D-Day was just a few hours away, and each one of the Operators was prepared to give their lives for their country. They were a hell of a long way from home, but Team Ghost was back, and they were ready to reclaim Europe from the monsters—or die trying.

Captain Reed Beckham checked the M4 propped up against a wheelbarrow near a row of recently harvested corn. He spat in the dirt and wiped his face on his shoulder. Fitz was about to lead Team Ghost into France against God knew what, and Beckham was digging fresh graves on Plum Island.

He looked toward the makeshift outhouse and trench separating the graveyard from fifty acres of farmland. Corn, beans, and other produce covered any evidence of the foundations that still remained of the Medical Corps laboratory buildings Colonel Rick Gibson had built. But just because Beckham couldn't see them didn't mean he would forget what had occurred there or the hundreds of men and women who had died—many of them buried here, each marked by a white cross.

He would *never* forget.

Guard towers rose over the beaches, and electric fences lined the coast. Water glistened in the distance, and a destroyer with a massive cage on the bow drifted across the horizon, likely heading for harbor to drop off new civilians.

Beckham looked at his M4 again. He had traded the weapon for a shovel today. He raised his new prosthetic hand and wiped the sweat from his brow. It was unusually hot for October. He glanced down at the carbon-fiber blade attached under his left knee. Standing on it was much easier now, but he still couldn't run better than a ten-minute mile. His goal was to keep up with Fitz on a jog around the island when he returned from the European front. For now, Beckham was just trying to keep up with Kate, and she was almost six months pregnant.

It was seven months since Beckham had led Team Ghost into Building 8 to investigate the breached bioweapons research facility. He could still see Sergeant Tenor transforming into a monster in his arms, and the look on his face when Staff Sergeant Riley put Tenor out of his misery.

Beckham hit his forehead with his prosthetic hand, trying to pound the memories away, but they kept coming in an endless stream, like the bullets from the MP5 he had fired that day. He saw Sergeant Jose Garcia back in the bunker beneath the Capitol Building, sacrificing himself so the rest of them could escape—a duty Beckham should have done himself. He saw Lieutenant Colonel Jensen gasping for air on the tarmac, bleeding out from a bullet Beckham wished he had caught instead. And he saw Riley on the gurney back on the *GW*, broken and bloody. He couldn't bear the thought of the kid like that...

Beckham hadn't been able to save any of them.

Tears welled up in his eyes, blurring his already damaged sight. The juveniles' corrosive toxins had taken his hand, his leg, and much of the vision in his right eye. He'd given all he could, and it still hadn't been enough to save his brothers.

No. Don't do that, Reed. They don't want your tears. They want you to keep living.

Beckham plucked his shovel out of the dirt, gripping it with his left hand. He speared the ground with the sharp tip of his left blade for balance and stabbed the earth with the shovel. He scooped up a chunk and tossed it to the side, then dug again and again, until a waterfall of sweat was pouring down his chest.

He was right-handed, and learning how to do everything with his left was maddening. It had taken him days to figure out how to use a freaking shovel, and he was still learning to shoot with his left hand. That was the hardest part—besides touching Kate. It didn't feel right using something that wasn't a part of him.

Drawing in a deep breath, Beckham filled his lungs. For three days straight he had worked on completing a new irrigation system for the crops. Now that he was done, he was working on graves for civilians. Plum Island had been hit hard with disease. Many of those being rescued from the mainland were suffering from dysentery. Some even had typhoid. There were rumors of hemorrhage virus infections in rural areas, but so far Plum Island hadn't seen any infected. In any case, the grave digging wasn't going to stop anytime soon.

A voice interrupted him midshovel.

"Boss, we're out of TP."

The door to the outhouse swung open, and Master Sergeant Parker Horn stepped out wearing a pair of fatigues and a white tank top with sweat stains around the pits. Faded tattoos covered his upper body and arms, but there was a glistening new Celtic cross on his chest above his heart with the names of all of their brothers and sisters lost in the war. He'd borrowed the idea from Garcia.

"I'd rather just shit in the bushes," Horn grumbled as he slammed the wood door behind him. "Place stinks like a dead Variant."

Beckham chuckled. It felt good to laugh, but he was still having a hard time not feeling guilty when he smiled.

Horn plucked his shovel out of the ground and joined Beckham. A few minutes later, they both looked up at the cough of a diesel engine. An army truck with an open troop hold plowed down the dirt road. The driver parked the beast of a vehicle on the side of the road. He jumped out, waved at Beckham and Horn, and then disappeared around the side of the truck to let a dozen civilians out the back gate. They were all carrying backpacks and water bottles, like the migrant workers Beckham remembered seeing in the Florida orange groves when Team Ghost was on leave.

The civilians fanned out across a field of carrots to harvest the vegetables. Horn went back to digging, but Beckham couldn't seem to look away from the fields of crops and the fresh graves. Life and death, separated only by a trench.

He went back to digging. Manual labor was one way to keep his mind off things. It wasn't as hard as Delta Force training, but it was tough given his injuries. It was also boring as hell. While he didn't miss the killing, he did miss shooting and training missions. And he really missed Apollo.

Letting him leave with Fitz three months ago was one of the hardest things he had ever done, but with Plum Island officially designated a safe-zone territory (SZT), he had felt compelled to let Apollo protect Fitz and his new team. Fitz needed the faithful German shepherd for protection. Beckham didn't.

He wondered how his two friends were doing now. The last time he'd spoken with Fitz was several days ago, and the call was only a few minutes. Not near enough time for an update.

"Boss, maybe you should've accepted the position from Ringgold," Horn said. "You'd be running this place as mayor of Plum Island, hanging out in that fancy air-conditioned embassy building. This heat wave is—"

"I'm not a politician," Beckham interrupted. "And I never will be."

"Well, I'm not a ditchdigger."

Beckham stabbed the ground with his shovel and looked at his best friend. "We're retired now, Big Horn. We picked this life for Kate and your daughters. Remember?"

"When President Ringgold personally promoted Fitz,

Davis, and us three months ago, I didn't think we'd be the ones digging ditches. We've spent our lives fighting. Now we're doing this shit."

"Would you rather be in Europe, with your girls worrying about you every night, wondering if this time Daddy wouldn't come home?"

Horn mumbled something under his breath and bent down to scoop another load of dirt. "No. I just miss it."

Beckham didn't need to ask what he meant. "I do too. Every damn minute. I wish we could be out there with Fitz. I wish a lot of things, brother. Pretty much anything beats this shit. But you wouldn't be happy sitting behind a desk. You wanted to be outside. Besides, we got your girls to think about, and I have Kate and my kid coming. Staying here was the right decision. We can protect them."

"Yeah," Horn said. "Sheila would want me to keep our girls safe. I can't do that from Europe. Didn't mean no disrespect, boss."

"It's fine, Big Horn. I understand."

They continued denting away at the earth in silence for several minutes. Beckham used the time to think. The only reason he hadn't immediately turned down President Ringgold's offer was out of respect for his commander-in-chief. He'd promised to consider it, but in the end, he had still turned her down. There were plenty of other capable people to serve as mayor.

A half hour passed before Horn spoke again. "You hear what Kate said last night about the hemorrhage virus still being out there?" He stopped to wring out the hem of his sweaty shirt. "What about VX9H9 and Kryptonite? I thought that shit was supposed to kill all of the Variants."

"Remember the *Truxtun*?"

Beckham locked eyes with Horn across the grave they were working on. Raw pain flooded Horn's gaze.

"How could I forget?" Horn said.

"The crew was infected with the hemorrhage virus because the ship was outside the range of VX9H9. I'm sure there are rural places that have avoided both bio-weapons. The rumors are likely true."

"Maybe we'll be fighting again after all."

Beckham bent down and struck the earth with his shovel. Kate was back at their new home, a small three-bedroom prefab house they shared with Horn and his daughters, Tasha and Jenny. They were supposed to find out in a few days if they were having a girl or a boy.

He dug faster, scooping, throwing the dirt, and bending back down for another shovelful until the motion became automatic. His back muscles ached, and his biceps burned with every scoop.

Fifteen more minutes passed, then thirty.

By the time he finally stopped to grab a drink of water, he was standing in a shallow grave, and the ship that had been sailing across the horizon was nearing port.

"Got some newbs," Horn said. "How many more of them can we take on here?"

Beckham shook his head and eyed the boat. Every rifle on the beach was aimed at the newcomers. But it wasn't Variants or juveniles that the security forces were worried about. It was the civilians they were ferrying in.

"You really think someone could be infected with the hemorrhage virus?" Horn asked. He spat in the dirt.

"Everyone has to go through decon and an interview about how and where they survived since the hemorrhage virus emerged."

Horn flared his nostrils. That was Hornspeak for skepticism.

"Disease isn't the only threat," Beckham said. "President Ringgold told Kate not everyone in the government has accepted her and Vice President Johnson with open arms. There are strongholds popping up and claiming the administration has no right to govern them since it just left them to die."

"Yeah, I know." Horn pulled a cigarette and jammed it between his lips. "You hear about those marines that got ambushed? They were liberating a survival post in Detroit. Gangs are coming out of the shadows. Most of the good people are dead, brother. The ones left out there had to do bad shit to survive. Which makes me very wary of all these new people coming to the island."

Beckham watched the boat maneuver into harbor. He still couldn't see what the name was, but it was an Arleigh Burke–class destroyer. The massive cage on the deck was loaded with civilians.

"Con artists, boss. I bet a few of those people are maggots that helped the Variants. Human collaborator fucks." Horn jammed his shovel into the dirt, his cigarette wobbling from his lips. "I should be working those interviews. If a human collaborator makes it onto the island, I'll rip their spine out."

Beckham kept his eyes on the boat while he sucked down the rest of his water bottle. Horn was right—and Kate was part of the interview team along with Ellis.

"Let's head back," Beckham said. "I don't want Kate out there without me. I don't care how many people they got guarding her."

Horn emptied his bottle over his head and shook the water from his red hair like a dog shaking his coat. Then he walked over to the wheelbarrow to retrieve his M249. Beckham grabbed his rucksack and flung the strap of his rifle over his back.

They walked back to their jeep in silence, both

exhausted from six hours of digging graves. Despite the fatigue and his strained muscles, Beckham felt good. He had missed the exhaustion that followed long training runs and workouts. And even though his new detail wasn't exactly Delta Force training, it felt amazing to be back outside. He had been cooped up in their house for most of the first month of his recovery after they got off the *GW*. That was before the power plant had been fixed on Plum Island, when power was run off generators. The sweltering heat made recovery hell.

Horn tossed him the keys when they got to their jeep. Beckham instinctively reached up to catch them with his right hand and had to fumble to keep them from hitting the dirt.

"Come on, boss, you know you want to. This jeep is *dope*."

Beckham hesitated. He hadn't driven a vehicle since his last mission, before he lost his hand. They climbed inside, sliding onto leather seats stained with the blood of the previous owners. Beckham eyed the manual transmission, then looked through the hole where the windshield ought to have been. There were still pieces of glass around the frame, but Horn had kicked out the shattered remains two days earlier.

You got this, Reed. No problem.

He grabbed the knob of the transmission, put his foot on the clutch, shifted into gear, and peeled out. Gravel spat out behind them. The jeep suddenly jerked forward as the transmission died.

Horn reached out to brace himself against the dashboard. "Holy shit. Take it easy, boss."

Beckham shook his head and turned over the engine again. He grabbed the gearshift, fumbling with it on his first try. He grasped the stick with his prosthetic hand on the second attempt.

The silence wasn't just awkward, it was embarrassing. How the hell was Beckham supposed to protect his family if he couldn't even drive a manual transmission?

Come on, Reed.

Horn reached for his seat belt and strapped in.

Beckham put his foot on the clutch and shifted into first gear by pressing with what was left of his arm. The jeep lurched, but the gear caught as his foot slipped off the clutch. The tires screamed, spitting gravel into the air. He grinned at that. It wasn't much different from when he had learned to drive a stick on his father's old Ford Ranger. Even the faces that looked his way were similar. The farmers stared as Beckham sped by the fields.

"Easy as shooting a Variant in the face," Horn said. He let out a bellowing laugh and pounded the outside of the door. Sticking his head out the passenger window, he drew in a long breath of air. "You smell that?"

Beckham shifted into second gear smoothly this time. "What?"

"The smell of freedom. America's back, baby!" Horn pulled his head back inside and smiled.

But Beckham didn't return the smile. He was too focused on driving and too preoccupied with his worries. Kate, Operation Beachhead, the rebuilding efforts. Retirement was supposed to bring with it peace of mind, but Beckham didn't have anything close to it.

He struggled to shift again.

Horn watched nervously with bated breath, his smile gone.

"Piece of shit," Beckham mumbled at the gearshift.

"Don't let it get you, brother. You're still the same man you were before DC," Horn said. "You can still fight if it comes down to it. You know that, right?"

"You think it will come down to it?" Beckham asked,

although he already knew the answer. He took his eyes off the road for a moment. Horn flexed his forearms, the tattoos stretching across his muscular flesh. That was his way of saying yes.

Beckham nodded. He shifted into the next gear, more smoothly this time, and turned the wheel to the left. The road curved toward Plum Gut Harbor on the west side of the island. To the north was the abandoned Animal Disease Center facility. The airstrip was located to the east, near more farmland that would be cultivated in the spring.

Mature trees framed the road on both sides, blocking out the view of the ocean and the rooftops of the new housing development nestled behind the harbor. The white-domed roofs of the Medical Corps facilities were all gone now, bulldozed at President Ringgold's orders. Only two laboratories remained for Kate and her team to work in.

Leaves cartwheeled to the ground in the rearview mirror, swirling in a colorful collage of yellow, brown, and orange. Like the changing seasons, the future of humanity was hanging in the balance of life and death.

Static from the radio crackled and pulled Beckham back to reality.

"All hands to Dock Three," came a female voice. "Repeat. All hands report to Dock Three."

Horn looked at Beckham's missing hand and grinned. "Don't worry, boss, they still mean you."

Beckham almost rolled his eyes. "A little too soon, Big Horn."

Horn laughed again. "Gun it, boss!"

Beckham punched the gas and raced down the final stretch of road, kicking up a tornado of exhaust behind them. The trees thinned, replaced by more fields and the tan roofs of houses tucked behind the harbor. Guard towers protruded over the growing town. Several M1A1 Abrams Tanks were positioned along the shoreline, their guns angled out over the ocean. One of them swerved toward the destroyer docking at the harbor. A cluster of civilians waited inside the cage on board, guarded by dozens of marines in CBRN suits. More soldiers were running toward the three electric-fence barriers separating the docks from the town.

"Looks like a lot of mouths to feed," Horn said.

"Every one of those mouths means something. They're more than pieholes, Big Horn. We're sitting at two percent of the pre-Variant human population. Worldwide."

Horn ran a finger over his freshly shaved face. "Two percent? Jesus. We really were on the edge, weren't we?"

Beckham let off the gas as they pulled into the town. He took a left on the main street and drove toward the barracks. Soldiers were coming and going, some reporting for duty, others returning home to crash. He parked outside the single-story building and pulled up the parking brake. Then he craned his neck to look at his best friend.

"We still are on the edge, Big Horn. That's why every single life we can save matters." He patted Horn with his prosthetic hand, then grabbed his rifle.

The thump of helicopter blades commanded his attention to the sky. Two Black Hawks soared over the island, moving toward the harbor at combat speed.

Beckham put his hand to his eyes to shield them from the sun. The blinding rays made it difficult to see the scientists and marines inside the open door of the Black Hawk, especially since they were all wearing biohazard suits, but he knew one of them was Kate.

"Goddammit," Beckham whispered.

Horn wiped his nose with the back of his hand. "Why are they wearing suits?"

Beckham didn't reply, but he knew the answer. Typhoid, dysentery, and malaria weren't the only threats to Plum Island. The hemorrhage virus was still out there. Kate was one of the most experienced scientists left in the world, if not *the* most experienced. She was the perfect person to help the government protect the SZTs from infection including their own Plum Island, but she was also going to be the mother of his child—and his wife someday soon, he hoped. She wanted to keep working, and he respected that. But it didn't mean he had to be happy about it.

The Black Hawk flew overhead and prepared to land on a pad adjacent to the docks. Beckham grabbed Horn's sleeve and pulled him to the back the jeep, where they kept their own CBRN gear.

"Suit up," Beckham said. " heading to the decon zone."

2

Dr. Kate Lovato forced herself to look away from Reed. Although she was a hundred feet off the ground, she could still see the pained look on his face. It wasn't from his injuries—it was from concern. Kate didn't blame him, but this was her duty, even though she didn't particularly want to be out here today. Her body hurt, and she was exhausted from countless sleepless nights. The nightmares, the pain in her lower back, and the sporadic sound of gunfire kept her up nearly every night.

She dreamed often of her parents. Sometimes they were alive, sometimes they were dead. Other times they were Variants.

She knew Fitz and the new Team Ghost would probably be too late to save them. Europe had reverted back to the Dark Ages, and her parents were almost certainly dead somewhere in Italy. She'd been put in charge of a team researching the new monsters popping up across the globe, beasts with wings and pincers. Creatures with webbed hands and gills that allowed them to swim underwater for hours. Armored monstrosities the size of horses.

But it wasn't the monsters that kept her up every night. It was rumors of the virus that had created them creeping back into rural areas across the States. If the hemorrhage virus was really back...

A hand pulled Kate gently away from the open door of the Black Hawk. It was her partner, Dr. Pat Ellis. A strand of black hair had fallen across his forehead behind his CBRN visor. He jerked his head to move the hair away from his eyes.

"You read the report this morning?" he asked.

"Didn't have a chance."

Ellis reached for a handhold above him. "The Medical Corps issued a statement about outbreaks popping up in the SZTs."

"Hemorrhage?"

He nodded. "There have been several documented cases."

The words made Kate draw back. She scanned the troop hold and put a finger to her visor to signal that Ellis should be quiet.

Several of their six marine escorts glanced up from their seats to look out the door.

"Damn, that's a lot of civvies," one of them said.

"Hope they've been checked out," said another.

"Those are marines down there. Not some turd army grunts," added a third man.

Kate held back the cutting remark she longed to make. She'd never understood the need to speak that way about another branch of service. It was just macho nonsense, she knew, but it still felt wrong to her ears.

The Black Hawk flew over the deck of the USS *Monterey*. It was full of marines in CBRN suits, all armed to the teeth. They were directing a line of civilians onto the deck as they streamed out of a massive cage the size of a school gymnasium. Inside were the tents where the people had been living for several days. There were several portable toilets, but she could also see buckets littering the deck. The conditions, from above, looked horrid.

"They've been checked for infection," Ellis said. "I'm more worried about the weapons they could be carrying."

The marine on the door gun chuckled, his breathing apparatus making his voice raspy.

"Shit," he said. "Those civvies were checked for weapons long before they ever made it on the ship." He glanced at Kate and then Ellis. "Sounds like the real weapon is the hemorrhage virus. I heard what you said, Doc. You think anyone down there could be infected?"

Ellis started to speak, but Kate cut him off.

"No. Those people have already been through decon, and if someone was infected with hemorrhage we would know it."

"But we are testing people," Ellis added. "Just to be sure."

Kate looked at her partner, and he shrugged back at her.

The door gunner stared at them for a few seconds before centering his weapon on the single-file line of survivors. They moved like prisoners being led down a plank as they slowly filed down the ramp. The marines then directed the civilians to a wide dock raised twenty feet out of the water by steel stilts and framed on both sides by a fence topped with razor wire. From there they followed arrows toward a much smaller metal cage built on a central platform about three hundred feet from the shore. Inside, two doctors and three marines had set up a checkpoint.

That's where Kate and Ellis were headed. Today their job wasn't researching new monsters. It was making sure they detected and isolated anyone with a disease or virus.

The door gunner continued roving his gun over the crowd. "Largest group yet. Look at all of those kids."

Kate followed the path the civilians would have to take to get to safety. She had been part of the planning committee, but seeing the system in operation was different from what it looked like on paper. It was only meant for about fifty people at a time, but there were easily double that many moving down the ramps.

"Like fish in a barrel," one of the marines said. The grin on his face bothered Kate, and she turned away to watch as the Black Hawk circled the port. Everyone on the dock would have to pass through the three chained doors in the twenty-by-twenty cage. If they were cleared, they would be escorted through a gate that opened to a final dock leading to the island. Anyone not cleared would be escorted to a biosafety Level 4 facility built on a large platform on the water. A bridge allowed vehicles to drive up to the building after they had passed through several security gates.

The white dome with its windowless exterior was a chilling reminder of the Medical Corps buildings Kate and Ellis had worked in. She looked toward the area in the distance where the old compound had once stood. Only one building remained—the Command Center where Lieutenant Colonel Jensen and Major Smith had held meetings.

"Prepare for touchdown," the pilot said over the comms.

Ellis glanced over his shoulder as the craft descended toward the helipad on a wide dock next to the USS *Monterey*.

"Ellis," Kate said. She put her hand on his shoulder and turned him toward her. "What did that report say? Is it bad?"

"It isn't good, Kate."

Her spirits sank further at the news, her tired heart sick of the abuse. After several months of relative peace, anything that threatened their fragile existence on Plum Island made Kate feel both exhausted and angry.

She had known before they deployed VX9H9 that it wouldn't completely eradicate the hemorrhage virus. Kryptonite wasn't a one hundred percent solution either. The virus was still out there. Hiding on ships in the ocean, in bunkers buried beneath the earth, and now apparently popping up around the SZTs.

The crew chief waved them away from the door as the Black Hawk landed on a pad adjacent to the ship. He jumped out, ducked down, and reached for Kate's hand. She took it and kept low. The six marines jumped out of the chopper and followed with their M4s angled at the ground.

"Go, go, go!" one of them yelled. He gestured toward the metal gate.

The Black Hawk took back to the sky as soon as they were clear. The draft slammed into Kate, wrinkling her CBRN suit and putting pressure on her already strained back. She moved as fast as she could, but she was carrying a lot of extra weight now. Every morning she made an effort to jog or walk with Reed. He was getting stronger and faster every day, and she was getting slower by the minute. She wasn't sure how women ran marathons pregnant, but several of her friends had proved the female body was capable of anything.

Kate eyed the adjacent dock where the line of survivors slowly made their way toward the central cage. The civilians had mostly looked the same from the sky, but now, up close, she could see the diversity in the group. There were young and old, men and women, and a mix of races here. Some wore fatigues, others T-shirts and jeans. Everyone was emaciated and filthy. A few wore dust masks and even garbage bags over their clothing like some sort of haphazard CBRN suit. If it weren't for her own suit, Kate imagined she would smell them from this distance. Flies buzzed around the crowd as it inched toward the first checkpoint.

Kate focused on a woman in a wheelchair and the gentleman pushing her down the dock. How some of these people had survived out there for so long was hard to understand. But they were finally safe. Plum Island was their new home.

A year ago she'd watched a video about the average American. Fifty-one percent of the country had been female at that time. There were forty million senior citizens and twenty-seven million disabled people. Those were just some of the numbers she remembered. She could see from the group in front of her that things hadn't changed much. America was still diverse, and while many from the older generations had perished, there were still some left, despite all odds.

She heard the grumble of Zodiac engines and looked to the water again. A trio of the boats slapped over the waves. Soldiers manning machine guns angled them at the civilians on the dock. Above, on the USS *Monterey*, marines in CBRN suits stood along the deck with automatic rifles. Snipers in guard towers zoomed in with their rifles. Two tanks centered their turrets at the raised docks.

There were a hundred guns of various sizes trained on the civilians, and Kate still didn't feel safe. She wasn't worried about anyone infected with hemorrhage—she was worried about the other diseases and the potential of human collaborators. Bad people getting onto Plum Island was supposed to be nearly impossible.

But now, she wasn't so sure.

Normally she was more empathetic, but there were

terrible people out there. What if there was a human collaborator amongst these people? What if someone was infected with—

Don't go there, Kate. Just do your job. These people need your help.

She looked to the children as a reminder of why she was really here. Most of these kids were probably orphans, but thanks to President Ringgold, they were guaranteed a better life here. The new school on the island was nearing completion. With twenty classrooms, a nursery, and a room that slept over one hundred kids, Plum Island wasn't just a beacon of hope—it was the future of America. The next generation of scientists, engineers, architects, doctors, and teachers would grow up here, including Kate and Reed's child.

Three of the marines ran ahead of Kate and Ellis as they approached the cage. The platform curved toward the central checkpoint, where the first of the civilians were waiting at the gate. The Zodiacs coasted to a stop two hundred feet away on both sides.

One of the soldiers pulled a bullhorn from the boat. "Stop at the red line. Stay five feet apart from one another unless you are a family. Do not approach the checkpoint until you are instructed. Parents and children must proceed separately."

There were a few raised voices and shaking heads in the crowd, but most of the civilians remained calm. Some shuffled forward, heads down, shoulders sagging. She could see the exhaustion and desperation in their eyes. But there was also hope. After surviving over seven months behind enemy lines, they were the lucky ones. The terror they had experienced ended here.

Clouds swallowed the sun, casting a shadow over the entire island. Kate guessed a storm was headed their way, but she hoped she was wrong. It was going to be a long night out here for these people, and for her team.

The squad leader waved Kate and Ellis forward into the first checkpoint. Marines on the other side of the fence unlocked the gate and let them into the cage. Two Medical Corps doctors were unloading their supplies and gear inside.

"Doctors Lovato and Ellis reporting for duty," Kate said.

"About time," one of the doctors said in a thick French accent without taking his gaze off his computer. The voice belonged to Dr. Aldric Durand. The Frenchman had been giving a lecture at Johns Hopkins when the hemorrhage virus outbreak stranded him in the United States. Since then he had been working with the Medical Corps and had just recently been transferred to Plum Island.

Dr. Leslie Case looked up from the crates she was unloading and nodded at Kate and Ellis.

"Do you know the routine?" she asked. "This is our biggest group yet."

"Which is why we're here to help," Ellis said warmly. "Just tell us where you want us and what you want us to do."

Durand glanced over his shoulder. "I'd like you two to be in charge of the blood testing. Doctor Case and I will conduct the interviews."

Kate would have preferred to be on interview duty, and she knew that Reed didn't want her anywhere near potential pathogens. But this was Durand's show, and she *had* volunteered to help.

"On it," Ellis said.

He walked over to help Leslie unload the medical crates, but Kate stood her ground, looking out over the civilians beyond the red line. There were so many children, and most of them were alone. Some swatted at flies, others stifled coughs and attempted to stand tall in an effort not to look sick. She had seen kids like this before, in Africa and South America when she worked with the CDC. But she never thought she would see something like this here in the United States.

A man with wild brown hair and a thick beard with streaks of gray approached the gate. He was dressed in a New York City police officer's uniform and had his arm around a small boy, no older than seven or eight. They looked familiar, but she couldn't remember where she had seen them.

Kate walked over to Ellis. He grabbed his medical kit and pulled out the volumetric bar-chart chips—a device that could run fifty blood tests in seconds, including one for the hemorrhage virus. Kate had used the device many times in developing nations. The results weren't immediate for everything, but this was only the first checkpoint. If these people made it past this point, they would be isolated in a well-guarded facility on the shore to await the results of the other tests.

"Are we all set?" Durand asked.

"Hold up!" someone yelled.

Kate knew that voice. Two men in CBRN suits lumbered across the dock, their boots pounding the metal surface. Make that three boots and one prosthetic blade.

"Reed, what the hell?" She worked her way to the back gate, but the two marines there blocked her way.

"Back up, bucko," Horn said from the other side. "We got access."

Reed held up his badge, and one of the marines stepped up to examine it. He nodded and unlocked the gate to let Reed and Horn through.

"What are you doing here?" Kate asked. She didn't

need to ask the question, really. He'd promised to protect her and their unborn baby, and Reed was a man who took his promises seriously. She watched as he unstrapped his assault rifle so he could get through the narrow gate.

Ellis and Case finished setting up, ignoring the commotion, but Durand had his hands on his hips. "What's going on here? Who are you two? The Medical Corps is in charge of this checkpoint, and I don't remember anyone else being cleared."

"Cool your buns, Doc," Horn said. "We're here to keep you safe."

Durand raised a gray brow. Horn took a step forward, towering a good foot above the small French doctor.

"Is there a problem?" Horn asked. His chest heaved, and hot breath clouded the inside of his visor like a bull snorting. Kate recognized the signs that he was about to blow a gasket.

"He's with me," Kate said, holding up a hand. "Both of them are. You're looking at two of the most decorated soldiers in the United States."

Durand glanced at her, then looked up at Horn. He turned back to his laptop and said, "Just stay out of our way."

Kate reached out and wrapped her arms around Reed, relaxing as a wave of calm washed over her. Although she had been briefly annoyed that he'd felt the need to protect her while she worked, in truth she was glad he was here. Together they could face anything.

Reed's gaze flitted over Kate's shoulder. He slowly pulled away from her and walked past the other doctors to the front gate leading to the civilian dock. He stopped and looked at the police officer and his son on the other side.

"Jake, right?" Reed said. "I thought you went back to the SZT in New York."

The man rubbed at his beard and said, "Who's asking?" He pulled his son back from the red line.

"Captain Reed Beckham. My team helped evacuate you and your son from New York during Operation Liberty."

The man's dull eyes suddenly brightened. He looked at Reed's hand, then the outline of the blade under his CBRN suit where a boot should have been.

"I'm sorry, sir," Jake said. "I'm—It's been a long few days. We were at the SZT in New York, but I requested a transfer to Plum Island. Things are bad there. Very bad."

"No need to be sorry," Reed replied, moving to the right to let Durand and Ellis pass. "I'm just glad to see you and your son again."

Jake let his son walk forward to the checkpoint. "Timothy, can you say hello?"

Timothy avoided Reed's gaze but nodded and muttered, "Hi."

"Good to see you, kid," Reed said. "We'll get you through here in a few minutes. Just hang tight."

"Come on, let's get this line moving!" shouted a man near the back.

Timothy flinched at the voice and moved closer to his dad.

"Hurry up!" someone else yelled. "We're starving and exhausted."

"My daughter needs water!"

The voices continued, and Durand gave a thumbs-up to the Zodiacs floating below. The soldiers centered their rifles on the dock, preparing to fire on anyone who stepped past that red line.

There were a hundred civilians, maybe more, stretching from the dock all the way up the ramp to the deck of the *Monterey*. To the east, rain streaked from the bulging gray clouds, the storm heading right for Plum Island.

The soldier with the bullhorn brought it back to his visor. "Move forward. One at a time."

Durand directed the doctors and marines into position. Kate and Ellis stood to the side of the desk where Durand took a seat. Case sat next to him. Horn and Beckham took up spots to the left and right side of the main gate, and the other three marines stood guard at the back of the cage. The police officer cautiously stepped over the red line, then turned and whispered something to his son that sounded like *Everything will be fine*.

Durand gestured for Jake to approach.

Two drops of rain pelted the clipboard in Kate's hands. It was supposed to be a smooth and quick process, but she could see the storm was about to throw everything off.

Maybe we should have done this in segments, she thought. But it was too late to send everyone back now.

"Proceed," Durand said.

Horn unlocked the gate and let Jake into the cage. Then Horn closed the gate, locked it, and directed the man to a blue circle in front of the desk.

"Please remain within the blue circle and do exactly as we say," Durand said. His voice was calm but firm. "Do you understand?"

Jake nodded.

"State your full name, age, and everywhere you have been for the past seven months," Durand continued.

"Jake Temper. I'm..." He paused for a moment and looked to the sky, blinking as if he was trying to remember, or possibly forget. "I'm forty-eight years old, and Timothy and I survived in New York City for the first month. We were then rescued by him." He pointed toward Reed. "From there we were taken to the *Wasp*, where we lived for several months before it was overrun by juveniles. We escaped on a small boat to New

England. We evaded the enemy for several days and were later rescued by Captain Rachel Davis of the *George Washington*. We were moved to the SZT in New York City, but I requested a transfer here."

"Noted," said Durand. "Doctor Lovato will now ask you some questions about your medical history."

"Have you had any contact with anyone infected with the hemorrhage virus in the past ten days?" Kate asked.

"No," Jake replied.

"I want you to answer the following question with a clear nod of your head if your answer is yes. If the answer is no, simply shake your head." Kate paused for a moment and looked at the list even though she had it memorized. "Do you have any of the following symptoms: headache, fever, nausea, itching, or abdominal pain? Again, if the answer is yes to any of these symptoms, then simply nod. If it is no, then shake your head."

Jake shook his head.

"Good. Now please hold out your right arm. Doctor Ellis is going to take a blood sample."

Ellis approached with a V-chip testing card. As he reached for Jake's arm, a man wearing trash bags and a dust mask collapsed on the dock. Four civilians around him moved away, pushing several other people behind them against the fence. The steel beams kept the metal chain links from buckling.

"Everyone stay calm," Horn ordered.

The fences were meant to keep people isolated, but they weren't built for so much pressure. If someone panicked, it could cause a stampede. With nowhere to go, the civilians would be crushed against the fences.

The soldier with the bullhorn yelled, "Step away from that man! Do not touch him!"

Beckham and Horn approached the gate but kept

their weapons angled downward. The crowd continued moving away from the fallen man, who lay limp on the dock.

Horn turned to Durand. "Yo, Doc, what do we do about this guy?"

Durand ignored him and spoke into his comms.

"Command, this is Doctor Durand. We have a civilian down on the dock. He is not moving but shows no obvious signs of infection. Please advise."

"Copy that. We're reviewing video footage to see what happened. In the meantime, send in someone to escort him to the biofac."

Reed pivoted toward the door, but Horn held up his hand. "I got this, boss."

"Go with him," Durand said to two of the marines standing sentry behind him.

Both of the men nodded and shouldered their M4s as they followed Horn through the open gate. Reed gestured for Timothy to move out of the way. The boy did as ordered, and the crowd slowly shifted to the left to allow Horn and the two marines through.

That gave Kate a better view of the civilian on the dock. An Atlanta Braves hat and a dust mask obscured his features.

"Careful, Big Horn," Beckham said.

Horn raised his M4 and approached in a crouch. Slowly, the three men made their way toward the downed man. More civilians parted to give them room.

Halfway there, the fallen man's tennis shoe suddenly twitched. Then it kicked, and he brought his left knee up. He sat up, his head cracking from side to side in a robotic fashion.

"What the hell is wrong with him?" someone yelled.

"Back up! Back up!" another shouted.

It only took a second for the screaming to start.

Kate reached out to grab Reed's arm, but he was already raising his rifle.

"Timothy," Jake said. "It's okay, son. Daddy's here. Just stay calm and don't move, okay?"

"Stay in the blue circle," Durand ordered.

A transmission broke across the main radio channel. "Cage One, video footage shows the civilian was stabbed with a syringe. The perp is wearing a gray sweatshirt and black pants."

"Oh my God," Kate whispered. She exchanged a meaningful look with Ellis. They both knew what was in that syringe.

"Cage One, you are authorized to use deadly force."

"Lock that gate," Durand ordered.

"Timothy," Jake said. He reached out for his son, but the marine in the cage pointed his rifle at the former police officer.

"Stay where you are, sir," he said in a shaky voice.

Kate's world slowed to an agonizing pace. She couldn't seem to move as she watched the man in the garbage bag leap to his feet like an acrobat and then crouch, head still at an awkward angle. Blood was dripping from his ears, nose, and wild, yellow eyes.

"He's infected!" someone yelled.

"Take it down!" came a voice over the line.

What had been a human being minutes before swiped at the closest person, opening up four parallel gashes on the poor man's stomach. Then he bounded forward on all fours and leaped onto a woman who was trying desperately to back away.

The gunner on the Zodiac to the left hesitated, but the other one opened up. The big gun barked to life. Rounds cut through the fences and tore into the infected man, blowing off his arm and his left leg at the knee. Blood splattered the civilians all around.

"NO!" Kate yelled at the same time as Reed.

Jake ran to the gate, but the marine behind him was too busy staring in shock to fire.

"Open it!" Jake insisted.

"Do not open that gate!" Durand shouted.

Reed fumbled with the keys. He found the correct one and opened the gate to allow Timothy through.

Horn and the two marines were already retreating with their rifles aimed at the civilians now covered in blood. One of them twitched and jerked, turning into a monster in mere seconds. The gunners on the Zodiacs focused their fire.

"Hurry!" Reed shouted. "Get those kids out of there!"

Horn backpedaled away from the carnage, but several people behind them were also running for the gate.

"Close that door!" Durand shouted. He hurried over and reached for the key. "That's an order, Captain."

Reed ignored the doctor and held the gate open.

A Black Hawk buzzed overhead, and the door gunner joined the slaughter as more civilians started clawing at their eyes—and each other. The crowd at the other end of the dock raced away from the gunfire and back to the ramp that led to the *Monterey*.

The radio flared to life. "Fox One to Five, you have permission to fire. Do not let anyone back onto the ship."

The civilians were torn to pieces as gunfire rained from above and below.

Kate fell to her knees, whimpering in a voice she didn't recognize. How could this be happening? How could someone have been carrying a hypodermic of the hemorrhage virus? And why?

She couldn't think over all the screaming and gunfire.

Horn lowered his rifle and grabbed a child. One of the marines seized the woman's wheelchair and pushed her down the dock. The second marine picked up a little girl in one arm and a boy in the other. They were ten feet away now, but the Zodiacs closed in.

"Hold your fucking fire!" Reed shouted over the comms.

"Shoot them! Shoot them all!" Durand yelled back.

The doctor pushed at the gate, but Reed held it open with his good hand. Then, in a swift motion, he punched Durand in the side of his helmet with his prosthetic. The French doctor dropped to the deck like a tree falling over.

Horn and the other two marines burst through the open gate with the remaining civilians in tow. Reed held it open to let several more through.

Kate sobbed as she watched blood-splattered men, women, and children crawling toward them, pleading for mercy. More blood spilled over the side of the dock and dumped into the sloshing ocean.

"My God," Kate said. "My God, what have we done?"

A panicked voice said from inside the cage, "You got a tear in your suit, man!"

The two marines with Horn backed away from him. He lowered the boy he was carrying and put him down, then looked down at his right bicep. A round had grazed his sleeve, leaving a bloody streak.

Kate could hardly hear anything over the gunfire, but she did pick up the next transmission over the comms.

"To those in Cage One, place your weapons on the deck and stay where you are. Do not attempt to leave, or you will be fired upon."

Reed helped Kate to her feet and then placed his gun down. Horn did the same, and the other marines complied. Case bent down to check Durand, who was holding his injured head.

The gunfire from the Zodiacs died as the craft fled the scene to avoid the bloody waves. Pops sounded from the deck of the *Monterey* as marines picked off the few bodies still moving on the dock.

Of the hundred or so civilians, only nine had made it into the cage. There were five children, Jake, two other men, and the woman in a wheelchair. And it wasn't over yet. She eyed the BSL4 facility on the platform to the east. In a few minutes, they would all be led there, with every gun on Plum Island pointed at their backs.

3

President Jan Ringgold sat in the new Oval Office, sipping a cup of hot green tea and looking out at the Allegheny Mountains.

There had been a lot of debate about the location. From the *George Washington* aircraft carrier to an ambitious plan to rebuild the White House on Plum Island, everyone had had an opinion. In the end, President Ringgold had chosen to return to the mainland. It didn't hurt that the Greenbrier Resort in West Virginia had a Cold War–era bunker under it, but it was the beauty of the mountains and their strategic location that had sealed the deal.

After a month of remodeling aboveground and another month and a half of hardening the structure below and updating security features, the new White House was finally operational. Much of the Classical Revival architecture of the resort had been salvaged, despite a fire that had ravaged the east building during Operation Liberty.

Ringgold stepped closer to the window and blew on her still-steaming tea. Floodlights illuminated the freshly mown grounds and flowers overflowing from the ceramic pots. She couldn't see them now, but the leaves on the trees framing the courtyards were changing.

The sight of a secret service agent armed with a shotgun walking along the stone path reminded her that threats still existed despite the beauty all around them. It might always be that way, but the country was slowly recovering.

She brought her cup back to her lips and sighed before taking a drink. The little luxuries kept her spirits up in a time of turmoil and uncertainty, but sometimes she wondered how much more she could take. She had been president for one hundred and two days. Every hour, no matter what time it was, she faced life-or-death decisions. Tonight her mind was jumping from worry to worry. Operation Beachhead was about to begin, and she would soon head down to the Situation Room for updates.

A knock at her door told her that she was probably about to face another challenge. She turned away from the windows and called for the visitor to come in. She pulled at her cuff links and brushed the wrinkles out of her suit to prepare.

Vice President George Johnson strode into the room, his expression grim.

"We have a situation, Madam President." He slowly shut the door behind him.

Ringgold took a final sip of her tea and set it down. "Have a seat, George." She gestured to one of the chairs in front of her desk.

Johnson stiffened his back and held out a folder marked *Confidential*. "All due respect, ma'am, I'd prefer to stand. I've been sitting in the Situation Room for the past hour with the Joint Chiefs and my generals."

"Is Operation Beachhead under way?"

"Actually, that's not why I'm here."

Ringgold narrowed her eyes and took the folder. It wasn't unusual for Johnson to meet with his team without her. That was part of the deal. He oversaw the military, and she oversaw the rebuilding efforts and handled civilian matters. Scooping her red-framed glasses from the desk, she put them on and opened the folder.

"Inside you will find a list of all our SZTs," Johnson said.

Ringgold skimmed the safe-zone territories, noting the red check marks next to several of them. They had constructed over seventy-five of the strongholds across the country, at least one in each state. The juvenile populations were slowly being eradicated in every major city, and any survivors they rescued were evacuated to the closest SZT, where they would receive housing assignments, food, and medical treatment. But not all of the strongholds were as secure as they had planned, and Ringgold had a feeling that was exactly what the red check marks meant.

Portland, Oregon. Chicago, Illinois. Des Moines, Iowa. Kansas City, Missouri. Denver, Colorado. Boston, Massachusetts. The list went on and on.

"The safe zones are reporting some very disturbing news," Johnson said. "We are receiving reports of the hemorrhage virus. There has been one documented case in every marked SZT."

Ringgold stopped reading in order to meet Johnson's eyes.

"The hemorrhage virus? How is that possible?"

Johnson cleared his throat. "VX9H9 was never one hundred percent effective."

"What about Kryptonite? I thought it was supposed to kill anyone left alive who had been infected."

He shook his head. "There were areas outside the range of both weapons. Underground, very rural areas, ships."

"Have you informed the Medical Corps at Plum Island?"

Johnson nodded. "Yes, Madam President. We just shipped over a briefing this morning."

"Good. Perhaps Kate can shed some light on this."

Johnson pulled at his collar before continuing.

"That's not the worst of it. There aren't packs of infected. Only individuals trying to enter the SZTs. It's odd. So far we have been able to contain all of them... until today."

Ringgold resisted the urge to pull at her own collar. "What happened?"

"It's SZT Fifteen, Madam President. Turn to page twenty-nine."

She quickly flipped through the pages, knowing exactly which SZT she was looking for. It was Chicago, and it was special to her for more reasons than one. Her cousin, Emilia, who had survived in the countryside and been rescued by a squad of marines, was living there.

"That's a transcript of the last transmission we received."

Ringgold looked up. "What do you mean, last transmission?"

"SZT Fifteen has gone dark, Madam President. And that's not all... Plum Island was attacked a few hours ago."

It was Captain Rachel Davis's forty-fifth day as captain of the USS *George Washington*. At thirty-seven she was young to hold the post, but President Ringgold had overseen the ceremony herself the same night Team Ghost received their promotions. That was the last time she'd seen her friends.

Davis still wasn't fully recovered from her gunshot wounds, or the actions that had earned her the service rank, but she was slowly getting better. Standing for long periods was painful, but she was fine when she was on the move. The cane her doctor had assigned her was jammed into her locker.

Stupid toothpick, she thought when she pictured it. If Beckham wasn't using a cane, she didn't need one either. She palmed a bulkhead to combat a wave of dizziness and looked out the porthole at Panama City Beach, Florida.

Rear Admiral Rick Humphrey was right next to her, staring through binoculars at the burning city. Flames licked the sky from relentless bombing. They were clearing the city and preparing to build SZT Seventy-Nine, but there wasn't going to be much left if they didn't stop blowing it up.

"Hit 'em again," Humphrey said.

Davis hesitated for a split second, then gave the order.

RIM-7 Sea Sparrow missiles streaked away from the aircraft carrier and curved into the sky. Another set followed close behind, the exhaust hissing behind the missiles. They glided three hundred feet over the water and then slammed into two buildings in the center of town, a crimson explosion lighting up the cityscape.

The raucous blast shook the Combat Information Center, rattling the portholes.

"That should have toasted most of the bastards," Humphrey said. He stroked his thick mustache and looked at Davis. She forced herself to watch the flames, praying there weren't any civilians in the vicinity.

"That the last of the coordinates?" Humphrey asked.

"One more, sir," Davis replied. She read the coordinates the Marine Recon team had identified.

"Finish it," Humphrey said. He pivoted away from the

CIC's window before the missiles launched, his hands behind his back. "I want to do a flyover in the morning. If it looks clear, we'll send in mechanized units to look for survivors. Then we get word to President Ringgold. They can break ground for SZT Seventy-Nine as soon as the flames recede and it's secured."

"Aye-aye, sir," Davis said.

Four more Sea Sparrows and a flurry of smaller RIM-116 Rolling Airframe Missiles raced away from the *GW*, lancing into the areas of the city that weren't yet on fire. If there were survivors out there, Davis hoped they were somewhere deep underground. She knew the juveniles would be. Their chances of finding a survivor stronghold in Panama City was unlikely, but like the other cities they had liberated, there were always a few people left to save. Humans were a lot like cockroaches that way.

"I'm retiring to my quarters. You have the bridge for now. Wake me up if you hear anything else about SZT Fifteen," Humphrey said. He looked exhausted, and Davis didn't begrudge him his rest.

"Aye, sir," she replied. She moved over to the station where Jay Belford, a new officer and recently reassigned to the *GW*, was seated. She still didn't know half the new staff on her own damn ship.

"Updates, Belford?"

"Nothing new, Captain, but there is chatter over the network about an incident at Plum Island earlier today."

Davis felt another wave of dizziness.

"What kind of incident?"

"An attack, ma'am."

Davis reached out to steady herself on the chair, doing her best not to draw attention to her condition. She couldn't appear weak to her staff, not with morale already at an all-time low.

"A yet-to-be-identified assailant was carrying a syringe containing the hemorrhage virus," Belford said.

Davis gasped, her already spinning head going into deep dive. "What? Why in the hell would ... ?"

Another explosion rocked the city, a mushroom cloud of fire booming into the air. "Jesus," Davis said. She pulled her gaze away from the destruction. "Do we know how bad the attack was?"

Belford nodded. "Ninety-four civilians were killed. All were being relocated to the SZT at Plum Island by the USS *Monterey*. The virus was contained, we think, but several residents are in quarantine just to be sure."

"Ma'am!" shouted a voice.

Lance Corporal Katherine Diaz stood at her station. The *GW* was so short on staff some of them held dual positions. Diaz was Davis's personal bodyguard and helped some of the communication officers.

"I'm picking up an SOS over the short wave," Diaz said. "There are survivors out there, Captain."

Davis pushed the thoughts of her friends at Plum Island aside. There wasn't anything she could do to help Beckham or Kate right now, but there were people she could save here.

Diaz handed over her headset and Davis took a moment to study the short lance corporal as she reached out to grab it. Diaz's face seemed unusually pale beneath her dusting of freckles, and Davis suspected she was about to find out why.

Davis wasn't the only one to lose her loved ones in this war. Diaz had seen her husband killed in an airstrike from the very government she swore to defend. That's one reason Davis had picked Diaz as her personal bodyguard. They both had nothing to lose.

A panicked female voice surged over the channel,

and Davis cupped the headset over her ears. What the woman said chilled Davis to the core.

"To the military or *anyone* that can hear this, stop firing on the city! There are over fifty children and adults at—" The message cut off, then restarted.

Davis pulled the headset off. She knew the survivors couldn't hear her. It was a one-way UHF transmission.

"Diaz, can you figure out where they are?"

"Maybe the general area, but not an exact location."

"Get it done," Davis said. She turned to Belford. "I want two marine fire teams prepped and ready to go on the hour. Everyone wears CBRN suits."

Belford stared for a moment, uncertainty in his watery blue eyes. "What about Admiral—"

"He left me in charge," Davis said. "That's an order."

"Yes, Captain," Belford said. His gaze shifted to someone standing behind Davis. She turned, half expecting to see Humphrey, but instead saw Marine Sergeant Corey Marks standing in the center of the room.

He cleared his throat and then rasped, "I'd highly recommend waiting until morning, Captain. You know better than anyone that juveniles hunt at night."

Davis understood why some of the marines called Marks "Two-Face" after the Batman villain. The left side of his face was hidden by shadow, but the right side was illuminated enough to see a scar running from his lip to his ear. He was a rough man with a layer of fat covering old stomach muscles, and a thick upper body from years of weight lifting. He was also smart enough to make sergeant, but something had stopped him from ever advancing past that rank.

"Ma'am, I lost two of my boys out there the other night. I don't think sending anyone out there right now is a good idea."

"You're not in charge," Diaz said. "Captain Davis gives the orders."

Davis gave her bodyguard a glance. They would need to work on the chain-of-command thing.

"I'm sorry about your men, Sergeant, but they died to give us the coordinates to bombard the city." Davis paused to reflect. "If they were correct, then the juveniles are dead. And any human survivors we were hoping to save will also be dead soon if we don't go out there to help."

Marks coughed and brought his hand up to cover his mouth. His lungs rattled. "Easy for you to say. You got no skin in the game."

"*Excuse* me, Sergeant?" Davis stood tall, her fingers tightening into fists. "I'm not sure I heard you correctly."

Several officers looked up from their stations, but Davis kept her gaze on Marks.

"I will be going out there with you, Sergeant. Is that enough skin in the game for you? Meet me on the flight deck at 0100 hours, and bring your CBRN suit. We have some civilians to bring home."

"Yes. Yes, ma'am," Marks grumbled. He ran a hand through his thin gray hair and retreated from the CIC.

Davis looked at Belford. "Tell Humphrey I'm going ashore. In the meantime, you have the bridge."

The corporal leaned back a little in his chair. "Ma'am, I would highly—" He stopped himself and said, "Good luck. And be careful, Captain."

Davis jerked her chin at Diaz. "Let's go, Lance Corporal."

Before they left, Davis eyed the burning city in the distance one more time, thinking of the husband and nephew she had left behind when she'd been called up for duty. Blake and Ollie had died in the outbreak, and she never had a chance to say good-bye. She had made a promise that she would save everyone she could since that fateful day, and there were people out there who needed her right now. She had no doubt that Beckham and Kate would be doing the same thing at Plum Island. She just hoped they were okay.

Diaz cradled her M4 across her chest like a pro as they walked out of the CIC.

"Don't worry about that turd Marks. He means well," Diaz said.

Davis smiled her pearly white grin. "Just watch my six, Lance Corporal. We have some people to bring home."

"Kate!" Beckham screamed. He fought the two Medical Corps soldiers dragging him down the white hall of the BSL4 facility.

"Reed!" Kate yelled back. She was near the end of the passage. Two men were leading her and the other surviving civilians to God knew where.

The grip under Beckham's armpits tightened. "Please calm down, sir, or I'll have to restrain you," one of the soldiers said.

"Try it, asshole!" Beckham said.

Horn was yelling elsewhere in the facility, but Beckham couldn't see his best friend. "Get your hands off me, you piece of shit!" A pause, and then, "I'll break your dumb chicken neck if you don't let me go!"

Hearing Horn's voice made Beckham even angrier. He struggled again, this time dragging his blade and boot on the floor. The blade caught against a tile and folded under his body. Beckham tried to get his weight onto his right foot, but he fell to his knees. He pulled one of the men down with him, tossing him head over feet onto the ground with a thud. Beckham pushed himself up as the other guy backed away. He pulled out a Taser and jabbed Beckham before he could react.

A jolt of electricity rocked through his body. He screamed in pain and threw a punch that connected with the soldier's stomach. They both went down and hit the floor together. Beckham tried to stand but stumbled, his arm wobbly.

Something hot stabbed him in the back.

"Reed!" Kate screamed.

"Hold on, I'm com—" Beckham began when another jolt of electricity surged through him. He went down face-first this time.

"Please, sir. Stay down!" one of the soldiers yelled.

Beckham saw two boots in front of his face, but he couldn't move. Waves of red and black encroached from the sides of his vision.

"Kate," he whispered. "Kate, I'm coming…"

There was darkness, and blinding pain, and then… nothing.

Beckham woke up naked in an isolation cell. He was shaking violently in the chilly air.

A voice came over the speakers. "Stay calm, sir. You're going to be okay and so will your friends."

Beckham raised his hand to shield his eyes from the bright LEDs. He squinted, winced, and felt his back where the bastard had shocked him. It took every ounce of his control not to stand up and pound on the door sealing him in the tiny room.

A blast of warm water hit him. He pushed himself up and said, "Where's Kate? Where's Horn?"

"They're being treated, sir."

Beckham turned slightly so the water could hit his back. "Treated for what?"

"They both suffered minor injuries and are now being checked for infection. Please, sir, hold out your arms so we can get you rinsed down. The sooner you cooperate, the sooner you can see them."

Beckham looked up at the video camera. The voice was kind and reassuring, but he didn't trust anyone who worked for the Medical Corps. He had only met two men in that uniform who could be trusted, but Jensen and Smith were both dead. "Sir, you are about to be covered in a disinfectant, so please raise your arms."

Grunting, Beckham tried, but he could hardly lift them up. He spun as the shower covered his body with a chemical-infused spray. A few minutes of soaking in the foam made his skin tingle. He did his best to hold his exhausted and sore arms out at his sides. Standing in the shower under the glow of a bank of LEDs gave him the opportunity to see every mark of battle on his body. There was no denying he was not the man he once was. While still lean and muscular, he was covered in scar tissue. Two claw marks crossed his chest like an X, and shrapnel wounds puckered his shoulder. What was left of his right arm was covered in burns.

The warm water kicked back on, rinsing the chemicals away. He sucked in a breath of steamy air and looked down. Foam flowed down his carbon-fiber blade. In the past he would have felt panicked to be trapped in a room like this and terrified at the thought of infection. But like his body, his mind had also changed. Old fears were gone, replaced by those of a man just trying to protect what was left of his friends and family.

No, he wasn't worried about infection, but he was sick with worry for Kate and Horn. The tear in Horn's suit could have exposed him to infected blood. To make things worse, Kate had been light-headed after the attack. She was under way too much stress, and he feared she could lose their child.

A wave of anger overtook Beckham, and he pounded the tile wall with his prosthetic hand. A Medical Corps soldier in a CBRN suit looked in through the glass window to the small isolation chamber.

"Sir, please stay calm," the man said. His eyes flitted across Beckham's ruined body. "We're almost done here."

Beckham finished rinsing off and stepped out onto the tiled floor in an area partitioned off by a curtain. A towel hung from a rack near the entrance. He used it to dry off and then wrapped it around his waist. He pulled the curtain back to reveal a dozen more stalls, all separated by glass windows.

Jake was toweling off Timothy's hair in one of the nearby cells. Beckham exchanged a nod with the police officer. Horn was in the next chamber, and the other two surviving civilian men were farther down. Dr. Durand was there, an ice pack on his head where Beckham had punched him. The only guilt Beckham felt was that he hadn't hit him harder.

Medical Corps soldiers stood guard outside the entry to each shower. Beckham looked back at the man guarding his.

"Sir, please put on the clothes provided," said the sentry. "Your blood test came back negative."

Beckham didn't even remember them taking blood. Must have been when he was out. He picked up a white jumpsuit from the bench. Sitting down, he took off his blade and rested it against the wall. He changed as quickly as he could, but getting his stump through the pant leg proved to be difficult without help. When he'd finished and attached his blade, he stepped up to the door and combed his wet hair back with his left hand.

A chirp sounded, the door unlocked, and the soldier on the other side pulled it open. One by one, the other isolation doors opened up. Jake and Timothy stepped out with the others, but Horn remained inside.

"What about Master Sergeant Horn?" Beckham asked.

"We are holding him for a while," the sentry said.

Beckham paused. "What the hell for?"

The soldier didn't reply, just waved Beckham forward. They walked down the hallway, but Beckham detoured toward Horn's door. The soldier guarding it held up his rifle.

"Sir, please do not step over the red line."

Beckham glanced down at the floor. His blade was on the outside of the line, and after seeing what had happened on the dock outside, he didn't want to push these people. They had their orders.

"It's okay," Horn said. He held up a paw. "I'll be fine, boss. Just look after Tasha and Jenny till I'm out of this shit hole."

Beckham hesitated, and Horn said, "Really, brother. I'm good."

"Follow us, please," another Medical Corps soldier said from the other end of the hall. Jake, Timothy, and the other civilians were already moving. Beckham's gaze flicked from the man guarding Horn's door and then to his own escort.

"Please, sir, I don't want any trouble," the soldier said.

Beckham didn't know his name or rank or anything about him, but he could tell the kid wasn't a killer. Beckham wasn't going to force him to become one. Flaring his nostrils, he stepped back into the line and followed the others. Horn sat on the bench inside his stall, his lumberjack arms wrapped around his torso. He offered a final nod of reassurance. Beckham returned the gesture.

"Stop at the red line," said a voice at the end of the hallway. Two Medical Corps soldiers walked around a corner, M4s cradled across their chests.

"I'm Corporal Ingersoll," one of them said. "You have all been cleared of infection and will be taken through these doors for a briefing." He directed his sharp gaze at Beckham.

"Captain, please follow me."

Beckham joined Ingersoll. The guards opened the metal doors and motioned for Jake, Timothy, and the others to go through. Durand stopped and looked at Beckham.

"You're not going to get away with what you did back there," he snarled. "We have protocols for a reason."

"Sorry about your head, Doc, but you deserved it."

A Medical Corps guard ushered Durand through the doors before he could reply.

"This way, Captain," Ingersoll said. He gestured for Beckham to follow him down a connecting hallway that curved toward another set of metal doors.

"Where's Kate?" Beckham asked.

"I'm taking you to her now. We have some news for you."

That made Beckham walk faster. His next words came out in a rush. "What news? Is she okay? Is it the baby?"

"I think you'd better hear this from her."

Beckham limped down the hall, heart stuttering in sync with the clicking of his blade on the white tiles.

When they got to the double doors, Ingersoll pushed them open. He nodded at Beckham and jerked his helmet toward a bright room furnished with medical equipment and a single bed. Kate was sitting with her legs over the side and her hand on her swollen stomach.

Beckham rushed over to her, almost slipping on the floor. "Kate, sweetheart, are you okay?"

Kate wiped away the tears rolling down her face. She smiled, and Beckham saw the tears weren't of pain, but of joy.

"We're having a boy, Reed," she said. "We're having a little boy."

4

Fitz sat in the radio telephone operator seat of the MATV, watching tracer rounds spit across the sky like shooting stars. RIM-7 Sea Sparrows and smaller RIM-116 Rolling Airframe Missiles were streaking away from the USS *Iwo Jima* toward the shore, the blasts blossoming into the air and bursting in exploding crimson bubbles. Operation Beachhead had officially begun.

The sight of Normandy reminded Fitz how far from home they were. He was a homebody, and was already missing his Southern roots. He would have done just about anything for some biscuits and gravy, and a good night's sleep right now.

But biscuits and sleep were going to have to wait.

Salt water spilled over the side of the Landing Craft Air Cushion carrying the MATV. Inside were two other all-terrain armored vehicles and a trio of armored Humvees, all mounted with M240s.

Flanked on all sides by dozens of other LCACs, the expeditionary force thumped over the waves, carrying over two thousand marines and dozens of vehicles and tanks. The other MEUs would be doing the exact same thing in Spain, France, and Germany. Tens of thousands of American soldiers were about to embark on the biggest operation in Europe since D-Day. But unlike the trained American forces in World War II, most of these men and women were volunteers with no basic training.

The boat rumbled as a wing of AV-8B Harrier IIs tore overhead, their single-engines screaming. A dozen Ospreys followed, along with a trio of Black Hawks. Next came the Bell AH-1Z Viper attack helicopters. They buzzed across the night like a swarm of angry bugs.

Fitz held on to the handle above his door as the LCAC jolted over a wave. Mist sprayed in through the open window and drenched the windshield. Stevenson turned on the wipers. They squeaked across, clearing the view just as more missiles screamed into the sky. The *Iwo Jima* and the other two destroyers were about a mile out, launching their arsenal at Variant coordinates provided by Marine Recon units. The USS *Forrest Sherman* still hadn't joined the expeditionary force, but it wasn't far behind now.

Apollo looked up from the floor, and Fitz patted him on his head. The dog had been through hundreds of hours of combat in the past few months, but this was his first invasion. It wasn't Fitz's first rodeo, however. He'd been there at the start of Operation Iraqi Freedom, rolling into Baghdad on the front lines with the other marines. He'd spent nearly six months in the hostile Iraqi city of Fallujah, sometimes waiting hours or even days to deliver death with a single shot as a sniper. But this time Fitz wasn't holed up in some shitty apartment building with his spotter. He was part of a much bigger force designed to deliver death to the enemy in a far more massive way.

Fitz couldn't deny he was terrified about what they would find in Europe. He felt a similar fear back in Iraq, but fighting Saddam's forces was much less frightening than facing the monsters of the new world, especially with the rumors of even nastier beasts emerging across the European front.

An icy ball formed in the pit of Fitz's stomach as he stroked Apollo's fur. He wasn't worried about losing his life. But he was responsible for more lives than just his own now. He was worried about Apollo, the members of Team Ghost, and all of the other young men and women with the MEU.

In the back seat, Rico was writing in a journal. Tanaka seemed oblivious to the assault, but Fitz knew the man was taking a measure of their approach while listening to his music. Dohi, stoic and focused, watched the waves for anything hostile. Stevenson kept his eyes on the water as he gripped the steering wheel like a race car driver waiting for the gun to go off.

"What you listenin' to, Tanaka?" he said.

Tanaka didn't reply at first. He looked up to the front seat like he was unsure if Stevenson was messing with him.

"Tupac," Tanaka finally said.

"You love that old-school shit."

"That's old-school?" Fitz said. "Shit, now you're making *me* feel old."

Stevenson grinned. "You are old, sir."

Rico rolled her eyes at Fitz. He cracked a half grin and went back to patting Apollo's head. As the boat slapped over the waves, he found himself not looking to the future but to the past.

"Seventy years ago, my grandfather was on a landing craft headed for a beach just like this on D-Day," Fitz mused out loud. "Makes you think, doesn't it?"

"My grandpa too," said Stevenson.

Fitz blinked in surprise. "For real? I didn't know that there were . . . I mean, I thought that . . ."

He trailed off, realizing his foot was firmly wedged in his mouth.

Stevenson just laughed. "African American soldiers fought in Operation Overlord, sir. Only the history books don't talk about it so much. My grandpa talked about having to dig graves for American troops, but trust me, he also killed his fair share of Nazis."

"Wonder if the history books will be talking about us someday," said Rico.

Fitz smiled, but his heart wasn't in it. He let his mind wander. Rumors of massive underground meat factories, eerily similar to the concentration camps of the Nazis, had reached them. The EUF had discovered several World War II bunkers filled with human prisoners, all being used to feed the growing juvenile armies that were eating their way across Europe. He knew they wouldn't all make it back from this mission in one piece. They were facing the worst threat humanity had ever seen.

A transmission crackled in Fitz's earpiece, a welcome distraction from his thoughts.

"Command, this is Delta One. First flyover shows no signs of juveniles or adults. Infrared is picking up zero. Over."

Another voice replied, "Copy that, Delta One. Fox One to Six, you have permission to land. Repeat, you have permission to land."

"Roger," Fox 1 replied. "We're preparing to dock."

The first wave was made up of the M1A1 Abrams Tanks, LAV-25 Light Armored Vehicles, Humvees, and Assault Breacher Vehicles. Team Ghost was part of the second wave. Most of the ground troops were in the second and third waves, held back to cut down on casualties in case there were any Variants lurking near the landing points. The plan was pretty simple: Let their eyes in the sky identify Variant nests and soften up those areas with heavy artillery. Then send in the troops to mop up the rest.

General Nixon's strategy didn't seem much different from those his predecessors had used during Operation Liberty, and every other mission since the hemorrhage virus raged across the States. Fitz had questioned the orders back on the *Iwo Jima*, but the commanders had shut him down, insisting they had learned from their mistakes and that this operation was different.

He sure hoped they were right about that. Commander Bradley was right about one thing at least—the juveniles were very different from their parents. And Europe wasn't just crawling with Variant offspring, it was still swarming with adults too. Which meant more of the little bastards would be coming.

Colonel Gibson, the man behind this nightmare, couldn't possibly have known what his engineered bioweapon would spawn. The colonel was dead now, but the terror he had helped create lived on. First the hemorrhage virus, then the Variants, and now the ever-evolving juveniles.

The nightmare is just beginning, Fitz thought as the boat skirted over the water. He remembered what Dr. Ellis had said about the offspring. They were far more intelligent than any serial killer or Nazi general, not to mention stronger and faster. Even worse, they were developing more weapons to fight against humans, from toxins to thicker armor and flame-resistant flesh. The beasts were more than a new breed of monsters—they were the ultimate predator. Kate and her team were studying the creatures and sending updates to the military, but that intel rarely got all the way down to Fitz, and he hadn't been able to talk to Beckham or Kate for several days.

"I'll be right back," Fitz said. He opened the door

and stepped out onto the deck of the landing craft. The vibration ran up his carbon-fiber blades and his thighs like the tingle from gripping a motorcycle throttle.

Fitz shut the door just as the back door opened and Rico jumped out. She tucked her small journal in her pocket, and they stood next to each other to watch the tracer rounds split the horizon. Sparrows and RAMs continued to fly overhead.

Rico blew a bubble that popped the same moment a trio of missiles hit a cliff. The sparks showered onto the beach, illuminating the rocky terrain and the first of the LCACs making up the first wave.

There was no sign of Variants or juveniles on the shore. Perhaps Command had been right about this one.

He unstrapped his MK11 and brought the scope to his eye, scanning the beach with the infrared optics. The juveniles could be difficult to detect because their armored shells blocked their heat signatures, but all he saw were smooth rocks and sand.

"Anything?" Rico asked. She gestured for his rifle.

He handed it to her and took a step back, using the moment to examine the other vehicles in the landing craft. There were fifty marines aboard, all inside their all-terrain vehicles. Some of them were just kids and hadn't even finished their training. Others were aging vets who had been saved from the cities and had answered Ringgold's call to serve. Doing so meant they got to eat better than the people back at the SZTs. Other than Plum Island, most of the strongholds were disease-infested communities plagued with violence and crime.

The boat jolted again as the bottom scraped over a rock.

Fitz cupped his hand over the radio to hear an incoming transmission over the distant explosions and the exhaust from the turbo fans at the rear of the LCAC.

"Command, this is Fox One, we've reached the shore. No sign of contacts. Preparing to disembark, over."

"Copy that, Fox One. You have a green light to proceed. Stay frosty."

Fitz patted Rico's shoulder and took his rifle back. He walked to the metal landing ramp at the right side of the craft. A middle-aged marine with his arm in a sling stood at the gate, his helmet and flak jacket soaked with salt water from the spray. Through the mist, Fitz could see the first wave of boats running ashore. The ramps opened, and Humvees shot out onto the beach. The tankers followed in the M1A1s, plowing over the sand.

"Master Sergeant, you're supposed to stay in your vehicle until we beach," the marine said. "Please get back to—"

A thud rocked the side of the landing craft, cutting the man off midsentence. He glanced over his shoulder, then back at Fitz. "You hear that?"

"Just a wave," Fitz said. He looked past the sentry, focusing on the ocean. It was difficult to see in the darkness, and he could only spot the outlines of the other LCACs to the east. Rico joined him at the ramp and grabbed the railing.

"Please return to your vehicle," said the marine guard. "We're going to be on the beach in a couple minutes."

"We're going, just give me a second," Fitz replied. He scoped the shoreline again and zoomed in on the tanks. They were crawling across the beach toward a dirt ramp that curved up and over the cliffs.

Fitz roved his rifle back and forth, when he saw a sudden flash of motion at the top of one of those cliffs. He jerked the gun back to a figure skittering up a jagged summit like a spider. The monster crested the peak and perched.

"Command, this is Fox One. Beach is clear of contacts, repeat…"

Another jolt hit the side of the LCAC.

"What the hell are we hitting?" Rico asked. "It's not supposed to be shallow out here."

Fitz didn't reply. He zoomed in on the biggest juvenile Variant he had ever seen. The beast, covered from head to foot in plates of armor, was crouched like a gargoyle on the rocks over the beach.

Fitz pushed his mini-mic into position to report the contact, when another transmission came over the net.

"Command, this is Fox One. Our tracks are stuck in something."

"Come again, Fox One."

Fitz centered his gun on the Abrams. Several of them were stopped about halfway up the beach, not far from the natural sandy incline leading out. Steam from the engines rose around them like steaks cooking in a skillet.

White noise crackled from his headset, the spotty transmissions breaking up.

"Tracks…Stuck in some sort of oil…" the tank commander replied over the comms. "Something's burning."

Fitz aimed back at the Variant. It was gone now. A pair of Black Hawks swooped over the spot where it had been and headed back to sea.

"This is all wrong," Fitz whispered. He lowered his rifle and opened the channel to Command. "This is Ghost One, reporting hostiles on the cliffs. Over."

"Copy that, Ghost One. How many did you see?"

"One," Fitz replied, realizing how silly it sounded.

The reply was shortly delayed.

"Ghost One, Command. Advise if you spot anything else. Over."

Fitz's cheeks flared with embarrassment. He turned to move back to his vehicle, but then he saw something that made him stop. The whitecaps near the LCAC looked strange. He elbowed the marine out of the way, squinting for a better look at what could have been fins in the water.

Flares suddenly shot into the sky in all directions from the second wave of the MEU. Their red light illuminated the water and beach.

Boom, boom, boom.

The sound of more flares fired above, and in their wake came a sight that seized the breath from Fitz's lungs. Those weren't waves at all—they were the turtle-like shells of juveniles swimming just beneath the water. Hundreds of them.

All at once they seemed to jump from the water, claws extended and puckered mouths popping. The beasts leaped onto the sides of the LCACs and clung like barnacles.

"CONTACTS!" Fitz screamed. He swung his MK11 up just as one of the creatures grabbed the marine guard by the back of the neck. The monster plucked his head off with the ease of a man popping the tail off a shrimp. The sound of the man's skull disconnecting from his spine made Fitz's stomach roll. He angled his MK11 up, chambered a round, and shot the monster in the right eye, blowing out the back of its head over the water.

Rico grabbed Fitz and pulled him away from the ramp as two more of the beasts emerged, their claws gripping the top gate of the landing craft. Their talons shrieked over the metal as they pulled themselves up.

"Move!" Rico screamed. "Get back to the MATV!"

Fitz fired off two more rounds as soon as a pair of bulbous eyes emerged over the side of the ramp. One of the creatures opened its mouth and sucked down a round that exited through the armor lining its neck. The second juvenile jerked to the left an instant too late, and

Fitz shot it in the skull. Chunks of armor and flesh peppered his helmet.

"On the Two-Forties!" he yelled, waving to the other vehicles. He pushed his mini-mic to his lips and opened the channel to Team Ghost. "Dohi, get on the big gun!"

Marines emerged from their MATVs and climbed into the turrets, swerving the automatic weapons into position. Within seconds the whine of 7.62-millimeter rounds sounded, echoing in the enclosed space. They streaked in all directions, smashing through armored plates and sending juveniles spinning down to watery graves.

"Don't hit the sides of the ship!" Fitz yelled. But it wasn't just the rounds he was worried about cutting through the delicate landing craft. It was the talons of the juveniles. He ran back to his MATV and opened the passenger door.

Stevenson beat on the wheel. "Close the door!"

Apollo was barking at the approaching monsters, saliva dripping from his maw. Fitz turned where he stood and fired. Two more of the juveniles vanished over the high walls of the LCAC. He chambered another round and was moving into the vehicle when an explosion on the beach commanded his attention. The Abrams had opened fire. Fitz zoomed in with his rifle at dozens of creatures mounting the bluffs. Several of the beasts jumped into the air as the shells punched into the cliffs, blowing pieces of rock sky high.

Another explosion flashed in his peripheral. He pulled his scope away to see the beach ignite in a massive blue fireball. The heat was fast and intense, and he could feel it on his face even a quarter mile from shore.

He shielded his eyes, squinting through a fort of fingers.

Fitz jumped into the MATV and slammed the door as the explosion died down, revealing the tanks, Humvees, and other vehicles caught in an inferno. A tank commander opened the hatch of his Abrams, his skin melting off like candle wax as Fitz watched helplessly through his scope. The man fell limply over the side of his tank, and Fitz lowered his rifle in horror.

"Jesus, this isn't happening!" Rico said.

Tanaka leaned forward. "It was a trap all along. That's juvenile toxin on the beach, isn't it? They knew we were coming."

Fitz couldn't wrap his mind around the facts. More of the juveniles were climbing the side of the landing craft. They were almost inside.

Lead, Fitz. You have to lead.

Black Hawks and Vipers returned to the fight. They flew over the smoldering wrecks of the first wave of the MEU, door gunners firing—but they were aiming into the sky. So what the hell were they shooting at?

Fitz pushed his scope to his eye and leaned back so he had room to move his rifle in the front seat. Something flapped across his crosshairs toward the Black Hawks, but it was too fast to capture.

One of the juveniles made it over the ramp and landed in front of their bumper. It let out a screech that opened a trio of armored slits on both sides of its neck. Fitz knew then how the monsters had avoided detection in the water. They had gills.

Dohi centered his gun on it and fired rounds that lanced into the creature's chest plate, punching through vital organs.

Fitz exhaled and raised his MK11. The Black Hawks were circling now, and their gunners were still firing into the sky. He zoomed in on the door gunner of the closest helicopter just as a bat-like creature twice the size of a man yanked the marine out of the chopper. It flapped away, holding the man in its talons.

Not bats. Juveniles. They can fly!

More of the beasts launched from the cliffs and took to the sky, plucking door gunners out and tossing them aside like rag dolls. The Vipers gave chase, guns blazing and missiles streaking away. The winged Variants were massive, but they were no match for a missile. Several of the creatures windmilled to the ground, frayed wings smoking as they plummeted.

A flurry of transmissions from Command overwhelmed Fitz's earpiece.

"What the hell is happening out there?"

"Fox One, do you copy? Over."

"Fox Two, do you copy . . ."

"Does anyone fucking copy?"

There was screaming, too, and desperate cries for help. All chain of command seemed to have been lost in the chaos. Fitz ripped the bud from his ear and realized that the hissing noise he'd been hearing wasn't static—it was the sound of air escaping from the cushion of their landing craft. But even worse, the M240s were going silent as juveniles fought their way onto the ship. The gunner from the MATV to their left was ripped from his turret and tossed to another juvenile standing on the hood like a violent, bloody game of catch. The beast ripped him apart in a flurry of slashes before leaping to the next vehicle.

Dohi roved his gun and blew both the monsters away, but it was too late for the marine gunner. His corpse crashed to the ground, now no more than a hunk of mangled flesh.

Their vessel jerked to the left, drawing Fitz's attention to the pilot station. Both of the navy pilots of the LCAC were gone.

Shit, shit, shit. You have to lead, Fitz. Get out there and lead!

Through the windshield, the burning beach was growing closer. He didn't know if they'd make it before the LCAC sank. But they had a more urgent problem. Another craft was on a collision course with theirs. Fitz grabbed his door handle and prepared to bail out.

Stevenson tried to pull him back. "What the hell are you doing?"

"Saving us," Fitz replied. He jumped out onto the deck and slammed the door before Apollo could follow him.

"Dohi, cover me!" he yelled.

Rico opened her door as Fitz approached. She raised her M4 over his shoulder and fired a burst that sent a juvenile behind him skittering away.

Fitz gripped his ringing ears. "Jesus, Rico!"

"You're welcome!"

Gunfire from the 240s streaked overhead. Fitz crouched down and ran with Rico for the back of the boat. A juvenile jumped in front of Fitz as he rounded the next Humvee. He skidded to a stop and went to raise his rifle, knowing it was already too late.

A blade struck the creature's armored neck, slicing through the organic plates. Warm blood squirted over Fitz. He wiped it away to see Tanaka standing behind the beast with his Katana out, the metal gleaming with crimson. He finished the monster with a stab from the smaller Wakizashi to the back of its skull.

Two more of the juveniles jumped onto the roof of the Humvee Tanaka was standing behind, crushing the metal. Both monsters looked to be over four hundred pounds, with sucker lips the size of Tanaka's head.

"Go!" he yelled, twirling his two swords and walking toward the juveniles confidently. Fitz looked back at the other LCAC still drifting toward them. Water bubbled around the cushion as the juveniles worked to sink the craft.

Fitz and Rico ran to the pilot station. She grabbed the door and pulled. Glass fell away from the shattered window. Fitz climbed through the missing windshield where a juvenile had yanked out the previous pilots. He grabbed the controls and twisted the steering wheel to avoid the oncoming craft. Gunfire cut in all directions as the M240 gunners fought desperately to keep the juveniles off the sides of the LCAC.

From this vantage, Fitz could see the entire battlefield. The ocean, beach, and cliffs were alive with monsters. Bubbles frothed and burst on the surface over submerged boats, and vehicles burned on the beach. Helicopters circled above the jagged cliffs, firing on the juveniles in the sky.

They passed the sinking LCAC on their left. It was going down, but there was a final marine still fighting from the turret of his MATV. The flash from the muzzle fire illuminated a youthful face that Fitz recognized from the *Iwo Jima*.

Fitz turned the wheel again, away from the craft. The marine continued firing even as water rose around his MATV. The ocean swallowed him a moment later.

There was nothing you could have done, Fitz told himself. But it didn't make him feel any better.

Their own LCAC was still in trouble. The ramp fell with a crash, letting in a dozen juveniles. The cold ocean flowed into the LCAC, gurgling around the vehicles. Fitz could see Apollo pawing at the window of the MATV. They were sinking less than a thousand feet from the shore.

Not like this, Fitz thought. *Please, God, not like this.*

He looked for Tanaka. The man was busy carving up

a Variant near the starboard side of the ship. He stuck his Katana inside the creature's sucker lips and twisted it before turning to strike the other beast as it lunged at him.

"Watch out!" Rico shouted.

She wasn't yelling at Tanaka—she was yelling at Fitz. He whirled as a shadow covered their craft. The outline of another ship emerged to the west. The massive bow of a destroyer cut through the water. At first he thought it was the *Iwo Jima*, but the silhouette was wrong.

"It's the *Forrest* fucking *Sherman!*" Rico shouted.

An M2 Browning .50-caliber on deck opened fire, rounds slamming through a wave of the flying Variants. Another M2 joined the fight. Together, the Ma Deuces cut the abominations from the sky.

The crew of the *Forrest Sherman* had arrived just in time to save what was left of the second wave of the MEU. But there wasn't anything they could do for the marines on the beach, and Team Ghost wasn't out of this yet.

"On me, Rico!" Fitz shouted. He climbed back out of the window and jumped into the cold water flooding their craft. The ocean surged around his blades. He waded forward, firing on a juvenile shaking the side of their MATV. Apollo barked furiously from inside. The beast reached back, then punched an armored hand through the window.

"No!" Fitz screamed.

Rico surged in front of him, tossing her M4 aside and unslinging the sawed-off shotgun from her back. She fired a blast into the juvenile's back. It fell off the MATV and whirled toward her. She pumped the shotgun and fired another blast that hit the beast in the face, its eyes exploding like egg yolks. The creature pawed at its head, then jumped over the side of the boat into the water.

"Tanaka!" Fitz yelled.

The man walked around the end of a Humvee, sheathed his blades, and pulled his M4. Neither Fitz nor Tanaka said a word as they raced back to their MATV.

Fitz opened the front door, and Apollo jumped into his arms. Stevenson clambered out, and the entire team climbed onto the roof of the vehicle as water rushed into the sinking craft. Standing above the MATV with Apollo in his arms, Fitz saw the hellish landscape before him. The beach was still on fire, and the charcoaled hulls of vehicles smoldered in an oven that didn't seem possible to shut off. Blue flames raged over the sand and rocks. Fitz could feel the heat on his face, despite the cold water surrounding him.

"Fitz, we need you!" someone shouted.

Something gurgled as more water rushed in, and Fitz felt it pulling them down. He set Apollo down and searched for a target with his MK11.

"Up here!" shouted a voice.

A rope ladder hit the opposite end of the LCAC as the *Forrest Sherman* maneuvered closer. It was shallow here, which meant Colonel Bradley was taking a major risk to save the scattered survivors of the MEU.

Marines climbed down from the side of the destroyer.

"Get to the ladder!" Fitz shouted.

Standing back to back on the roof of the MATV, the team fired at the juveniles swimming around the vehicles. The war for Europe had just begun, but if Team Ghost didn't get moving, they weren't even going to make it to the shore.

5

"Come here, little buddy," Piero whispered.

He bent toward the skinniest mouse he had ever seen and slowly set his emergency candle on the brick floor of the access tunnel. The light danced over damp walls covered with dripping green stains. Graffiti, both modern and old, tattooed the ancient walls. There were designs of Roman soldiers, cartoon animals, and religious symbols. The abandoned sewer had existed for hundreds of years with these markings, and would continue long after Piero died here.

But he wasn't ready to die just yet.

A draft of cold air whistled down the tunnel, causing the flame to flicker out of control. He reached out with a crumb of granola bar to bait the mouse. In his other hand, he gripped his knife, ready to strike.

The tiny creature glanced up, pink ears perked and curious black eyes centered on the piece of food. It cautiously sniffed the air.

Piero had always had a soft spot for animals, but he hadn't eaten anything but granola bars for days now. It was amazing how the mind worked when it was in distress. Especially when the body was starving.

You're going to taste delicious, he thought. *The two bites*

I can get off your ribs. He imagined eating the creature would be a lot like eating chicken wing. There was never enough meat on them.

Piero wasn't a big man, but he had a large appetite. Food was life to an Italian, and he hadn't had a proper meal in more months than he could count. The mere thought made his stomach grumble.

He studied the tiny creature, tilting his head like a Varianti watching its prey. Maybe mice really did taste like chicken, or maybe they tasted like something else entirely. The pigeon he'd eaten sure hadn't tasted like chicken.

Shut up, Piero. Focus.

It was getting harder and harder to concentrate. He had to remain vigilant if he ever hoped to escape this wretched city, but he felt himself drifting further and further into insanity.

The mouse stood on its hind legs and reached up with little white paws, sniffing the air voraciously.

"That's right," Piero whispered. "You're almost there. Just a little farther."

He scooted forward on his knees, his knife clenched tightly in his hand. Gritting his teeth, he slowly pulled it from the sheath and prepared to skewer his dinner.

Like the starving creature before him, Piero had let his guard down for the chance at a meal. Years of Special Operations training had prepared him to survive for days without food in the field. But not months. And not on his own in a city ravaged by monsters.

The mouse inched forward until the morsel of food was a centimeter away from its nose. Just as Piero prepared to knife it, a distant thud echoed in the dark passage. As slowly as possible, he reached for the candle and picked it up. The frail creature craned its small neck and peered into the moving candlelight that illuminated the narrow sewer passage. The sewer seemed to stretch on and on. Now was Piero's chance to kill it, but the distant banging stopped him.

He sheathed the knife and reached for his rifle. He'd made himself go back to the river a few days after Antonio's death. There had been no sign of his friend left. At least he'd found his rifle.

Boom. Boom. Boom.

The mouse's ears perked, and so did Piero's. For a moment he had forgotten that he wasn't the predator. Like the mouse, he was the prey. And the juveniles had finally found his hiding spot.

He blew out the candle with a shallow breath. The light receded, and darkness swallowed Piero as if he had jumped into a black hole. He felt a tug on his finger. The brave mouse wasn't going to let the food go without a fight.

"Stupid little idiot," Piero whispered. He pulled the granola bar away, but the mouse didn't let go. It held on as he put the precious piece in his vest pocket. Inside too went the small creature.

"I'll save you for later, then," Piero said. He rose to his feet, gripping his Beretta ARX160 assault rifle, and raised the night-vision optics to his eyes. The green-hued pane came into focus. He centered the crosshairs on the end of the passage, where it curved to the northeast.

It sounded like the thumping was coming from the secret trapdoor that led to the Vatican, but he couldn't be sure. The narrow passages made it difficult to locate the noise. If it was coming from the door, he would hear a warning. He had rigged up an alarmed barricade just in case the monsters made it through.

Scanning the passage, he saw no sign of movement. The sewer tunnel weaved under the city streets along the edges of the Vatican. After living down here for months, he had the layout memorized. He had been using the tunnels to get from place to place, but he wasn't the only one. Although the juveniles now controlled the streets above, they also dwelled in the darkness.

Piero hadn't seen sunlight for several days. Or was it longer than that? Sometimes he thought of himself as Gollum from *Lord of the Rings*. Other times he pictured himself as a Varianti.

No, Piero. You're not a monster. You're still a man.

Another distant boom thumped down the passage. The mouse struggled in his vest pocket at the sound. Piero turned to run, but he froze at the screech that followed. The secret metal door leading to the Vatican had been broken off its ancient hinges. A siren wailed, louder and louder with every beat. That only seemed to enrage the monster on the other side of the barricade. Over the sound of the alarm came the shattering of wood crates and the shriek of the beasts tearing through them.

Piero's heart fluttered.

The juveniles were inside.

In seconds, they had destroyed the barricade he'd spent an entire day building. He stood there, frozen in terror, unsure if he should run or stand his ground and fight. There were fifteen rounds left in his last magazine. If there had been only one juvenile, he might have been able to kill it before it killed him. But there was no way he could defend himself against a pack of the beasts, especially if they were the other kind...

Don't say it, Piero. Don't you say it.

The winged horror that had ripped Antonio apart wasn't the only one. He had seen others topside, which was another reason he no longer ventured above the streets, even during the day. The juveniles were still growing, still changing, developing wings and horns and God knew what else.

Piero made the sign of the cross and then raised his rifle. Somewhere overhead, the heart of the Catholic Church had fallen. Hell on earth was real, and no prayer was going to save him. The Pope, the cardinals, and all the priests were long dead—or turned into Varianti.

The mouse quivered in his pocket, and Piero made a decision. In all his years of fighting, he had never run from an enemy. But that was before he had faced the monsters. He turned and fled.

He tried to lighten his footfalls, but everything echoed in the narrow tunnel. And the juveniles would hear him regardless. They knew he was there.

He tried to imagine how they saw the world. It was all too easy to slip into the mind of a monster. The yellow-hued view, similar to his own night-vision optics, narrowed as it raced down the tunnel on all fours, joints popping and armor creaking. Lips the size of a bowl smacked, and a warty, bulbous nose sniffed the air, picking up Piero's gamey scent. It rounded a corner and snorted at a heat signature ahead—a heat signature with a second, smaller signature near its chest. The monster's vision changed from yellow to white, and now Piero could see a heartbeat—his heartbeat. The vision homed in on the second, tinier heartbeat.

Stop it, Piero. Stop it!

There was no denying he was going crazy. Maybe he'd already gone over the edge. He knew the monster couldn't see his heartbeat, and especially not that of the mouse in his pocket.

He closed his eyes briefly. The vision was gone, replaced by the darkness of the tunnel. He pushed the scope back to his eye. Somewhere behind him, claws scraped over the walls. He couldn't resist looking over his shoulder, but the movement threw him off balance. He reached out to brace himself as he tripped. In the last second before impact, he palmed the ground, saving the mouse in his vest from certain death. Using a scraped, bloody hand, he pushed himself up and kept running.

His hideout wasn't far, just around the next turn, but the beast was getting closer. He could hear its armor scraping against the walls.

Piero sucked in air as he ran. The trick was steady breathing. Steady was how he survived.

But why would you want to survive? You could be the last person left alive in Rome. Maybe even the last person on the planet.

Another steady breath. Another steady exhale.

You're not the last person alive. There are others. You will find them.

Piero gasped for air as a stitch tore at his side.

He had found someone last week, but the priest he'd stumbled across wasn't really a man. Not anymore. At first, Piero had thought he was one of the Varianti. He had been shambling down a passage to the east, covered in blood and filth. It wasn't until Piero moved in with his knife that he saw the eyes of a man staring back at him—crazy eyes, but human.

The priest had started screaming when he saw him. Screaming so loud that Piero had been forced to do something he didn't want to think about...

He could almost hear Antonio's voice in his head now. *Run! Stop thinking and run!*

Piero gripped his rifle tighter and ran around the next corner. The mouse continued clawing at the inside of his vest pocket, but its tiny nails weren't going to get through the lining.

The passage curved into a long tunnel that connected to Saint Peter's Basilica. His hideout was directly under the church, not far from the priest he had killed. It was by chance that he had found the spot. If it hadn't been for the priest, he would never have found it at all.

Piero smelled the rot before he saw the corpse in the green hue of his night-vision optics. The body lay just outside the iron grate of his bunker.

No, not a bunker. A tomb.

The monster behind him shrieked, shocking Piero into a sprint. It didn't sound like mindless squawking. It sounded almost like...

Oh no, Piero thought, his heart slamming against his rib cage. *Please, God. No.*

A second shriek answered the call of the first.

There were two juveniles in the tunnels, and they were communicating.

Piero kept his scope to his eye as he closed the distance to the grate. He held his breath in an attempt to keep out the wretched smell of the corpse. The stench was almost unbearable, but it served to camouflage his own scent.

The mouse continued to scratch at his pocket, desperately now, like it knew the monsters were closing in.

"It's okay, little buddy. We're going to be okay."

Piero stopped at the grate and lowered his gun. He moved the priest out of the way, grabbed the bars, and pulled them away from the entry to the ancient tomb. With those out of the way, he got on the ground and began scooting through the narrow gap between the brick wall and the floor.

Sparks suddenly rained from the ceiling of the tunnel to the east. He froze, stuck under the entry. He couldn't see the beast, but he knew it was coming. The sound of snapping joints, like massive tree limbs cracking, filled the tunnel as the monster darted horizontally across the stone.

As Piero wiggled through, his vest caught on a chunk of broken brick that had come loose.

Come on, come on.

The mouse squirmed in his pocket.

A second screech sounded from the opposite direction. The other juvenile was moving in. This one was larger. He could tell by the crunch of claws over the bricks. Wind rushed down the tunnel. It whipped up the scent of rot, filling Piero's nostrils again with the awful smell.

He sucked in a breath—and his nearly nonexistent gut—and continued wiggling. Using his left hand, he felt for the loose brick and pushed up on it so that the mouse would not be crushed. He shoved himself free and shot through the gap, crashing to the floor on his back a few feet below.

His rifle bit into his shoulder, but he ignored the pain and got up. He moved back to the entrance. The sparks showering from the ceiling provided him a brief glimpse of the monster outside. It was about two hundred pounds, maybe more—small compared to the other beast he had heard.

He fumbled for the grate and pulled it back into place. Then he reached through the gap in the bars and pulled the dead priest's body into position.

"Forgive me, Padre," he whispered as he dragged the rotting corpse in front of the entrance.

Just as he finished, the second juvenile raced into the tunnel.

They stopped to talk to each other, a high-pitched sort of squawking that sounded like hissing vultures, only ten times louder.

Piero wanted to cup his hands over his ears to block the horrifying sounds, but he grabbed his rifle and brought the scope to his eye to scan the room that had become his home. It was maybe twenty feet by forty. The sarcophagus of some long-dead Italian stood at the back of the tomb. Latin was inscribed on the ceiling, and the remains of stenciled artwork covered the stone walls.

He ignored the artistic details and searched for the exit. There was a stone staircase that wound up several stories into the basilica. Rising to his feet, he slowly turned to check the passage outside with his scope, making sure the coast was clear to run.

The piercing shrieks of the talking juveniles faded away, replaced by the sniffing of their wart-covered noses. A paw that looked like it belonged to a bear slapped the ground, and its talons scratched across the flagstones.

Even the mouse in Piero's pocket froze at the sound.

A horned snout dripping saliva moved into view. The beast bent its gargantuan armor-plated head to sniff the dead priest.

Sprouting from its shoulders was an enormous pair of wings. Not the kind that he had plucked off the pigeon he had caught a month earlier. There were no feathers. These wings were like that of a dragon, covered in skin and reinforced with a layer of armor. The tips were frayed and bony.

Piero ducked down farther and gently put his back against the wall. The second monster arrived a moment later, sniffing the priest and then squawking angrily.

Another sneeze plastered the ground above with saliva that smelled like dead fish. Piero did his best not to breathe. The mouse went back to struggling in his pocket, clawing and squeaking.

Be quiet, he thought. Reaching down, he cupped the small creature in his hand. He didn't want to squeeze it to death, but...

The mouse suddenly stopped as the sound of footfalls stomped along the hallway outside the grate. The beasts were prowling now, still sniffing for his scent.

Piero closed his eyes and pulled his hand away from his vest to grab the stock of his rifle. Ever so slowly, he raised the gun and moved his finger to the trigger. Maybe he could shoot them both in the head before they made it through the narrow space. He would need to be fast, accurate, and smooth—but maybe he had a chance.

He waited, his finger tight against the trigger. The beasts continued to hunt outside the grate, and one of them brushed against it. Dust rained down on his matted brown hair, but Piero kept his eyes closed.

Just as he was about to leap up and blast the monster in the eye, a distant shriek sounded. It came from the west. Both juveniles stopped sniffing.

Silence consumed the tomb and the tunnel above.

The screech came again. This wasn't a random cry of a monster. They were calling to each other with a message of some sort. He could only pray the message wasn't about him.

Beads of sweat dripped down Piero's face. He didn't dare blink, move, or even breathe. The mouse remained still in his pocket.

A rush of wind whipped through the grate, rustling Piero's filthy hair, as the beast's wings began to flap. He remained with his back to the wall, sweat dripping down his head, heartbeat quickening. He risked a shallow breath, inhaling the sickly stench of decay.

As the beasts retreated, Piero carefully stood and pushed the scope to his eye just in time to watch the larger juvenile flapping down the hall, the tips of its wings barely clearing the walls.

The sounds of the monsters faded away, leaving him once again in silence, his only company a mouse and the corpse of a priest he had killed.

He kept his rifle tucked in his armpit and pulled the mouse from his pocket by its tail. The creature squirmed upside down in the darkness. Piero couldn't see it, but he could feel it wiggling.

It squeaked at him. Piero could guess what it meant: *Put me down, human!*

He crouched and set his rifle against the wall. Instead of skewering the mouse with his knife, he grabbed a small piece of granola out of his side pocket and gave it to the mouse. It ate rapidly, then looked up for more.

Piero smiled. He wasn't alone anymore. He had a friend.

Kate was curled up on the couch in their prefab house, wrapped in Reed's arms, listening to the hum of the furnace. It was odd hearing the rattle of the air-distribution system. The residents of Plum Island were lucky to have access to power and luxuries like running water and heat. Most of the SZTs were under strict energy curtailments with generators powering critical facilities for just a few hours a day.

She rested her head on Reed's chest, thinking of how she didn't ever want to leave this spot. It was the one place in the world she felt safe—the one place Variants and humans couldn't hurt her.

No one had said much since they returned home from the Medical Corps BSL4 facility. The clock was ticking toward nine, and the temperature had plummeted with the rain. Tasha and Jenny sat in front of the crackling fireplace, playing with a puzzle.

"Don't get too close," Horn said. He sat on the edge of a recliner with a shotgun on his lap and his M249 propped up against the wall behind him. Reed's rifle was next to the couch within easy reach.

The guns no longer made Kate nervous. She had

her own now, a small pistol that Reed insisted she keep on her person at all times. They had talked to the girls many times about never touching the weapons.

Horn checked the dressing on his left arm. "I think I'm almost out of lives, boss."

Reed nodded. "You're lucky you didn't lose your arm."

"One centimeter to the left and I'd look like you." Horn cracked a half grin, but Reed didn't smile back.

Kate was still in mild shock after the attack on the docks and the nightmare of decon. She kept her head on Reed's chest, listening to his heart beating, realizing how lucky they all were to still be alive.

Reed ran his fingers through her hair.

She thought of their baby boy, wondering whether he'd end up looking more like his daddy or her side of the family, but her thoughts quickly jumped to the innocent lives lost on the dock.

"To think I was starting to trust the Medical Corps again," she said. "Those *bastards*. How could they just open fire like that?"

Horn bowed his head, the hint of a grin gone.

"It's my fault," Kate continued. "I was part of the planning committee. We should never have let so many people on the dock."

"We were on that committee too," Reed said quietly. "But we couldn't have stopped this. Terrorism is something that's very difficult to plan for."

Tasha and Jenny glanced up from their puzzle, eyes roving from face to face. There was still innocence there, despite everything they had seen and lost.

Reed shook his head and sat up. Kate sat up with him and pulled a blanket over her lap.

"I've been trying to wrap my mind around what happened, but I just don't get it," he said. "I want to listen in to see if there's any chatter about it."

He grabbed the radio from the side table and turned it on. For several minutes Kate listened with him, but no one was talking about the attack.

"Command, this is Post Fourteen. Possible bandit spotted along the fence in Section Four-Four."

"Roger that, Post Fourteen. Sending Alpha Four to check it out."

"Try the Freedom Air Waves," Horn said.

Reed turned the channel to the independent radio station run from an SZT in California. The broadcaster was in the middle of a message.

"If you're out there listening, remember to make your way to the closest SZT. There are medical supplies, food, and safety for all."

"Safety," Horn said, shaking his head. "Yeah, right."

The broadcaster listed off the locations of the SZTs in California, Oregon, and Washington. Reed turned the channel to a military station, and Kate nestled her head back on his shoulder.

The transmissions continued, but she tuned them out. Tonight was supposed to have been a time of celebration. She had planned on using their rations to make a spaghetti dinner the evening they learned the sex of their child. But instead they were confined to their house listening for news of Operation Beachhead or the attack on Plum Island. President Jan Ringgold had promised she wouldn't let something like this happen. She had promised Plum Island would be a beacon of hope for future generations.

Tears welled in Kate's eyes, but she blinked them away. She didn't want Reed to see her crying.

Not tonight.

She sat up with Reed at an announcement from the military channel.

"Operation Beachhead begins in just a few hours.

Please pray for your brothers and sisters about to embark on a mission to take back Europe from the Variants."

Horn nodded. "We should say a prayer. Come here, girls." He reached out and gently took their hands in his own. Kate wrapped her fingers around Reed's left hand and smiled at him sadly. She hadn't heard him pray often, but she knew his faith was important to him.

"Dear Lord, tonight we pray to you and ask you in your divine mercy to look after our friends overseas. Please protect Team Ghost and all of the men and women in our armed forces as they embark on a mission to save mankind."

"Amen," Horn said.

Tasha and Jenny echoed the word, and Kate joined in. It was hard to imagine what Fitz and the others were about to go through, or what they were thinking. Being so far apart made Kate feel helpless. She closed her eyes, trying to fend off painful memories.

They all sat quietly for several minutes, even the girls, until the rap of a knock on the front door interrupted the silence.

Horn stood with his shotgun. "You expecting company, Kate?"

She shook her head. Reed pulled a gun from the holster on his hip and limped over to the door with Horn.

The pounding continued, and Kate gestured for Tasha and Jenny to follow her into the kitchen. A tree branch scratched at the window over the sink. She almost flinched at her own reflection in the glass. The woman staring back could have been a stranger. Her eyes were swollen from crying, their normally bright blue washed out and dull.

Another knock snapped her from her trance.

"Who is it?" Reed asked. He raised the revolver and used the hallway to partially shield his body. Horn took up position behind him.

"It's Pat," came a voice. "I need to talk to Kate."

Kate sighed and led the girls out of the kitchen. Reed shot her a glance and lowered his pistol at her nod. He unlocked the bolt and inched the door open.

Ellis was shivering on the stoop, collar up to his chin. He had a folder tucked under his right arm. Reed looked over Ellis's shoulder and scanned the dark street. Across the road, the Browns, a family Kate hardly knew, were playing cards in their living room with some of their other neighbors. For a moment things seemed like they could be normal, like this was just another American city in a time before the war, but the searchlights from a Black Hawk passing overhead and the rumble of a Humvee's diesel engine reminded Kate of the new reality. They were still at war.

Sometimes she thought they would always be at war.

Jack Brown glanced up from his hand of cards, walked over to the window to look at the sky, then closed the curtains over the steel-barred windows.

"It's freaking cold out here. Can I come in?" Ellis said.

Reed stepped aside and let Ellis through. He shut the door behind the doctor and latched it, then looked through the peephole.

"You're not supposed to be outside," Reed said with his eye pressed against the door. "That squad could easily pick you up for breaking curfew."

"I still have some authority around here," Ellis replied. "Besides, I need to talk to Kate."

"This late?"

Kate loved that Reed was protective of her, but sometimes it was a bit too much. Whatever Ellis had to say was likely important.

"Come in, Pat," Kate said. She gave Horn a meaningful look. He quickly nodded back.

"Time for bed, girls," Horn said.

"But we want to stay up and finish the puzzle," Jenny whined.

"You can tomorrow." Horn gestured down the hall-way. "Come on, I'll read you a story."

"Good night, girls," Kate said.

"Night, Auntie Kate," they said in unison.

"Thank you, Horn," Kate said.

Horn smiled at her, then held Reed's gaze for a second before vanishing down the hallway, leaving Ellis, Kate, and Reed to talk. She took a seat at the kitchen table and moved a stack of reports out of the way. Reed holstered his revolver and grabbed a pistol he'd left lying on the table. He pulled the magazine to check it. There were boxes of ammunition stacked next to empty magazines. This was what domestic life had become: she and Reed at the dinner table, each doing their respective homework for the night.

Ellis took a chair, opened the folder, and slid it across the table to Kate. He looked down the hallway to make sure the girls weren't listening just as Horn shut the door.

"This is the report I was telling you about earlier," Ellis said. "I grabbed the updated version from the lab after the attack."

Kate opened the folder and scanned the memo first.

CLASSIFIED—TOP SECRET—EYES ONLY

Examination by unauthorized persons is an act of treason punishable by fines and imprisonment up to 15 years and $100,000.

She had seen the language before, but she wasn't worried about Reed seeing anything he shouldn't. They were a team. Everything she knew, she shared with him—and vice versa.

Reed held the magazine in his prosthetic hand and placed a bullet in the top with a click. Kate had watched him struggle with the same action for weeks now, but he finally had the hang of it. He continued to slowly fill the magazine as Kate read through the document.

"The attack today wasn't an isolated incident," Ellis commented. "According to this report, there have been others."

Beckham placed a full magazine on the table. "What do you mean?"

"You heard about someone being stabbed with a needle, right?" Ellis ran a hand nervously through his hair.

"Yeah, some random psychopath on the dock. But that—"

"Not random," Ellis interrupted. "The person responsible knew they were committing suicide by doing this. They waited days for the opportunity and did it to inflict the greatest possible damage."

Kate scrutinized her partner. He was talking fast and sweating despite the chill in the air.

"But where would they even get the virus?" Reed asked. "And why commit suicide?"

"There are dozens of reports of cases of the hemorrhage virus mentioned here. VX9H9 and Kryptonite killed over ninety-nine percent of the infected and Variant populations, but there were some places outside the kill zones. We thought that's all it was at first, but now we know they are most certainly deliberate attacks."

Ellis flipped through the pages and pointed. Kate passed over another confidential warning and read the text below his finger. SZT 15 in Chicago had a solid black line through it, followed by the word *COMPROMISED*.

Kate felt a sinking feeling in her gut. She instinctively

put a protective hand on her stomach as Ellis kept talking.

"There have been coordinated attacks on SZTs nationwide. Someone is trying to sabotage the rebuilding efforts."

"But why?" Reed asked. "And who?"

"I'm not sure. That's why I'm here," Ellis said. "You got any ideas, Kate?"

She shook her head. Kate was used to the baby moving, but not like this. He was kicking hard. The sudden motion scared her more than the news. She was under way too much stress. Reed and her doctors had warned her about this.

"Kate?" Reed asked, putting his hand on hers.

She kept rubbing her stomach with her other hand. She could think of several men who might try to sabotage the rebuilding efforts for their own twisted agendas. Colonel Gibson and Colonel Wood were the first to come to mind, but the evil bastards who had started this nightmare were dead now.

"I'm not sure," she finally said. "But if I had to guess…what about surviving Alpha Variants or even juveniles that are still out there? Could they be capable of this level of coordination and sophistication? I mean, what type of human would kill innocents like they did today and then take their own life unless something was being held over their head? Like the safety of their family, for example."

Ellis looked to Reed.

He shrugged. "You're the one who said the juveniles are more cunning than serial killers."

The thought of an Alpha or a juvenile Variant using human prisoners to attack SZTs made her feel nauseated. She gasped as her baby suddenly kicked harder than ever.

Reed gave her a worried look. "Are you okay?" He scooted close and placed his hand on her shoulder. He squeezed it gently. "Are you in pain?"

Kate shook her head. "No...I...I think the baby is just restless." She looked up to meet his eyes, but Reed was already bending down next to her and placing his hand on her stomach.

Footfalls sounded from the hallway, and then Horn walked into the kitchen. He opened the fridge and grabbed a beer. Cracking the can open, he took a swig, wiped the foam off his lips, and burped, not realizing or not caring that everyone was looking at him.

"Girls are asleep," he said. He turned to Ellis. "So, Doc, what's the bad news?"

6

It was 0100 hours and thick clouds were streaking across a sky choked by smoke, but Captain Davis didn't need her night-vision goggles to see. Panama City Beach blazed. Underground gasoline tanks continued to go off like fireworks, new infernos igniting every few minutes. Flames licked the few structures that had survived the bombing from Operation Liberty.

Davis could already hear what Admiral Humphrey would say about this mission: *You risked your life and the lives of a team of marines for a few civilians?*

It wasn't the first time she had done something like this, and it wouldn't be the last. There were plenty of men and women who could serve as captain of the *GW*, but there weren't many who would go out in the middle of the night into a burning city to rescue stranded civilians. At least the mission would keep her mind off the front in Europe—and Master Sergeant Fitzpatrick. She hadn't seen him for months. Davis could only hope that they would meet again someday, but first she had a stronghold of survivors to locate.

"Let's go!" she shouted as she crossed the deck of the aircraft carrier. Two Black Hawks waited, rotors already thumping. Davis and Diaz strode past a row of F-18s.

Behind the two women were the marines of Fire Teams Rhino and Scorpion. Led by Sergeant Marks, the two recon teams included some of the most experienced men the USMC had left to offer.

Between them, they had killed over two hundred juvenile Variants and saved over a thousand human survivors. Davis felt a rush of heat at the thought. She was finally leaving this floating hunk of metal to go back out there, where she belonged: hunting monsters and rescuing civilians.

A concussion sounded in the distance, and Diaz paused midstride as another gout of flame and smoke rose into the sky over an industrial area. She was the least experienced of the group when it came to fighting juveniles, but Diaz had made her mark during Operation Liberty. She had ten kills under her belt.

"I told them to avoid that area," Davis muttered, shaking her head. "It's full of oil reserves."

There was no time for a full mission briefing tonight. As they approached the big black birds, Davis stopped to give her orders. The two fire teams circled around her.

"The SOS was narrowed down to the Bay County Courthouse. The building is still standing, but fires are quickly approaching and the smoke there is really bad." She looked to Sergeant Marks. He was cradling his SAW.

"Sergeant, you have Team Rhino. Scorpion, you're on me," Davis said. "Let's move out!"

The two fire teams separated and fanned out toward the choppers. Davis grimaced at the pain running up her legs and shoulders as she climbed inside the troop hold. She was hurting, but she wasn't going to let it hold her back. She took a seat, reached into her vest, and pulled up her CBRN visor to swallow another handful of painkillers. That earned her a concerned look from Diaz, who took a seat next to her. The other four men of Fire Team Scorpion piled inside, and a crew chief gave the pilot a thumbs-up. Davis sucked down a gulp of water as the bird lifted off the deck.

"Command One, this is Scorpion One. We're in the air."

"Roger that, Scorpion One. Good luck."

Several people watched them from the windows of the CIC tower on the flyover. One of them was Belford. Davis knew he would handle things while she was gone, but she cringed at the thought of Humphrey waking up with him in charge. That's why she planned to be back before Humphrey's nap was over. This was going to be a quick in and out.

She looked across the troop hold at the shadowed faces of men she hardly knew. Everyone was dressed in camouflaged CBRN suits over a layer of body armor. On top of the suits, they wore vests stuffed with magazines, frag grenades, and the sleep grenades the military had developed for use on the juveniles.

Davis recognized one of the men, Lance Corporal Nick Black, only because of the thick Mohawk smashed under his domed CBRN helmet. He offered a sly grin and heaved his M249 across his chest. A Benelli M1014 twelve-gauge shotgun hung from a strap around his back. The other members of the fire team held modified M4s with grenade launchers.

"You're Scorpion Three, Four, Five, and Six on the comms," Davis said, pointing down the line. Four helmets nodded back at her.

Davis looked to Diaz. "You're Two on the comms."

"Yes, Captain."

She took a moment to study the lance corporal. Davis could tell Diaz was nervous even though she wasn't showing it. She saw a lot of herself in the younger woman, and they shared more than losing their husbands to this war. They both had problems following orders.

Davis felt her stomach growl. She cursed under her breath, remembering for the first time that she had skipped dinner during the bombing of the juvenile strongholds. The pills she'd swallowed were going to eat at her guts. She fished a power bar out of a pocket on her vest and pulled her helmet up again to take a bite. The nutrition would tide her over for a few hours. She washed it down with another mouthful of water.

"We're about two minutes out," one of the pilots said. "We'll circle once before touching down."

"All right, people, lock and load," Davis ordered.

She pulled her helmet back down and grabbed a magazine from her vest. She slammed it into her M4 with a satisfying click. Then she stood and crouch-walked to the open door, her CBRN suit crinkling as she moved. Wind forced smoke from the burning city into the troop hold.

The crew chief pointed past Bunkers Cove and Massalina Bayou. "LZ is down there, Captain!"

Davis raised her scope to her eyes as they flew over North Cove Boulevard. Millions of dollars' worth of boats burned in the water, some of them capsized, others on their sides in the oily water. The tip of a burning sail slowly sank to its final resting place, the water swallowing the flames and bubbles frothing to the surface.

Another explosion bloomed in the distance, sparks raining down over derelict city streets. Smoke drifted across the harbor, masking her view of the courthouse. The Black Hawk carrying Rhino Team flew ahead.

"Scorpion One, this is Rhino One. Be advised. We

have eyes on a pack of juveniles moving along the intersection of North Cove and East Sixth Street."

Sergeant Marks waved from inside the other helicopter and then pointed to the road below.

Davis flicked her muzzle in that direction. Fires framed the asphalt on both sides, and flames continued to dance in all directions. There was motion halfway up the street, but she couldn't tell if it was the smoke or something else.

"Making our first pass," one of the pilots said. They banked to the left and followed the other Black Hawk over East Fourth Street. The bridge sagged into the water, the center a charred crater where a bomb had blown it in half. The west side was clogged with charred vehicles, but there was only a single car on the east side.

"There!" Diaz shouted. "They're making a run for the bridge."

At first Davis didn't see them, but as she zoomed in and switched to infrared, she saw the four heat signatures. She pulled her visor away from the scope, squinting at the juveniles galloping toward the bridge. Their armored bodies were covered in soot and ash.

"Holy fuck, those are the biggest I've ever seen," Black said.

"Not so little anymore, are they? We might need to stop calling them juveniles," Diaz replied.

"Scorpion One, Rhino One. We got four bandits on the East Fourth bridge," Marks reported. "Requesting permission to engage."

"Negative, Rhino One. We got this," Davis said. She turned to Black. "Get on the Two-Forty, but conserve your ammo. We may need it."

"With pleasure, Captain."

She stepped out of the way to allow the large man past. He grabbed the gun and didn't hesitate to fire.

"For my mother!" he yelled. "And my father!"

Diaz looked at Davis with wide eyes, but Davis slowly shook her helmet from side to side. She had seen soldiers deal with their losses in different ways, and Black wasn't the first to avenge his lost family members.

The green streaks of tracer rounds shot across the bridge. A barrage of 7.62-millimeter rounds followed, kicking concrete into the air and raising the street as if a massive animal was moving under the pavement. The crack of the gun filled the troop hold.

Black centered his fire on the beasts and closed in. One of the rounds clipped the slowest creature in the back leg. Blood painted the concrete as the juvenile tripped and crashed to the ground. Black fired again, and a salvo of rounds hit it in the midsection. It spun into a guardrail, flipped over the other side, and plummeted into the water.

"Oorah!" Black yelled. "Oo-fucking-rah!"

Davis patted him on the back to remind the marine to focus. "Three left! Don't let them in the water!" she yelled in the respite of gunfire.

He raked the muzzle back and forth as the other beasts spread out and zigzagged. The wave of smoke cleared across the road on the other side of the bridge, giving Davis her first glimpse of the yellow brick building that was their target.

The beasts sprinted right for it. Davis remembered the message they'd received from the survivors:

To the military or anyone that can hear this, stop firing on the city! There are over fifty children and adults at . . .

Black continued to unload a barrage of fire. He hit the smallest of the remaining juveniles in the head with a lucky shot. It crashed to the pavement, sliding limply to a stop.

"Hell yeah! Nice, Big B!" yelled one of the other marines.

The final two creatures made a run for the ten-foot-wide gap in the center of the sagging bridge. He killed the one on the right with three rounds to the back, but the final juvenile was faster than the others. If it made the leap across, it would have the abandoned vehicles on the other side for cover.

"Hurry!" Davis shouted.

The beast suddenly increased its pace, limbs blurring as it raced for the edge. In a last-ditch effort, it launched its body into the air and leaped over the missing section.

Black raised the gun slightly to correct his aim and fired a burst that sent the beast cartwheeling through the air.

Davis whooped, unable to control herself. Black let up on the gun and roved it back over the terrain.

"That's all of them, Command," Davis said into the headset. "We're preparing to land, over."

The next transmission froze her to the core. "Scorpion One, this is Wolverine One. Get your ass back to home plate, ASAP."

Every eye in the troop hold focused on Davis.

"Guess Humphrey couldn't sleep," she said with a grin. "Take us down over there. We'll head back...as soon as we've got those survivors."

Fitz threw up out of the open door of the Black Hawk. The taste of bile burned his throat and tongue. Sniffling, he ran a sleeve across his nose as a hand clapped his back. He knew it was Rico, but he couldn't look her in the eyes. Not with tears in his own. He wasn't the first man to lose his breakfast this morning. Stevenson had coughed up his several minutes earlier.

"Here," Rico insisted. She waved a stick of bubble gum in front of Fitz.

Stevenson reached out with a gloved hand. "You got an endless supply of that shit or what? I'll take a piece."

"He can have mine," Fitz said.

The Twenty-Fourth MEU had survived the night, but it had come at a horrible cost. On the horizon, the sun peeked over the cliffs of Normandy, spreading the first rays of golden light over the scene of the massacre. Team Ghost clustered together in the troop hold to stare at the beaches. The bodies of dead marines bobbed up and down in the water. Hundreds more dotted the sand. Bones protruded from the charred flesh of those who had been caught in the deadly inferno.

Throughout the graveyard, the tanks, Humvees, and MATVs looked like overcooked lobster tails, their armored guts flayed open from the hellish fires that had blown the vehicles apart from within. Everything was covered with the green residue of the juvenile toxins.

Of all the battles Fitz had seen, this was the worst. Even Operation Liberty didn't compare.

"Unreal," Tanaka said. He continued cleaning a sword with a bloody rag. "I thought Command knew what they were doing this time."

Fitz nodded silently, his gloved hand on Apollo's head.

"Never did say thanks for what you did back there," Rico said. She clapped Tanaka on the back. "You've got some pretty sweet moves."

Tanaka ran the rag down the Katana one last time, leaving the blade so clean Fitz could see his pale reflection.

"You would have been better off using your rifle," Stevenson said.

"Didn't see you firing yours," Tanaka replied with a glare.

Fitz directed his gaze back to the beach, too exhausted to intervene. Normally crews would already be on shore cleaning up and preparing the KIA for transport, but the flames and the sand were toxic. Colonel Bradley had ordered survivors to regroup farther down the beach at a new location for the FOB.

How could this have happened? How could the juveniles have known we were coming? I told those assholes at Command...

Fitz swallowed the anger as they passed over the *Mesa Verde*, the *Ashland*, and the *Iwo Jima*. They were anchored a quarter mile away from the shoreline.

The *Forrest Sherman* continued searching the waters to save any marines who might have survived. But Fitz wasn't holding his breath. They hadn't pulled a survivor from the ocean for over three hours.

"How many?" Fitz muttered. "How many did we lose?"

Ospreys, Black Hawks, and Viper attack helicopters patrolled overhead. Fitz glanced up at the black birds. They had lost several of them in attacks from the winged juveniles, but in the end, the newly evolved monsters had been no match for Stinger missiles and 7.62-millimeter rounds.

The thumping blades drowned out the chatter over the open comm channels. Tanaka cupped his ears with his hands and then pulled them away. "Recent report isn't good, sir."

"Numbers?"

"Three hundred confirmed KIAs and twice that many MIA," Tanaka said. "The first wave of mechanized units was completely wiped out. Zero survivors, sir."

Fitz felt the bile rising in his throat again. He thought

about asking Rico if she had another stick of gum, but she was too busy staring at the nightmare below. He swallowed instead, straightened his back, and took a deep breath as the Black Hawk passed over the *Forrest Sherman*.

The deck was stained red from the injured and dead. Boot prints marked a path through the carnage. Medics ran from tent to tent on the flight deck. A team carried a stretcher with a marine who had lost a leg. He was holding the stump and screaming what sounded like, "Mama!"

Fitz closed his eyes briefly. "You will fight again, brother. Hang in there," he whispered to the marine below.

A transmission cracked in Fitz's earpiece.

"Ghost One, Tango One, report to the FOB, ASAP."

"Copy that, Tango One," Fitz replied. He rose from his crouch, his blades groaning like the bones of an old man.

Team Ghost gathered around as the pilots changed course. The bird flew over the burned mechanized units, providing another grisly glimpse of the final resting places for the men and women of the first wave.

Stevenson made the sign of the cross, and Tanaka closed his eyes and bowed his head. Fitz focused on the open hatch of an M1A1 Abrams below and the skeleton sticking halfway out, nothing but green bones left. Reaching down, Fitz patted Apollo on the head and whispered, "It's okay," although he wasn't sure who he was trying to reassure.

If Beckham could see this...

But Beckham wasn't here. The man had given everything to fight the Variants, and he'd more than earned his retirement. It was up to Fitz to carry on his legacy and lead Team Ghost. He felt the weight of that responsibility more than ever as he looked down on the battlefield.

This was just the beginning...

The bird continued for the FOB to the west. Another wave of LCACs was ferrying a second group of vehicles from the anchored ships. Tanks, LAV-25s, Humvees, and Assault Breacher Vehicles were already cruising across the beach. Marines in bulldozers worked on building a perimeter.

Colonel Bradley was down there. Fitz didn't blame the commander of the MEU for the attack or the decision not to risk extra marine lives to bury the dead— even though it broke the rule to never leave a man behind.

"All it takes is all you got, Marine," Fitz said, echoing the motto of Sergeant Jose Garcia. He finally understood why the French and European Unified Forces weren't here waiting for them with wine and cheese on the beach. Europe had fallen into darkness because the juveniles here had grown up. They were adults now, and they were smarter, bigger, and more deadly than any Fitz had faced back in the States.

Another transmission crackled in Fitz's earpiece. Scouts advancing up the beach reported a pack of Variants prowling the cliffs above the FOB. A pair of attack Vipers peeled off to engage the bandits.

Fitz looked up at the cliffs and then returned his focus to the beach. More marines had washed ashore there, torn apart by the claws of the monsters. There were also juvenile corpses amongst the ranks of the dead. The shadow of the Black Hawk passed over one of the winged beasts. It lay on a sand dune, wings spread like a shroud over its back. Entrails spilled onto the sand beside it.

"You see that?" Fitz asked.

Dohi whistled through his teeth.

"What the hell is that thing?" Rico asked.

"Some sort of hell-spawn bat," Stevenson replied. He rubbed at his hairline and took another slug of water from a canteen.

"I bet France is full of those freaks," Tanaka said. "That's why the EUF didn't show up."

Rico nodded. "That's why they sent us."

Stevenson shot her a glare. "Yeah, it's working out really well, isn't it? Already lost a third of our manpower, and we aren't even onshore yet. We'd be better off back home saving our own people."

"What did you say?" Fitz asked.

"Nothin'," Stevenson replied, avoiding his gaze.

Fitz wasn't used to arguing with his teammates, but Beckham had warned him of this. He wasn't just a marine or a member of Team Ghost anymore. Fitz was the leader, and he still hadn't gained the full respect of his people.

Rico steered the conversation back toward the juveniles. "I can't believe those things have freaking wings."

"Wings, toxins. Shit, I don't care if they start breathing fire. I'll kill 'em in every shape and form," Tanaka said.

"Not if you keep using those toothpicks," Stevenson said with a chuckle. "You're lucky you didn't break them on their armored hides."

Tanaka stood on his tiptoes to look Stevenson in the eye.

"Put your headphones back in before I—"

"Before you what?" Tanaka said.

Fitz stepped between the two men before a fight could break out.

"Cool it! I know everyone's on edge. We lost a lot of brothers and sisters last night, but we aren't going to let them die in vain, are we?" Fitz paused to look at both Stevenson and Tanaka in turn.

The members of the new Team Ghost met his gaze and shook their heads.

Fitz pointed out the open door. "Are we going to let our petty differences spoil their sacrifice, Sergeant Tanaka? Sergeant Stevenson?"

"No, Master Sergeant," both men replied simultaneously.

Rico clapped Stevenson and Tanaka on their arms. "Sometimes I don't understand men."

"Little lady, I'll never claim to understand women," Stevenson said.

They cracked half smiles, but the weak grins quickly faded away. Rico offered a nod to Fitz, and he nodded back. He was really starting to appreciate the easygoing sergeant. She had shown bravery in every battle Fitz had fought with her, and her quick thinking on the LCAC had likely saved everyone's lives. He had high hopes for Tanaka and Dohi, but so far Stevenson was just proving to be a pain in the ass.

"Prepare for landing," said one of the pilots. They descended over the beach, rotor wash whipping up a tornado of grit. Fitz waved Team Ghost toward a central tent in the middle of the FOB. Bulldozers and other heavy equipment rumbled in the distance, building a fort of sand around the base.

Once they were clear, the chopper pulled away to join those already in the sky. The crack of gunfire and explosions from missiles sounded in the distance as the Vipers found their targets. Flames emerged from the cliffs overhead, but the marines setting up the FOB weren't distracted.

Fitz jogged with his men, blades sinking in the loose sand. He thought of Beckham again as he neared the

Command tent. What would he say to Colonel Bradley after what had happened the night before? And how would he mentally prepare for whatever mission the commander had in store for Team Ghost next?

He stopped a few feet from the tent, readying himself to find out just how bad things were about to get. Two lance corporals stood outside the tent with a marine Corps flag and an American flag hanging overhead.

"Master Sergeant Fitzpatrick. Colonel Bradley inside? He's expecting me."

The man on the left nodded. "Yes, Master Sergeant. I'll let the colonel know you've arrived." The marine snapped to attention and ducked under the flap of the tent.

Fitz scratched Apollo's ears and whispered, "Don't go to the bathroom, okay?"

The dog wagged his tail.

"Master Sergeant," came a rough voice from inside the tent. Colonel Bradley walked out into the morning with a flask in one hand. He offered it to Fitz. "Whiskey?"

Fitz considered the offer. He could use a stiff one right now, but he wasn't sure if this was a test. There was also a rule he had learned in boot camp. Never make an officer wait.

"Sir, thank you, sir," Fitz said, reaching out. He took a gulp and handed it back to the colonel, remembering another rule, this one something his mom had taught him when he was growing up: Never stare.

Bradley didn't just have a rough voice. The left side of his face was divided by a long scar that had taken his eye and carved a ravine in his dark skin. He didn't wear a patch over the missing eye.

"Hell of a morning for the Marine Corps," Bradley said. He took a long swig, wiped his lips, and glanced at the other members of Ghost. Then he gestured for them to come inside the tent. "Bring the dog, too."

"Follow me, boy," Fitz said. He led his entire team under the flaps held open by the lance corporals. The man on the left eyed Apollo doubtfully.

"Hold up," Fitz said. He looked at his dog and pointed toward a mound of sand with weeds growing out of it. "Apollo, go take a piss over there."

The dog trotted away, lifted a leg, and then ran back.

Fitz nodded at the sentries and ducked under the flaps. The inside of the tent was furnished with a war table littered with maps. A marine manned the radio equipment on a desk in the corner. He continued listening to chatter without getting up from his seat.

Bradley shook his head and sat the flask on the table. "I wish I had good news, but we got our asses kicked last night. The juveniles laid some sort of corrosive liquid on the beach that burns hotter than jet fuel." He paused for a moment, took another gulp from his flask, and let out a sigh.

"But we're marines, and marines don't lay down and die. We keep moving forward. We keep fighting."

"Damn straight," Rico said.

Bradley's eye roved toward her, then back to Fitz. All trace of emotion vanished from his hard face. "Some of you *aren't* marines, but I hear you're the best we got left. If Captain Beckham vouches for you, then that's good enough for me."

Fitz stiffened his back and waited for the orders he knew were coming.

"I'll be frank," Bradley said. "I have a special mission that is very important and very dangerous. This one was approved by General Nixon himself. He has a plan to get to Paris, but we need your help."

He pointed on the maps at a town called Lisieux. "The EUF has put us in touch with a rebel unit called the Ombres. Apparently that means 'shadows' or something. They're operating out of the Basilica of Saint Thérèse."

Fitz raised his brows, but before he could speak, Stevenson fired off a question. "Why the hell didn't the EUF warn us about the coast?"

Bradley scowled, and Fitz felt his face flush. He and Stevenson would need to have a serious talk before the man's mouth got them all into deep shit.

"The EUF has their own problems. Paris got hit hard yesterday by those winged creatures, which they are calling Reavers. Recon units are tracking an army of Variants moving north toward the city." Bradley put the whiskey back down and pulled a picture from a folder and held it up for everyone to see.

"Forget about the EUF for now and their lack of intel. Your mission is to find these rebels," Bradley said.

Fitz studied the picture. Was this some kind of joke?

"Kids?" Rico asked, beating him to the punch. "These Ombres are *kids*?"

"And a woman they refer to as *Maman*."

Bradley set the picture down. "I'm sending a CH-53K King Stallion transport with an MATV this afternoon. I want Team Ghost in that MATV. Your mission is to find the Ombres and see if they can provide intel to help us make our way safely across the countryside to Paris. The next phase of the war, Operation Reach, depends on it. General Nixon is planning on dropping radioactive dirty bombs on strategic locations to kill pockets of Variants. But we need to know where they are first."

"Understood, sir," Fitz said.

"What about civilians?" Rico asked. "Dirty bombs won't just kill the juveniles and adults in the area."

"That's why your mission is so important," Bradley replied. "We need to know where they are and where the enemy is. Operation Reach is a two-part mission: Phase one is to cook the Variants with radioactive bombs. In phase two, we advance to Paris and save as many people as possible on the way. We will meet the EUF there, rearm and regroup, and then work with the Europeans to take back more cities. After Paris, we hope to secure Rome, Berlin, and Barcelona. Our success hinges on that intel. Understood?"

"Yes, sir," Fitz said again. He threw up a salute with the rest of Team Ghost.

The old colonel dipped his chin, dismissing them.

As Fitz went to leave with the rest of his team, Bradley called out after him.

"Hold up, Master Sergeant."

Apollo paused, but Fitz nodded at the dog to follow the others out of the tent.

"Sir?" Fitz said, pivoting back to the colonel.

"I'm going to be honest with you, son. You're going deep into enemy territory. The EUF has relayed some pretty fucking terrifying images of the creatures they're facing out there. Which is another reason this mission is important."

Fitz nodded. "We won't let you down, sir."

"I don't think you understand, Fitzpatrick. Those Reavers aren't the only thing out there, and I want you back in one piece. I made a promise to Captain Beckham, but there isn't much I can do for you when you're out there. Team Ghost will be on their own."

7

Tactical lights penetrated the smoke swirling around the courthouse as Scorpion advanced. Captain Davis directed her M4 at the barricade covering the front door. Someone had gone to great lengths to block off the entrance. She flicked her light across the steel plates that had been welded over the front doors.

"Rhino One, Scorpion One. Did you find a way in?" Davis said into her headset.

"Negative, Scorpion One," came Marks's reply.

Davis held up a hand to her team. Black and Diaz froze in the smog. Behind them were the other three marines. They took knees and raked their guns back and forth at eye level for contacts.

Distant pops and snaps sounded all around them, like they were in the center of a forest fire. Embers rose into the night sky. The flames were closing in. Davis felt like she was slowly cooking in her suit. Her skin itched from the sweat running down her body.

So this is what hell is like, she thought.

She took in a hot breath through her mask and gave an advance signal to her team. There were fifty kids inside waiting for rescue, and she was wasting time.

Black ran ahead with his SAW shouldered. His

footwork was that of a well-trained marine—fast but steady. Davis kept Diaz by her side. She felt responsible for the younger woman, even though technically Diaz was her bodyguard.

Halfway to the building, Davis reached up to wipe ash from her visor. The flames were encroaching from the west, and the smoke was thickening. Her visor clear for the moment, she increased her pace, scanning the brick façade of the courthouse as she moved. The twenty-foot-tall white pillars were covered in soot, and three floors of windows were boarded up. Graffiti reading *Repent* and *The End Is Nigh* marked the brickwork.

"Not for these people," Davis whispered to herself.

Black stopped at the stairs and waited for orders. Davis ran past him and crouch-walked to the windows on the right of the barricaded front door. A transmission from Marks stopped her midstride.

"Scorpion One. We found a way in. Heading inside now."

"Copy that," Davis said. "We'll meet you inside."

The window to the side was covered with two-by-fours. She grabbed one of them and pulled, but it wouldn't budge.

"Over here," Diaz said. She stood at the second window, holding a board that had been pried back. Another piece of wood hung loosely from the windowsill. Diaz leaned down to examine them.

"Looks like someone beat us here," she whispered.

Davis hurried over to take a look. Scratches crisscrossed the charred brick like chalk marks on a blackboard.

Were they already too late?

There was never enough time to think in the field, even when everything around her seemed like it was moving in slow motion. In a split-second decision, she decided to move forward cautiously, hoping they hadn't come all this way for nothing.

"Rhino One, Scorpion One, watch for hostiles inside." She looked to her team and gave her orders with hand signs. Her fingers carved through the smoke.

Black stepped up to the window and ripped the other boards off like they were just sticks. He set them on the ground softly. Diaz used the butt of her gun to break the remaining pieces of glass.

"Watch your suits," Davis said. "Diaz, you have point. Check it out."

Black cupped his hands, and Diaz used them as a makeshift step stool to reach the window. She jumped inside and vanished. The crackle of flames and swirling smog surrounded Davis as she waited anxiously.

Diaz returned and gave the all clear a few seconds later. Black held out a hand and helped Davis through the window. The big marine followed them while the other three men held security outside.

Davis took a cautious step over the broken glass and directed her light down a hallway covered in debris and trash. Two other beams joined hers, dancing across walls and ceiling. Every surface was caked with dried blood. Ahead, a red path snaked across the floor.

"Jesus," Diaz whispered.

"More like Satan," Black mumbled.

Davis raised a finger to her visor, then directed Diaz and Black to flank her. Taking point, she pushed her scope to eye level and hurried down the passage, heel to toe, heel to toe.

Quick and steady, she reminded herself. *Always quick and steady.*

Her muscles screamed as she moved, her injuries flaring up with each step. The deeper they advanced into the courthouse, the more she began to wonder if she had made a terrible mistake. The SOS had been so desperate, and the thought of rescuing over fifty survivors so tempting. But this place looked like a slaughterhouse. She swept her muzzle up and down and left to right to check the hallway for contacts. The beams revealed more dried blood and gore.

Davis spotted a map on the wall ahead. Using her gloved hand, she carefully cleared it off. A radiation symbol marked the location of a fallout shelter. That was the most likely location.

"Rhino One, sitrep," Davis whispered into her mic. The response took several seconds between waves of static.

"Scorpion One, we're clearing the west wing."

"Copy, Rhino One. Scorpion is advancing to the fallout shelter."

Davis glanced back the way they had come to check the three marines standing outside. They stood with their weapons raised, the smoke making them look like specters.

The eerie sight unsettled her.

She continued down the hallway when another transmission hissed into her ear.

"Scorpion One, this is Wolverine Two. Where are you? We're picking up something on radar, over."

Davis stopped midstride. It was Belford on the comms.

"Copy, Wolverine Two. What are you picking up?"

"Inconclusive. Actual says for you to get back here as soon as you can. Over."

"Roger." Davis motioned Black and Diaz around a corner to a pair of doors that led to the basement. Belford hadn't sounded overly concerned, but then he never did. There were hundreds of ghost ships in the area, most of them harmless and drifting aimlessly. She wasn't going to let that stop her from saving these kids after she'd risked so much to get here.

Black took up position on the left of the doors and looked for her signal. At her nod, he grabbed the handle and twisted. It clicked. Locked.

He kicked it open. The door hit the inside wall with a thud that told any lurking juveniles of their position. But the screech she thought would follow never came.

Heart stuttering, Davis maneuvered back into point position and aimed her rifle into the stairwell, finger hovering over the trigger. The tactical light filled an empty concrete passage with a white glow.

She hesitated in the open doorway when she saw more blood. Labored breathing echoed in her helmet as she tried to catch her breath.

What the hell happened here? Where is everyone? And where are the monsters?

Questions raced through her mind, but she pushed on, knowing that if anyone out here had survived this long, they had likely done it by keeping out of sight. She continued down two more passages to a steel door marked with a radiation symbol.

Another transmission crackled in her earpiece as she approached, this one nearly lost in static.

"Scorpion One...Scorpion Four...Helicopter... Reinforcements..."

"Come again, Scorpion Four," Davis said. She tapped the side of her helmet, white noise burping into her ear.

"Scorpion One, there is a Black Hawk en route from the *GW* and an unidentified vessel in the water."

Great. That's just freaking great, Davis thought.

Diaz put a hand on her arm. "Captain, do you think we should go topside?"

"We're right here. We finish the mission first," Davis said.

"But what about the other vessel?"

She shook her head. There were kids in this building. Turning back now wasn't an option.

Black waited for orders, his hand on the door. Davis gave him a stern nod. When he pulled on the blast door, Davis saw the talon marks. The door was already open.

Black cursed. He let go of the handle and backed away, shouldering his SAW and aiming it at the door. Davis and Diaz raised their M4s simultaneously.

She was slowly approaching the door when a distant crack of a gunshot made her flinch. She aimed a glance over her shoulder at the stairwell.

More gunshots.

"Scorpion, do you copy, over?" Davis said into the comms.

There was no answer.

"Wolverine Two, Scorpion One. We have small arms fire near our location. Please advise, over."

This time the answer came back almost immediately— and it wasn't Belford. Admiral Humphrey barked an order into Davis's ear.

"Scorpion One, Wolverine One, you are to return to home plate right *fucking* now. We've made contact with the USS *Zumwalt*. She's headed our way." There was applause in the background and some whistling.

The *Zumwalt*? The stealth guided-missile destroyer had gone missing months ago, right after the outbreak. It had been christened not long before the world went to hell, but no one had heard from the advanced ship since.

Davis looked at the blast door, her mind racing. They were so close. So freaking close.

"Captain, all due respect, but maybe we should go topside," Black whispered.

Davis nodded, but instead of turning to run, she reached for the door handle. She had to know for sure.

Diaz and Black took up position with their rifles when they realized what she was doing. She waited a moment before pulling the door open. The screech of metal would have made Davis cringe if it weren't for the adrenaline pumping through her veins. The trio aimed their muzzles inside. Beams from their tactical lights illuminated a long room furnished with bunk beds, desks, and chairs.

Dust whirled in the still air. She took a breath and exhaled inside her visor. The pane fogged around the edges, narrowing her view.

She took a step inside, slowly moving her light back and forth. The rays cut through the dusty air and fell upon one empty bed after another.

"No one's here, ma'am," Diaz whispered.

"We better move out," Black added.

Davis centered her light on a desk with scattered radio equipment. Even if there had been someone here to send a distress signal, the damned radio was smashed to pieces.

None of it made any sense.

"Let's move," Davis said. "I'll take point." She paused when she stepped on a furry lump. Bending down, she grabbed a teddy bear stained black with blood. Her already aching heart broke in half as the tattered toy fell to pieces in her hand. It confirmed what she knew, but had been pretending wasn't true—the juveniles had broken in.

Any survivors were long gone.

But that didn't make sense either. The SOS mentioned the bombing, which meant it had to be recent, but the blood here was dry. So who sent the message...and why? Had the juveniles set some sort of a trap? Were they capable of that?

Davis tossed the remains of the teddy bear to the

ground and rushed out of the room. She loped up the staircase two at a time, her legs screaming in pain.

An explosion sounded just as she got to the top landing, but it wasn't until she reached the hallway that she realized the blast wasn't coming from the gasoline facility nearby. It came from just off the shore.

The boom faded away, giving rise to another sound not unlike someone choking on a chicken bone. The gurgling echoed down the hallway. She instantly flicked off her light and instructed Diaz and Black to do the same.

She could only imagine what kind of creature was making the noise. Darkness and smoke closed in, and with it came a gripping fear that Davis hadn't felt since the Earthfall facility. She flipped her NVGs into position, held in a hot breath, and peered around the corner with her finger on the trigger of her M4.

Instead of a beast, her gaze fell on a marine crawling across the floor. Scorpion 4, who was supposed to be holding security, was dragging his legs behind him, smearing blood across the filthy floor.

Davis almost burst around the corner to help him, but froze when she saw three men in black CBRN suits striding down the other end of the passage. They wore gas masks and four-eye NVGs over their helmets. There were no markings or identification on their CBRN suits or helmets that she could see.

Who the hell were they?

The men raised black SCAR-L rifles and painted the downed marine's back with red dots. One of the soldiers stepped out from the group and leaned down next to Scorpion 4 with a Beretta M9. He pointed the suppressed barrel at the marine's head. In a robotic voice filtered by the gas mask, he said, "Where's the rest of your team?"

Scorpion 4 continued crawling, choking as he moved. Bloody spit peppered the inside of his visor.

Three more men in black suits climbed through the open window and entered the hallway. The soldier with the suppressed M9 watched the injured marine squirm a few feet, then aimed the gun at the back of his helmet and fired two shots.

"No!" Davis gasped. Her panicked voice drew the attention of the soldiers. The leader pointed his M9 and shouted, "Over there!"

A salvo of gunshots punched into the brick wall as Davis turned. She stepped out from the safety of the corner and returned fire with a burst that hit the man with the M9 in the chest. Blood sprayed the floor, and she turned before he hit the ground. Another volley punched into the wall. The shrapnel clanked off her helmet.

"What the fuck is happening, Captain?"

Davis waved Black's question away. Even with Diaz and Black's help, there was no way they could take five men without suffering more casualties. They had to survive first and avenge the rest of her team later.

"Run!" Davis shouted. She pointed to the other end of the hallway. "Now!"

"Who are you shooting at?" Diaz yelled back.

Davis grabbed her bodyguard and heaved. "MOVE!"

Black was already running. He raised his SAW and took point, moving low with his muzzle roving across the smoke-filled hallway. Halfway down, a transmission broke over the comms. It was another robotic voice like the man that had executed Scorpion 4.

"Tell us where the rest of your team is, and we won't kill you."

"Fuck your mother," Marks replied.

A crack followed that could have been a pistol whip to the helmet. Marks grunted, and white noise crackled over the channel.

Another message broke into her ear. Humphrey's

voice sounded panicked, and that alone frightened Davis more than anything else.

"Scorpion One, we're being boarded! The *Zumwalt* has been compromised." There were gunshots, then Humphrey shouted, "Davis, damn it, get your ass back here!"

Davis cursed. The entire thing, from the SOS to the arrival of the long-lost ship, had been a trap. Who would do such a thing, and how had they taken control of the *Zumwalt*?

She angled her M4 at the other end of the hallway as more soldiers in black emerged. Red dot sights flickered across the passage, falling on Diaz and Black. The large marine took a knee and opened up with his SAW before Davis could get off a shot. The rounds tore through the three soldiers, splattering blood over walls already caked with dried crimson. They crashed to the ground.

Black was up and running with Diaz on his six, but before Davis turned the corner she grabbed a grenade from her vest, pulled the pin, and listened to the approaching footfalls.

"Captain, come on," Black yelled. "We need to—"

Davis cut him off with a shout of her own as she tossed the grenade around the corner. "Eat that, you assholes."

8

Ringgold sat in the Situation Room surrounded by members of her cabinet and military officials. The lights dimmed as the monitor brightened on the north wall.

News of Operation Beachhead and the slaughter of the Twenty-Fourth MEU had reached the Greenbrier in the early-morning hours. The other MEUs hadn't fared much better in Spain or Germany. General Vaughn Nixon, like General Kennor before him, had been caught with his pants down. Despite this failure, he was still pushing Operation Reach.

She laced her fingers together and waited anxiously to hear more about Europe and the attack on Plum Island, but she also desperately wanted an update on SZT 15 in Chicago and her cousin, Emilia.

Several more staffers filed into the small room and stood at the back. Across the table sat Vice President George Johnson and Joint Chiefs of Staff General Jay Allen. The other joint chiefs were seated around the long table.

Ringgold reviewed the names of all the new advisors and officials. She had made a point of sitting in on every interview and had spent hours reading resumes and bios. Ben Nelson, a rising star in the CIA before the outbreak, was her new National Security Advisor. His background in counterterrorism had helped him hit the ground running, but this morning he had every reason to be nervous. He straightened his tie and tucked it into his black suit.

Last time she had seen him was at a meeting about the threats to the safe-zone territories. He'd assured her that security measures were in place to keep the hemorrhage virus and remaining juveniles out of the strongholds. While they still didn't know exactly what had happened to SZT 15, Nelson was calling the incident at Plum Island a terrorist attack.

He wasn't the only one sweating. Ringgold felt perspiration drip down her own forehead. She touched the American flag pin on her lapel. It always helped calm her.

James Soprano squeezed in behind Nelson and Ringgold. He took a seat to her right and offered a smile. James was overweight, had bad teeth and a receding hairline. He also loved his cigars. But although he was incredibly unhealthy, he was also brilliant. That was exactly why Ringgold had picked him to be her Chief of Staff.

Ringgold donned her red glasses and scanned the room. Her gaze lingered on the American flag above the door. It was a symbol of pride and hope, and she deeply respected the traditions it represented. But there were those out there who didn't respect it, who didn't believe in the things America stood for. Someone was attacking the SZTs that Ringgold had worked so hard to build. She knew that Emilia and the other survivors at SZT 15 were likely dead, and she felt sick for not being able to stop whatever had happened there and at Plum Island.

Ringgold had promised survivors homes. She'd promised them safety. Instead, they were plunged into a new nightmare.

Johnson's voice interrupted her thoughts. "Madam President, Raptor One is en route to SZT Fifteen. We'll have a visual in a moment."

General Allen typed on his laptop, and the main screen on the north wall flickered to life.

"It has now been twelve hours since SZT Fifteen went dark," Johnson said. "All attempts at communication have failed. Our drone flyovers have shown nothing."

Ringgold regretted not sending troops earlier, but Johnson had advised against it unless it was a last resort. With the failure of the flyovers, they now had no other choice. The closest outpost was twenty miles west of Chicago. It was operated by Lieutenant Jim Flathman and a skeleton crew of battle-hardened men. They had held the small military outpost against overwhelming forces for over seven months. Captain Rachel Davis had landed there to refuel on her way to the Earthfall facility, and she'd been impressed with the unconventional lieutenant and his operation. Ringgold trusted her recommendation—but his help came at a price. Flathman wanted more food, more ammo, more men... and a lifetime supply of whiskey.

Ringgold wasn't used to negotiating with soldiers, but in this situation she had agreed without a counteroffer. She looked at Johnson, who was running a hand over his bald head, and nodded at her second-in-command.

"Go ahead, General," Johnson said.

Allen brought up a series of grayscale images of SZT 15. High walls topped with razor wire surrounded a three-block area. There were half a dozen buildings within the perimeter. In the center was the embassy, and on top of that were empty nests with idle machine guns. There wasn't a soldier at any of the posts. FEMA semitrailers, military vehicles, and civilian cars lined the road, but the sidewalks were vacant. Not a person—or a body—in sight.

"As you can see, it's like everyone just disappeared," Allen said. "We see no evidence of a battle or Variants. Raptor One is almost to the target. Lieutenant Flathman reports his team is ready to deploy."

"Transfer us to the feed," Johnson said.

Ringgold thought of her missing cousin, the only living family member she had left. Growing up, they had been very close, but college and careers had separated them over the years. She'd hoped to visit SZT 15 soon, but now the only visit Ringgold was going to make was via video feed.

And she already suspected it was too late for a reunion.

With a short nod, she gave her orders for Flathman's team to drop into the fray.

"Find my cousin alive, and I'll give you every bottle of whiskey you could ever drink, Lieutenant," Ringgold whispered.

The morning sun rose into the sky above the destroyed skyscrapers of Chicago. From above, it could have been Baghdad or Kabul. The husks of buildings lined the horizon like chipped teeth. The streets were still clogged with the burned hulks of cars left over from the fire-bombing of Operation Liberty.

Lieutenant Jim Flathman had seen a lot in his four tours of Iraq and Afghanistan, but nothing had prepared him for what he saw when he returned from the War on Terror. His platoon had hurried back to the States when the hemorrhage virus first emerged at O'Hare, but by the time he reached Chicago, the virus had ravaged the metropolis he called home. He'd grown up in the hood, worked construction starting at fourteen, and joined the army at eighteen. He'd served his country ever since.

Coming home to a place overrun with monsters was worse than any war in foreign lands. The only thing that came close to the Variants were his two ex-wives. They'd taken him for every penny. Not that it mattered much now.

Flathman leaned out the door of the Black Hawk for a better view. PFC Stone and Staff Sergeant Bosse crouched next to him. The two men represented a quarter of his crew. The other six soldiers were back at Outpost 46, holding down the fort.

"Jesus," Bosse whispered. "I used to play baseball down there." He pointed toward a crater with gloved fingers. Metal bleachers, black with soot, surrounded the gaping hole in the earth where a baseball field had been.

"You've seen it all before," Flathman said. "Stay focused. We got a mission."

Bosse gave a haphazard salute. "We're with you, Ten Lives." It was Flathman's nickname and a running joke at the outpost, given to him after surviving just about everything the apocalypse could throw at him. Flathman wasn't a superstitious man, but he *had* escaped some dicey situations.

He pulled off his helmet and touched the Cubs hat he wore underneath it. Maybe he was becoming a bit superstitious after all.

The pilots flew over the remains of a high school and a residential area that was pancaked from what looked like a tornado. Trees, cars, and buildings were flattened in a wide arc around the dirty bomb a team of Army Rangers had detonated three months earlier to wipe out the main pocket of juveniles. Fences and signs surrounded the zone with radiation warnings.

"Two minutes to target," said one of the pilots.

Flathman put his helmet back on and looked to his men. "Alright, you know the drill. We drop in, collect intel, then bug out. This is *not* a rescue op. Our mission is to figure out what the fuck happened down there."

He was too hungover to give a pep talk. Stone and Bosse nodded, but he saw them exchange a look. His men knew he was an alcoholic, but he was a functional one, and he had held his post against the Variants for over seven months. That had to count for something. That post, however, was shit out of whiskey, leaving him with only a single bottle of shitty vodka. He'd asked for a lifetime supply of whiskey—although how long a lifetime might last now was debatable. When Ringgold had agreed, he'd smiled for the first time in months. A lifetime supply of the sauce? Now that was something he would risk leaving his small sliver of paradise for.

"This area really took it in the ass," Stone said.

The bird passed over another street choked with abandoned vehicles and framed on each side by crumbling buildings.

"There," Bosse said. He pointed to the rusted metal walls at the edge of Millennium Park. The chopper passed over Cloud Gate, the mirrorlike metal sculpture everyone called "The Bean."

Flathman caught the chopper's reflection on the stainless steel exterior as they flew overhead. He scoped the walls of SZT 15. Where there should have been soldiers manning flamethrowers, M134 Gatling guns, and M240s, there was nobody.

"Doesn't look like anyone's home," Stone said.

"Hold us here," Flathman ordered the pilots. He scanned the zone for motion. His crosshairs fell on the main entrance—the twenty-foot-tall steel doors were sealed shut. The two checkpoints outside the gate were vacant.

He zoomed in on M240s mounted behind the sandbags, both barrels angled at the ground like someone had left them and never come back.

"What the hell?" Flathman whispered to himself. "Where did you sons of bitches go?"

There was no evidence of a battle. No spent shell casings, no bodies, and no blood. It was like the soldiers had straight-up vanished. He had heard about the same thing happening at the Earthfall facility three months prior. Turned out there were Variants and human collaborators there. But Flathman saw no evidence to suggest the juveniles were here. No matter how smart the monsters were, they always left behind signs.

"You getting this, Command?" he said into his comms. "I'm not seeing anything at all from up here."

"Copy that, Lieutenant. Proceed inside the SZT." The southern drawl of General Allen answered him, but he knew President Ringgold and Vice President Johnson were watching his every move.

Just my fucking luck. Government forgets about me for seven months, and now they need me to do their damn dirty work. There better be some good single malt on the rocks when I get back to the post.

Flathman wasn't a stranger to disobeying orders; it was how he had managed to survive. But these orders had come from the very top. You couldn't just say no to the commander-in-chief.

That didn't mean you couldn't negotiate and make a few requests of your own. He grinned at that thought and held up a hand toward the cockpit.

"Take us in," he said.

The bird rose back into the sky and flew over the steel gates. Rows of FEMA housing trailers were set up on the park lawn across the street from the embassy. Rusted barrels used for fires were positioned on sidewalks and alleys where those who weren't fortunate enough to have a trailer had set up tents and makeshift shelters. It reminded him a bit of the block he had grown up in—the block he'd escaped.

Funny how life could bring you back to where you started.

He scanned the area to the west, checking the rooftops. Satellite dishes and communication antennas were rigged on top of the structures. Flags whipped in the wind from poles over the side of the embassy building. In the center of the rooftop, a large red radio tower rose into the sky.

"Do you see that?" Bosse said. He directed his muzzle at what looked like a scarecrow about two-thirds of the way up the tower.

"Raptor One, what's that on the radio tower?" Allen asked a moment later.

Flathman pushed his mic to his lips. "Checking, standby." He didn't even have time to zoom in before Stone shouted.

"Jesus, is that a fucking body?"

Flathman centered his crosshairs on a crucified human corpse stretched across the west side of the tower. Sunlight fell on the exposed muscles. A crow landed on the corpse and began picking at it.

"Shit," Flathman grumbled. It was likely the handiwork of the juveniles in the area. He'd been hunting a pack for weeks and seen grisly totems like this before. But where were the other bodies? There had been hundreds of soldiers here, and they couldn't have all been killed by a handful of juveniles, not unless they had been tricked...

"Take us down," Flathman said.

The pilots looked back from the cockpit.

"Sir?" one of them said.

"I said take us the fuck down."

A second of hesitation passed, the pilots exchanging a glance before they lowered the bird toward the street. Three feet off the ground, Flathman jumped out onto the concrete. The two Rangers followed him out of the chopper.

"Bosse, you and Stone take the left. I'll take the right. High and low, clear the windows and watch the rooftops. We rally at the embassy."

Flathman ducked low, crouched behind a Humvee, and used a stolen moment to scan his surroundings. The embassy was four buildings down, near the front gate. FEMA trailers were set up in the park across the street. There were half a dozen vehicles between him and the building, plus eight rooftops and over a hundred windows. Plenty of places for a sniper or a juvenile to be hiding.

Raising his rifle, he took off at a run, scanning the windows on the right side for motion. Above, the crow continued to pick at the dead man on the radio tower.

Gotta be those fucking juveniles.

He wasn't just here to claim his reward of whiskey, he realized—he was here to kill the bastards that had been tormenting his post for months. Just the other day he had lost PFC Collins. The shy kid from Iowa had been taking a piss during a patrol when he was dragged into the sewers by the beasts.

Collins had been a lousy soldier, but he was just a kid and Flathman had tried to protect him. Bosse and Stone, on the other hand, were men he could trust with his life. That's why they were here. Like any coach, Flathman had his favorite players, and he'd brought his MVPs on this mission.

The sun continued to rise over the city. Flathman pulled his sunglasses from his vest pocket and put them on. He made a dash for an old Nissan Pathfinder, his tennis shoes slapping the pavement.

Despite his bad habits, Flathman was a dedicated runner. He'd traded his boots for a pair of Nikes and jogged around the inside of the fences countless times, earning him another nickname at the post.

Flathman, the Running Man. Ten Lives. Evel Knievel.

He didn't mind the nicknames. There was a place in the apocalypse for adrenaline junkies and drunks. In fact, he was faring just fine in the End Times. Some would say he fit right in.

Bosse flashed a hand signal to indicate the area near him was clear.

Flathman bolted toward the rally point. With every step, his guts sank a bit lower. The nausea wasn't from the hangover, either. He was getting a bad feeling about this mission. And no matter how many shiny bottles of hooch he imagined, he was starting to wonder if it was worth it.

Of course it's fucking worth it.

He stopped at another vehicle to catch his breath, scanned the area, and then took off across the final stretch of asphalt. The embassy building towered above him. It had once been a bank. Prisonlike bars covered the windows on each floor, and two fenced-in checkpoints separated visitors from the front doors. The cages were all empty, and there still wasn't a bullet casing in sight.

The front gate creaked in the wind, the locking mechanism clicking as it hit the metal fence. He stopped in front and flashed signals to his men. Their weapons arched across their zones of fire with a precision that calmed Flathman's rolling stomach. He could trust his boys in the field. Whatever was waiting for them, they could take it.

"On me," he said.

Bosse and Stone fell into line behind him, their weapons trained on the building. Flathman stopped to check his six. A piece of trash whirled in the empty street. Nothing else moved.

He pulled the gate open and stepped into the checkpoint. With his weapon ready, he kept low and moved toward the second gate, then onto the steps that led up to the building.

The first gate creaked again, and this time a scratching sound answered the creak. Flathman pivoted toward the street with his rifle.

"You hear that?" he whispered.

Stone and Bosse glanced around, their muzzles moving horizontally across the street, scanning for contacts.

"Negative, sir," Bosse said.

"I didn't hear—" Stone began to say.

A metallic thud sounded from the direction of the FEMA trailers. Flathman silently directed Bosse and Stone to follow him. Together, they slowly retreated from the gated checkpoints and made their way into the road.

The sun cast a brilliant glow on the carmine metal walls surrounding the SZT. Flathman used the dawn light to search for more clues. He checked the pavement again for signs of gunfire, but saw nothing. No bullet casings or chunks of concrete chipped away from rounds.

Nothing.

He cursed and spat on the ground. Then he flashed another round of hand signals. Bosse and Stone fanned out toward the dozen white FEMA shipping containers. Flathman used the cover of vehicles as he approached, stopping to listen and scan before continuing.

His tennis shoes crushed the recently trimmed lawn. As he moved, he took in a breath. Hell, the park even smelled like fresh-cut grass! Whatever had happened to these people, it had been sudden.

Caw! Caw! Caw!

Flathman flinched at the screeching bird. He shouldered his rifle and aimed it at the tower, where the crow was now flapping away from the corpse.

Heart pounding, Flathman slowly lowered his rifle to turn back to the trailers. As he moved, an echoing whistle came from the sky. The sound rose on the wind, and Flathman recognized it. Helicopters, moving in fast. He directed his team down into a crouch near a pickup truck for cover.

"Ten Lives, this is Raptor One, do you copy?"

"Roger, go ahead."

"We got three bogies bearing 090."

Flathman prepared to respond when a trio of AH-6 Little Birds emerged over the buildings to the east. They buzzed overhead with soldiers clipped to the sides, their weapons angled down on the street.

"Hide," Flathman ordered his men. He crawled under the nearest truck, his guts tightening. Over the past seven months, the Variants had never gotten the drop on him. Not once. He'd been lucky—Ten Lives Flathman, the man who was too stubborn to die. But he'd forgotten that the monsters weren't the only threat out there, and he had the feeling his last life had just run out.

It wasn't the first time in her life that Dr. Kate Lovato didn't want to go to work, but she would have given anything now to be curled up at home in bed with Reed. She hesitated at the end of the corridor leading to her lab, where she gently put a hand on top of her belly and glanced at Ellis. He was standing at the entrance to the clean room in the new lab facility, using the new fingerprint scanner by the door.

"Come on," he mumbled. The pad flashed green, and he bent down to put his eye up to the second recognition slot.

The door chirped, then opened, revealing the clean room partitioned off by glass walls from the labs beyond. An air-filtration unit clicked on above, humming quietly. They were the only two scientists in the BSL4 lab this morning. Durand and Case were working later that afternoon. Kate wanted to be out of here before they arrived.

"You coming, Kate?" Ellis said. He stood in the doorway and glanced back at her.

"Yes, sorry. I was just...thinking."

She had been thinking about the children who died on the dock. It was because of her protocols that the soldiers had opened fire. No matter what Reed said, it was her fault. Just like it was her fault the bioweapon she'd designed had killed her brother—and likely her parents, too. Javier had been infected with the hemorrhage virus during the early stages of the outbreak. She'd known, when she created the weapon, that it was a death sentence for him and all the other innocent people transformed into monsters by the plague.

Kate had become a doctor to help people. But now every time she did her job, people died.

She reluctantly followed Ellis through the doors. CBRN suits and sealed boxes waited inside. In the past, entering a Level 4 Bio facility wouldn't have bothered her. But it wasn't just her anymore. She had her son to think about. The slightest mistake could put her child at risk. Normally a pregnant woman wouldn't be allowed even close to a BSL4 lab, but this was the end of the world. She was here because there was no one else to do her job. Her country—no, the world—needed her.

But Reed and their baby needed her too.

"I got here at the crack of dawn and went through the overnight reports," Ellis said. He sat on a bench and began putting on his protective suit.

Kate grabbed hers from the wall and took a seat.

"And?"

Ellis rolled the suit up his legs to his waist. "And it's not good. Operation Beachhead was a spectacular failure, and the EUF is retreating from dozens of major cities. The list is massive, Kate. Istanbul, Manchester, Madrid." He paused and then added, "And Rome. I'm so sorry, Kate. They're pulling out of Italy for now."

Kate had prepared herself for this. She'd accepted her parents were dead. It didn't hurt anymore. Not much, anyway. If she kept telling herself that, she might start to believe it.

"The Variants set a trap in Normandy, and the Twenty-Fourth MEU fell right into it," Ellis continued. The words pulled her back to the bright, clean room that reeked of chemicals. She put her hand on her chest, feeling her beating heart through the CBRN layers.

"Did Fitz and Apollo make it?"

Ellis shook his head.

"What!" Kate exclaimed, pain breaking through her wall of calm.

"I meant I don't know. Sounds like they had to leave a lot of bodies on the beaches due to toxin saturation."

She loosened her grip on her chest, her hand falling to her stomach. "Does Reed know yet?"

"I don't think so. I may be the first to have read the report this morning. It came in with the specimen."

"Specimen?"

"We got video feeds, field reports, and a tissue sample from one of the winged creatures they found over there. Something they've dubbed a Reaver." He finished suiting up and walked over to her. "You sure you don't want to go home today, Kate? You don't look so good. I already started the process for DNA sequencing. You don't have to be here. I can complete it on my own."

Kate zipped her suit up and picked up her helmet. Of course she wanted to go home. But she wouldn't, not while there was even a chance she could do some good.

"Let's go," she said. For what seemed like the millionth time, she secured her CBRN helmet with a click. The first breath of cold, filtered air filled her lungs. She took in another slow and steady breath. She could do this. Everyone had a job to do, and this was hers.

The six-station lab was still empty when Kate and Ellis entered. He walked straight to the sequencing machine. There was a bag on a tray next to the station marked LEVEL 4—HANDLE WITH EXTREME PREJUDICE.

"The report came from the top. We are to determine what type of genetic modifications we'll see next. They also want to know what the hell this thing is. I'm honestly surprised we aren't being asked to find a way to kill it."

"We're out of time to develop anything," Kate said. "It's too late for bioweapons in Europe. They'll have to kill these monsters the old-fashioned way."

"You're starting to sound like General Kennor."

Kate ignored his comment and examined the specimen bag from a distance. A brownish liquid filled the inside. Ellis discarded it in the infirmary slot. Then he returned to the sequencer.

"I've already incubated the tissue in the centrifuge tubes. I could use some help with the detergents to separate the DNA from the cellular components, though."

Kate took in another long breath. As long as she was safe and cautious, everything would be fine. The Variant blood wasn't infectious, but that's not what worried her. It was everything else stored in liquid nitrogen-cooled cryogenic freezers. The Medical Corps kept a sample of every Level 4 virus known to man, including Ebola and now the hemorrhage virus.

"Have you checked the biometrics?" she asked.

"Still filtering through the raw data I entered last night."

Kate nodded. The biometrics tools aided them in comparing genetic and genomic data, which in turn allowed them to understand the evolutionary aspects of the Variants. Every time a new creature was discovered, it was analyzed, catalogued, and integrated into the pool of data.

Today, however, they weren't just studying field reports. They actually had a sample to study—a sample Kate guessed had cost a lot of lives.

Ellis finished setting up the tiny plastic centrifuge tubes. She joined him at the lab counter and grabbed a pipette. It had been a month since they had worked on anything new. Part of her enjoyed the meticulous detail DNA sequencing required. It was a good change of pace from reading reports and data mining.

She used her pipette to put the separated DNA into the sequencer. It took two hours to complete the process, but Kate found she didn't mind. It was a repetitive process that didn't require much thought: pipette the liquid in, spin it in the centrifuge, then discard the supernatants and pipette new liquid in. Rinse and repeat. Kate didn't have to think about Fitz, Apollo, Reed, her parents, or anything other than the task in front of her.

When they were finished, Ellis turned the machine on and crossed his arms.

"Now we wait." He pivoted away from the machine and eyed his computer monitor across the room. "Ready to get back to research?"

"We don't have a choice. The report on the new Variants is due to Vice President Johnson in forty-six hours."

"I haven't had a chance to watch any of the new footage from the MEUs yet, but I read the report from Colonel Bradley of the Twenty-Fourth. There were over thirty of those Reavers at the landing."

Kate leaned closer, biting the inside of her lip. She had never seen one of the creatures before, but just the name sent a prickle of fear across her skin. And she had a feeling they weren't the only things ravaging Europe.

"Apparently there are more adult Variants in Europe than we thought. The EUF did an awful job deploying Kryptonite," Ellis said.

He shifted through his notes and ran a gloved finger down the page. "Looks like this feed was taken from a Black Hawk at the same beach where Fitz and Team Ghost landed."

On screen, the door gunner's helmet-mounted camera shook violently as the chopper rolled to the right, providing them a view of the moonlit cliffs of Normandy. Below, several destroyers carved through the water. Dozens of smaller craft skirted toward the shore, all of them filled with vehicles.

Several had already beached, disgorging tanks and armored trucks onto the sand. Although Kate couldn't see them, she knew Fitz, Apollo, Rico, and the new members of Team Ghost were down there somewhere.

The camera rolled back to the sky.

"There," Ellis said. He pointed to a flurry of shadows that could have been bats passing in front of the moon.

Kate leaned even closer.

"Reavers," she whispered.

A brilliant ball of fire flashed below, blinding the feed. When it cleared, the door gunner was firing at a sky full of armored Variants with wings.

"Darwin would be amazed," Ellis said. "Those things are…"

Kate brought her hand to her helmet, her breathing raspy. Her heart was pounding and sweat dripped down her forehead.

Her friends were out there facing monsters unlike anything her imagination could have conjured.

Another Black Hawk crossed in front of the door gunner's feed. The troop hold was full of soldiers, all firing their weapons into the sky. One of the beasts swooped up from below and plucked the door gunner away like a child grabbing a doll. A second soldier reached out to pull him back and plummeted into the darkness.

"Those things are incredible," Ellis said in a tone that made Kate wonder if he was talking more to himself.

She narrowed her eyes at him and snapped, "What the hell do you mean by that? Those things are monsters, not some wonderful new species. And our friends are out there, my parents…"

Her voice trailed off as she realized she still hadn't accepted their fate. She'd been lying to herself for months, but in her heart there was still a flicker of hope.

Ellis dipped his helmet. "I'm…I'm sorry, Kate. I didn't mean to upset you. I just haven't ever seen anything like it before."

A chirp interrupted the slaughter on screen. Kate and Ellis both turned toward her laptop. The biometrics report from the night before had finished running.

"I'm sorry, Kate," he said again.

She ignored his apologies. He didn't have anyone left. It had to be hard being alone. But the insensitivity of his comment, as if he was almost *happy* to see how the Reavers had evolved…

"I'm going to check the data," Kate said. She got up

from his station and moved to hers. After typing in her credentials, she clicked on the report.

REPORT FROM PARIS, FRANCE

10.19.15

PREVIOUSLY UNIDENTIFIED SPECIMEN

RUN AGAINST 300 MILLION OTHER SPECIES

CONCLUSION: NEW VARIANT SPECIES

"What's it say?" Ellis said.

Kate turned to look her partner in the eye. "It says the French have discovered an entirely new species."

"The Reavers?"

"No," Kate replied. "Something even worse."

9

President Ringgold watched the video feed from SZT 15 with a growing sense of horror. It was almost too much to process. Lieutenant Flathman and his team were pinned down by mysterious helicopters, which was bad enough. But the real mystery was where all the people had gone. She'd looked in vain for her cousin, but there was no sign of Emilia.

There was no sign of anyone.

Not many people knew her cousin had been at SZT 15. But then again, most of her staff didn't know anything about their president's personal life. They didn't know she had grown up in Harlem in an apartment building infested with bedbugs and drug dealers. They didn't know, because she didn't tell them. She had never wanted to use her past for political gain, but she wasn't ashamed of it, either. By the grace of God and a hard work ethic, she and Emilia had escaped hell. Now Ringgold feared she had inadvertently condemned her cousin to an even worse fate than the one they'd escaped.

There's always hope.

She had reassured Dr. Kate Lovato of that many times, but Ringgold wasn't sure she believed it anymore.

She palmed the table and stood. Across the room,

General Allen was whispering something to Johnson. Neither of them looked happy.

"We have an incoming video message from an unidentified source," Allen announced.

"How'd they get this frequency?" Johnson asked.

Allen shook his head, unsure. They both looked at Ringgold, and she nodded for them to proceed.

The main screen divided in two. To the left was Flathman's feed from the ground, and to the right was a man with sun-reddened skin and a head of graying hair. He'd been bound and forced onto his knees, but his gaze was defiant.

Johnson's mouth hung open. Ringgold had never seen him so shocked.

"Dear God. Is that Admiral Humphrey?"

"Yes, sir," Allen confirmed. "The video is from the *George Washington*."

The camera panned to the right to show a soldier dressed in black fatigues. He sat in the captain's chair, one leg crossed over the other. He nonchalantly nodded at someone out of view.

Ringgold flinched at the crack of gunfire from the wall-mounted speakers and brought her hand up to her mouth as the admiral crashed to the floor, part of his skull blown off.

"Jesus Christ," Allen said.

Johnson took another step toward the screen, his hands balling into fists. "No!" he yelled, his usual calm failing in the face of such an atrocity.

The man in black uncrossed his legs and leaned forward, providing a view of dark brown eyes, short-cropped gray hair, and a face pockmarked with acne scars.

"Jan Ringgold," the man said, raising his eyebrows. "It's about time we met."

Johnson reached for Allen's headset.

"You're speaking to the President of the United States," Johnson said. "Identify yourself."

The man shook his head and leaned back in the chair. "Not my president. You don't recognize me, do you, Johnson?"

Johnson didn't reply, just glowered at the screen.

"Lieutenant Andrew Wood of the ROT. Resistance of Tyranny, if you're wondering what the acronym means. You knew my older brother, Colonel Zach Wood. But that's not important right now. What's really important is what I'm about to say. So listen up. You too, Jan."

Ringgold grabbed a mic from the table. "I remember your brother," she said. "And I remember what he did on Plum Island. You don't want to follow in his footsteps."

"I have control of the USS *George Washington*," Wood said, continuing as if she hadn't spoken. "You've had a real hard time holding on to it, haven't you, Jan?"

Johnson went to speak, but Ringgold raised her hand to silence him.

"What do you want?" Ringgold asked.

Wood paused for dramatic effect, seeming to enjoy his captive audience. "I want the presidency."

"That's not going to happen," Ringgold said sternly.

Wood nodded once, then flashed a smile that vanished so fast it could hardly be considered one. "I figured you'd say that. So I'm going to show you something that might make you reconsider. Take a look at SZT Fifteen. You're not the only one with choppers in the vicinity."

Her gaze flitted to the left side of the screen, where Flathman was still hunkered down.

"Pay close attention to those FEMA semitrailers. Have your lackey come out for a better look," Wood said. He crossed his legs again and folded his hands on his lap, waiting.

Allen gave the order, and Flathman crawled out from under the truck and focused his cam on the trailers. All at once the lift gates opened and figures stumbled out.

Flathman retreated as the streets came alive with movement. Hundreds of men and women with duct tape over their mouths and hands staggered into the street, blinking and unsteady like they'd just woken up from a nap.

"This might take a few minutes," Wood said. "Those people have been sleeping for a while. They're going to be very hungry."

Some of the civilians broke their bonds immediately and raised their hands to the sky to shield their eyes from the sun. A few others snapped their restraints to crouch in the street, hissing and snarling. But the majority dropped to all fours. Free now, most of them skittered away and leaped to the walls of buildings, the tops of cars, and the metal fences surrounding the safe zone.

Allen looked up. "Flathman's asking for orders."

Johnson exchanged a glance with Ringgold, but she was too stunned to reply. Flathman raised his gun and opened fire a second later. On his right, the two other soldiers did the same.

Emilia, I'm so sorry. She scanned the diseased faces for her missing cousin and then shook the shock away. She had to do something.

"Tell Raptor One to get in there and pick those soldiers up right now!"

Johnson nodded at Allen, who relayed the message. Flathman looked up at the sky as Raptor 1 emerged over the SZT wall. The pilots dipped toward his position, but as soon as they did, the AH-6 Little Birds fired on them with chain guns. The rounds punched through the windshield and troop hold, sending the chopper whirling out of control.

For a moment Flathman just stood there, staring, his camera focused on the falling Black Hawk. It hit the SZT wall a moment later, and a massive explosion bloomed across the screen.

"No," Ringgold whispered. "This can't be happening."

Flathman's screen vibrated. He was running again, but everyone in the room could see there was no escape. The creatures were too fast, despite having been under sleeping gas or whatever it was Wood had used to sedate them. They prowled on all sides, clawing, and testing him as he fired burst after burst to fend them off.

Wood let several moments pass before he spoke again.

"Jan, as secure as you claim your SZTs to be, it was remarkably easy to compromise this one," he said, shaking a finger. "Actually, that's a lie. We had a little trouble at first. We tried to sneak in the hemorrhage virus by infecting some poor bastard we captured living outside the walls like we did at Plum Island. Sometimes you just have to offer an incentive to get people to do awful things, like threaten the lives of their loved ones. Like your cousin, Emilia Ringgold. *Such* a distinctive last name. When I saw it on the official census, I just knew I had to meet her. But I digress. At SZT Fifteen all we had to do was bait Mayor Kaylor."

Ringgold felt her hands shaking. She knew Kaylor, had thought him to be a good man.

"It didn't take much to get him to let us in. A few favors and a promise of a seat in my cabinet. By the time the guards knew what was happening, we had them surrounded. Didn't even fire a single bullet. Then it was just a matter of getting everyone inside those trailers. Didn't turn out real good for Kaylor, though. It was pretty easy getting under his skin, so to speak."

Ringgold now realized it had been Kaylor hanging from the radio tower. She closed her eyes for a moment but forced them back open to face the monster in front of her.

"Now that I have your attention, I'm going to tell you again, one more time, what I want. There are about seventy-five more SZTs, and I have more than enough vials of the hemorrhage virus to take them all down. Not to mention two destroyers. I think I'm going to rechristen this one the *Zach Wood*. What do you think?"

Ringgold wanted to reach into the screen and rip Wood's arrogant smirk off his face but she spoke in the calmest voice she could manage. "Why? Why are you doing this? To avenge your psychotic brother?"

Wood wagged a finger again. "You don't get it, do you, Jan? You gave us no choice but to use guerrilla-warfare tactics." His voice rose into an angry snarl. "You took the presidency by murdering our military leaders, including my brother, and then rewarded the man who killed him with a goddamn medal."

"This isn't guerrilla warfare. This is terrorism," Ringgold snapped back.

Johnson glanced in her direction, shaking his head subtly. He was warning her to back off. She felt her legs wobbling, but she remained standing.

"Everyone but Johnson get out," she said firmly.

The list of people she trusted had three names on it: Dr. Kate Lovato, Captain Reed Beckham, and Vice President George Johnson. And the first two were hundreds of miles away. It took a minute for everyone to leave the room, but as soon as the door shut, Ringgold brought the mic back to her mouth.

"The United States of America has never negotiated with terrorists in the past, and we're not going to start now. I don't know what kind of sick game you're playing, but you won't win. We will find you, and we will stop you. Just like we stopped your brother."

"You can try, Jan. I'm counting on it, actually. But if a single aircraft comes within striking distance of my growing fleet, I will launch every missile on board at your precious SZTs."

Wood winked at the screen, and the feed fizzled off.

Johnson pounded the table with a fist as Ringgold sank into her chair.

Flathman's screen continued to jolt violently as the lieutenant ran. The man on his right was tackled to the ground by three infected that ripped at his flesh with razor-sharp claws. The smallest of the three—he must have been a child, Ringgold realized—clamped sucker lips around the soldier's neck and tore away a ribbon of meat.

She had seen many people killed by the monsters, but she had never seen a child feed. Flathman raised his rifle, but instead of killing the creatures, he shot the soldier in the head to end his suffering.

The beasts crawled over the limp corpse and tore into the flesh. Flathman sprayed the monsters with bullets as he ran. Ringgold had to force herself to look away, terrified that she would see Emilia with wild yellow eyes and misshapen features.

"What is ROT?" she asked. "Who the *hell* are these people?"

Johnson took in a long, deep breath. "When Lieutenant Andrew Wood left the Medical Corps, he became CEO of a private military contracting company about the same time his brother Colonel Zach Wood was working with Colonel Rick Gibson on refining the VX-99 program. I don't know a lot about ROT, but I do know they had a bunker with a lot of vehicles, aircraft, supplies, and weapons."

"But how did they capture the *GW*? And which destroyer is he talking about?"

Johnson shook his head. "I'll get Allen working on this to see if we're missing any other ships. As for how Wood captured the *GW*...probably the same way he got Mayor Kaylor to open the doors in Chicago."

Ringgold couldn't believe what she was hearing, but she did know what she had to do next. She stood again and looked at the flag for a moment, gathering her courage.

"Send the message out to all of the SZTs to raise their security alert to Level Red. And get me the best Special Forces troops you have left. I want Wood tracked down and neutralized," Ringgold said. She could think of a couple of men on Plum Island who would be able to get the job done, but Beckham and Horn were retired now.

Back on the main screen, Flathman was running hard, pausing only briefly to fire into the mob behind him. One of the creatures, a large half-naked male, leaped onto a car hood. It chewed at its own chubby arm, ripping off a piece that stretched out in a web of tendons and flesh. The lieutenant shot the creature in the stomach and then fired on a smaller, female Variant skittering across the side of the embassy building. It fell onto the top of one of the cages and twisted fiercely in the razor wire.

A flash of motion came from the left, knocking Flathman to the ground. Ringgold brought her hand around her mouth.

"Get up, Lieutenant," Johnson said.

Flathman did just that, but his helmet remained on the ground—and with it his camera. Side by side, Ringgold and Johnson watched the lieutenant dart down the street. His tennis shoes pounded the pavement and he held on to his Chicago Cubs hat with one hand as he ran. He did not look back.

There was a knock on the door, which made

Ringgold flinch. Flathman rounded a corner and vanished from the feed as she turned to see General Allen peeking inside the room.

"What is it?" she asked.

Allen stepped into the room. "We just intercepted an SOS from Captain Rachel Davis of the *GW*. She's alive, Madam President, and she's going to try to take the ship back. But she's saying there's a second ship already leaving the area."

"The other destroyer," Johnson said. "That's how they were able to capture the *GW*."

Allen nodded. "It's the *Zumwalt*, sir. I just listened to the transmissions. Wood hailed the *GW*, pretending to be friendlies. Humphrey had no idea what was coming. Wood also had AH-Six Little Birds in the area." He paused and then said, "If the *Zumwalt* goes off radar and they escape, then we have more than just the *GW* to worry about…"

Johnson dipped his head in defeat. "Guess we know where the stealth ship vanished to all those months ago. These ROT bastards have been planning this for a long time."

Captain Davis moved on all fours in the dense grass along the shoreline. Diaz crawled to her right, and a few feet ahead, Black's thick Mohawk cut through the torpedograss like a shark fin through water.

In the distance, heavy smoke streamed out of the city. Davis coughed into her hand, wishing she hadn't removed her CBRN suit. But she'd had no choice. The white suits made them stand out like ghosts in the night, and it wasn't just the monsters hunting them now.

The buzz of a helicopter sent Davis to eating dirt. She

flattened her body in the mud and craned her neck to the sky. Two AH-6 Little Birds shot overhead with soldiers clipped to the sides. One of the men pointed in her direction, and Davis quickly averted her gaze.

They had managed to evade the patrols all morning, but with the sun up it was only a matter of time before they were spotted. She was lucky Diaz had been able to get a call through to President Ringgold about the ambush with their satellite phone. As a communications officer, the lance corporal always carried it with her into the field.

Davis kept her head down as the choppers circled. She still didn't know much about this ROT, but she could see they were well trained and well equipped. Plus, they had her ship *and* a stealth destroyer.

As soon as the birds passed over, Davis got back up and continued crawling. The *GW* was still anchored, but the sleek gray body of the *Zumwalt* was long gone. She had watched the ship sail hours earlier. There was no telling where they were now.

This is your fault, Rachel. You should never have left!

She had let her guard down. Part of her had thought rescuing those children might help relieve some of the pain from choosing duty over family at the start of the outbreak. Nothing could bring Blake and Ollie back, but maybe if she could save just one more person…

Gritting her teeth, she fought back the painful memories. Her weakness had killed brave men and women on her ship. She had fallen right into ROT's trap. Now she was on the run in a city still burning from the missile strikes she had ordered. If that wasn't bad enough, there were men and monsters prowling the streets, hunting for her team.

Quick and steady. Keep it quick and steady.

If there was one thing she had learned in the past

seven months, it was that she was never out of the fight. Even now, with enemies closing in from all directions she retained her killer instinct.

The Little Birds finally abandoned their search. Black slowly rose out of the torpedograss and waved to Davis and Diaz from the muck. He waded through knee-deep water, then ran up an embankment toward a bar called Bayou Joe's. Docks with boat slips emerged to the west. She eyed the ride she'd chosen to get back to her ship, but first she needed a diversion.

Davis and Diaz ran at a crouch toward Black. He propped a shoulder against a tree with a base that was twisted like a Twizzler. Slowly, he moved around the side and aimed his SAW toward a gravel road. Diaz took a knee and sucked down the rest of her water bottle. She dragged a sleeve across her lips and said, "What's the plan, Captain?"

"We have to get back to the ship before they leave," Davis said. "I'm guessing that's going to be soon, but they must still have soldiers in the field."

Black shot her a glance. "All due respect, but you gotta be kiddin' me, ma'am. They got at least fifty men, bunch of them Little Birds, and hostages."

"What about the rest of the strike group?" Diaz asked.

"Too far away," Davis replied. "I'm sure they're already inbound, but by the time they get here, it'll be too late."

"Maybe we should consider the *GW* a loss, ma'am," Black said. There was fear in his voice, but he held her gaze. "Maybe we should let the big dogs handle this."

Davis shook her head. "Absolutely not. That's *my* ship. I lost her once, and I got her back. I'm going to get her back again. I understand if you want to stay here and hide…"

"I'm with you, Captain," Diaz said.

Black sighed. "So what's your plan? Steal a boat and—"

Raised voices cut him off. He ducked down and fell to his stomach. Diaz took up position behind a second tree, and Davis joined her.

To the north, several soldiers in black CBRN suits walked down the gravel road. Several more men in white suits trailed them, hands bound, and heads bowed.

Davis centered her M4's optics on the prisoners, focusing on a face that looked even worse than when she had seen it aboard the *GW* a few hours ago. Blood dripped down Sergeant Marks's battered features. He shuffled along with the other two marines toward the docks.

The hum of engines came from the south. Two black Zodiacs coasted over the waves away from the *GW*, packed full of ROT soldiers. There were two fire teams—far too many to engage.

Black looked to Davis for orders. It pained her to do it, but she flashed the signal to stand down. He pushed his eye back to the optics on his SAW. She wanted to tell him to open fire, but she couldn't risk it. Not with those reinforcements on the way.

Davis waited in silence, listening to the chirp of bugs and the buzz of the distant helicopters. Flames ate the city to the west. Her skin was coated with soot and ash, and her lungs burned from the smoke. Diaz and Black were waiting for her next orders, their faces filthy and apprehensive.

They had to do *something*. Davis refused to just sit there while a bunch of terrorists stole her ship.

Diaz's eyes suddenly went wide, and she jerked her mud-streaked chin toward the water about two hundred feet away from the Zodiacs.

Waves moved across the surface as if miniature submarines were gliding underneath. They fanned out into three, then six different arrows. Davis spotted rough, armored shells just beneath the surface.

"Juveniles," Diaz whispered.

Davis centered her M4 back on the dock. Sergeant Marks stood at the edge, a gun pointed at his back. The other two marines stumbled up to his side. The team of ROT soldiers hung back with their weapons shouldered. They were going to execute the marines.

Marks turned toward the men. "You're not going to get away with this, you sons of bitches! Admiral Humphrey will have you all hanged for treason."

Davis shook her head. Sarge was about to get himself and the other two marines shot.

One of the ROT soldiers let out a muffled laugh. "Humphrey is dead, you old prick. Now, shut your mouth, or I'll put a bullet in it."

Marks took a step backward, and Davis lowered her rifle, her stomach dropping as if she were about to jump out of a plane. Humphrey was dead?

This is your fault. You're the reason he's dead. You should never have left the ship, you selfish . . .

The anger and shame almost caused Davis to do something stupid. She was halfway to pulling the trigger, and damn the consequences, but she forced herself to stand down. She took in a smoky breath and reminded herself of the truth.

You didn't kill Humphrey. These terrorists did. Quick and steady, Rachel. You got this.

The curved backs of the juveniles cut through the water as the beasts surfaced. They were swimming toward the Zodiacs. Despite their armored shells, they were fast—much faster than their Variant parents.

Davis waited for the monsters to attack. It would buy her a window to take out the soldiers guarding Marks, but it could also end up giving away their position. If things went south, she didn't want to engage half a dozen juveniles and three teams of ROT soldiers.

She had two choices: Fight, or sit here and watch whatever happened next.

It took a glance at the horizon, where the *GW* waited in the sparkling water, for Davis to make up her mind. They would kill the ROT soldiers guarding Marks and the other marines as soon as the juveniles attacked the men in the Zodiacs. Then they would steal the ROT uniforms as disguises to get back onto the *GW*. It was a long shot, but this was the best and only opportunity she would get.

The craft coasted over the waves, drawing closer by the second. The soldiers in the bow jolted up and down, unaware that Davis was already choosing which of them would die first. She zoomed in on a face obscured by a gas mask and made her decision.

"Black and Diaz, you take the assholes on the dock. I'll focus my fire on the Zodiacs. Cover those marines. Try to keep the juveniles away from them."

Together, the trio crept into position.

Davis kept her crosshairs on the soldier at the helm of the lead Zodiac. She was preparing to fire, when the craft suddenly burst into the air, sending the occupants cartwheeling in all directions. A pair of juveniles surfaced, their maws snapping. One of the beasts jumped out of the water like a great white shark and clamped its teeth over the helmet and shoulders of a soldier. It dove back into the water with its prey and vanished under the surface.

The boat landed a second later with a splash.

Screaming, gunfire, and the screeches of enraged, hungry monsters filled the smoky morning air. The soldiers in the second Zodiac fired at the circling juveniles. Bullets connected with targets Davis couldn't see.

She trained her gun on the dock, where Marks and the two marines were being pulled away by their captors. Four ROT soldiers forced their way past the men and took up position on the end of the dock.

"Now," Davis ordered.

She centered her crosshairs on the two soldiers guarding Marks and his men. Her first shot clipped her target in the back of his helmet. Marks seized the opportunity to grab the rifle from the other soldier. An instant later, the other two marines wrestled the final ROT man to the ground. Marks pulled the soldier's knife and silenced him with a swift stroke across the throat.

Black unloaded on the four men at the front of the dock. Splinters exploded as bullets tore up the wooden platform. One of the soldiers clutched his chest and fell into the water. The other three turned to fire on Davis's position. Black killed another man with a shot to the throat before he was forced to take cover.

Diaz let out a screech and dropped to the ground. Two rounds bit into the tree above Davis's head. She cursed but didn't have time to check on her bodyguard. She squeezed off three shots and crouched as another round punched into the bark where her helmet had been. Her next shot hit one of the ROT soldiers in his visor. She looked back at Diaz.

"You okay?"

"I'm good," Diaz said. She quickly pushed herself off the ground. "Round hit my weapon. No harm, no foul."

Davis felt a swell of pride. The woman had conviction, a true warrior. She roved her gun back to the Zodiacs. Bloody bubbles frothed around the capsized boat. The men in the second craft continued to unload their weapons into the water around them. The three soldiers had no fire discipline, and the juveniles seemed to be waiting under the surface for them to run out of magazines.

Smart, Davis thought. *Too smart.*

Black continued to fire on the dock, taking out the last of the ROT soldiers. The men crumpled in heaps of twisted limbs.

"Over here!" Davis shouted. She waved at Marks, who was busy relieving a dead man of his radio and SCAR. The other two marines grabbed weapons, then followed the sergeant toward the shore.

"Let's go!" Davis shouted. She yanked Diaz to her feet, and with Black on point, they took off running.

The guns on the Zodiac behind them went silent, one by one. Davis risked a glance over her shoulder just as a juvenile leaped from the water and tackled the final soldier. Bubbles surrounded the sinking craft. A hand broke the surface, and then a face.

"Help me!"

Davis would have shot him to end his suffering if it had been one of her marines, but this man didn't deserve an ounce of mercy. For the first time since the outbreak, she felt no sympathy for a human killed by the monsters. The ROT terrorists deserved to be ripped to shreds.

10

Horn and Beckham made their way through the streets toward the central embassy building. Dressed in civilian clothing, the two former Delta operators walked unnoticed through the throngs of soldiers and the citizens of Plum Island. If it weren't for their weapons, they might have been mistaken for farmers in their jeans and sweatshirts. But today they weren't working the fields. They were headed to a meeting called by Mayor Antoine Walker. Every man and woman who could fire a gun had been invited to the embassy to discuss the recent attack.

The event cast a dark shadow over the island. Everyone was paranoid. Civilians huddled together, talking in hushed voices. On a normal day, the market would have been a bustling hotspot. Usually carts full of fresh produce would line the streets, and government employees would hand out boxes of government-issued food to citizens in exchange for ration cards. Beckham had been looking forward to cashing in some credits for a pumpkin as a surprise for Tasha and Jenny.

"Think we'll hear anything about Fitz and Ghost?" Horn asked. He walked through the town square sucking on a cigarette and showing off his muscles and tattoos beneath rolled-up sleeves.

"Not sure, but I'm going to ask."

"I wouldn't worry too much, boss. Fitz knows what he's doing. And the folks he's got with him on Team Ghost are supposed to be some of the best." He paused. "I mean, besides us. Obviously."

"Shit, I can barely even walk a straight line today. That son of a bitch tased me twice."

Horn chuckled. "I can't believe you punched Durand in the face. Not saying he didn't deserve it."

Beckham grinned back, but even that was painful. His entire body ached from digging the day before and from the shocks from the Tasers. He still hadn't fully recovered from the toxins that had ravaged his body, either. The pain was worse than he let on, but he didn't want to be put on permanent desk duty. *That* might kill him.

They continued through the deserted market quickly, passing stall after stall of corn, potatoes, squash. It was all there, and there was plenty to go around, but no one was buying today. Everyone was either at the embassy or at home with the doors locked.

"So you're going to have a boy," Horn said. He took a drag off his cigarette, then exhaled smoke through his nose. "I really thought you guys were going to have a girl."

Beckham smiled. "I think Tasha and Jenny are disappointed. They better not gang up on him. Having two older sisters isn't easy."

Horn laughed again, but then his expression turned serious. "I just wish Sheila was here to see them grow up with your son."

"I know, Big Horn. I do too."

"I also wish Sheila would have met Kate. I think they would have really liked each other."

Beckham looked down at the ground, not sure what

to say. Horn rummaged in his shirt pocket and pulled out a small envelope. He opened it and tipped out a ring set with a modest diamond.

"Had this all this time. Chow brought it back for me from Bragg. He couldn't, you know, bring Sheila home, but this was the next best thing. I want you to have it. I think Sheila would have wanted that too."

"Ah, man, I can't accept..."

Horn pushed his hand toward Beckham. "You're gonna marry Kate, and you're gonna need a ring."

Beckham picked up the band with trembling fingers. "Thanks, brother."

"Love you, bro," Horn said.

Beckham slipped the ring into his pocket with the picture of his mom, then reached out and gave his best friend a one-armed hug.

"I love you too, Big Horn."

They pulled away and continued through the market, walking in silence for a few minutes, both of them lost in their memories. As they approached the end of the market, Horn said, "So, you got a name in mind for your son?"

"We've talked about it..." Beckham hesitated, not wanting to bring up more painful memories. But hell, it wasn't like they were gonna forget the ones they had lost if they stopped talking about them.

"Javier Riley," he said at last. "After her brother—and our brother."

For a moment, Horn didn't say anything. Then he clapped Beckham on the shoulder and said gruffly, "That's a good name, boss. But why not Javier Alex?"

"We considered using his first name, but in the end decided it would be better to use Riley to help carry on his family name..."

A gust of wind bit into them, providing a momentary

distraction. Horn shielded his precious cigarette with a hand and eyed a pair of Medical Corps officers walking by. The two soldiers smirked at them.

"Fuck you lookin' at?" Horn asked.

One of the men hesitated, but the other said, "Come on, we're going to be late."

"That's right," Horn said after them. "Keep walkin'." He took a long drag on his cigarette, then flicked it on the ground.

Horn stomped the cigarette. "We get no respect anymore. I'm really starting to hate this civilian bullshit."

They continued toward the embassy building at the end of the street. Unlike the prefab houses FEMA had shipped to the island, the embassy was a beautiful structure with white columns out front and large windows. Workers on scaffolds were putting the finishing touches on the exterior of the building. Those gorgeous windows were all being covered with metal bars.

Two marines on the bottom steps directed Beckham and Horn into a line. Another set of marines were checking IDs outside the large steel doors leading into the building. The line inched up the stairs. Beckham kept his hand on his aching back the entire way. His body was falling apart.

At the top step, he pulled his badge from his pocket and handed it over to the stony-faced marine at the door. The man looked at it quickly, glanced at Beckham's face, back at the ID, and finally to Beckham's prosthetics. He was growing used to the judgmental stares now, but this was too much. Now he knew exactly how Fitz felt.

"You want to say something?" Beckham asked.

Instead of a condescending smirk, the marine offered a warm smile. "I heard the stories about you, sir. Thank you for everything you did to save our country." He handed the ID back to Beckham.

"You hear any stories about me?" Horn said. He pulled his ID card.

The marine's eyes roved to Horn. "Yeah, you're that star college football player from Team Ghost, right?"

Horn slapped his knee and looked at Beckham. "Hell yeah! Finally some respect."

The soldiers in the line behind them fidgeted, and the marine jerked his chin after looking at Horn's badge. "You're both clear."

Beckham and Horn strode into an auditorium packed with soldiers and civilians. Everyone inside had the battle-hardened look of people who'd fought the Variants.

"Please take a seat," came a voice from the front of the room.

Beckham grabbed a chair next to Horn as Mayor Antoine Walker, a tall African American man with glasses and salt-and-pepper hair, took the stage. He stepped up to the podium, surrounded on all sides by officers of the Medical Corps. Army Lieutenant General Miles Rayburn stood right behind Walker. They were supposed to share control of the safe-zone territory, but there was no doubt who was really running the operation here. Walker was a puppet, a paper pusher. Rayburn, on the other hand, was the one who had ordered the civilians shot on the docks during the attack.

Beckham had a hard time stomaching that, but after the rage had dissipated, he could understand the decision. Rayburn had done what was necessary to save the island.

"Plum Island endured a horrible tragedy yesterday," Walker said. "We now know this was an act of terrorism, and we also know it was not the only act of its kind."

Beckham gave Horn a sidelong glance. "You hear anything about more attacks?"

Horn shook his head.

"I'll let Lieutenant General Rayburn explain," Walker said, stepping aside.

Rayburn straightened his cuffs and stepped up to the podium. He looked like a career officer with his slicked-back hair, neatly trimmed mustache, and sharp gaze, but he had started off as a Delta operator, just like Beckham. After sustaining an injury that left him unable to fight, Rayburn had moved into commanding a Ranger Unit and quickly climbed the ranks.

Looking out over the crowd, Rayburn said, "Today we received information that SZT Fifteen in Chicago has been compromised. Everyone there is infected with the hemorrhage virus, or dead."

Raised voices instantly followed this statement. The room broke into chaos.

"How could that happen?" someone yelled.

"They're *all* dead?" said another.

Rayburn held up his hands, but he couldn't get the room under control. He pulled his side arm and pointed it to the ceiling. That got everyone's attention.

"Calm down!" he shouted.

Mayor Walker crossed his arms nervously.

"I understand that you're all scared and frustrated, but now is not the time for unrest. We think the same people are responsible for the attack on Plum Island. Their weapons aren't bombs or bullets. They're using the virus to commit biological terrorism."

Beckham shifted uneasily in his seat, not wanting to believe what he was hearing. Horn balled his hands into fists, and Beckham felt phantom pains from his missing hand as he tried to do the same.

"A few hours ago, we were informed by Vice President Johnson that the enemy is a group called the Resistance of Tyranny, or ROT," Rayburn continued. "They are led by a man named Lieutenant Andrew Wood. He is the younger brother of Colonel Zach Wood, a man I believe is familiar to many of you. He claims President Ringgold is not the rightful leader of this country. I've also been informed that the same group commandeered the *George Washington* from Admiral Humphrey and Captain Davis."

Beckham's heart stuttered at the news. While he had been busy digging ditches and graves, everything had gone to hell.

"Not all the other territories see ROT as the enemy," Rayburn said. "Lieutenant Wood has been on the Freedom Air Waves telling a very different story. According to him, Ringgold stole the presidency."

Beckham rose from his chair. "That is bullshit."

"Captain, I'm going to have to ask you to sit down," Rayburn said.

Horn stood as well. "Why the hell would they believe Wood? The guy's brother was a madman!"

A burly man wearing denim overalls stood. "Can't we recall troops from Europe?"

Rayburn shook his head. "The war for Europe has just started. Our MEUs and other forces have landed, but they didn't land to empty beaches. From what I'm hearing, it was a slaughter. General Nixon is busy with the next phase of the war, Operation Reach, and trying to advance east. We can't count on their support anytime soon."

Beckham wanted to ask more questions about Operation Beachhead and the crew of the *GW*, but this wasn't the time. Rayburn probably wouldn't know anything about Team Ghost or Davis anyway.

The man in the overalls rubbed the back of his bald head, squinting like he wasn't sure what to say next.

"So why the hell are we here?" Beckham said. "What's your move, sir?"

Rayburn grabbed the sides of the podium, locked eyes

with Beckham, and leaned forward. "We're here to start planning a war, Captain."

They played the video over and over, and each time it ended, Kate told Ellis the same thing.

"Again."

He hit the rewind button, and then Play.

The grainy, green-hued feed had been captured right before a French unit was overrun by unidentified Variants about one hundred miles south of Paris.

On screen, the six French AMX Leclerc tanks rolled through the countryside at combat intervals, breaching stone walls that had stood for centuries, smashing through barns, and pancaking shrubs.

Seventy years ago the German Tigers had done the same thing. Kate had watched a lot of documentaries with her dad when she was growing up. He was a connoisseur of anything World War II, and this footage reminded her of the black-and-white films from that era. Her dad had always said the Nazis were the worst enemy Europe would ever face.

He had been wrong.

She looked back to the screen, where Reavers were flapping across the sky. If it weren't for their tails, Kate might have mistaken them for oversized bats. The spiked cords whipped back and forth as the beasts flew in a V formation to meet a squadron of French helicopters.

Missiles hissed from the launchers and fanned out toward the enemy. Explosions flared like fireworks as the missiles connected with the armored beasts. Several of the creatures wheeled away, wings burning. One dropped into a nosedive and smashed into the dirt not far from the Leclerc tank taking the video footage.

Half the Reavers made it through the barrage. They swarmed the choppers, spraying toxins, wrapping their bodies around windshields, and plucking gunners out of the doors. Fearless, one of the monsters used its armored back to spear the rotors of a chopper. The spike sheared through the blades, sending the bird into a tailspin.

The feed panned back to the battlefield.

Kate chewed her nails as she watched the video for the tenth time, her thoughts turning to Fitz and Apollo. How could they possibly win against an enemy like this?

Dad always said no one thought we could beat the Nazis at first. But we did.

Tracer rounds streaked overhead like shooting stars. On the ground, the tanks plowed through a hedge. They charged through the rubble and advanced across a farm field overgrown with weeds.

A chopper spun from the sky and crashed in a heap of mangled metal a few hundred feet from the lead Leclerc, but the tank didn't slow. It kept rolling forward, turning slightly to avoid the debris.

"Here we go," Ellis said. His finger hovered over the computer mouse, ready to pause the frame.

Another tank pulled out in front of the Leclerc taking the footage. It curved around a mound of dirt, then jolted to a halt. The tracks were stuck. It sat there for several moments trying to back up, move forward, and back up again.

Two minutes into the effort, dirt exploded around the tracks. The earth gave way and the tank sank, leaving only the cannon turret aboveground. Another blast of dirt, and then the ground swallowed it whole.

The Leclerc capturing the footage halted, and the cannon roved across the green-hued view for a target. The gun shifted back to the left, where another tank rolled across the field. The tracks had crushed a fallen fence post, and it was dragging tangled wires behind it.

The video feed began to pan away when the ground sank in front of the Leclerc dragging the fence. The cannon speared into the hole, wedging the tank in. The driver tried to reverse, but the tracks kicked out dirt like a dog digging a hole.

The hatch opened, and a French soldier jumped out. He bolted across the field, weaponless and without his gear. In the blink of an eye, the ground swallowed him too. A geyser of dirt rose into the air above the area where he had been standing a moment before.

A third Leclerc moved across the feed, the cannon firing on a target out of view. The camera swiveled to follow the gunfire as it peppered an embankment that shouldn't have been in the center of the field.

Kate stopped chewing on her nails and folded her arms across her chest to rest on her belly. She was already shaking in anticipation of what came next.

She almost missed it this time, but Ellis slowed the video down. The Leclerc firing at the embankment rose slightly on a mound of dirt. At first Kate could hardly see it, but something massive was pushing up on the tank, slowly lifting it into the air.

"Those things have to weigh fifty tons," Ellis said.

"More than that."

In slow motion, the feed showed the tank tipping onto its side, the tracks continuing to run. A pair of massive creatures pulled themselves out of the ground, but the video was too grainy to see them in detail.

The Leclerc taking the footage fired on the monsters. The gunfire ricocheted off the armored flesh of the abominations. It fired its cannon with a jolt. The blast and the following explosion blinded the night-vision feed. Sparks rained down in the green-hued view.

"Now," Kate said. "Pause it."

Ellis paused the frame and they both stared at the silhouette of a monster unlike any they had encountered before. It looked a little like a beetle, with its rounded back and small, bulb-like head, but the thing was massive.

"We're sure that's it?" Kate asked.

Ellis kept his gaze on the screen. He was inches away, studying every pixel. "Yeah, that's it," he said. "A French recon unit collected a blood sample a day after the battle when they went to search for survivors. That sample made it back to a lab in Paris, where the EUF then entered it into the shared database."

"So besides the blood, this video is the only evidence the creature even exists."

"Yup," Ellis said. He leaned back and scratched his chin thoughtfully. "We better put this in the report to Vice President Johnson."

"And say what? There are insect-like Variants in Europe?"

Kate noticed the gleam in Ellis's eye. Her partner had a theory.

"What are you thinking, Pat?"

"That type of genetic change...I don't know. Whatever caused those mutations wasn't just the chemicals in VX-99. There's something else going on here. And we need to figure out what it is before the Americans advance east for Operation Reach."

11

The Sikorsky CH-53K King Stallion rose into the eastern sky and lifted Team Ghost's new MATV off the sandy beach. It was still technically in development, with the first production model still years away, but the military had needed every resource it could get. Fitz reached for his seat belt as the bolts tightened. He wouldn't ever tell his team, but he had an aversion to heights. He was fine on flights when the plane was already in the air, and skydiving didn't bother him for some reason, but there wasn't much in life that made his stomach drop like standing on the edge of a tall building or watching the ground sink below him like this.

Something wet brushed Fitz's hand, distracting him from the view. He looked down at Apollo, nestled between his blades on the floor. The dog nuzzled his hand again. Fitz wasn't the only one who didn't like heights.

"It's okay, boy. Don't worry. This won't take long."

Fitz turned to check his team. Tanaka, Dohi, and Rico were in the back seat, prepping their weapons and double-checking their gear. Stevenson sat behind the wheel, absentmindedly twisting it like he was actually driving.

"They see me *rollin'*. They *hatin'*." Stevenson was

muttering with a goofy grin as he continued to turn the wheel.

"Thought you didn't like rap," Tanaka said, looking up from his rucksack with a wounded expression. "I feel like I've been lied to."

Fitz couldn't help but chuckle along with his team.

He looked out the passenger window at the FOB they were leaving behind. The tents and vehicles were like toys from this height. Abrams tanks and Humvees snaked up the beach. Marines the size of ants trailed the mechanized units. Behind them, the fleet glided through the now-calm water. The beach ended in cliffs sharper than Variant teeth. The MATV cleared the rocks, and the green French countryside rolled into view.

Fitz brought a hand to his face to shield his eyes from the afternoon sun. A transmission crackled into his earpiece, bringing with it the first shot of adrenaline through his fatigued body.

"Ghost One, Lion One. We just made contact with the EUF. They gave us coordinates for the Ombres. Last known location was the Basilica of Saint Thérèse. EUF hasn't been able to raise anyone. Nothing on the comms for over forty-eight hours."

The message was from Colonel Bradley. Between the static and his rough voice, Fitz couldn't get a read on him. Normally he could tell by his CO's tone how bad things were going to get. Forty-eight hours was a long time to be silent.

There was a pause before Bradley said, "Ghost, watch your back out there. Good luck."

Fitz almost sighed with relief. For a moment he had thought Bradley was going to kill the mission, and he was itching bad to get back out there.

The King Stallion's main pilot, Delta 1, informed Team Ghost that they were thirty minutes away from the insertion point. Fitz sat back and breathed deeply, mentally preparing himself for the mission. The MATV rattled as the helicopter pulled higher into the sky.

"You sure this thing can support our weight?" Stevenson asked, looking out the side window.

Fitz checked the cables attached to the front bumper that angled back up toward the belly of the chopper. The big gray bird continued to ascend, and their escorts—a pair of Apaches—rose with them. Fitz threw up a two-finger salute to the pilot of the chopper to his right. The man nodded back, then pulled ahead to scan the flight path for threats.

Clouds drifted across the horizon and then parted to make way for the blazing sun. The rays beat down on their MATV, and Fitz flipped his sunglasses down over his eyes. He was glad to be fighting in the daylight. The Variants hated the sun, and he hoped the evolved beasts were still sensitive to it. They needed every advantage they could get.

"Pretty deserted down there," Tanaka said. He had his face pressed against the back window.

The shadow of the King Stallion, the two Apaches, and their MATV crawled across overgrown fields. Tractors and other machinery sat rusting where their owners had left them. There wasn't an animal in sight. Frayed ropes hung loosely from posts where livestock had been tied up. The pens were empty, and Fitz imagined the horror the poor creatures had felt, trapped like worms on a fishhook.

Although Fitz couldn't see them, he knew the Variants were still watching, their bellies empty and their reptilian eyes constantly searching for their next meal.

Seven months ago Fitz would have felt the prickle of fear.

Not today.

The faster he started killing the monsters, the faster he could return to his friends at Plum Island.

All it takes is all you got, Fitz thought. *Do what Beckham trained you to do: Lead and sacrifice.*

He watched the landscape and tried to recall as many details as he could about his previous missions. They'd all been successful, even the one that took his legs from him. He'd come back missing part of himself, but he'd lived to fight another day.

Fields and farms turned into a solid green blur as Fitz stared out the window. Would he come back from this one? Would any of them? One day, he knew, his ticket would be punched. Men like him didn't die in their beds of old age. But he'd keep fighting until the end.

"Listen up, Ghost," Fitz said.

Everyone in the back seat turned their attention to Fitz. Stevenson shifted to look at him but kept his hands on the wheel.

"I'm not going to lie. I don't know exactly what we'll face when we get down there. We all know that VX9H9 and Kryptonite weren't sprayed effectively over this area, so we should expect hostiles. The Ombres have gone dark, so we should also expect to do some searching when we get to Lisieux."

"ETA ten minutes, Ghost," the main pilot announced.

Fitz angled his rifle over a city polka-dotted with gaping craters. The steeple of a church had been sheared off. He leaned closer to the window to focus on what looked like an arm sticking out of the rubble. He raised his scope to confirm but saw only bones. The Variants had plucked it dry like a chicken wing.

He lowered his rifle. "Remember, our mission is to find the Ombres, collect intel, and return that intel to the FOB. Recon, not extraction. Got that?"

"They're kids, right?" Rico asked. She pointed out

the window. "How the hell did kids survive in this wasteland?"

"And we're going to leave them behind?" Stevenson said.

Fitz didn't have an easy answer. He didn't like the idea of leaving anyone behind, especially not kids. "Our orders are clear: Get intel and call in air-evac. But... if there's room, we will personally get the Ombres to the FOB."

He didn't need to glance to the back troop hold to see there wasn't much extra space, especially with the gear already back there.

"Kids are resilient," Dohi said. "My ancestors survived many years hiding from the US Cavalry in the *Dinétah*. Many of them were on their own after the army slaughtered their parents."

"Where's Dinay-whatever? I thought you were from Arizona," Stevenson said.

"*Dinétah*," Dohi said. "It means 'homeland.' Part of it is in Arizona."

Stevenson looked in the rearview mirror, his brows crunched together like he had no idea what Dohi was talking about. But Fitz got it. There were uncomfortable similarities between the way the US government had eradicated the indigenous people of America and the way the Variants had swept over the globe. Fitz loved his country, but he wasn't always proud of the things it had done. He gave Dohi a solemn nod to show he understood.

"ETA five minutes," a pilot said over the open line.

"Once we set down, I want Dohi on the Two-Forty. Everyone else, you keep an eye on your zone of fire. No one fires a bullet until I give the order," Fitz said.

He did a final inventory of his gear. The gas grenades they had used in Washington hung from his vest next to extra magazines of armor-piercing rounds. Meg's hatchet was clipped onto his duty belt. He had his M4, M9, and trusty MK11 with him, but after the massacre on the beach he still felt unprepared.

"That's Lisieux," Rico said, pointing to another ruined city in the distance. "I always wanted to travel here, see the city and the basilica. It's a damn shame the EUF bombed the shit out of it."

They passed over the highway leading in to the town, drafts from the rotors kicking up tornadoes of ash around the charred hulks of vehicles. Buildings with moss-covered tiled roofs faced a ring road littered with debris. The structures still standing had been licked by flames that left a black residue like charcoal. At the north end of the plaza stood a lopsided building with a clock tower. The glass face of the clock was shattered, and the hour and minute hands had twisted like bent silverware.

"Delta One, tell Black One and Black Two to stay clear of rooftops," Fitz said into his headset.

"Roger that."

The King Stallion ascended higher into the sky, pulling the MATV with it. Fitz focused on the tiled roofs that were still intact below. Both Apaches were circling the outskirts of the city, scanning it for hostiles.

Half the zone was covered in a carpet of ash. The majority of the buildings in the center of the city were burned down to their frames, but the town square had mostly survived the devastation.

"Area looks clear," reported a pilot from one of the Apaches.

"Black One sees a clear LZ near the target," Delta 1 said.

"Copy," Fitz replied. "Prepare for insertion, Ghost."

He pulled a magazine from his vest and slammed it into his M4. Next he loaded his MK11 and finally his M9.

Rico slapped a magazine into her rifle and then grabbed her sawed-off shotgun and pumped in the buckshot shells she'd used to kill a juvenile on the LCAC the night before. Two more clicks sounded, from Tanaka charging his M4 and Stevenson palming a magazine into his SAW. A thump followed from Dohi loading a grenade into his M4 launcher. Apollo sat up, knowing damn well what was about to happen.

"Ready, boy? Just like old times." Fitz strapped an armored vest around the dog's back. In its pouches were extra magazines, medical supplies, and rations.

Apollo licked Fitz on his cheek as he leaned down. Fitz searched the dog's amber eyes to see if he had any idea how far into enemy territory they were. Judging by his wagging tail, Apollo didn't know, and that was fine with Fitz. He didn't want his best friend to worry.

"Ghost One, change of plans. Best spot for insertion looks like a courtyard about two blocks from the Basilica of Saint Thérèse."

"Copy," Fitz said. He looked back at Dohi. "Up top, oorah?"

Dohi nodded and said, "Rah."

He flipped the hatch open and climbed up into the turret. Wind rushed into the vehicle. Rico and Tanaka angled their weapons at their windows, and Stevenson bent low over the steering wheel, ready to start driving the MATV for real.

Across the city, the two Apaches continued to search the outskirts for hostiles. The King Stallion flew low over a street blocked with destroyed vehicles and an old overturned wagon. Fitz raised his MK11 to scope the massive church rising in the distance. Unlike the broken steeple he had seen earlier, the bell tower was still standing.

"How's it looking up there, Dohi?" Fitz asked.

"All clear so far."

Fitz loosened his seat belt and twisted for a better view. The street was a couple hundred feet below, racing by so fast it made his guts tighten. He pivoted back to the windshield as Black 1 approached the Basilica of Saint Thérèse. Set on top of a hill at the edge of the city, the white stone structure looked almost like a fortress. It was a beautiful cathedral, even with nothing but ruins all around it. The building stood tall and proud, overlooking the town of Lisieux. A wide path led from a roadway through overgrown gardens and up to the entrance. Small towers jutted from the rooftop, matching the steepled tops of the evergreens that grew along both flanks of the building.

"Hot damn," Rico said. "It's even more gorgeous than in pictures."

"My grandpa told me about this place," Stevenson said. "That church survived World War Two."

"And now World War Three," Tanaka said.

"Stay focused," Fitz said. "We can discuss history when we get back to the FOB."

Despite his own orders, he couldn't stop looking at the basilica. Extravagant, brash, and intriguing—the church was one of the most impressive buildings Fitz had ever seen. Seventy years after the Nazis bombed it, it was still standing, but not without damage. Now that they were closer, he could see that the war with the Variants had left its mark. The grounds were pockmarked with black craters. Jagged pieces of stained glass surrounded boarded-up windows. The stone pillars framing the entrance were cracked and crumbling in places, and the two towers flanking the vestry were blown away completely.

The chopper pulled the MATV closer, giving Team Ghost a better view. Burned vines climbed the side of the building like dead, shriveled veins. Against all odds, the basilica had survived whatever battle occurred here.

But where were the Ombres?

Nothing stirred in the wasteland below, and the only sign he saw of people was the occasional skeleton stretched out on the grounds. The Variants never left anything more behind.

"Take us over the gardens," Fitz said. He wanted a better look before they dropped down there.

The Apache flew toward the back end of the church.

"Does anyone have eyes?" Fitz asked.

"I don't see shit," Stevenson said. "Looks like a ghost town to me."

"Same," Rico added.

"Nothing up here," Dohi replied.

Fitz adjusted his sunglasses and moved back to his window to watch the Apache vanish behind the bell tower of the basilica. It hovered there for a moment, rotors whipping through the air out of view.

Ding! Ding! Ding!

The sound caught them all off guard. Fitz raised his rifle at the bell tower. It chimed, over and over.

"Is someone doing that?" Rico asked.

Stevenson ducked down for a better look. "Can't be."

The scouting Apache suddenly jerked to the right. The entire nose, including the windshield, was covered by what looked like a wrinkled plastic bag.

"The bell is a warning signal!" Fitz shouted. He zoomed in with his MK11.

"Bandit at three o'clock!" Dohi called from above.

The church bell chimed again, the noise echoing over the burned-out city.

"I can't see!" shouted Black 1.

Fitz attempted to follow the Apache in his scope as it banked hard to the right. His crosshairs centered on a grotesque Reaver wrapping its wings around the cock-pit, blinding the pilots.

"Black One, watch out!" Delta 1 yelled.

The weight of the monster pulled the Apache toward the ground. The beast flapped away at the last moment, giving the pilots only a second to react. They pulled up and narrowly cleared a building adjacent to the church, but the rotors clipped one of the towers, sending the Apache whirling out of control.

"Bandits to the north!" Dohi shouted.

Shadows peeled away from burned buildings as Black 1 crashed to the ground. The nose slammed into the cob-blestone street, breaking the ancient bricks like a bull-dozer busting through concrete. The chopper skidded to a halt without catching fire. Fitz expected an explosion, but there was only smoke rising from the ruined metal. Dozens of Reavers took to the sky, flapping toward the other Apache.

Motion in the center of the city commanded Fitz's attention. All at once, adult Variants squeezed out of sewer openings and bolted from ruined buildings. They galloped toward the downed chopper.

"Open fire, open fire!" Fitz roared, his heart rising to his throat. The time to fight had come at last.

12

President Jan Ringgold walked through the gardens outside the new White House, her hands clasped behind her back. She was sick to her stomach over the events of the past three days. She laced her fingers together too tightly, pain racing up her right arm. The bullet that Lieutenant Brett, the monstrous first victim of this war, had fired into her shoulder still stung from time to time. She didn't mind the pain. It was a reminder of the evil that had reshaped the world.

Now that evil was back. It might have a new name and wear a new face, but the motivations behind it were still the same. Power. Vengeance. How many more lives would be lost because of these ROT terrorists?

Ringgold felt paralyzed by the same darkness she had felt when she was hiding at the bunker in Raven Rock. She refused to let that darkness consume her. Instead, she paused by a rosebush and bent down to inhale the sweet scent of the blossoms. Perhaps stopping to smell the roses was a cliché, but it served as another necessary reminder.

There is goodness and beauty in the world. There is hope. That's why you have to keep fighting.

She looked up from the flowers to find her National

Security Advisor, Ben Nelson, standing before her, dressed impeccably as always. Ringgold wondered where he managed to find his vast assortment of colorful ties. Today's was the same bright red as the roses. Chief of Staff James Soprano rounded a hedge of bushes a moment later, sweat dripping down his bald head. He flattened his gut as he approached and stood up straighter.

"Madam President," Nelson said.

Soprano, out of breath, joined them. "Good afternoon, ma'am."

"Is it?" Ringgold asked. She unclasped her hands and looked at the men in turn. Though she had personally vetted them, she didn't fully trust them. There was no doubting their intelligence, both men were brilliant. But in a way that only made them more dangerous. They hadn't risked their lives for anyone. They hadn't taken bullets or killed like she had. Maybe it was a lot to expect, but that was the type of loyalty she was looking for. Until then, she would remain on her guard.

"We have an update, ma'am," Nelson said. "We've reached out to all of the SZTs to warn them of the threat from ROT. We've also increased security and diverted several marine brigades from city-clearing duty to protect the uncompromised SZTs."

"That's good," Ringgold replied. She crossed her arms. Then Nelson's words hit home.

"Wait, did you say 'uncompromised'?"

"Yes, Madam President. There's bad news too," Soprano added. He dragged a handkerchief across his forehead. "SZT Sixty-One has declared sovereignty."

Ringgold's eyes shot up. "New Orleans has...seceded?"

Nelson chimed in. "We knew it was coming, ma'am. SZT Fourteen is on the fence. SZT Thirty-Three and Forty-Nine are threatening the same thing."

Ringgold cursed under her breath. Those last two

safe-zone territories were in Texas. Their mayors were congressmen who had served on the opposite side of the aisle from Ringgold. But old-school politics was supposed to be a thing of the past. The war against the Variants and their offspring had brought politicians together and created allies out of old enemies.

At least, that's what she'd thought.

Marine One flew overhead, distracting her for a moment. Vice President Johnson was back from a meeting at SZT 45, just fifty miles east of the new White House. A sniper stood in his crow's nest on the roof and flung his rifle over his back to climb down the ladder. Another man took his place for the change in shift. Everywhere she looked there were snipers and marine sentries. Secret service agents patrolled the gardens. There were hundreds of men and women here to protect her, but she still would have traded them all for Beckham and Horn.

The *whoosh* of the helicopter waned, and Ringgold directed her gaze back to her chief of staff. "What else?"

Soprano hesitated like he was afraid to tell her. He hooked a finger under his collar and said, "It's the *Zumwalt*, ma'am, but the ship's disappeared off radar. By the time we sent our destroyers, she was gone. The *GW* is on the run too. We're tracking her toward Louisiana."

"I understand it has stealth capabilities, but how does a ship the size of the *Zumwalt* go missing?"

Soprano looked to Nelson.

"Well?" Ringgold asked, waiting.

"It was built to disappear, Madam President," Soprano said.

"Do we not have aircraft that can search for it?" Ringgold asked. "I still don't understand how a ship can go missing in broad daylight."

Nelson took over. "There are hundreds if not thousands of derelict ships in the ocean right now. Finding the *Zumwalt* without radar is like finding a needle in a haystack. Besides, I wouldn't advise testing Lieutenant Wood. He said no aircraft within striking distance. We simply can't risk it."

"Yes, I heard him. But you're telling me the *Zumwalt*, which is armed with some of the most advanced weaponry left in the world, is gone. And we have no idea where it went. I'm sure you can understand why I'm not happy."

The execution video of Admiral Humphrey replayed in Ringgold's mind. Wood and his men were animals, and now they had the weapons to inflict damage on an unfathomable scale.

"Let me make one thing clear," Ringgold said. "We *cannot* fight this war on two fronts. If we are forced to split our resources between the Variants and these terrorists, we will not prevail."

"Vice President Johnson will know more now that he's back," Soprano said. "He should be here in a few minutes."

Nelson grabbed his satellite phone. "If you don't mind, I need to make a call. I have one scheduled with Mayor Walker of Plum Island."

"Good. Tell him I want to talk to Captain Beckham," Ringgold said. She unfolded her arms and pointed at the phone when Nelson hesitated.

"Now," she ordered.

"Yes, ma'am," Nelson replied. He stepped to the side, punched in a number, and tapped his foot on the ground.

Footfalls pounded the brick walkway of the garden a moment later, and a team of marines and secret service agents rounded the corner with Vice President Johnson in tow. He walked with his head down, reading a document in a buff folder.

"Should be just a few minutes," Nelson said, taking his ear away from the phone.

Ringgold nodded and hurried to meet Johnson. "Hello, George," she said.

Johnson glanced up from his folder, his forehead a line of creases. His eyes were flinty, like they had been the first time Ringgold had met him, back when the enemy was mostly just mutated monsters. She'd never thought to look back on those days with fond nostalgia.

"Madam President," he said with a nod. "I'm assuming you already got the bad news about the *Zumwalt* and the *GW*?"

"Yes," she said softly. "Why does every briefing have to be bad?"

He closed his folder and sighed. "Because we're still at war."

The sobering words made Ringgold let out her own sigh.

"ROT is more organized than we thought," Johnson continued. "I've already sent Special Ops teams in for recon at their known facilities, but I'm almost positive we won't find anything there. They are likely operating out of the *Zumwalt* now. According to Captain Davis, they also have a considerable number of men on board the *GW*. She's tracking the vessel now."

"And the *Zumwalt*? Do you have any idea where it is yet?"

Johnson rubbed his wrinkled forehead. "No."

"When did you last hear from Captain Davis?"

Johnson kept rubbing the same spot. "A few hours ago. She's trailing the *GW* in a Zodiac. She's with a small team of marines, all dressed in uniforms they stole from dead ROT terrorists."

"But we haven't heard from her for two hours?"

"Afraid not," Johnson said. "I wouldn't worry too much. She's probably trying to keep out of sight."

Ringgold had to believe Davis was still out there, fighting to take back the ship, but how could she possibly expect to take on an aircraft carrier with a rubber raft and a handful of marines?

"We need to find the *Zumwalt* and destroy it," she said. "Not tomorrow, not the next day. Right now! Every second that passes is another second closer to an attack on the SZTs. You're in charge of the military, George, and I respect your opinion and experience. But this is not a request. You will find the *Zumwalt*, and you will destroy her—and the *George Washington*."

Johnson dipped his head slightly. "A private word?"

He directed her away from the others to the nearby fountain. The soothing sound of the water helped calm her nerves, but she was still seething with anger. She hadn't just lost Emilia—she had lost her peace of mind. The country was falling apart again on her watch.

"Madam President, we're dealing with terrorists that have proven they will stop at nothing until they get what they want. On top of that, Wood isn't just a professional liar, he is a con artist. He is on the Freedom Air Waves saying horrible things and convincing SZTs to turn against us."

"What things?" Ringgold asked.

"It doesn't matter. They aren't true, Madam President… Listen, I have every available asset looking for the *Zumwalt*, and we are watching the situation on the *GW*. The SZTs still loyal are all on the highest alert, but we have to be cautious about what we do next. In some ways, this situation with ROT is more dangerous than the juveniles. If Wood fires his missiles on our SZTs before we neutralize him, he could destroy everything we have worked to build." Johnson paused. "They could kill *everyone*."

The words chilled Ringgold to her core. She couldn't speak, she could hardly breathe.

"They waited until just the right moment," Johnson said, shaking his head. "They knew we were weak. And now I've been backed into a corner. I think we should think about delaying Operation Reach and recalling some of our troops from Europe. After the catastrophic failure of Beachhead, no one would blame you."

Ringgold considered the proposal for a single moment before shaking her head. "No. We have a duty to humanity. We started this. Our military will end it. General Nixon needs to focus on Operation Reach. We have the forces here at home to track down and destroy these terrorists. I don't believe for a second we won't be able to find them."

"Damn straight we will. But what about the damage they do in the meantime?"

"I will not recall our forces from the war in Europe, George. We will solve this problem on our own with the resources we have."

Ringgold looked back to Nelson, who was speaking rapidly into the satellite phone.

"Come with me," she said to Johnson. He followed her back to Nelson and Soprano. "Do you have Captain Beckham on the line?"

Nelson cupped his hand over the receiver. "No, but Beckham is in the room."

Ringgold reached out for the phone. "This is President Ringgold, I'd like to speak to Captain Beckham."

"Hello, Madam President, this is Mayor Antoine Walker. I've been wanting to speak with you about—"

"Now, please."

White noise crackled in her ear, and then she heard Beckham's voice.

"How's West Virginia treating you, ma'am?"

"I can't complain. How are you recovering?"

"Good, ma'am. How about you? Is your shoulder healing?" His voice was calm, but cautious. It was the tone of a man who was about to be the father of a child in a world at war.

"Still got a shard of bullet inside me, but I'll live." She thought of Beckham's injuries and quickly changed the subject. He had lost far more than she had. "How's Kate?"

There was a pause, followed by, "We're having a baby boy."

"That's fantastic. I'm so happy for you both." There was so much more she wanted to say, but they didn't have time for any more small talk.

Beckham must have realized that too. "Thank you, Madam President. As great as it is to catch up with you, why are you really calling?"

Ringgold closed her eyes. She was the president of the United States of America. Her country needed her now more than ever, and she needed the best operative left on the planet.

"I'm sorry, but we have a situation. I'm recalling you for active duty, Captain Beckham."

Beckham held the receiver in his sweaty left hand. All he had planned to do today was work the fields and come home to dinner with Kate, Horn, and the girls. But maybe he wasn't made for a simpler life. Maybe there was no escaping the fight after all.

"We have a situation and I need your help," Ringgold repeated. "The USS *Zumwalt* is on the loose, and the *George Washington* is heading toward Louisiana. On top of that I have safe zones declaring sovereignty and swearing allegiance to ROT. Wood's been on the comms slandering me to anyone who will listen—and it seems quite a few people *are* listening. This could escalate into a civil war if we don't quash this thing quickly."

Beckham wanted to reassure her that everything would be okay, but he respected President Ringgold too much to lie. If ROT had commandeered a stealth warship, they could be anywhere right now. And the weapons on board could wreak havoc. They were already on the cusp of extinction. A civil war would tip them over the edge.

"In my experience fighting against terrorists, whatever you do has to be fast and fierce," Beckham said.

"That's why I'm talking to you. I'm surrounded by dozens of advisors and generals, all telling me different things. What would you do if you were in my shoes?"

Beckham felt the burden of that question settle on his shoulders. He was supposed to be just a civilian now. Questions like this were meant for soldiers. From the corner of his eye, he saw Horn leaning against the wall of Mayor Walker's office. His tattooed arms were crossed, and he was chewing on a toothpick. He raised his eyebrows at Beckham as if to say, "Well, boss, what you gonna do?"

"Captain?" she said.

"I would give Davis a chance to take back the *GW*, and I would direct all my resources to finding the *Zumwalt*. If Lieutenant Wood is half as bad as his brother, we can't afford any mistakes."

Another pause on the line. "What if I stepped down? I could end all this."

"Absolutely not," Beckham replied. "I seriously hope you aren't considering that, ma'am."

"Not for a second, but I wouldn't be surprised if some of my staff are," she said quietly. "We have been at war too long now. We have lost so much."

Beckham thought of the graves on the shoreline of Plum Island. The sacrifices his friends had made would not be for nothing. Without meaning to do it, he stiffened his back and stood a little straighter.

"What do you need me to do?" he asked.

There was no hesitation in Ringgold's voice this time. "I know you and Master Sergeant Horn are retired. You have your families to think about. But I need you both now more than ever. Take control of security at Plum Island. The United States can't afford to lose it."

Beckham fingered Sheila's ring and glanced over at his best friend. Next he studied Walker and Rayburn. Both men were watching him, their expressions giving nothing away. Could he trust them to have the president's back?

"Can I count on you, Captain?"

"Yes, Madam President. You can always count on me."

13

"Open fire!" Fitz yelled again.

The 240 whined to life from the hatch of the MATV, and a stream of rounds sped toward the monsters.

Fitz opened his window and stuck the muzzle of his MK11 outside.

"Get us on the ground!" he ordered the King Stallion pilots.

Instead of descending, the pilots pulled up. The MATV swayed, the cords above tightening. The MATV moved up and down like a carnival ride. Rico screamed and Apollo howled. Fitz tried to steady himself and pointed the rifle at a Reaver. A spiked tail whipped back and forth as the beast cut through the air. He locked his crosshairs onto the abomination. Oval yellow eyes blinked at him, and a sucker mouth the size of a basketball popped open revealing strings of saliva and a maw full of needle-sharp teeth. The creature brought its legs up like a bird of prey preparing to scoop a fish from the water.

Fitz held in a breath and fired a shot that punched a gaping hole in the monster's right wing. It whirled away, tail slashing through the air. Another quickly took its place. The beast let out a piercing roar that Fitz could hear even over the thunderous sound of the rotors.

"Dohi!" he shouted. "Three o'clock!"

The 240 opened up on the monster before it could get close to their MATV. The rounds punched through the wings and chipped away at thick armor, but the creature stayed aloft.

Fitz lined up a head shot that finally stopped the beast. It smashed into the windshield of their vehicle, sucker lips clamping onto the glass. Blood gushed from a golf-ball-sized hole where its right eye had been. Dozens of jagged teeth gnashed together so hard the tips broke off.

Stevenson let out a high-pitched yelp and turned the windshield wipers on. The blades hit the creature's armored cheek repeatedly, back and forth. If Fitz hadn't been scared shitless, he might have laughed.

The King Stallion pulled up again, making the MATV sway wildly. The Reaver's lips popped off the glass. It slid down the hood of the truck and plummeted to the ground.

"Holy shit," Stevenson said. "Holy. Fucking. Shit!"

Through the blood-streaked windshield, the sky was alive with the monsters. The remaining Apache released a salvo of missiles that blew several of them to pieces. In the streets, the Variants closed in on the downed chopper. Everywhere Fitz looked he saw the diseased beasts: on the top of burned-out vehicles, perched on rooftops, and climbing from the sewers. It reminded him of the first days of Operation Liberty.

Fitz went to move his rifle when he saw movement in Black 1. He zoomed in on one of the pilots, who was still alive. The wave of pale flesh quickly consumed the Apache and he saw there was nothing he could do to save him. Fitz aimed the crosshairs on the pilot just as a scrawny beast with a mane of thin hair pulled him from the cockpit.

All it takes is all you got, Marine, Fitz thought. Garcia's words gave him the courage to end the man's suffering. It took him two shots to kill the man. The first clipped his shoulder, and Fitz silently apologized. The second hit the pilot in the visor.

Fitz quickly moved his gun back to the sky, unable to watch the Variants tear the corpse to shreds. In the back seat, Rico and Tanaka were firing their M4s on semi-auto. The *crack crack* echoed inside the armored vehicle. Stevenson kept his hands on the steering wheel, prepared to drive the moment they hit the ground.

"Get us down there!" Fitz shouted.

"You crazy?" one of the pilots yelled back.

"YES!"

The King Stallion jerked to the right, sending their MATV swinging through the air. The big gun overhead went quiet for a moment.

"Dohi!" Fitz yelled, looking up at the turret.

The 240 roared back to life as Dohi unloaded another barrage at a pair of Reavers swooping toward the MATV. Variants on the streets swiped at the air, talons raised and saliva dripping from their sucker lips. Hundreds of yellow eyes followed Team Ghost's progress.

The six of them against an army of monsters. It was just like old times.

"Focus on your zones!" Fitz shouted. "Keep the Reavers away from the King Stallion!"

He fired off shot after shot, wondering how the Ombres could have survived out here. Had the EUF sent Team Ghost into a trap? Or maybe this is why the Ombres had gone silent. Maybe they were dead.

He thought the second option was the most likely, but they wouldn't know for sure until they hit the ground. He squeezed off a round that hit a Reaver in the back of the skull.

Boom! Boom! Boom!

The explosions commanded his attention. Black 2 fired another torrent of missiles that hit rooftops and sent more of the creatures cartwheeling through the sky. Despite the hellfire being rained upon them, the monsters still came, fearless and enraged.

The comm channel was full of panicked voices.

"We have to get out of here," said Delta 1.

"Black Two, you got bandits on your six!" yelled Delta 2.

Three Reavers were trailing the Apache, and two more took off from rooftops as the bird passed overhead. If Fitz hadn't been looking through his scope, he would never have seen the acid hit the side of the chopper.

A scream sounded over the comms and the helicopter plummeted toward the town center. It hit the ground belly first before exploding into a fireball that sent shrapnel whizzing into the sky.

Fitz was too shocked to move.

"What do we do?" Rico asked. When he didn't answer, she said more urgently, "Fitzie, what are we supposed to do?"

Fitz stared at a city consumed once more by flames. The Variants clambered over the bones scattered in the streets. It looked like hell on earth.

If the Ombres were out there, they weren't going to show up now.

The Reavers turned their attention to the King Stallion. There were still at least twenty of them, and Fitz didn't see how Dohi and the rest of Team Ghost could hold them off.

What would Beckham do?

While the pilot brought them around, Fitz used the moment to think. They were surrounded, and there was no way they could fight through the hordes below.

Forced into a decision, Fitz gave his order, "Get us the hell out of here!"

The reply was a jerk of the MATV as the King Stallion pulled them skyward. Apollo looked up from the floor, amber eyes searching Fitz for reassurance. They had been in some sticky spots, from hiding under a pile of dead Variants in the New York Public Library to the sewers beneath Manhattan. Now they were a hundred feet in the air over a city infested with adult Variants. He should have left the dog with Beckham.

Anger, guilt, and helplessness washed over Fitz as the King Stallion pulled them away from the basilica. He'd failed Team Ghost. He couldn't even handle a recon mission.

A Reaver shot out of nowhere, claws slashing through the air and cutting through one of the straps holding the MATV. It snapped from the front bumper.

"SHIT!" Stevenson shouted.

Fitz's guts knotted as the vehicle dropped toward the ground. The MATV jerked again as it hung by the cables still attached to the back bumper and the roof. Apollo crashed against the windshield and yelped in pain. Fighting his seat belt, Fitz grabbed the dog and pulled him back onto the seat. Dohi cried out as he slipped, hanging halfway out of the turret.

"Help Dohi!" Fitz shouted over his shoulder.

Rico and Tanaka were already pulling him back. When Dohi was safely inside, he reached up and locked the hatch.

"Get us lower!" Fitz yelled into the comm. If they couldn't go up, their only choice was to go down. They were already dropping, the pilots having realized the exact same thing.

The King Stallion rolled left and then right to avoid a

swarm of Reavers. Fitz gritted his teeth and watched the rooftops below. Variants tilted their heads to look at the swaying MATV. It was like dangling meat in front of a pack of hungry wolves.

Fitz couldn't fire without letting go of Apollo. All he could do was pray. Then something streaked past the windshield and angled into the sky. An explosion sounded, and a piercing screech that Fitz could hardly hear followed.

His mind raced, but it wasn't until he saw several human figures standing on rooftops below that he understood. Fitz heard more missiles arc into the sky. How the hell did those kids get RPG launchers? Helpless, he hung from his seat belt and watched as the Ombres emerged from their hiding spots.

A winged beast dove toward one of the buildings, plucking a figure off the roof and carrying it away upside down.

"Get us lower. Now!" Fitz yelled.

"I'm working on it," one of the pilots snapped.

Their MATV slowly inched toward a street full of rusting vehicles and skeletons.

"Cut us loose when I tell you, Stevenson," Fitz said.

The big man nodded, his eyes wide.

Variants were galloping toward them, jumping onto cars, picking up bones and tossing them at the MATV like crazed animals.

Fitz held his breath, his fingers buried in Apollo's furry coat.

"Fire her up, and as soon as we hit the ground, floor it!" Fitz yelled.

Stevenson nodded again. He cranked the MATV, and it roared to life.

They were close enough to the road that Fitz could see

the slitted eyes of the Variants. The monsters squawked and slashed at one another, their starving bellies sending them into a ravenous frenzy.

"Faster, Delta One!" Fitz said. The King Stallion increased its speed, swinging the MATV forward ever so slightly.

"Now, Stevenson!" Fitz ordered.

Stevenson pulled the manual override, and the MATV snapped loose from the two remaining restraints. The front tires hit the ground with a violent jolt. The bumper clipped the back of a car, sending it crashing into a building.

Fitz bit his tongue and tasted blood, but that was the least of his concerns. In seconds, the beasts were on them. A Variant jumped onto the hood, cracking the windshield with its thick talons. Another smashed into Fitz's door, and a third rammed the back gate with its head.

"Gun it!" Rico shouted.

Stevenson steered to the right, then punched the gas to plow through the line of Variants stampeding toward them. The brush guard on the front bumper smashed into the bony, naked beasts. They spun away like bowling pins, blood painting the cracked windshield.

At the end of the street, the bell tower of the basilica rose into the sky. Rockets peeled away from the smaller towers over the church's nave. The Ombres were still fighting.

In the rearview mirror, the King Stallion had pulled ahead, outpacing the flock of Reavers pursuing it.

"Thank you, Delta," Fitz said into the comms.

"Good luck, Ghost," replied Delta 1, his voice hoarse from yelling.

Dohi popped the hatch open, but Fitz reached back and grabbed him. "Let me."

Fitz's mother had always told him never to delegate

a task if he could do it himself. That lesson had been reinforced by Beckham, who was always the first into the fray. It was time for Fitz to lead by example—and to take out as many Variants as he could.

Fitz unstrapped his seat belt, set Apollo on the floor, then jumped into the back seat. He took Dohi's place and rose into the turret, only to duck as the claws of a Reaver swooped down. One second earlier and it would have caught him. Cautiously, he peeked back out and grabbed the 240.

The MATV squealed around a corner, kicking ash into the air. Fitz pulled his laughing-skull bandanna up over his mouth and nose. It was a memento from Riley, the kid and joker of Team Ghost. Fitz wore it with pride.

Fitz yelled wordlessly as he fired. Rounds tore into the remaining Reavers. He counted three of them, and one was injured, its left wing on fire. Easy pickings. It was the beasts on the ground he was more worried about.

Variants smashed into the sides of the MATV as Stevenson tore through the streets. Rico opened her window and jammed her shotgun outside. Tanaka did the same with his M4. Like a wagon from the Wild West firing at robbers on horseback, Team Ghost unloaded on the Variants.

Fitz eyed the rooftops for the Ombres, but they were nowhere in sight.

"Changing!" Rico shouted.

"I'll cover you," Tanaka said. Fitz saw the flash of light on steel. The sword impaled a Variant clinging to the door. He twisted the blade, opening a hole in the beast's neck that fountained blood over the side of the MATV.

The creature fell away and was crushed under the back tires with a sickening crunch.

"Take us to the basilica!" Fitz yelled. He directed his

fire at a Reaver that was on the retreat, hitting it in the back before it could escape. The final two took off in opposite directions, and Fitz trained his fire back on the Variants on the streets.

The European Variants looked slightly different from those in the States. Their spines protruded from their veiny skin like the knobs on a prehistoric animal's back. Some had hairy manes running up their necks and skulls like Mohawks.

Bullets punched through their ropy muscles and sent them spinning across the path of the MATV. High-pitched cries sounded as the monsters were crushed under the weight of the armored vehicle. Without an Alpha or their more intelligent offspring to guide them, the monsters soon retreated to their lairs beneath the ground, leaving the injured to bleed out.

Stevenson kept his foot on the gas, smashing into beasts on the run. "Yeah, that's right, you ugly shits!"

The truck jolted up and down over fallen monsters, but they didn't slow until they reached the final street. Stevenson navigated around the parking lot, driving cautiously toward the towering Basilica of Saint Thérèse.

Fitz grabbed his MK11 and zoomed in on the towers. When the Ombres had retreated, they had covered the windows back up with wood.

"Hold up," Fitz ordered.

Stevenson pulled around a military vehicle with a skeleton hanging out of the door and put the truck in neutral in front of the stone steps of the church.

Fitz centered his rifle on one of the three front doors at the entrance as it creaked open. Team Ghost waited inside the vehicle, weapons smoking, ready to fire.

A slender figure with long gray hair and dressed in a leather trench coat walked out onto the landing. At this distance, Fitz couldn't make out how old the person was, but he could tell it was a woman. Several smaller shapes flanked her on both sides—maybe eleven or twelve years old, judging by their size. They carried AK-47s. A taller person stood in the open doorway behind them with a rocket launcher. The woman held up her hand and gestured for them to stay back. She walked down the steps toward the MATV.

Fitz climbed back inside the vehicle and ordered his team to stay put and cover him. Then he opened the door and stepped outside. His carbon-fiber blades sank into soft ash. He glanced at the sky and saw nothing but an ocean of blue and the occasional puffy white cloud.

Satisfied, he pulled his bandanna down and approached the church. She mimicked his action, removing her gas mask to reveal the wrinkled face of a woman around sixty. Dark-green eyes that were both kind and curious studied Fitz.

"I'm Master Sergeant Joe Fitzpatrick with the United States military, ma'am."

In perfect English, the old French woman said, "What brings you to Lisieux?"

"We're told you would know of enemy movements in the area and western France. Anything you can tell us about the Variants, especially the ones with wings, would help the military take back your country. Where do they nest? How long have they…"

His voice trailed off as every gun in the church suddenly pointed at the MATV. Including the monster of a rocket launcher.

"You came for info? That's why Jacques died?"

Fitz remembered the figure that had been plucked from the rooftop. "I'm sorry about him," he said. "But we need your help."

14

Captain Davis shifted in her wet uniform. The worst part about wearing the salvaged CBRN suit from the dead soldier wasn't the blood. No, it was the stench of the man's cologne. The musky scent was worse than the rotten smell of Variants.

Who fucking wears cologne in the apocalypse, anyway?

Their Zodiac coasted over the waves, drenching Davis in salt spray. The small craft carried the surviving members of the *GW*. Sergeant Marks and his two marines sat in the back with SCARs shouldered, scanning the waves for swimming juveniles. Diaz and Black rested with their backs on the bow.

Their first objective was to find her ship. Keeping up with an aircraft carrier in a Zodiac was nearly impossible, but they had plenty of extra gas and the *GW* wasn't moving at full speed. The real trick was staying out of sight.

The distant rumble of fighter jets sounded over the sea. She searched the sky for them but could see nothing in the muddy clouds. An oil tanker coasted through the ocean several miles to the west. They had passed a cruise ship earlier. There were hundreds of derelict ships out here, making it all too easy for the terrorists to hide from

Command on radar and satellite. "There she is," Black said. He pointed at a long blot of metal on the horizon.

Davis breathed a sigh of relief, then said, "Stay back, but don't lose her again." She considered using their satellite phone, but she didn't want to risk it. Her specific orders from Vice President Johnson were to remain out of sight and look for an opening. If and when she had an opportunity, she would request a green light to board the ship and take it back. Davis knew how risky it was. The ship was armed with enough munitions to blow up half the SZTs in the country, and ROT had already threatened to do just that.

Davis cursed under her breath. She still couldn't believe she'd lost her damn ship to a bunch of terrorist assholes.

"Where are they headed?" she asked.

Diaz unfolded a laminated map from her vest. Pointing to the beach to their right, she said, "That's Pensacola Beach. We're coming up on Fort Pickens. Fort McRee is on the point ahead."

"So where do you think they're heading?"

Diaz studied the map. "If I had to guess...New Orleans."

Black hefted up his SAW to make way for Sergeant Marks. He sat down next to Davis and pulled off his gas mask. The sergeant's bruised face twisted into a scowl as if he was trying to say, *I fucking told you so.*

Instead, he said, "What's your plan, Captain?"

Davis removed her own mask to speak freely. "Follow the ship and sneak aboard at nightfall, assuming Command gives us the all clear. If we get caught, at least we're wearing uniforms that might give us a chance to shoot first."

Marks chuckled. "Shoot first, ask questions later. I like it." He pulled a cigar from his vest and unwrapped the plastic. "I was saving this for later, but since we're going to die, I might just as well smoke it now."

Diaz shot Marks a glare. "All due respect, Sarge, but do you remember who you're talking to? Captain Davis seized the *GW* from the enemy back when it was armed with nuclear weapons. She will—*we* will—take it back again."

Davis held up a gloved hand to silence her bodyguard. She knew Diaz meant well, but now was not the time to start an argument with Marks.

A mile ahead, the *GW* was beginning to turn. The bow of their craft caught the larger vessel's wake, sending the Zodiac a foot into the air. They landed with a splash and then smoothed back out.

Marks eyed the marine on the engine as he pulled a Zippo from his pocket. "Watch it back there," Marks grumbled with the cigar jammed between his lips. He went to light it, but Davis nabbed the cigar from his hands.

"You want to draw attention to us?"

Marks glared at her like a kid who had been robbed of a piece of candy.

"You can smoke this later—after we take back our ship." She stuffed it in her vest pocket.

Marks's swollen jaw moved, but he didn't say another word.

The *GW* was rounding a peninsula thick with lush trees and overflowing underbrush. The eastern shore featured a white sandy beach surrounded by a teal lagoon. Seven months ago there would have been sunbathers, but now monsters lurked in the torpedograss. The bow of the ship vanished, and Davis looked back at the marine on the engine.

"Can't this thing go any faster?"

"We're maxed out, Captain."

Diaz raised her M4 to her visor. She quickly pulled it away and pointed to the sky.

"We got contacts!"

Everyone in the craft followed her fingers to a pair of black dots rising over the peninsula.

"Little Birds," Davis said. "Get us to the shore, fast."

The Zodiac curved hard to the right, the engine humming as the driver pushed it to the max. They shot over the waves, jolting up and down. Every free hand in the boat raised rifles toward the sky, but it only took a moment to see the small helicopters weren't heading for the Zodiac.

"What's that hanging from the bottom of the second one?" Black said.

Davis zoomed in with her M4. "My God," she whispered. She slowly pulled the scope away from her eye, unable to look any longer at the man hanging from a noose tied to the bottom of the Little Bird.

"Those animals," Black said. He looked to Davis. "When I get on board, I'm going to kill every single one of those bastards."

"That a sailor? One of ours?" Diaz asked, her eyes wide behind her visor.

"It's Admiral Humphrey," Black said. "Check the bars on the sleeves. That's his uniform."

Davis looked toward the shoreline, unable to think much past the anger. She pointed to a cluster of downed trees in the water. "Stop us over there until those Birds are out of sight."

The driver directed the boat toward the beach, carving through the water at an angle. He eased off the gas and coasted to the trees. Davis immediately regretted the choice of cover—it stank of rotting fish, and there were a number of manatee carcasses, each one picked clean, on the nearby beach. There were juveniles hunting here.

Maybe even adults that had survived by swimming out to sea when Kryptonite was dropped.

The Little Birds continued inland, Humphrey's corpse swinging from the rope like a pendulum. The thump of the rotors faded away, the sound replaced by the chirp of bugs and calls of exotic birds Davis couldn't see. Waves slapped against the shore, and the Zodiac rocked back and forth as the surf crawled through the fallen trees.

It would have been peaceful, almost serene, were it not for the sense she had of being watched. Davis scanned her team. Weapons were shouldered, and muzzles raked back and forth, covering every direction.

She flashed hand signals, and the marines raised their rifles into zones of fire. The afternoon sun baked the surviving members of the Scorpion and Rhino teams as they sat in the boat, waiting for Davis to give her next orders. The radio towers on top of the *GW* moved in the distance, just visible over the green canopy of trees. The aircraft carrier had rounded the peninsula.

Her ship was getting away again.

"Where are they headed now?" she asked.

Diaz looked at the map. "Maybe Pensacola. Hard to say. There's a few bays they could be trying to anchor in. Escambia Bay, East Bay . . ."

Davis motioned for the driver to turn the engine back on. The Zodiac hummed back to life. She did a final check for the Little Birds before flashing an advance signal back to sea. The boat backed up, then jolted forward.

Waves slapped against the bow, salt water misting the occupants. Davis kept the butt of her M4 in the sweet spot of her arm, ready to center in on a target at a second's notice. She was frosty, but she was also on edge. If they fell too far behind, they would never catch up to the *GW*.

Another peninsula and an island came into focus at

nine o'clock. She couldn't see nearby Fort McRee, but she spotted Fort Pickens at one o'clock. Brick walls, stained black from nearly two centuries of exposure to the maritime elements, surrounded the fort. Cannons still poked from the walls. They were there for the tourists, but once, those cannons had protected this spot from hostile ships.

More bloody carcasses of manatees dotted the sand below the fort. She zoomed in on the remains. Not a single ounce of meat was left on the creatures.

She flicked her muzzle to the wooded area up the beach, expecting to see eyes staring back from the foliage, but all she saw was tangled weeds and branches swaying in the wind.

"Faster," she said.

The driver turned the throttle, and the craft zipped over the waves. Storm clouds rolled in from the west. Rain that looked like rays of light hit the ocean on the horizon. Davis turned her attention back to the peninsula to scan the water for hostiles. She scooted closer to Black, who stood at the bow, his SAW trained on Fort Pickens.

She balled her hand into a fist to tell the driver to ease off the gas as they rounded the corner. The Zodiac crested a wave, slapped the water, and coasted toward the shallows. The marine on the engine navigated the craft around boulders sticking out of the clear water. Schools of fish swam by, just small enough to avoid interest from the monsters.

Davis held in a breath as they cleared the edge of the peninsula, letting it out into her mask when she saw the stern of the *GW*. It was already moving through Pensacola Bay toward the natural harbor.

Diaz looked up from the map. "They're definitely not heading toward—"

The thump of a helicopter cut her off. A Little Bird

rose from the center of Fort Pickens and climbed into the sky, Humphrey's body still hanging from the skids.

Davis clenched her jaw and pointed toward the shore. The boat turned sharply, engines humming and water spraying. Davis took a seat and grabbed a handle as the boat accelerated. The *GW* was now in the bay, and there was a flurry of movement on the deck.

"They're anchoring," Diaz said.

Zodiacs and black speedboats raced from Fort Pickens with more men and supplies. ROT soldiers lowered ladders from the hangar decks of the *GW* to quickly transfer the boxes.

"Up there," Diaz whispered. She pointed to the deck where a dozen of Davis's crew were being marched to the starboard side with guns to their backs.

Marks rose from his position, but Davis pulled him back down.

"No," she grunted.

"We have to help them," Marks said. He squirmed in her grip, and eventually Black helped restrain him.

"Stay down, Sergeant," Davis said. She watched as her men knelt on deck with guns to the backs of their heads.

Davis flinched at the crack of gunfire. To her right, Diaz cupped a hand over her face and wept, but Davis forced herself to look as the ROT soldiers executed twelve members of her crew. The bodies plummeted over the side of the ship into the water. It took every bit of her self-control not to open fire, but now was not the time.

Soon, she silently promised. Soon these bastards would get what was coming to them.

Beckham was supposed to be preparing corn on the cob and vegetable stew with Kate. His mouth watered at the thought. Instead, he was riding with her to the BSL4 lab, where she would be continuing her research on the European juveniles. She was in the back seat, arms crossed over her swollen stomach, frustration painted on her face. Horn was behind the wheel, his expression neutral. He clearly didn't want to get in the middle of this particular fight.

"You're both supposed to be retired," Kate huffed. "President Ringgold blessed the decision herself. Now she's asking you to put your uniforms back on."

Horn's eyes flicked from the road to Beckham, but he kept his mouth shut.

"And you're not supposed to be in a biohazard lab," Beckham said. "We all have our duty."

Kate looked toward the roof, then back at Beckham. "What about Tasha and Jenny? What about the baby?" Her hand caressed the outside of her stomach. "If something happens to you..."

Beckham's heart ached, but he had already made his decision.

"Kate, if the *Zumwalt* shows up in the harbor or the *GW* launches their arsenal at us, then we're all going to end up dead. ROT already tested our defenses once. Next time we might not be so lucky."

"You call that lucky? Hundreds of people were killed."

Beckham reached back with his prosthetic hand, hesitated, and pulled it back. He reached out again with his left hand, but she reared away.

"Damn it, Kate, I don't want to go back out there either. But if I have to kill every one of those ROT bastards to keep you safe, that's what I'll do. I *have* to do it."

Those words made everyone in the jeep pause. Horn turned the steering wheel slowly, his breathing heavy.

The *whoosh* of a chopper in the distance broke the uneasy silence.

Beckham ducked down to see a trio of Apaches raced out to sea. A transmission over the open line followed in his earpiece. "Bogey spotted five miles north of home plate. Sending Rogue One, Two, and Three to check it out. Over."

Horn turned down the road that dead-ended at the BSL4 lab. Several marines in CBRN gear were positioned at the gate. The largest of them approached the jeep, and Horn rolled down the window to flash his credentials.

"Evenin'," Horn said.

The marine looked in the window, studying each of them.

"Good evening, gentlemen. Doctor Lovato," the man said, his voice raspy from his breathing apparatus.

He stepped away from the jeep, nodded at the gate operator, then gestured for Horn to proceed. The lift rose into the air, and Horn drove onto the bridge that extended out to the lab on its raised platform. A second gate slowly opened.

Beckham and Horn both looked at the dock connecting to the facility from the west. The USS *Monterey* had left the island, and the docks where its civilian passengers had perished were shiny from the rigorous spraying of chemicals.

A marine waved Horn through the next gate, and he pulled up to the windowless facility. A white dome marked with the Medical Corps symbol rose above them.

Beckham stepped out onto the pavement and gently touched Kate's arm. She glanced up, blue eyes avoiding his for a moment.

"You and I both know there are monsters out there,"

Beckham said. "You and Ellis are fighting them here in this lab, and our friends are fighting them half-way around the globe. My fight is here, protecting this island."

"It's not the same thing," Kate said.

"We all fight in our own ways."

Kate looked at her stomach and shook her head. "I just...I thought you were done fighting."

"I can't promise I'll ever be done," Beckham said. "You're needed in the lab, and President Ringgold needs me to manage security here at the island. That's the reality of our situation, Kate. We can't just quit with the world falling apart around us."

"Okay," she said after a moment's hesitation.

"Okay."

She put her palms on his chest and leaned in to give him a quick kiss on the cheek.

"We'll pick you up in a couple of hours. Be careful."

"Always am." She moved away, but he pulled her back.

"Please don't be mad at me. I love you, Kate."

Her rigid posture relaxed and her eyes softened. "I love you too."

She followed two marine escorts toward the building but stopped and held up a hand before vanishing into the lab.

Fifteen minutes later Horn was speeding down a gravel road on the way to the island's forward oper-ating base, near the cemetery, overlooking the water. He parked the jeep in a gravel lot already filled with Humvees and pickup trucks. Neither of the men said a word when they saw the white crosses on the hill in the distance.

The ocean was rough tonight, whitecaps stained red by the setting sun. The *Zumwalt* was out there somewhere, waiting to strike. There was no telling where, when, or even if ROT would hit Plum Island, so Beckham had to prepare for every possible scenario.

He got out of the jeep and retrieved his gear from the back. It had been a few months since he'd carried his rucksack. It felt heavier, or maybe it was all the muscle he had lost.

The two Delta operators walked in silence past the graves of the heroes lost in the war against the Variants. They paused at one grave in particular to look down at the white marker.

Alex T. Riley
"The Kid"

Closing his eyes, Beckham sucked in a breath through his nostrils. He felt one of Horn's massive hands on his back.

"If I had been there," Beckham said, bowing his head.

"You have to let that guilt go, man. It will eat you up."

Beckham dragged his sleeve across his face and nodded. "You're right, Big Horn. Our job is to make sure we don't have to keep digging graves."

It was hard to believe he would never see most of his men again. He hadn't even been able to bring their remains home. The only one they had buried from the original Team Ghost was Riley. He'd died not far from here, at the hands of the Bone Collector.

If none of this had happened, they would all be down at The Bing right now, Team Ghost's favorite Florida watering hole. Riley would be on a table, dancing in his underpants. Tenor, Edwards, and Panda would be arguing over who was up for the next lap dance. And Beckham would have been right there with them, laughing and knocking back beers with his brothers.

Beckham carried the guilt of all their deaths, and he couldn't help thinking about how he could have done things differently. War was a series of decisions with unpredictable outcomes. A single step in the wrong direction could earn you a bullet. Some men could make it all the way up a beach unscathed with thousands of rounds zipping by them. Others might get hit the second they jumped out of the boat. He'd been luckier than most. Maybe luckier than he deserved.

"Captain Beckham!" shouted a voice.

Army Lieutenant General Miles Rayburn stood on the beach in front of the Command Center Building with three dozen troops surrounding him. An M1A1 Abrams growled down the shoreline about a quarter mile away. Guard towers dotted the shoreline like light poles, the muzzles of sniper rifles angled out over the water.

Rayburn waved two fingers, the large silver ring of his old military unit glinting. He was all army, the type of guy who didn't get along well with other branches. But his history as a former Delta operator and his speech back at the embassy proved he was supportive of President Ringgold. That earned him, if not Beckham's respect, at least the chance to prove his loyalty.

"Boys, this is Captain Reed Beckham and Master Sergeant Parker Horn," Rayburn said as the two men approached.

The soldiers on the beach all turned. Some of them raised their eyebrows at Beckham's prosthetics. He had expected that, and was ready for the stares. Fitz had taught him what courage really was—not just fighting an army of monsters, but standing proudly after you had been torn apart by them.

"Good evening everyone," Beckham said. "Tonight we stand in front of the graves of those who gave their lives to protect Plum Island and everything it represents. Our job is to do everything we can to honor their sacrifice by making this island secure for future generations."

Every eye on the beach remained focused on Beckham. He had their attention now. Just like his CO at Fort Bragg, he had learned how to evoke emotion in his team without saying much.

"I'm not going to waste time explaining our situation. Operation Reach is about to go down thousands of miles away, but here at home we are planning for our own battle. It's time to get to work."

"You heard Captain Beckham. Let's get moving!" Horn shouted. He clapped his hands, and every grunt on the beach began filing toward the Command Center Building. An American flag snapped on its pole as a helicopter shot overhead.

Beckham stopped to watch as the Apaches flocked toward the crimson sunset. A transmission came over the open comms while they were still in view.

"All hands to your stations. The bogey spotted fifteen miles north of home plate is an Arleigh Burke–class guided destroyer. Looks like the *Monterey*. Repeat, bogey incoming."

Rayburn looked at Beckham and Horn.

"She was supposed to be heading to Maine," Rayburn grumbled. "Why the hell would she..."

Rayburn's words trailed off, and Beckham said, "I have a feeling Lieutenant Wood just added another ship to his fleet, and he's sent it our way."

15

Fitz set his rucksack down on a dusty church pew and told Apollo to stay. The dog sat on his hind legs, eyes never leaving Fitz as he followed the leader of the Ombres down the center aisle. He performed the sign of the cross as he walked. Never in his life had he been in such a beautiful church before. His blades clicked over the marble floor, echoing in the cavernous space.

It was only late afternoon, but the church was shrouded in darkness. Planks of wood covered the shattered stained-glass windows. Even the massive rose window had been covered from the outside, muting its vibrant colors. Upended church pews barricaded the entrances. These people had been living in hell for months on their own with no running water or electricity. The reek of body odor and feces filled the ancient church.

"This way," the woman said, waving Fitz toward the altar. He wanted to stop and marvel at the mosaics covering the walls and the paintings of religious iconography, but the woman's pace was brisk.

They passed row after row of pews. Stone columns framed the three-story nave on all sides. There was a balcony on each side. Children, hardly taller than the wood railings, patrolled the walkways, carrying weapons too big for them.

Fitz cradled his MK11 across his chest and walked faster to keep up with the woman. She still hadn't said much, and his patience was starting to wear thin.

"When the EUF said they would send soldiers, I assumed there would be more of you," the woman said at last. She stopped at the bottom step leading up to the altar. She flashed a pair of hand signals to the kids above. They darted away, keeping to the shadows. Fitz had no doubt they were still watching.

"I'm sorry to disappoint you, ma'am, but we took a beating on the beaches," Fitz said. "I don't mean to be rude, but we're on a timetable here. Your intel can help save lives as General Nixon pushes toward Paris."

The woman brushed her curtain of gray hair aside and glared at him.

"Intel? I'll give you intel," she said, speaking rapidly, her French accent growing thicker. "Three days ago those things descended on Lisieux. They killed five of my children as well as every adult left in the group. Another boy, Jacques, died today. He died trying to save *you*. We'd been hiding in the crypts, but when you showed up, you led them right to us."

Fitz leaned back slightly from the onslaught. "Madam, I'm really sorry for your losses. Truly. But we did not lead them to you. They were already here."

"They know we're here now," she replied. "They will come for us, and when they do, they will bring more."

"I'll call in evac before that happens." Fitz was careful with his words, not wanting to make a promise he couldn't keep. After losing the Apaches, Colonel Bradley would be wary of authorizing air transport.

She raised a skeptical eyebrow but said nothing.

"Look, ma'am, I think we got off on the wrong foot here. What's your name?"

She hesitated for a moment before answering, "My name is Mira."

He reached out to shake her hand, but she just stared at him until he dropped it.

"Nice to meet you, Mira. I'm—"

"Master Sergeant Joe Fitzpatrick. Yes, you said."

He made a point to always be a gentleman, but apparently chivalry had died with the apocalypse.

"We don't have much time," Fitz said quietly. He took a seat on a nearby pew and propped his MK11 and M4 up next to him. He didn't feel right about bringing a weapon into God's house, but he figured the big guy would understand.

"Mira, I need to know where the enemy is so we can advance across the countryside and liberate any survivors."

Fitz pulled a map from his vest. Unfolding it, he then flapped it out and looked for their location.

"Liberate," Mira said. She said something in French under her breath that Fitz didn't understand.

"It means we're here to help you."

She scoffed, shaking her head as she stood. A quick glance at the balcony above sent two children darting away to hide in the shadows.

"Many months ago, I told them help would come. The soldiers who came died. Dragged away at night by the monsters. The parents of these children, too. I am the only adult left in Lisieux. I taught the Ombres to fight. I taught them to hide. Now you come here and demand information. What could you, barely half a man, and these few soldiers do to protect us?"

"We don't look like much," Fitz said, trying to keep his temper in check. "But Team Ghost is the best out there. The Twenty-Fourth Marine Expeditionary Unit trusted us with this mission. Now, I understand *you* may not trust us—"

Mira cut him off with the click of her tongue like she was scolding a child.

One of the kids glancing through the wood posts above smiled at Fitz, then vanished from view. He trained his eyes back on Mira.

"Ma'am, I need to know about enemy movement in this area." Fitz pointed to the section on the map the Command staff had identified back at the FOB.

Mira eyed the document with obvious distaste. Fitz held it out, but she sighed and pushed it away.

"I'm not helping you until I have some guarantees for my children. You don't fool me, boy. You can't take all of us in that truck, can you?"

Rico approached the pew where they were sitting. "How many of you are there?"

"Twenty." Mira's green eyes flitted toward the ceiling, then refocused on Fitz. "Nineteen now."

He flashed back to the tiny tennis shoes of the child who had been picked off the roof of a nearby building. Jacques had died risking his life to help Team Ghost.

"There are nineteen of them, plus me. But my seat doesn't matter. Get the children out of here. I will stay," Mira said. She let out a weary, mirthless chuckle. "Maybe someday they'll talk about Saint Mira of Lisieux, eh?"

Fitz hadn't been sure what to think of her until now. She was prickly and cautious, but she was also serious about giving up her shot at rescue. She would die for these kids. He could feel Rico staring at him, but he avoided meeting her gaze. They both knew the MATV couldn't carry that many.

"Our MATV was built for a crew of three and up to twelve additional troops. We will try to squeeze everyone into the truck," Fitz said. "That's assuming Command sends the King Stallion to retrieve the MATV. If not, we'd need a Black Hawk, and those are in short supply right now."

Mira didn't answer right away. Fitz lowered the map and set it on the bench where she could see it. Then he stood and walked up to the altar. A life-sized crucifix hung under the stained-glass window.

God, if you're listening, I could really use some help right about now.

Fitz made the sign of the cross again.

"You're a religious man?" Mira asked.

Fitz dipped his helmet. "I have faith."

Mira cracked a sly grin. "You won't when you see what's out there." She picked up the map. Holding it in one wrinkled hand, she used the other to point at the red line Command had marked from the FOB to Paris.

"There are things you have never seen before out there. Unspeakable things. The ones outside…" She scoffed again. "You have no idea what lurks in the shadows."

Rico chomped on her gum impatiently. "Oh yeah? So how about you tell us exactly what you mean by that?"

"Wormers," said an adolescent voice.

A boy no older than thirteen with shaggy red hair came from the shadows and leaned against the opposite edge of the altar, curious blue eyes studying Fitz.

"Michel, I told you not to talk about those things. You're going to scare the other kids," Mira said.

"I'm not a kid," he fired back.

"I suppose I should introduce you all to my second-in-command," Mira said.

"I'm Michel," the boy said, planting his hands on his hips. "The captain of the Ombres."

"Do you all speak English or what?" Stevenson asked from the balcony above.

Tanaka, who was checking one of the boarded-up windows, turned to look at them. "America is one of the only countries where most citizens speak just one language."

Stevenson shrugged. "Whatever, man, I know some Spanish."

"And I know five languages," Tanaka said. He paused, then added, "Fluently."

"Is one of them French?" Stevenson said with a smug grin.

The piercing howl of a monster silenced the men. Fitz looked toward the ceiling as a thud sounded from somewhere up above. Dust rained down on the pews like dirty snow. A chorus of shrieks and growls followed, coming together in a symphony that made the children take shelter under pews and in the shadows. It was unlike anything Fitz had ever heard. These sounds were guttural and primal, as if a pack of hyenas had somehow become infected with the hemorrhage virus.

"What is that?" Rico whispered.

"The rest of them," Mira replied. "I told you they would be coming."

Michel raised his AK-47 and chambered a round. "C'mon. I'll show you the crypts."

Piero awoke to pitch-black darkness. He pulled the blanket over his shoulders and closed one eye, but kept the other open. That's how he'd slept for the past month. Half the time he was so tired he wasn't sure if he was awake or dreaming. But he had a lookout now. The mouse squeaked again. That was what had woken him up.

"*Piccolo amico*," he whispered. "It's all right, little friend."

The same squeak sounded. He couldn't see the mouse, but he could hear it skittering across the ground. The furry creature brushed against his nose, and Piero had to hold in a sneeze.

Sitting up, Piero held his nose shut until the urge to sneeze passed. The mouse jumped onto his shoulder, which had become its favorite resting spot.

"You have a bad dream?" Piero asked. He struck a match and lit a candle in his new hiding spot. The glow blossomed to illuminate the four-by-eight-foot tomb.

The mouse chirped back. He tilted his button nose up, sniffing the air and narrowing his eyes at the dancing flame. Piero wasn't sure how old the mouse was. He wasn't even really sure it was a boy mouse, but he was going to keep thinking of his new friend as *he*.

"I need to give you a real name," Piero whispered. The mouse tilted its head, still sniffing and studying him curiously. "You're right, we should eat first."

Piero got to his knees, plucked his knife off the ground, and sheathed the blade. His pistol was out of ammunition, but he grabbed it and placed it in his bag nonetheless. He might get lucky and find more rounds.

Their new shelter was three stories beneath Saint Peter's Basilica, in the catacombs most tourists never saw. So far, the Varianti hadn't found it either.

"And they aren't going to find us, are they, little friend?" Piero's voice was a whisper that he hardly recognized. His father had told him that the voice was the first thing you forgot about someone after they passed. But what about your own voice? If he didn't recognize it anymore, did that mean he was dead?

No, you're still alive. You're Piero Angaran. You're a soldier.

The mouse climbed higher onto his shoulder as Piero crossed the room, his tail brushing against Piero's ear.

The candlelight guided them to the crawlspace they used as an entrance and exit to the tomb.

The winged creatures always hunted at night, but the sun would be coming up soon. He hadn't been above-ground for days now. He was almost out of water, and his gurgling stomach reminded him he hadn't eaten anything for ... how long? He'd lost track.

The mouse squeaked again, his way of telling Piero to hurry up.

He petted the mouse with a fingertip, and felt its ribs and bony spine just beneath the fur. Piero wasn't the only one that needed to eat.

The creature didn't protest when Piero put him in a small pouch and zipped it up almost to the top. Piero wished he could climb inside there with his little friend.

He placed the pouch in his backpack, then crawled through the dusty passage. A cobweb stuck to his face, but he didn't bother wiping it away. No matter how many times he crawled through the narrow tunnel, the spiders would rebuild their webs.

Piero had already scavenged the eastern passages beneath the Vatican. It was time to try the western side. But there was no telling what lurked in the shadows there.

"Probably something worse than spiders, eh?"

Three stories of stone and dirt above, a new day was dawning over Rome. The winged beasts would be returning to their lairs, and the Varianti on the ground would seek refuge in their nests. It was time to leave his own nest for the hunt.

In the beginning he'd had to flatten his stomach and remove his gear to get through the crawlspace, but now he was so skinny that it was quite easy to carry the essentials as he went through: his rifle, his knife, a water bottle, and a small pack containing medical supplies, ammunition, and the pouch containing his friend.

The candle flame flickered as he continued squirming, threatening to go out. If it did, he wouldn't be able to strike another match until he got to the other side. Not that it mattered much. Piero was accustomed to the dark.

Grunting, he crawled the final stretch and dropped the four feet to the ground by sliding down the wall, his hands hitting the floor first.

He stood and raked the candle back and forth, illuminating a low stone ceiling and walls that had been built countless years ago. It was difficult to know exactly how old everything was down here. He had always thought humans would last forever, but he realized how naive he had been.

For all he knew, he could be the last human in the world. When he was gone, the walls would be all that remained.

Sighing, Piero walked slowly across the room. He switched hands with his candle and rifle, jamming the stock into his right armpit and raising the muzzle toward a staircase that led to a hallway above. He walked on the tips of his boots, avoiding the click of his heels. It was habit more than precaution. If there were monsters above, they would hear the sweat drip off his head.

Halfway up the winding staircase, he stopped to listen to the silence. There wasn't even the whisper of drafting air or the skitter of an insect. It was like being in outer space, or maybe like being dead.

You're not dead. Your name is Piero Angaran. You are a soldier.

The silence was unnerving, but it was better than the alternative.

He continued up the stairs, the weapon wobbling in his weak grip. He'd lost so much muscle and body weight that holding the gun had become a challenge.

You're still a soldier. You're still a man.

The reassuring thoughts—not to mention the pangs of hunger in his belly—gave him the strength to continue climbing the stairs. There was nothing like hunger to drive a man to desperation. The Varianti were also driven by a primal need to feed. At least he didn't share their disgusting appetite for human flesh.

"That's something, isn't it?" he asked the mouse.

It didn't answer.

He tensed as he rounded the final corner, listening for any sign of the demons. The candlelight danced in the narrow passage, like hands reaching out for him. A distant drip, drip of water echoed, but besides that he heard nothing.

Raising his rifle, he stepped into the hallway and held his candle out to the east, then to the west, muzzle sweeping over the dark passages. The light only reached a few hundred feet, and there was no sign of the monsters.

For the first time, he took a left to head west, starving, scared, and unsure if he would ever see the sun again.

16

Captain Davis was still shaking from shock and anger. Three hours ago, she'd seen a dozen of her crew executed. Since then she'd remained hidden in the tall grass on an embankment with nothing to think about but revenge. Her small team flanked her on both sides, all watching the brick walls of Fort Pickens. They had abandoned their Zodiac in a canal and covered it with a camouflage tarp Marks had discovered onboard. So far they had avoided detection, but patrols of ROT soldiers were combing the area.

She wasn't sure how long they could remain hidden, and she didn't want to try walking up to the terrorists in a stolen ROT uniform either. But they couldn't stay here forever.

She crawled through the grass and scoped the deck of the ship where the ROT soldiers had airlifted two MGM-140 Army Tactical Missile System delivery vehicles. Several men carefully unloaded crates around them. Zooming in, she saw the same surface-to-surface ballistic missiles she'd encountered at the Earthfall facility, which could carry a payload like the bioweapon they'd used to exterminate most of the surviving Variants. But these looked more advanced, with larger fuel chambers for a wider range.

But why would ROT have those? Unless...No, even they wouldn't be that insane.

The only reason they'd have them would be to arm them with the hemorrhage virus. Firing even a few of them at SZTs would wipe out every man, woman, and child left in America. With most of the American forces overseas, there was no way they could stop another outbreak here in the States.

Davis bit down on her lip. She would not let ROT destroy everything President Ringgold had worked to rebuild and the military had fought and bled for to defend.

She flattened her body against the embankment, her finger creeping toward the trigger of her rifle. A patrol of six ROT soldiers walked down the shore, their SCARS roving back and forth. In her mind's eye, she could picture her rounds tearing through the men. But even then, she wouldn't feel satisfied. Davis wanted to gut them—to paint the beach with their blood.

Never in her life had she felt anger like this. It burned in the very marrow of her bones. The itch to jump up and empty her magazine into every ROT soldier she could see was overwhelming. Revenge was all she could think about.

Get your head on straight, Rachel. You need to be smart about this. There is too much at risk to do something stupid.

There were still members of her crew alive on the ship, and she still had Black and Diaz, as well as Marks and his men to think about. Not to mention the fate of the human race.

The patrol was fifty yards away now, walking through a cluster of trees.

"We can take 'em, Captain," Marks whispered.

"Not without firing a shot. I've counted over fifty soldiers so far. We can't kill them all by ourselves, and the ones we don't take down will make short work of us."

"Look, I know you have your orders, but even you can't be this cold. The admiral is dead and they displayed his body like a fucking dog. Then they executed a dozen of our crew in front of us. I'm just a sergeant, but even I know sometimes orders are meant to be broken."

Davis heard Diaz suck in an angry breath, but she held her tongue this time.

"Those were my men, too," Davis said. "*My* responsibility. I'm going to get the *GW* back, and then we're going to kill every last one of those sons of bitches. But not until we have the right opportunity. Understood?"

Marks stared her down for a moment longer, but in the end he looked away and grumbled, "Understood."

Davis wasn't sure she believed him.

Part of her wanted to charge in with guns blazing just like him, but she knew that was the wrong move. These ROT soldiers had been baiting her by displaying Humphrey's corpse and executing the crewmen. They were terrorists, and their currency was fear.

The only way to fight them was through superior strategy. Ideally, President Ringgold would have sent a Special Ops team to retake the ship. But Davis and her motley band of soldiers was the best they were going to get. Luckily, she had learned a thing or two about situations like these when Lieutenant Colonel Kramer had commandeered the *GW*.

Quick and steady, she thought, and then mentally added *quiet* to the list.

She waved Diaz over.

"Diaz, where's the closest SZT?"

"There's one in New Orleans and one in Tallahassee," she answered promptly.

Marks scooted closer. "Both are way too far from here to get help, if that's what you're thinking. And New Orleans has sided with the enemy."

Diaz looked back down at her map. "There is a small outpost here." She pointed to a blue dot on the map that was marked *OP119*.

"What do we know about it?" Davis asked.

"It's only twenty miles from here by boat, or thirty if we had a car, but there's no way to know if anyone is actually manning the post. There are hundreds of these stations, and many of them have fallen in the past few months to juveniles or raiding parties. I think the standard crew is twenty soldiers."

"They say soldiers go there to die," Black said. "They're basically outposts, like the traders used back during the Revolutionary War. Deep in enemy territory and away from the help of the military."

The team flattened as the beam from a flashlight hit the top of the embankment. Davis put a finger to her lips as voices muffled by gas masks came over the hill.

"Man, I don't know if I like this. I mean, executing those sailors is one thing. That's all about sovereignty. You can't let the tyrants have anything over you, right? But turning kids into monsters is where I draw the line."

"Wood won't do it. He's just using the missiles as leverage," said someone else.

"What about Chicago?"

Another voice, rougher and deeper, replied, "Stop being a pussy, Morgan. This is war. We got to do what we got to do to take our country back from that bitch."

"Ringgold ain't so bad," said the first voice.

There was a sound of a scuffle, and then an *ooph*, like someone had been hit in the stomach.

"Lieutenant Wood would have you killed for that comment, Morgan. You're lucky I don't slit your throat to shut your stupid ass up."

Davis heard coughing. "I'm just sayin', man. Jesus."

"Cut that shit out," said the rough voice. "We're supposed to be at the checkpoint in ten minutes."

The muffled voices faded with the wind, but their words stuck with Davis like a fire that wouldn't go out. She knew she had to make a decision quickly.

"Sergeant, you and your men stay here and watch the *GW*. Diaz, Black, and I will head to OP119 to see if we can get some help. Hopefully they will have some firepower there."

Davis didn't voice the rest of her plan out loud. She wasn't ready to blow her ship up yet—with the rest of her crew still on it—but she couldn't let Wood fire any of those missiles at civilian targets. If it came down to a choice between saving the *GW* and saving the country... well, that was no choice at all.

The kids in the Basilica of Saint Thérèse had seen a lot since the monsters came to Europe. Fitz could tell by their hollow, haunted eyes. But the way their faces lit up when they saw Apollo warmed his heart. The dog was a well-trained combat veteran, but he was also a big, good-natured animal that loved attention. The kids stroked the German shepherd and cooed over him in French until a stern word from Mira made them scatter back to their posts.

Most of their group had moved to the crypts while Fitz waited for Command to return his transmission. Dohi was upstairs with Stevenson, watching the grounds for movement. Fitz didn't feel much safer underground, but he couldn't hear the howling.

"What is that?" came a voice.

Fitz felt a tug on the bandanna around his neck and

looked over to Michel. While most of the kids were fascinated with Apollo, the boy had taken an interest in Riley's laughing-skull bandanna.

"I like it. Where did you get it?"

"From a very good friend," Fitz replied. As much as he wanted to tell the story, there was work to do. He glanced at the blockaded doors where Tanaka and several kids stood guarding the entrance. The children chatted with each other, but Tanaka remained silent in the shadows.

Rico and Mira studied the map, their heads bent over it, the younger woman's bright blue hair a stark contrast against Mira's silver gray. Mira still didn't want to talk about the beasts that had overrun her country. Fitz had to get her to talk, and fast. Enemy forces were heading their way, and it was only a matter of time before they broke into the basilica.

He looked at his watch. The sun had gone down hours ago, and whatever was coming would move in the early-morning hours.

They were running out of time.

"Lion One, this is Ghost One, do you copy? Over."

A response hissed into his earpiece this time. Static at first, then a voice.

"Copy, Ghost One, this is Lion One. Over."

Fitz looked at Mira. She was still holding her cards tight, unwilling to tell him any details. Not that he blamed her. She was doing what any mother would do to protect her children.

A second transmission came across the channel. Colonel Bradley growled, "You better have some good news for me." There was a pause of static, then, "Have you completed your mission?"

"Working on it, sir."

"Have you located the Ombres?"

"Yes, sir."

"So what's the problem?"

Fitz hesitated. "They want a ride out of here."

"How many are there?"

"Twenty."

There was a pause that seemed to stretch forever.

"If you get me the intel I need to advance across France, I'll send the King Stallion to pick up that MATV," Bradley finally said. "You got to cram everyone in, though, because I can't risk sending any Black Hawks. Get back to me when you have what I need."

There was cursing and a shout on the other line. White noise followed, then the transmission cut off. Fitz almost tore his earpiece from his ear.

Fitz hated being a hard-ass. He'd been raised to treat people—especially women—with respect and courtesy. But the time for being a gentleman was over. He turned to the Frenchwoman and gave her a steely glare.

"If you want your kids to leave this town alive, you'll tell me everything you know. Right now. I want enemy movements, coordinates. What type of monsters we're dealing with, and how many." He pointed to the ceiling. "Those things outside, whatever they are, they *will* find us. They will kill everyone in this church. And Command isn't coming to help unless I give them something."

Mira blinked and took a step back. "Your commander would leave you out here?"

There was no hesitation in Fitz's response. "Absolutely."

Rico pulled the map closer to Mira. "Show us where these 'unthinkable' things are so we can bomb the hell out of 'em, okay?"

"And show us the best route from our FOB to Paris," Fitz added.

"I have your word you will get us out of here?" Mira asked.

Fitz nodded and held her gaze. Mira swiped her long gray hair over her shoulders and leaned down over the map. Michel followed her with his hands on his hips and the AK-47 dangling from a strap over his shoulder.

"About five months ago the French military retreated to Paris," Mira said. "They cleared and held on to several *arrondissements*. Those areas were their final stronghold."

"They put up a good fight," Michel said. "My dad was there. He was a hero."

Fitz looked at the boy, who stood proudly despite the AK-47 weighing down on his shoulders. Disheveled red hair stuck out in all directions as he stepped into the light. Freckles dotted his sharp nose. He reminded Fitz a lot of his brother at that age.

Mira smiled at Michel, and Fitz forced himself to do the same thing, even though his heart ached for the kid.

"Your father was very brave," Mira said. "If he had known you were still alive, he would have come here instead."

Michel nodded solemnly, and she looked back to the map.

"This area," she continued. Her finger slowly crossed the map from their location in Lisieux to Paris, and then south to Orleans. She traced a circle around the Saint-Laurent and Dampierre nuclear power plants. "The government blew up these plants as a last resort. I remember the disaster at Chernobyl. The radiation here…it is worse than that."

Mira traced another, larger circle that reached from Bourges to the south all the way to the outskirts of Paris. It was an area of nearly fifty thousand square kilometers.

"Jesus," Fitz whispered. "That's like setting off a

small nuclear weapon." He nodded at Rico to make note of the area so they could avoid it.

"Doesn't radiation kill the juveniles?" she asked.

Mira clicked her tongue and folded her arms across her chest. "A nuclear bomb would have been better. The leaked radiation, it did not kill all of these monsters. It transformed some of them. Before, I was in communication with resistance in the area. They told me of the things they saw. Their transmissions have all stopped coming now."

Rico's voice sounded high and thin as she asked, "What did they see?"

"They reported things I don't discuss with the children. Wormers, Pinchers, and Black Beetles."

Fitz looked at Rico and tried to process this information. If what Mira was saying was true, then the Twenty-Fourth MEU was going to have more than just juveniles, Reavers, and battalions of grunt adults to think about.

"The mutated army has been moving northwest, out of the nuclear zone," Mira said. She pointed to the Parc Naturel Régional du Perche. "If there is one area to avoid, it's this. Stay very clear of it. There are other creatures there that have no name. An EUF recon unit was deployed to document them. I listened to the comms. They encountered some sort of creature with bark for skin. Your commanders should set the entire forest on fire."

Mira continued to point out areas to bomb and places where new breeds of monsters had been reported. The picture she painted was grim. France was completely overrun.

When she finished, Fitz thanked Mira and then gestured for Rico so they could speak in silence.

"The leaked radiation," he whispered. "Why would it not kill these juveniles?"

Rico shrugged. "Maybe it killed some of them but wasn't strong enough to kill the others. Maybe that's why they mutated? I have heard of juveniles back home surviving the dirty bombs."

Fitz scratched at his chin. "I'll relay this to Bradley so it can be passed up the chain of command. Some scientist like Kate will probably make the call whether to continue with the plan to drop the dirty bombs during Operation Reach."

They both looked up at a voice at the door across the room. Fitz reached for his M4 and MK11 that were propped up against the wall of mosaics behind him. Rico's hand went for her M9, but they both paused as Stevenson poked his big head through the open door, wearing a mask of worry.

Fitz straightened his back in anticipation of even more bad news.

"Whatever was on the roof is gone, but we've got new movement outside, sir," Stevenson said. "Dohi is reporting motion in the gardens."

"Variants? Reavers?" Rico asked.

Stevenson shook his head. "Don't think so."

Fitz turned back to Mira. "What else is in this area?"

The woman unfolded her arms, her shoulders sinking. In the dim light, she looked far older. How she had kept these kids alive was beyond Fitz. Maybe this church was sacred—maybe God or Saint Thérèse had protected them.

Fitz was starting to think the place was cursed.

"Dohi said the ground is moving out there," Stevenson said.

Mira narrowed her eyes. "What did you say?"

"Wormers," Michel said. He was already pulling his loaded AK-47 from his shoulder. He spoke in a low but confident voice for a thirteen-year-old and then signaled to three of the older kids in the back of the room. They started checking their weapons.

Wormers? Fitz imagined juveniles with tails, wiggling across the ground, sucker mouths popping as they neared their prey. It didn't sound that scary.

Rico chewed her gum violently like it was an overcooked piece of steak. "Reavers, Wormers, Pinchers, Black Beetles. Shit, you got all the creepy-crawlies here."

"Great, that's excellent," Stevenson said. "More monsters that want to eat us."

"More to kill," Tanaka said. He reached back to check the draw on his blades.

Fitz considered going topside to see things for himself, but first he had to get any remaining intel from Mira.

He gestured at the map. "What's the best route to Paris?"

Mira looked at Michel and nodded for him to stand down. Then she pulled the map back to her. She used a pen to draw a diagonal line that snaked from the FOB northeast of Lisieux all the way to Paris.

Michel walked around the table, one hand holding his rifle, the other scratching his filthy face. That's when Fitz noticed the red Superman cape the boy was wearing. The rifle had covered it up earlier.

"I have a better idea," the boy said. "I think we should take your truck out there and drive to Paris as fast as we can."

Mira put her hand on the boy's caped shoulder and spoke rapidly in French. The comm link fired into Fitz's ear before she could finish. He held up a hand and pushed his earbud in.

"Ghost One, Ghost Three. Something outside you'll want to see."

"I'll be up shortly, Ghost Three," Fitz said. He then

opened the line back to Command to relay the intel and request evac.

"Lion One, Ghost One, do you copy? Over."

Static hissed into his earpiece.

Fitz tried a second time, but got the same white noise.

He caught Rico's worried gaze, and then very calmly said, "Come on, Apollo. Everyone else, stay down here. I'm going to check this out."

Kate could hear the air raid sirens through the lab walls. She waited on a bench next to Ellis in the safe room designed to protect them from airborne contaminants. Red beams circled the dark room from an emergency light in the center of the ceiling, which cast blood-colored shadows into the corners. Kate cupped her head in her hands and breathed deep. She exhaled slowly, looking for any calm she could find.

"If it's bad, Beckham would come for you," Ellis said. Kate wanted to believe him. He kept trying to reassure her, but neither of them had any idea what was going on outside. All she knew was there was a "bandit." It could be a juvenile, someone infected with hemorrhage, or something even worse.

"We really need to get back in there," Ellis said. "We left the specimen samples in the radiation-delivery machine. It'll ruin them, and we have a limited supply."

He stood and pressed his finger against the keypad. It beeped angrily back at him. "We're freaking locked in here?" Ellis kicked the door. "When the hell is someone going to tell us what's going on?"

It wasn't like Ellis to lose his cool, but they were both under a lot of stress. Kate stood and caressed her stomach while Ellis sent another weak kick at the door and slumped against the wall.

The wall-mounted speaker above his head buzzed. Banks of LEDs clicked on, spreading a white glow over the room. Kate rushed forward and pushed her thumb to the comm. "Hello? Can anyone hear us?"

"Kate! It's me."

Her heart leaped at the sound of Reed's voice. "Are you all right?"

"I'm fine, yeah. You and Ellis holding up okay?"

"No. We're locked in. What's happening, Reed?"

"The *Monterey* is back. I sent choppers to check it out. So far we can't reach anyone on board."

"You're not sending a team out there, are you?"

His response came after a second of hesitation. "We're still analyzing the situation."

"You are *not* going out there, Reed." Her voice was firm. "You and I both know that ship is compromised."

"I know, and I won't. Try not to worry. You're in the safest building on the island. I'll come get you in a couple of hours unless something develops. If anything happens, I'll come get you immediately, okay?"

"Okay. Just do me a favor and have someone unlock the doors. We have work to do."

Reed spoke to someone out of earshot, then said, "It's done."

Ellis pressed his finger back to the identification keypad. The door clicked open and he stepped into the vestibule. Kate stayed next to the comm, waiting for the words she needed to hear.

"I love you," Reed said.

"I love you too. Be safe."

Kate followed Ellis back to the lab. They had a hundred things to do, and all of them had to be done right now. The most important task was figuring out what they had found in Europe. It was only a matter of time before Fitz's team faced one of the creatures. Assuming he was even still alive. Kate slapped the thought aside as soon as it entered her mind. She couldn't dwell on worry. Not now.

"So we're in the clear?" Ellis asked.

"For now. Reed says this is the safest place on the island."

"I sure as hell don't feel safe here," Ellis said with a shake of his head. He changed the subject as they approached the lab doors. "That creature in the database is a juvenile, that's certain, but it's a different type of species than any we've discovered. Which begs the question—does this thing only seem like a new species because we haven't found it over here yet?"

"My thoughts precisely. I've wondered the same thing about these Reavers. Why don't we have them here?"

"My theory is that juveniles have had longer to develop in Europe. That means epigenetic changes could have activated genes we haven't even identified yet. The wings and everything else we're seeing have to be due to that. Right?"

"I'm not sure. Those things could be here and just hiding out, or they're content and well fed in whatever part of the country they've evolved in. Hopefully we'll know more in a few hours," Kate said. She stopped to put her finger against the recognition panel outside their lab. It chirped and the pad blinked green. Next she bent down and pressed her eye against the sensor. A red light scanned her pupil.

"Welcome back, Doctor Lovato," said a robotic voice.

Kate stepped into the clean room with Ellis. They were suited up and at their stations within fifteen minutes—a new record.

Ellis went straight for the radiation-delivery machine

and Kate crossed over to her computer. She keyed in her information and scanned through the DNA sequencing data. It pulled up a list of animals with genes that matched the juveniles in Europe. The first was a brown bat with a spear-tipped nose. The next, a massive armadillo.

She pulled up her report and added the information. Time passed quickly as she worked. Not since developing Kryptonite had she found herself so completely focused on her work. Maybe it was because, for the first time since the outbreak, she was using her skills to do something other than develop a bioweapon.

When she had finished typing, she read over the document. A half-dozen new Variants had been identified and entered into the database throughout the world in the past week, bringing the total to over fifty. Kate's shoulders rounded under an all-too-familiar sense of hopelessness, pressing her down like a heavy weight. She pushed back against the urge to give up. The world needed her, maybe more than ever.

Kate brought up the reports and photos of the many different Variants they had catalogued before the deployment of Kryptonite. There were the Variants in the desert with camel humps, others in arctic climates covered in fur. Those in temperate woodlands had developed a bark-like skin that let them blend into their surroundings. Some in tropical climates had gills. Perhaps the oddest of them all was the thin green monster with triangular forearms that looked remarkably similar to a praying mantis. Then there were the Alphas, the massive and terrifyingly intelligent creatures that were able to coordinate attacks and command armies of lesser Variants. The Bone Collector was there. So was the White King.

And yet, somehow, their offspring had evolved into even more terrible monsters.

"Kate, you've got to see this."

"Give me a minute, please. I'm finishing up the report."

He twisted to look at her from the radiation-delivery machine. His face told her the report could wait. She hurried over, moving as quickly as her aching back and swollen feet would let her. Ellis pecked at the machine's keyboard with a purpose.

"I used tissue samples from juveniles in the US and the juveniles in Europe. Then I ran panels of chemical analyses and exposed the samples to a broad range of radiation, just like we did months ago."

"And?"

He stepped away and gestured toward the computer monitor. The screen was divided into two frames.

"US sample is on the left. European is on the right," he said. "Take a look."

Ellis clicked the button to activate the radiation-delivery machine. The two dime-sized samples started to cook. The sample from the United States began to vibrate from the gamma radiation. But the one from Europe sat idly in the dish.

A hissing came from the machine, and Kate's eyes went wide as she stared at the image on Ellis's screen. The US sample had melted. Ellis increased the rads on the European sample. They waited for several minutes before it began to react. By that point, the specimen on the left was nothing more than a sizzling mess of red flesh.

The sample on the right began to bubble, but instead of melting, the exterior hardened into a crusty layer, much like an overdone steak. Tiny, needlelike structures poked out of the surface. In a matter of minutes, the sample had mutated into a chunk of blackened, spiky flesh.

"What on earth?" Kate whispered.

"Fascinating, isn't it?" Ellis stepped closer to Kate. "The European juveniles are sensitive to radiation too. But instead of compromising their flesh, it mutates them."

Kate gasped. The EUF had been blowing up nuclear power plants to kill off massive pockets of the breeding monsters, and Operation Reach planned to drop thousands of radioactive bombs on strongholds.

"If the military proceeds with Operation Reach, they are going to create an army of mutated monsters we won't be able to stop."

Kate felt the baby kick. Leave it to Reed Beckham's son to understand how much this changed the war effort.

"Come on," she said. "We have to get a message to Vice President Johnson and the EUF before it's too late."

17

Beckham nearly dropped his binoculars when he heard that Team Ghost had survived Operation Beachhead. He'd been watching the USS *Monterey* from the glass window of the Plum Island CIC with Horn and Mayor Walker. He turned to smile at Lieutenant General Rayburn. A few faces looked up from the piles of paper on the table across the room, but most of the dozen soldiers seemed focused on their tasks.

Beckham felt like he had just dropped his rucksack after a forced march. He knew what an uphill battle Team Ghost and the rest of the military still faced in Europe, but at least his friends hadn't been lost in the massacre.

"Sounds like they're on a new mission, but I wasn't able to get any information," Rayburn said.

"Thank you, sir, for letting us know," Beckham said.

Rayburn nodded. It may have seemed a small favor to some, but for Beckham this spoke volumes about Rayburn's character. The lieutenant general had gone out on a limb to determine the fate of Team Ghost. That also told him that Rayburn wasn't too salty about having to hand off security details.

Beckham brought the binos back to his eyes to

watch two Apaches hovering over the water north of
the destroyer. He'd already scanned every corner of the
Monterey, but there wasn't a soul in sight. He handed the
binos to Rayburn, who in turn gave them to Walker.

"Command, this is Badger One," one of the pilots
said. "No sign of contacts below."

"I don't know what to make of it," Rayburn said.

"I know exactly what to make of it," Horn said.
"Wood's got multiple sleeper cells out there. He had
more than one unit hiding on that ship."

Walker approached the window. "I say blow it out of
the water."

"That's one hell of a valuable ship," Rayburn said,
stroking his jaw.

Horn looked at him like he was crazy. "Ain't worth
jack shit if it's been compromised . . . sir."

Rayburn didn't seem put off by Horn's attitude, but
Beckham had hoped his friend would know better than
to blow his top around the lieutenant general. For now,
at least, they needed to try to work with him.

"We could board with a Special Ops team. Clear any
hostiles and then send in the Medical Corps to scrub it
down," Rayburn suggested.

Beckham and Horn both replied no at the same time.

"Way too risky, sir," Beckham added. "We tried to
salvage the *Truxtun*. It did not end well."

Rayburn nodded once. "Alternate course of action?"

"My recommendation is to keep the ship in sight,"
Beckham said. Then he remembered that his role was no
longer to offer recommendations but to make decisions.
When it came to the safety and security of the island, he
was in charge. "If it comes closer, we'll sink her. Chances
are it's crawling with infected. Wood wants us to waste
our troops and ammo on the *Monterey* so we'll be easier

to kill when he comes for Plum Island. Our best move is not to play his game."

Walker glanced over from the window. "Have you heard what he's been saying on the Freedom Waves?"

"Yes, and it is all lies," Beckham said firmly.

"I've spoken to some of my counterparts at other SZTs, and most of them agree with him about President Ringgold."

"And what do you believe, Mayor?" Beckham asked.

"I believe Wood is a terrorist," Walker said. "But I also believe we might have to rethink our negotiation policy. I won't risk the lives of the innocent souls on this island for the sake of one woman in a West Virginia bunker."

Horn crossed his tattooed arms. "Is that so?"

Rayburn cut in. "We don't negotiate with terrorists. The only choice we have is to kill the son of a bitch."

A tense minute passed before Beckham jerked his chin toward the war table. He walked over and put his prosthetic hand on the smooth surface, remembering all the meetings they had held here before. Jensen, Smith, Chow, Jinx, Riley . . . so many of his brothers had sat here with him. Now they were buried in the island's over-flowing graveyard. The pain continued to eat Beckham's insides. His blood pressure had risen during the discussion, and he could feel his pulse pounding in his ears.

"Boss?" Horn said.

Beckham pulled out the chair at the head of the table and sat down. He gestured for Rayburn, Walker, and Horn to take seats with the other soldiers who were reading reports. It was the first time Beckham had sat at the helm of the war table. He looked down at the seat that had once been filled by Lieutenant Colonel Jensen. His friend had given his life to protect the island.

Now it's my job, he thought.

"Gentlemen, we're here to discuss the safety of Plum Island," Beckham said. He took a second to scan the faces around the table. This meeting wasn't just about securing the island. For Beckham, it was about getting a read on the lieutenant general and mayor. He'd already decided not to trust Walker, but he wasn't sure about Rayburn.

Beckham pointed to the USS *Monterey* and said, "ROT is growing stronger. We're not just facing a group of terrorists threatening our very fragile existence. We're talking about a civil war. The things Lieutenant Wood has been saying about President Ringgold aren't true, but people at the SZTs are listening. Some of them have already made up their minds to side with the enemy. That cannot be allowed to continue."

Several men exchanged glances around the table. Beckham took note of their names and then continued.

"Our primary job is to protect this island, but our duty is also to protect and support the president of the United States. Under her guidance, we have built and secured over seventy-five SZTs. She has answered the calls from our allies that are still battling the monsters overseas. Working with Vice President Johnson, she has helped eradicate the majority of the Variants here at home. Now she needs our help."

Beckham stood and let his words sink in, scrutinizing the reactions to his speech. Walker nodded enthusiastically, as if he'd been on Beckham's side all along. Rayburn remained stone-faced, and his soldiers kept silent.

Was it possible that Wood had a sleeper agent here on the island? Or even in this room? Beckham pushed the questions aside for now and continued.

"Expect the worst and then plan for it. That's what I've always told my men. Tonight we will reassess our defenses. Not just against Variants but against an invasion by ROT. There are still vulnerable areas of the island not covered by patrols or guard towers. Fences and cameras won't prevent an attack. I want every available man and woman who can fight assigned to those areas," Beckham said.

Rayburn pointed to a map. "My men have already identified all the weak points."

"I'd like to conduct my own analysis, sir."

Rayburn's nostrils flared above his mustache, but he didn't reply.

Horn shifted in the seat next to Beckham. Rayburn hadn't formally objected to the change in chain of command, but he clearly didn't like being questioned.

"I also want recon boats," Beckham said, using his prosthetic to point at four locations surrounding Plum Island. "If Wood decides to use the *Zumwalt* in an attack, we won't see it coming on radar. We need lookouts to warn us."

"Sir?" said a tentative voice.

Beckham looked across the table at a young man with short-cropped brown hair and blue eyes. He wore a Medical Corps uniform.

"Go ahead," Beckham said.

"Sir, I've heard a rumor..." He trailed off, glancing uneasily at Rayburn and Walker. Beckham gestured for the young soldier to continue. "Well, sir, people are saying that Team Ghost killed Colonel Zach Wood in cold blood. Isn't it possible his brother is specifically hunting for you and your men?"

Beckham felt Horn's gaze, but he didn't look to his friend. A moment of silence passed. He used it to think of Fitz, Kate, and everyone else Lieutenant Wood could connect to his brother's murder. If it came down to it, Beckham would turn himself over to the ROT leader if it meant saving the people he loved. But he had the feeling the terrorist would happily strike the entire island with a barrage of ballistic missiles just to make his point.

"This is about more than one man's search for revenge. If Andrew Wood is anything like his older brother, and it seems that he is," Beckham said, "then we have to assume he wants the worst for anyone who stands opposed to his vision of the future."

He glanced out of the large glass window overlooking the ocean. The *Monterey* continued to drift through the calm water, drawing ever nearer to the shores of Plum Island. The island had seen more than its share of tragedy and betrayal, but Beckham had believed they could rise from the ashes better and stronger than before. For a little while, he had thought they might be able to build something good here.

Beckham sighed and rubbed his hand across the stubble on his jaw. Wood didn't want to build anything. He was like a greedy child who'd rather break a toy than let anyone else play with it. If Andrew Wood didn't get the presidency, Beckham had no doubt he'd destroy every safe zone in the country, even if it doomed humanity to extinction.

Captain Rachel Davis and her team crouched low and raised their weapons to eye level. They moved quickly out of the forest and toward a distant road in the final rays of sunlight. Shadows lurked in every direction as they wove between wrecked cars and trucks. They cleared each one, switching their aim from back to front as they moved. Trash swirled in the gusting wind, but there wasn't anything alive out here. Nothing that she could see, anyway. She flashed a signal to Black and ordered him toward a pickup truck blocking the street ahead.

They needed a ride to OP119. Otherwise they were going to be walking for the next two hours through enemy territory. The longer they were out here, the higher the chance a juvenile would find them. Worse than that, she didn't know how much time they had before the *GW* departed. For all she knew, Wood had already finished loading the 140s onto the ship and could take off at any time.

Commandeering a vehicle was a risk, but letting the *GW* escape was an even greater one. The fate and future of America rested on her shoulders, and she was not going to fail.

Davis crouched behind a sedan and waited for Black to clear the pickup. He shouldered his SAW and approached slowly. After checking the cab, he motioned for Davis and Diaz to join him. They crossed the street in combat intervals, with Diaz covering their rear guard. Davis raked her sights over the road and the forest beyond. Satisfied, she approached the passenger door of the truck. Black was already working on hot-wiring the vehicle.

"Did you try this?" Diaz said. She reached into the cab and flipped the sun visor down. A key was hanging from an elastic band. She grinned and handed it to Black.

Feeling edgy, Davis lifted her M4 and checked their six for contacts. The terrain appeared to be clear, but once again she felt the sensation of being watched.

"Let me drive," Davis said. She switched places with Black, who handed her the key. "Come on, baby," she whispered as she cranked the ignition.

The engine coughed to life and rattled under the vibrating hood.

"And now every juvie in Florida knows we're here," Black muttered.

The engine soon settled into a low purr. Davis climbed into the cab and buckled herself in. "Get your ass in back, Black," she said. "Diaz, you're up front with me."

Black unfolded the bipod on his SAW and climbed into the bed of the truck. The clank on the top of the cab told Davis he was ready to roll. She checked the gauges and almost grinned when she saw a full tank of gas. That was their first piece of good luck in a long time.

Davis shifted the truck into first gear. The intersection ahead was mostly clear of vehicles, but there were plenty of places for juveniles to hide in the acres of forest that flanked their route.

If they knew you were here, you would already be dead.

Davis pulled back the slide on her M9 and kept it at the ready while she drove. Wind gusted through the broken passengers'- and driver's-side windows. Both women removed their gas masks to breathe in the fresh ocean air. Each breath brought with it guilt for the crewmen she'd left behind, and as she drove in the opposite direction of her ship, she felt an almost magnetic pull to turn around.

You'll get your chance, she reminded herself. *Quick and steady, Rachel. Quick and fucking steady is the name of the game.*

Davis weaved around an abandoned motorcycle and then a truck with a fishing boat on a trailer. The boat had overturned and slid clear across the roadway, coming up against the trees on the other side. Once they were past that obstacle, Davis gunned the engine to take advantage of the stretch of open road.

"How far are we from the outpost?" she asked.

Diaz was already looking at the map. "Take your next right. Then it's another ten miles down a frontage road on the left."

Clouds rolled across the sky, and Davis felt another storm moving in. That wasn't a bad thing. The clouds would help block out light that would reveal her position when they returned for the *GW*.

"Alright, Diaz," Davis said. "Call Command."

Diaz pulled the satellite phone from her vest. She dialed in the number Davis had given her and reported the 140s and the coordinates of the *GW*. By the time she had finished, the sun was dying on the horizon. Darkness washed over the road, and Davis flipped her NVGs into position.

"Command says to continue recon," Diaz said. "They asked us to contact Sergeant Marks and his men for an update on those One-Forties."

Davis gave the order with a nod.

Diaz pulled the ROT radio and scanned through the channels. She brought it up to her mouth and said, "Rhino One, Scorpion Two, do you copy? Over."

Static filled the cab of the truck. Marks wasn't answering.

Diaz tried again, to the same result, and shook her head.

A hundred thoughts ran through Davis's mind, but she had to focus on the task at hand. She steered around a police cruiser that was tipped on its side before returning to the center of the road.

"You think Marks and his men were compromised?" Diaz asked.

"I don't know," Davis said heavily, but in her gut she felt the silence on the other end of the radio could only mean the worst had befallen the gruff sergeant.

Diaz looked out the window. "You're going to blow up our home, aren't you?"

"We *can't* let ROT fire any of those One-Forties. Doing so could destroy everything we've fought for."

Davis thought of Team Ghost—of Beckham, Horn, and Fitz, especially. She could really use their help right now. She wondered how Fitz was doing in Europe and hoped he was having better luck than she was. The red-headed marine was someone she'd like to get to know better, if she ever got the chance, and she would have been proud to have him by her side now.

"Watch out!" Diaz suddenly shouted.

Davis slammed on the brakes as something white darted in front of the truck. A thud sounded from Black hitting the back window. The truck screamed to a stop, the smell of burning rubber filling the cab.

"What the hell was that?" Diaz asked. She grabbed her M4 and roved it back and forth across the windshield.

Heart kicking, Davis reached for her M9, grabbed the steering wheel in her other hand, and turned to look at Black.

"You okay up there?"

The reply came back in a grunt.

"You got eyes?"

"Negative. But that was definitely a juvie."

Diaz angled her M4 at the shoulder of the road. "I don't see anything."

"If there's one, there are more. Hold your fire unless you have a target," Davis said. "I'm going to try to outrun them."

The truck had just started moving again when Black said, "Hold up. On the road at nine o'clock."

Davis looked out the window at a dark, wet streak on the pavement.

"Blood," Black said. "It's injured."

"Good," Diaz replied.

Pushing down on the gas, Davis steered back onto the road. The tires squealed, and the truck jolted forward. She drove away with her gun still in her hand.

"OP119 is probably going to be a loss," Diaz said. "Are you sure we shouldn't go back to the ship? Maybe we can figure out a way to stop them without, you know, blowing the *GW* to smithereens."

"Even if there isn't anyone manning the post, we could still find explosives, ammo, and other gear."

Davis wrapped her fingers around the steering wheel and turned slightly to avoid a car. The moon split the clouds again, illuminating a gap in the forest on the left side of the road. Acres of marshland stretched into the distance.

"We got about four more miles to go," Diaz said.

A tap on the cab roof made Davis flinch. She eased off the gas and stopped the truck as Black leaned down.

"Captain, did you see that?" He pointed to the marshes. "Back up a bit."

Davis threw the truck into reverse and then backed up about a tenth of a mile.

"Slower," Black said.

The wetlands came into view once more. Boulders speckled the muck, but nothing moved in her green-hued view.

Davis put the truck in neutral and set the parking brake, but she kept her foot over the accelerator just in case. Diaz scooted next to her for a better look. They sat there listening to the sounds of chirping bugs and croaking frogs.

One of the rocks suddenly moved and an armored face rose out of the water, a snake dangling from its jaws.

The reptile twisted and jerked as the juvenile slurped it through its sucker lips.

"There's six of them," Diaz whispered.

Davis dearly wanted to give Black a dressing down. He should have known better than to risk their lives for a glimpse at these monsters. Then she saw something that made her pull down her NVGs to get a better look.

One of the juveniles was lit up by more than just moonlight. Its armor radiated a white glow like a night-light, and blood was seeping from cracks in the plating. A piercing wail silenced every living creature in the marsh.

Davis threw the truck into first, popped the brake, and punched the gas. In the rearview mirror, the juveniles broke into a frenzy. But instead of following the truck, they all scampered away from the injured creature.

Pushing down on the pedal, Davis sped away down the empty road. Her mind was racing. She had no idea what was wrong with the juvenile, but if she had to guess, it had something to do with the radiation they had been exposed to during Operation Extinction. She'd heard of creatures that had survived the blasts with horrific radiation burns, but she had never heard of them glowing.

Diaz pointed toward a radio tower protruding out of the forest about a half mile away on the left. Davis drove for another quarter mile before pulling off the road. She turned off the truck and slipped the key back under the visor.

The pavement was still wet from the earlier rain, and her boots slapped in the shallow puddles. She grabbed her M4 and moved quickly around the vehicle with the scope at eye level, sweeping the road, the forest, and finally the radio tower. A barbed-wire fence surrounded the small station. A sign hanging off the fence marked it as OP119.

"Diaz, on me. High and low, watch the cars and the trees. Black, you're on point. Clear the left side of the road. We rally up ahead on either side of the main gate. If things go south, double-time back to the truck."

Black and Diaz put their gas masks back on and nodded at Davis. She pushed her filter over her face as Black took off at a crouch. The road was clear, and besides the rustling of tree branches, there was no movement.

Diaz kept close, her M4 moving from car to forest to car, just like Davis had ordered. She had held her own so far, and Davis trusted the younger woman to have her back. But she couldn't ignore the unease she felt having someone so green by her side. They ran at a stealth crouch after Black. The gas mask crushed his Mohawk, but strands still jetted up like fins on the back of some prehistoric dinosaur.

He stopped, balled his right hand, and dropped to a knee. He signaled that there were two contacts near the fence ahead. Davis nodded and pointed at a sedan ahead of them. It looked like it had been driven off the road on purpose and nosed into a ditch.

Davis signaled to Diaz, who ran across the road to take up a position behind the sedan. Davis then moved to the left and hid behind a tree.

The sounds of nature rose around them. It was peaceful, but Davis knew the noise might disguise the monsters lurking in the darkness. The juveniles were still out there in the marsh, and their unusual behavior put her on edge.

Black flashed another signal, motioning to advance. Davis shouldered her M4 and slowly moved around the side of the tree. Black was a few paces ahead, creeping along the barbed-wire fence.

Crack! Crack! Crack!

The gunshots came so fast Davis didn't have time to react. Several rounds slammed into Black. He went down hard with a grunt. Return fire came from across the road where Diaz was hiding.

Davis peered around the tree and quickly located the hostiles. She spotted two of them, both wearing army fatigues and using barrels for cover. They weren't ROT soldiers, but they had shot Black.

"Hold your fire!" Davis shouted. "We're friendly!"

Another gunshot lanced in her direction, kicking up dirt by her boot. Black was crawling toward her, reaching up with a shaking hand. Another shot punched into the ground next to him.

"Stay down," Davis whispered. "And hold on."

She raised her gun to lay down suppressing fire. In a swift motion, she sprayed a three-round burst at the barrels, careful not to aim too well. She didn't want to actually hit either of the men if they were army.

Davis yelled, "Diaz, covering fire now!"

More pops came from across the street as Davis bolted toward Black. She grabbed him under his arms and pulled as hard as she could, dragging him across the dirt by the fence. The men popped up, but a flurry of shots pushed them back down.

Thatta girl, Diaz.

Davis heaved Black to the safety of the trees. He lay on his back, gasping for air. She threw her shoulder against a broad tree trunk, anticipating another salvo of rounds to chip away at their hiding place.

"Hold your fire!" she shouted again. "My name is Captain Rachel Davis of the USS *George Washington.* I'm a friendly, okay? But by God, if you fire another shot, I'll blow both your damn heads off."

The gunfire she expected never came. There was only the sound of Black still gasping for air. She bent down to check on him. Instead of bleeding out on the ground as she had feared, he was making a thumbs-up sign. Between panting breaths, he said, "Took 'em to my vest . . . I'll be okay."

She let out a sigh of relief.

"If you ain't here to take our post, then why you wearin' ROT uniforms?" one of the men shouted.

Davis cursed her stupidity. No wonder. They looked like the fucking enemy. Now she had to figure out how she was going to explain their situation without making things worse.

"We stole these uniforms from some dead guys!" Diaz shouted back.

Davis cursed under her breath, and even Black shook his head.

"ROT commandeered my ship. I need help taking it back. Please, lower your weapons and let us inside," Davis said. "There are juveniles a few miles from here."

"Lower *your* weapons and come out into the open with your hands up," one of the men replied.

The two soldiers stood with their rifles cradled across their chests.

"Do it, Diaz," Davis ordered. She looked down at Black. "You see anyone else in there?"

He shook his head again, still holding his chest.

"Can you walk?"

This time he nodded and struggled to his feet.

"We're coming around," Davis said. "Hold your fire."

Davis and Black slowly walked into the road, weapons at their sides. She pulled up her gas mask. Beside her, Diaz did the same thing, letting her mane of dark hair spill around her shoulders.

Both men looked at her like they hadn't seen a woman in months. That scared Davis almost more than the thought that they might shoot her.

"Hold on," one of them said. He came around the barrels and worked a lever. The gate slowly creaked open.

"I'm Sergeant Sanders," said the man on the left. He was thin and sharp-featured. A tattered baseball cap with a Miami Dolphins logo rested on his small head. "This here is PFC Robbie."

The other man, thicker set than Sanders, nodded at them but said nothing.

"Welcome to OP119, Captain Davis," Sanders said. He glanced over at Black. "Sorry about shootin' ya, brother. Thought you were one of those bastards from ROT. They slaughtered everyone else and destroyed our radio. It's just the two of us now."

"How'd you two survive?" Diaz asked, her hand moving slightly toward her sidearm.

"We were on a patrol with PFC Mantel and heard the gunfire. By the time we got back … it was too late."

"Where's Mantel?" Davis asked.

"Juveniles got him a few days ago."

Davis scrutinized the man for a lie but saw nothing on his face but the truth.

"So what is it exactly that you need from us, ma'am?" Sanders asked.

"You got any ordnance?"

Sanders whistled. "You're my kinda gal. I got a few crates of C-Four. The ROT assholes never found it."

"Show me," Davis replied. She had just stepped through the gate when a new sound emerged over the chirping insects. The noise pulled her gaze to the sky. It started off as a low hiss and rose into a growl.

Everyone watched, stricken, as a missile rose from the direction of the *GW* toward heaven, its fiery exhaust trailing it into the night. A second missile followed shortly behind. They curved off in different directions, leaving nothing but cylinders of dissipating smoke in their wakes.

Davis's stomach dropped, and she had to put a hand on Diaz's arm to steady herself.

They were already too late to stop Wood.

18

Panicked voices echoed down the long hallway as President Ringgold and her staff marched to the elevator that would take them to the underground President's Emergency Operations Center. She hated the PEOC, it made her feel claustrophobic. "I want updates," she said. "What the hell is happening out there?"

"The *GW* launched two missiles," Soprano said. "One is heading for SZT Sixty-One in New Orleans."

"And the other?"

"It...appears to be heading here."

Ringgold halted in the middle of the carpeted passage, her heart beating so hard she felt the rush of blood in her ears.

"Madam President," Nelson said firmly. He touched her elbow and said, "We need to keep moving."

Soprano echoed Nelson's comments. "We've got to get you belowground, Madam President. According to Captain Davis, those missiles are likely armed with hemorrhage."

"Jesus," Ringgold whispered. "We have to *do* something."

"President Ringgold, please," Barnes, the head of her

security team, urged. "We have approximately twenty-five minutes until impact, ma'am."

She looked at the first of the vault doors at the end of the hall. Seven months ago, back when she was just secretary of state, she had been evacuated to a similar facility that was eventually overrun with the Variants. She had barely escaped Raven Rock, and the idea of sealing herself underground once more made her breath come in quick, sharp gasps.

Ahead, a secret service agent was ushering staff through the steel doors. Another agent inside punched in the biometric access codes for the control systems. He swiped his card, and the final vault door opened to reveal a red elevator.

The agents waited at the elevator doors, every eye on her, but she couldn't move. She felt paralyzed, overwhelmed by the horror of what Wood had done.

Instead of coming to kill her himself—and risking his men in the process—he was letting the hemorrhage virus do the job for him. Even if she somehow avoided being turned, the infected would tear the Greenbrier apart in their mindless drive to feed.

And while she was hiding, the country could fall into civil war. Wood was proving himself to be ruthless, intelligent, and completely insane. The most dangerous type of enemy leader.

She could not let a man like that take the presidency.

That thought propelled her forward. She jogged down the hallway and entered the cramped elevator. Soprano sucked in his gut the best he could and got in next to Nelson, who was fiddling with his purple patterned tie.

The doors sealed and a slight jolt rocked the elevator as it descended. The old west wing had been six stories beneath the White House, but this time they had built the PEOC nearly twice that depth. It had taken a month and a half, but it would protect them against the missile attack.

They would also be stuck down here. At least she could still lead from the bunker. Rally her commanders, coordinate with the SZTs. There would be innocent casualties, and she would bear the guilt for every single death. Safe zones would fall, but the United States of America would survive.

The elevator jolted again and the doors whispered open. Ringgold stepped out and was immediately surrounded by agents. Their footfalls echoed down the tiled floor, speeding up when they rounded a corner and the red blast doors came into view. Inside, her staff was already busy working at the big screen monitors. The inbound missile was a red blot on one of the screens, its trajectory traced by a dotted line. On a screen to the right, there was video footage of SZT 61 in New Orleans. The streets were mostly empty, but she saw several civilians running down the sidewalks.

Get inside, just get somewhere safe.

"We were able to get a message to the mayor," Nelson said. "Because of the water table, SZT Sixty-One doesn't have any underground bunkers. As soon as that missile hits, it's going to cause chaos. We can expect a fifty-percent infection rate within two hours, and ninety-five percent in eight."

"How long do they have?" Ringgold asked.

"Five minutes, Madam President."

She forced herself to look away from the screen and walked to the long war table. Several of her cabinet members were already seated there, fingers laced together, looking at her for orders. She walked past them to Vice President Johnson and General Jay Allen, who were huddled around another monitor with radar data.

"We have twenty more minutes before impact," Johnson said. "Plenty of time to get almost everyone down here."

"Almost?" Ringgold asked.

"There are snipers and a marine patrol in the blast zone who may not make it in time."

Voices came from every direction. Ringgold slowly turned, taking it all in.

"Wood is on the Freedom Air Waves saying it was us," Allen said.

"What do you mean *us*?" The idea froze Ringgold.

"Those missiles came from the *GW*, Madam President," Allen said. His voice was measured but firm. "Not all of the SZTs believe we lost the ship. They think we fired on SZT Sixty-One."

Ringgold closed her eyes briefly. She couldn't believe the fiendish audacity of Wood's plan. Not only would this attack completely destabilize the country, but he'd even managed to make it look like she had ordered the strike on New Orleans. As the first territory to declare sovereignty, it would be the obvious target if she wanted to send a message to the other SZTs.

"We're getting a message from ROT," Allen said.

"Bring it online," Johnson said. He and Ringgold stood side by side as equals to face Lieutenant Wood.

The main monitor showed the face of the man Ringgold hated more than any other. Andrew Wood had his left leg crossed casually over his right. Behind him were stacks of boxes and weapons.

He grinned at the camera. "Guess you didn't believe me, Jan. I'm kind of shocked, actually. Sending in just three marines? I figured you would risk more lives. That is your MO, isn't it?"

Ringgold's heart skipped a beat. Had he caught Captain Davis?

"Sergeant Marks and his men put up a bit of a fight, but

in the end we got under their skin, too. I'll spare you the details because I have more important things to discuss."

"Trace that transmission," someone whispered behind Ringgold.

"I figured since you aren't going to hand over the presidency, I'll just take it from you. Most of the SZTs are coming around, but for those that don't, I have no problem killing a few more people in order to succeed in the mission to take back the country from a tyrant," Wood said dryly. "Those people will thank me later."

"You really think you're going to get away with this?" Ringgold snapped. "People will learn the truth about what you did."

"From who?" Wood tilted his head and waited for an answer. He grinned when none came. "You're about to go dark. Good-bye, Jan."

The lights flickered, and then the screens blinked and went off. Static broke from the speakers.

"Someone tell me what the hell is going on," Ringgold said, her voice rising just shy of a shout.

Allen conferred with a young communications officer named Sarah Jean. He nodded at her to report.

"They're blocking our outgoing transmissions," Jean said. "But we can still listen. The comms are full of chatter between SZTs trying to figure out what's going on. They're scared. They're saying..."

Ringgold studied the woman. She was putting on a brave face, but she could tell that Jean was too frightened to finish her report.

"It's all right. Just tell me what you heard."

"They want blood, Madam President. They think the government launched an attack against our own people."

"SZTs Eighteen, Thirty-Three, Forty-One, and Forty-Nine have seceded," called a voice from another comms station.

"That missile might be a blessing in disguise," Allen said. "Wood knows it will keep us down here long enough to turn every SZT against you, but it will also prevent anyone from storming the bunker for your head if they think there are infected here."

Everyone was looking to her for answers. Ringgold tried to pull herself together, but how could she combat a man like Wood? He wasn't just a terrorist, he was a sociopath. He had been setting her up for this all along. Steal the *GW*, hit Chicago first, then New Orleans, and put the blame on her. Even if she could get a message out, the other SZTs would be panicking. Mob mentality and bloodlust would take over.

Allen was right—threat of infection was the only thing preventing her own generals coming for her head. Ringgold paused to consider every possible strategy, knowing the clock was ticking. The only way to win against Wood was to make moves he couldn't predict.

A thought occurred to her. "Won't the other SZTs know it wasn't us if we get hit with a missile, too?" Ringgold asked.

Nelson looked toward the ground, and Soprano avoided her gaze.

"What? Someone answer me," she said, her voice rising with anger.

"Madam President, if we can't communicate with anyone out there, then it won't matter. They won't know anything other than the lies Wood tells them. At this point the other SZTs are already rallying around him."

Ringgold closed her eyes to think. The definition of *crazy* was doing the same thing over and over again. She had to do something to break that cycle. She snapped her eyes open and said, "How much time do we have before that missile hits?"

Allen looked back at the radar. "Fifteen minutes and thirty-two seconds."

"We're moving," Ringgold said.

"What? Where are you going?" Allen said, his face going red.

"I'm going to do exactly what Wood won't expect me to do." She paused and scanned the room. "Nelson and Soprano, you're with me. Barnes, grab your two best agents and follow us. Vice President Johnson will stay here and assume control of the PEOC. In the meantime, I'll get the truth out to the other SZTs and a message to General Nixon. I *will* make this right."

She approached her right-hand man and lowered her voice so that no one else could hear them. "George, I trust you to keep these people safe. If I don't make it, I know that you'll take Wood down before he destroys everything we've built."

Johnson held her gaze. For a moment it seemed like it was just the two of them in the chaotic Command Center. She had known him for only a couple of months, but together they had been through so much. He wasn't just her second-in-command. Johnson was her friend, and she knew that after she left the bunker they might never see each other again.

"Good luck, Madam President," he said. "It's been an honor serving with you."

He held out his hand and she took it, clasping it between her own.

"This isn't really good-bye," she said. "I'm just going to go visit some old friends."

Piero stumbled down the long corridor, rifle clutched in one hand and a lit candle in the other. If he didn't find food soon, he would crash. There would be no more adventures for Piero Angaran, the last man on earth.

Antonio was dead. His entire squad was dead.

His sister, his parents. His friends. The pretty girl at the gelato shop who always gave him an extra scoop for free.

All dead.

If he was truly the last man in the world, then why go on living?

You should end this now. End it all.

The candlelight flickered as he rounded a corner into a new tunnel. A cockroach darted up the wall. Piero licked his lips.

He halted and held up the candle. His hand shook as he searched for the bug. It must have vanished into a crevice he couldn't see.

End it. End it all, he thought again.

It wouldn't be difficult to make the nightmare stop. He could stick the muzzle in his mouth and blow off the top of his skull in less than five seconds. What was there left to live for? He was like a cockroach himself, scurrying through the shadows underground. That was no way for a man to live, even the last man on earth.

The mouse ran up his shoulder and chirped in his ear.

"Shhhhh, *piccolo amico*," Piero whispered. He still needed to come up with a name other than "little friend." The mouse moved again, claws scratching his vest.

"You just want me to find you food. You don't care if I kill myself."

The mouse chattered back as if it understood. Piero set his rifle against the wall. He opened his pocket, picked up the mouse, and dropped him inside. The tiny creature looked up at him, his little black eyes pleading.

"Fine," Piero said. "I'll find you something to eat, but you have to be quiet."

He picked his rifle up and continued down the tunnel. The warm glow of the candle spread over damp walls, revealing more ancient art of religious figures.

Piero recognized one of the images as Judas Iscariot. The farther he walked, the darker the scenes became. He saw a demon with horns and flames around its eyes. Feathered wings hung from the monster's back. He roved his candle back and forth to illuminate the entire battle between demons and angels.

He shivered and turned away from the fresco to check his map. The tattered paper he had picked up in the church overhead months ago was almost unreadable. He held up the flame and studied the wavy lines and blurred markings, but it was no use—he was lost. He only knew he was in a passage under the western part of the Vatican.

Raising his rifle, he pushed on. He took a right at the next bend and entered a familiar-looking tunnel, pausing for a second to study a cross on the wall that he swore he'd seen before.

Have I been here already?

Piero shook his head and kept moving. He hadn't ever been this far west.

A drop of water hit him in the face a few paces later. He backpedaled and opened his mouth. He waited for several seconds, and was rewarded with a drip that stung his tongue. The water tasted like metal. But he was too thirsty to care. His tongue arced, anxious for more.

The mouse moved again inside the pocket of his vest.

Another drop hit Piero's tongue. He stood there for what could have been a minute or an hour. He lost track of time as he waited for drip after drip. His arms shook from holding the candle and the rifle, but he didn't dare put either of them down.

It wasn't until the mouse started squeaking that Piero

finally set the candle down and wiped his mouth off with a filthy sleeve. He licked his cracked lips and opened his vest pocket. Then, very carefully, he positioned it under the dripping water.

The mouse sniffed the air and poked its head out of the pocket. A drop landed on the small creature, slicking its whiskers to its cheeks. It reached up with tiny paws and scooped some of the water into its mouth.

Light from the flame fell on a puddle at Piero's feet. He bent down and set his little friend next to the puddle. It scampered over and began drinking greedily.

"Stay," Piero whispered. He raised his rifle and turned on the night-vision optics to scope the tunnel. They flickered at first, the battery was dangerously low. Nothing moved in the green hue. He clicked off the optics to listen for the monsters. There was only the sound of dripping water and the mouse lapping up the puddle at Piero's feet.

The silence had grown on him over the months. He wasn't just used to it—he enjoyed it. And anything that broke the quiet sent Piero diving for the shadows.

Once, he had been a brave man. He had been a Special Operations soldier with the Fourth Alpini Parachutist Regiment. But the months of solitude had taken their toll on his mind. He knew he was going mad—but then, if he knew it, then was he really mad?

"What do you think? Am I crazy or not?"

The mouse continued drinking.

The *slurp-slurp* reminded Piero of his childhood dog, Ringo. The dog had been a hundred times bigger than the mouse, but they drank the same way, lapping water up like it was the last bowl on earth.

Piero bent down and held out his hands. "Time to move, Ringo."

The mouse looked up but then went back to drinking.

It might take Ringo some time to get used to the new name, but Piero already felt pleased by it. He felt the tickle of a smile on his face.

"Let's go, Ringo."

The mouse's white ears suddenly perked, and his black beady eyes went wild. Before Piero could pick the creature up, the mouse scampered into the darkness, squeaking in terror.

"Ringo!" Piero cried. He spun at another sound that the mouse had already detected—the scratch of talons on stone.

Piero scooped the candle up and blew it out. Darkness washed through the tunnel like a tidal wave. He raised his rifle toward the noise and clicked on the NVG optics.

Motion flickered in his crosshairs. A meaty creature with a bulbous torso clung to the ceiling like a vast, hairy spider. It dropped to the floor and bolted forward on all fours before he could see more of it.

The soldier Piero had once been would have stood his ground and fought. But now he turned and ran. The piercing wail of the monster followed him down the passage.

The shrieks continued as another joined the fray. The terrifying noises struck his ears like poorly tuned instruments. They were so loud he couldn't think straight.

He nearly tripped, his boots sliding across the ground. Piero regained his balance and then raised the scope to darkness. Fumbling with the optics, he clicked it on, over and over.

His heart caught in his chest.

The battery had finally died.

He was blind, but those creatures could see in the dark.

The sounds of the monsters closed in from both directions.

"No, no, no!" he said, slamming the side of the gun. He fired off a shot to the west, and then another to the east. The muzzle flashes lit up the passage for barely ten feet, and the afterimages lingered like sunbursts in his eyes.

"Ringo," Piero called. "Ringo, where are you?"

Clicking joints echoed all around, and Piero released another burst. Rounds chipped away at the stone ceiling and punched through flesh.

The creature shrieked in pain. A hissing noise, like air being let out of a tire followed. Piero ducked down, waiting for the sting and burn of acid to spray his flesh. But it didn't come. He stayed crouched and pivoted on his heels, jerking his rifle first in one direction and then the other. He had to choose: left or right?

There's another option.

Piero had nine bullets left. Not nearly enough to kill the monsters if they were armored juveniles, but plenty to end his own life.

But he had to make a decision now.

In his mind he saw the faces of all his friends and family. They sat on the steps overlooking the Trevi Fountain, eating gelato in the late-summer sunshine. The pretty girl from the shop waved at him, beckoning Piero over.

He angled the smoking muzzle toward his mouth, but before he could pull the trigger, he heard a chirp and a curious squeak. Ringo jumped onto his arm, climbed up his shoulder, and then dove into his vest pocket.

Piero pulled the gun away from his face and fired a shot to the west. This time the flash captured the creature stalking him. An emaciated Varianti with a swollen, hairy belly crept toward him. Every inch of its bony flesh was covered in rashes. Yet another creature that had escaped to the tunnels to avoid the bioweapon they had dropped on Rome.

He squeezed off two more shots, which missed. The creature seemed to twist and distort in the waning light. It jumped to the wall in a swift motion.

Piero tightened his grip on his gun and centered it in the direction the monster had leaped.

Six more bullets, make them count!

He fired again, and this time the flash lit up a mangled corpse wearing tattered vestments.

The sight made Piero's heart kick even harder. It was the priest he had killed. That meant his old hiding place, which he had abandoned days earlier, wasn't far. But how was that possible? He *had* been going west, not east. Had he been wandering in circles?

The scream of the Varianti dragged him back to the present moment. He fired bullets five and four. The blasts captured the creature hanging upside down from the ceiling. The *smack-smack* of swollen lips covered in open sores made him cringe.

He lined up a shot and squeezed the trigger just as something grabbed his leg.

Piero fell so fast he had no time to brace himself. He only just turned in time to land on his left shoulder so he didn't crush Ringo. His bones ground together at the joint, but the hot slash of a talon on his ankle was what made him scream.

He remembered the horror of three Varianti stripping one of his old friend's legs to the bone.

No, I will not go out like that!

Piero kicked at the beast and tried to struggle free. Another claw grabbed his shoulder from behind. He was lifted off the ground, squirming and screaming at the top of his lungs. The pair of beasts pulled him in different directions like two hyenas fighting over meat. His left shoulder flared with agony, and claws sank deeper into his ankle.

"Run, Ringo! Get out of here!"

The mouse squirmed in his pocket, squeaking frantically. Piero's left leg went numb as the monster behind him gave a mighty heave.

"Please, please let me go!" Piero yelled. Hot tears blurred around his eyes. He swatted with his free right hand, striking the cold, clammy flesh of a creature that had no ability to reason and no capacity for mercy.

The numbness worked its way up his body. This was it—his time had finally arrived. Where there should have been terror, Piero felt only a strange, floating sensation. It felt a lot like relief.

After avoiding death for so long, the last man on earth, Piero Angaran, was about to die.

The monsters pulled harder, stretching his muscles and tendons to their limits. He stopped screaming, or maybe he just couldn't hear himself anymore. He went limp. There was a silence, almost peaceful, until a screech shattered it into a million pieces.

Piero felt the pressure release on his arms and legs. Claws struck sparks on the walls as the two monsters retreated into the darkness.

"Ringo," he whispered. "Are you okay?"

The mouse moved in his pocket as he sat up. Piero reached over his shoulder and felt blood running from a deep gash. His legs weren't in much better shape, but he got to his feet and scrambled for his rifle.

A blast of air caught him in the face as he stood. It carried the sour, rotting fruit scent of the monsters.

Piero pulled a lighter from his pocket and struck it to look for his rifle. He found his candle in the process. He snatched it off the ground and lit it with a shaking hand. He grabbed his rifle and ran for the bars of his old hiding spot.

Another draft of air hit him as the approaching

demon flapped wings nearly the width of the hallway. He didn't dare turn to look.

"Hold on, Ringo. Don't jump out," Piero whispered. He set the candle near the bars, slung the rifle over his back, got onto his belly, and crawled under the gap.

His boots hit the floor of the tomb below with a thud. He snatched the candle and pulled his rifle through just as the winged juvenile reached the passage. It bent down to sniff the bars and grabbed them with claws the size of butcher knives. A quick yank ripped the entire pallet away from the stone.

Piero fell on his butt and palmed the ground to scoot backward. The candle fell on its side, but the flame continued to burn. He tried to grab it, but the monster stuck its bulbous head through the opening and snapped at him.

He stared in horror at the creature's horned nose and wart-covered face. It tilted its head and let out a bellowing shriek that covered him in mucus.

Piero pushed himself off the ground and called for Ringo to hold on. He limped across the small room and jumped onto the stairs as the beast tried to squirm through the entry into the tomb. Armor screeched against the stone behind him. He stopped on the fourth step when he realized he had left the candle. He looked back and saw the beast's head and shoulders were stuck in the opening.

You're still a soldier. Stay and kill it.

The mouse chirped for him to run.

No, run. Run and hide. Ringo is right.

His last candle was on the ground just feet away from the monster's jaws. But the monster was wedged in the gap. There was no way the thing could get inside.

Raising his rifle and taking stuttering breaths, Piero slowly walked back down the steps. Ringo kept up his desperate chirping sounds, but Piero had made up his mind. The creature watched his every move, lips popping and jagged teeth dripping saliva. The reptilian eyes focused on him as he aimed his rifle.

Piero saw a flash of something like fear in its gaze.

Does it know it is about to die?

Piero didn't care. He was done running and hiding like a cockroach.

He approached the beast as it squirmed again, armored shoulders cracking the foundation around the grate. Flecks of stone pattered the floor at Piero's feet.

For the first time in as long as he could remember, he stayed to fight.

Piero pushed the rifle into the monster's sucker mouth and pulled the trigger, once, then again just to be sure. A cracking sound echoed as the bullets ping-ponged inside the monster's skull. The beast let out a final breath, which smelled like a fish market left to rot in the summer sun. Its eyes were still locked onto Piero, even in death.

He almost fired another bullet for good measure, but he needed to save it for himself. If and when the time came, he wasn't going to let them take him—or his friend. His knife would do for Ringo first, and then he would end this nightmare once and for all.

He grabbed the candle and limped up the staircase that snaked up through Saint Peter's Basilica. Piero and Ringo were returning to the light. They weren't going to live in the darkness anymore.

Piero Angaran was a man, not a monster.

And if he was going to die, he was going to do it on a full stomach.

19

Fitz did his best to keep the impact of his blades minimal on the narrow stone steps leading up to the balcony, but they had been built when humans had shorter strides—and he doubted the medieval architects had considered mobility prosthetics like his in their plans. Every time Meg's hatchet clanked against his thigh or the speared tips of his blades scraped across a step, Dohi glared at him.

Fitz paused to reposition the hatchet, and Michel bumped into him from behind.

"What's the holdup?" the kid whispered. "We're almost there."

"Sorry," Fitz mumbled. He patted Apollo and let the dog go ahead. Moonlight streamed through small gaps between boarded-up windows and filled the balcony with ghostly rays of light.

Fitz stopped and pressed his eye against a gap, but he could only make out indistinct shapes and shadows below. Wind whistled past the basilica, followed by something else he couldn't quite place—a rumble, like a far-off earthquake.

He continued on, moving slowly up the balcony. Michel hurried past Fitz to the next set of windows, where a girl with braided blond hair sat on a crate. She stood as they approached, a revolver in her hand. She acknowledged their presence with a contemptuous glare.

"It's okay, they're friends," Michel whispered.

The girl sat back down on the crate and said something in French that didn't sound friendly at all.

"Take a look," Dohi whispered, beckoning Fitz over to another window.

Fitz raised the loose top board and leaned forward. It took a few seconds for his eyes to adjust to the darkness.

"What am I looking for?"

Dohi's response was lost in the same rumbling sound from before.

Fitz squinted and focused on a bulging mound of soil. He stepped back, then pushed his rifle out of the small opening to zoom in using the scope. The raised earth suddenly moved toward the wall of the basilica right underneath them. He cursed as a dozen more of the mounds emerged and darted forward. Something was moving just below the surface.

"What the hell are those things?" Fitz whispered.

Michel stepped up. "Let me see."

At first he just stood there looking through the gap in the boards, his shoulders subtly rising and falling as he took in calm breaths.

How is this kid so calm? Fitz wondered.

"Yup, those are Wormers," Michel announced a moment later. "The most I've ever seen. And if they're out there, the Pinchers and Black Beetles aren't far behind."

Fitz caught Dohi's worried gaze. It was the first time Fitz had ever seen a hint of fear in the man's features.

"I'll try Command again." Fitz flicked his comm mic back to his lips. "Lion One, Ghost One. Does anyone copy? Over."

Fitz bent back down to the small window while he

waited for a reply. Static rushed into his ear, then a muffled voice, more static, and finally a response.

"Copy, Ghost One. This is Lion One. We've been hit by another wave of Reavers. Took down our comm tower for almost an hour. How about a sitrep?"

"Roger, Lion One. I have the intel."

"Good job, son. Relay your intel to Lion Two. Wait one."

"Wait, sir. We have enemy-forces movement, and, uh—" Fitz didn't know how to describe what he'd just seen. What could he say?

"You there, Ghost?"

"Roger, Lion One. I'm here. These things... whatever they are, they're big, and they're moving underground now."

"Repeat. Underground?"

"That's right, Lion One. They're tunneling."

"We'll cook those ugly bastards no matter where they're hiding. Our bombers are standing by. Operation Reach is a go. We are just waiting on your intel and the intel from several other recon teams in Spain and Germany."

Fitz remembered what Mira had told him about the radiation.

"Lion One, there's something else. The creatures here seem to have mutated, and the locals think it's from radiation."

"Copy that, Ghost One. That's no surprise. We're getting a ton of reports of new Variants out there. But don't worry, our bombs will kill all of them."

"The dirty bombs, though. What if they make things worse?"

"Ghost One, you just focus on staying alive until I can get you an evac. You let me worry about the other shit. I'll pass your concerns up the chain of command."

"Roger that, sir. How long until our evac?"

There was a pause, then, "You'll have to wait a few hours. We lost another Apache, and the King Stallions were damaged. They're being repaired now. I got one in service and can't risk it right now."

Fitz's heart sank as he watched the approaching Wormers. The gardens were a network of brown veins webbing toward the basilica.

"We have hostiles closing on our location," Fitz said. "We aren't going to last out here."

"I'll get you that evac as soon as I can. Until then, hunker down. Good luck. Lion One out."

Bradley's transmission ended, and a woman's voice came over the channel.

"Ghost One, Lion Two. Ready to receive your report. Over."

Fitz was so stunned he couldn't manage a reply. Apollo whimpered and sat back on his haunches, sensing his handler's anxiety.

"Ghost One, Lion Two. Do you copy? Over."

"Lion Two, this is Ghost One," Fitz said heavily.

He did his duty and finished his mission by relaying the coordinates Mira had given him. Command now had the information they needed to take out the Variant and juvenile armies with radioactive bombs in the next phase of the invasion. Operation Reach was meant to kill the majority of the monsters, allowing the MEUs and supporting forces to advance toward Paris. He just hoped General Nixon knew what the hell he was doing.

After Fitz gave the last set of coordinates, his shoulders sagged and he found himself unable to meet the eyes of the people watching him. Bradley would wait to drop those bombs until they got out. He wouldn't break his promise to Beckham to get Team Ghost home in one piece. Or would he?

No... Team Ghost is expendable.

Fitz swallowed hard, knowing he might have just called in a death sentence for his team and these kids.

The greater good. That's what being a soldier is all about.

"Are we going to take your truck, Mister?" Michel asked. His gaze flitted to Fitz's laughing-joker bandanna, then to his eyes.

Fitz had considered taking the MATV, but now he wasn't going to risk leaving the building with all those things out there. He tried to think of other options. Maybe they could survive the Variant army by hiding in the crypts like the Ombres, but they would still be within the blast zone of Operation Reach.

Even if they did fight their way outside to the MATV, not all of them would fit inside. He couldn't leave a single one of these kids behind.

Apollo whined at his knee. The dog's tail was between his legs, and Fitz quickly saw why. A shadow had blotted out the moonlight streaming in through the gap in the boards. Dohi slowly replaced the board over the hole and took a step back. More shadows shrouded the room on all sides. The buffeting wind of the Reavers' wings slammed into the basilica like a brewing tornado.

Fitz motioned for everyone to move down the stairs, but he himself waited to get a final look at what they were facing. At the far end of the gardens, a pack of frail adult Variants prowled along a fort of bushes. To the north, a juvenile perched on a stone ledge, its head tilted to watch the sky. A dozen more of the armored beasts moved in from the parking lot. In the small wood to the west, a tree suddenly sagged into the earth. The branches swayed and vibrated as if the trunk was in a blender. It jolted violently before the base of the tree vanished into the earth, leaving only the top branches.

"Come on, sir," Dohi called.

Fitz raised a finger, watching as a black beast with a curved beak for a mouth emerged from the hole in the ground. It was almost twice the size of an average juvenile, but instead of the rigid, turtle-like armor he'd come to expect, this one had the smooth shell of a beetle.

"Jesus," Fitz whispered.

Dohi tapped him on the arm. "What do you see?"

He pulled his eye away and slowly lowered the board.

"The devil," he whispered back.

Ringgold ran as fast as she could across the new White House lawn. Her lungs burned with every chilly breath. Soprano had already stumbled twice and was now leaning on a secret service agent.

"Hurry!" Nelson yelled.

They ran toward an unmarked Sikorsky UH-60 Black Hawk. It had the same stealth modifications as the one SEAL Team Six had used to raid Osama Bin Laden's compound. Nelson claimed it would get them out of here without being detected.

"How much time?" Ringgold asked.

"Five minutes to clear the infection zone, Madam President," Nelson said, running smoothly beside her.

"What about the teams out here?"

"We lost contact with them."

Ringgold cursed. Snipers and marines were somewhere in the woods, rushing to get back, but with the comms down there was no way to know where they were. In five minutes, that missile would hit. And then they would start to turn...

An image of her cousin, her eyes turned yellow and bloody, flashed across her mind. She shook the nightmarish images away.

I will not *become a monster.*

The thump of rotors forced her thoughts back to the tarmac. Nelson was already at the chopper. He motioned for Ringgold to duck, then held out his hand to help her into the troop hold.

She took a seat and strapped the buckles across her chest. The lights of the old resort glowed warm and bright in the distance. Ringgold hated to leave it with nothing but the clothes on her back, but she hated leaving behind the majority of her staff even more.

"Three minutes!" Nelson shouted. "Hurry!"

Barnes jumped inside and took a seat next to Nelson. The remaining two agents heaved a wheezing Soprano inside and climbed in after him.

"Let's go!" Nelson held up a thumbs-up sign to the cockpit.

Ringgold watched the gardens fall away below them, saying a silent farewell to the roses she had loved. Then movement caught her eye.

"Down there!" she shouted.

Soprano was breathing heavily, his hand gripping his chest. He twisted to follow her finger to the eastern fences. A team of marines was opening the gate. They were still at least a quarter mile from the White House.

As she watched their progress, praying they'd make it to safety, Ringgold saw the fiery trail of the missile emerge over the horizon.

"Move it!" Nelson ordered. "Get us the hell out of here!"

The bird rolled hard to the right, making the harness tighten across her chest. Pain raced across her injured shoulder, but it seemed distant, like none of this was actually happening to her.

To the south, the missile was already descending

toward its target. Ringgold twisted to follow its trajectory as the pilots turned hard to the east.

"Thirty seconds!" Nelson yelled. "Punch it!"

"Fast as we can go!"

Ringgold barely heard the pilot's reply. She was watching the team of marines below. They had crossed the gardens and were running toward the door of the main building.

"They're almost inside!" Ringgold shouted.

She lost sight of the men as the missile exploded in midair. A brilliant blast blossomed over the gardens. The heat wave scorched the trees.

The chopper turned again, blocking her view.

"We're clear!" one of the pilots said.

Ringgold turned to look at the White House. The roof was smoking, but it wasn't the fire she was worried about. It was the viral payload.

"Did anybody see if those men got inside?" she asked.

"I'm sure they made it, ma'am," Nelson said, but she could tell he didn't really believe it.

Ringgold couldn't even find the words to reply. If Wood had his way, he was going to send humanity beyond the brink of extinction. She couldn't let that happen—she had to find Beckham. He had stopped Colonel Zach Wood, and now he was the only man she trusted to stop his lunatic brother before it was too late.

She watched in silence as the helicopter sped away from the smoldering resort, wondering if, even now, the hemorrhage virus was wreaking havoc on the people she had left behind.

Beckham touched the pocket containing Sheila's ring, wondering if he would ever find a quiet moment to propose to Kate. He'd thought about doing it tonight after dinner, but once again a crisis had intervened.

The beams from the jeep's headlights cut through the night as they pulled away from the lab building. Kate and Ellis were in the back seat discussing their findings, and Beckham was doing everything he could not to interrupt or ask questions.

As he watched them talking animatedly, their heads bent together, he felt a flicker of emotion. Not jealousy exactly. Ellis wasn't a romantic rival, but he did get to share something with Kate that Beckham couldn't. He'd always considered himself to be an intelligent guy, but those two were on a whole different level.

Beckham looked down at his ruined leg and his prosthetic hand. He'd been a different man when he'd fallen in love with Dr. Kate Lovato. Would she still want to marry him now?

Fitz had warned him about feelings like this. After the young marine had lost his legs in Iraq, he'd also lost a lot of his self-confidence. The important thing, he'd told Beckham, was not to pretend like nothing had happened. People would look at you differently. You'd look at yourself differently too.

What did Kate see when she looked at him now?

As if sensing his troubled thoughts, Kate glanced up and smiled at him. Her eyes were tired, and there were wrinkles on her forehead that hadn't existed seven months ago. She was still the most breathtaking woman he'd ever seen.

Beckham smiled back, a lopsided grin, and felt his dark mood lighten.

"So lemme get this straight," said Horn from the driver's seat. Unlike Beckham, the big guy had no problems with interrupting the scientific discussion in the back seat. "You're saying there are giant killer bats and bug-like Variants in France?"

Ellis began a scientific explanation of how the Variants had mutated from the radiation that had poisoned much of the country when the EUF blew up nuclear power plants. Beckham tried to follow it, but a hissing in his ear alerted him to a transmission for Command staff. He cupped his earpiece and saw Horn doing the same.

"There has been an attack on SZT Sixty-One in New Orleans," said a voice over the comms. "President Ringgold has reportedly launched a missile armed with the hemorrhage virus. All attempts to reach the Oval Office have gone unanswered. Plum Island is on Level-Four lockdown until further notice."

Horn locked eyes with Beckham. In the back seat, Ellis was still talking about radiation and epigenetic changes.

"Shut up, Doc," Horn said.

Ellis dropped his hands to his lap. "What? What'd I say?"

Air raid sirens answered his question, wailing from towers all across the island. Beckham relayed the news about the attack to Kate and Ellis.

"She would never do that," Kate said. "There's no way."

"This was Wood," Beckham said.

"Doesn't the mayor know that? What about General Rayburn?"

"They know. But I don't trust Walker, and I'm still not sure about Rayburn."

"If the White House is compromised, there's no one to relay our findings to the EUF. They'll proceed with Operation Reach and make things even worse," Ellis said, raking his hand through his slicked-back hair.

"Goddamn Andrew Wood," Kate said. "Damn that whole family."

Beckham felt Kate's rage and frustration in his own chest. If Operation Reach went ahead as planned, the radiation from the bombs could fuel even more nightmarish mutations in the juveniles.

The situation stateside looked grim too. And if Wood had really launched those missiles...How far would he go to avenge his brother's death? What did he really hope to gain? The White House going dark at the same time as the attack on New Orleans was troubling. If he'd been planning the campaign to destabilize the country, then framing President Ringgold for a bioweapon attack on her own people was a smart tactic. Through Beckham's muddled thoughts came the words of the soldier back at the Command Center.

Sir...Is it possible that Wood is hunting for you and your men?

"Reed?" Kate said.

"Not now. I'm trying to think."

In the rearview mirror, he saw her blue eyes flare with hurt and then look away.

"I'm sorry, Kate. I didn't mean to snap, I just—"

Another transmission hissed into his ear.

"Captain Beckham, we need you back at Command. ASAP."

It was Rayburn, and there was something about his voice that Beckham didn't like. As of right now, the only people he trusted on the island were in this jeep.

Horn yanked the steering wheel and took a right back into town.

"Captain Beckham, do you copy?"

"Yeah, I copy. I'll be there in twenty," Beckham replied.

Static hissed over the channel.

The silence was telling. Sometimes the words that weren't spoken were the biggest clue to a man's plan.

"Head back to the house," Beckham ordered. "We don't have much time."

"But Rayburn just said..." Instead of finishing his sentence, Horn twisted the wheel again and sped toward the residential area of the island.

"We'll get the kids, food, and supplies, and then we'll make our way to the Animal Disease Center buildings. Nobody goes out there anymore, but the structures are sound. Once you're all safe, I'll return to Command. Horn will stay to protect you until I come back."

"No!" Kate said. "You can't do this alone, Reed."

Horn nodded. "We should stick together, boss. Fuck going back to Command. I don't trust *nobody* there."

Beckham pulled Jensen's Colt .45 Peacemaker from his holster. He flipped open the loading gate, thumbed the hammer, and spun the cylinder to inspect the chambers. It had been months since he had used the gun for anything but target practice, but he'd kept it well maintained just in case.

"I think we have to assume Walker and Rayburn have already been or will be compromised. Walker's loyalty to the president is 'fair weather' at best, and Rayburn..." Beckham shook his head. "I'm just not sure about him."

He holstered the revolver. "What I am sure of is that Wood is coming here on the *Zumwalt* to get revenge for his brother."

There was a hard silence broken by Kate's no-nonsense voice, the one she used when she'd already made up her mind about something. "Then we face him with you. We're a family, all of us. We stick together."

"Fitz and Captain Davis aren't coming to save the day this time. They're both thousands of miles away," Beckham said. "And I'm not going to let Wood hurt any of you. Kate, you have to trust me on this. If I don't report in, they will come looking for me. I have to get ahead of this thing, and my first step is to go to Command to gather intel."

Kate raised an eyebrow. "And if it's a trap?"

"Then I fight my way out and rendezvous with you all later."

"You against how many men?" Horn said with a snort. "Boss, I hate to break it to you, but you ain't the soldier you used to be."

Beckham gritted his teeth. The words stung, but they were true. He was lucky if he could take on one trained opponent, let alone an entire post of them.

"Reed, you are staying with us or else we're coming with you." Kate's lip trembled as she sucked in a breath. "You are *not* leaving me to raise this baby on my own."

Hot tears prickled in his eyes. He cleared his throat and turned back to the windshield to think.

Horn pulled the jeep into the residential area. The streets and sidewalks were empty. Drapes were pulled across the windows of every house on their block.

"We make this quick," Beckham said.

Horn pulled up to their small house and killed the engine. "Do I have time to grab a beer? I sure as hell could use one."

Beckham almost laughed, but his chest was so tight he could hardly breathe. He got out of the jeep and opened the door for Kate, then offered his hand to help her out. A cold rush of wind rustled her hair. She looked fragile in the light from the street poles, but he knew she was stronger than she looked. Holding her hand in his left, he walked with her to the house.

Inside, Donna and the kids were just finishing dinner. She and her son, Bo, were a regular fixture at their house.

"There's some macaroni left over," she said. "Hope ya'll are hungry."

Tasha and Jenny sprang up from their chairs and rushed over to hug Horn. He wrapped his arms around the girls and bent down to whisper something to them.

"Thanks for babysitting," Kate said.

Donna smiled. "My pleasure. Bo is finally starting to talk again, and I think it's mostly because of the girls." She lowered her voice and whispered, "I think he's got a little crush on Tasha."

Kate forced a quick smile. Beckham could see that she was just barely holding things together.

He sat down next to Bo, who was picking at a piece of cheesy macaroni on his plate.

"Hey kid, how you doin'?" Beckham asked. "You want to go on a field trip?"

Bo shrugged. The little boy had been through hell, surviving the Variants on the mainland and then losing his father during the fight with the Bone Collector a few months ago. A kid his age should be out riding bikes and playing baseball, but Bo mostly clung to his mother's shadow.

Donna gave him a worried look. "What kind of a trip?"

Kate pulled her aside to explain, while Beckham followed Horn into the bedrooms. Their gear was already packed and ready to go. They grabbed the Bug-Out Bags, along with some extra weapons, and hurried back into the living room.

Beckham dropped his bag and, at the sound of a rap on the front door, pulled his Colt .45. He gestured for everyone to get back. Horn herded the kids into the hallway along with Kate, Ellis, and Donna. Then he grabbed his SAW and took up position in the family room.

They exchanged a glance, and Horn slowly walked up to the door to check the peephole.

"Holy shit," he whispered, stepping backward.

Beckham raised the gun, ready to put a round in anyone that threatened his family. His heart pounded so hard he thought it might break through his chest.

"Get up here, boss," Horn whispered.

Beckham pulled the hammer back and joined Horn at the door. He looked through the peephole. On the front step was a woman dressed in a rumpled suit. Two men waited at the end of the walk, watching the street. An American flag pin gleamed on the woman's lapel, but she had a shawl wrapped around her head like a hood, hiding her face.

"I'll be damned," Beckham said.

He had a pretty good idea who she was. He just had no idea what she was doing on his doorstep. He opened the door and stood aside. The woman let her hood fall, revealing a face Beckham hadn't been sure he would ever see again.

"Jan?" Kate's disbelieving voice called from the hallway. She rushed forward and embraced President Ringgold.

"It's good to see you," she said, patting Kate's back, then holding her out at arm's length to take a look at her. "When are you due?"

"Another three months," Kate said.

Ringgold smiled, but she looked exhausted. She turned and called to the men who had followed her to the door. "Barnes, you stay outside. Soprano, Nelson, come with me."

The man she'd addressed as Barnes nodded and stepped back outside, while the two men in suits followed Ringgold inside.

"I wish this was just a social call," Ringgold said, "but we have a situation. No, that's an understatement. We have a *catastrophe*. I assume you've already heard about New Orleans?"

They nodded, and Ringgold wasted no time in briefing them on the full situation. The missile attack on SZT 61 wasn't the only one Wood had launched.

Beckham looked over at the fearful faces of Donna and the children, who were watching them from the hallway. He jerked his chin at Horn, who shepherded them to the master bedroom. Horn joined Beckham, Kate, Ellis, and Ringgold a minute later. Beckham gestured for them all to take a seat in the living room.

"How did you get here?" he asked.

"We almost didn't. I...I ordered these men to accompany me and left Vice President Johnson in charge of the PEOC. We got out just in time, just as the missile came in. Almost everybody made it belowground, but there was a patrol..."

She trailed off, her voice breaking on the last word. Beckham felt her pain. He'd been forced to make hard choices on missions, too. He'd never intentionally left anyone behind, but sometimes there was no other choice. The president wasn't a Delta operator. She couldn't be expected to behave like a combat veteran, especially not with the threat of hemorrhage raining down on her.

"You did what you had to do, Madam President. But what I meant was, how did you land on the island without being spotted? We have checkpoints and patrols everywhere."

"Stealth helicopter. We landed not far from the abandoned Animal Disease Center buildings." Ringgold took a deep breath and squared her shoulders. "Captain

Beckham, you are the only man I can entrust with my safety. I've already asked you to protect this island, and now I am here to ask you to shelter me until Lieutenant Wood is stopped."

He held the president's gaze and said, "Ma'am, I wish to God I didn't have to tell you this, but Plum Island *isn't* safe anymore."

20

Captain Davis sat in the passenger seat of the pickup while Diaz drove. She checked and rechecked her weapons. It was the only thing that seemed to calm her down.

She felt like a rabid animal on a chain—a chain ready to snap.

Diaz stomped the pedal as they passed the juvenile-infested marsh. The beasts crouched in the muck. Davis watched them curiously as they passed. One of the creatures glanced up, but then went back to fishing for prey in the swamp. For once Davis directed her anger at something other than the monsters. ROT was a much bigger threat than the Variants now.

"Still can't get anyone at the PEOC?" Diaz asked.

Davis shook her head and put the satellite phone back in her vest. "They've gone dark."

"How about Marks?"

Davis shook her head again, trying not to think the worst about the silence on both ends.

Diaz tightened her grip on the steering wheel, like she was holding in another question.

"What?" Davis asked.

Diaz jerked her chin toward the back. "You think the White House is gone and Marks is dead, don't you?"

Davis took in a breath of the cool night air.

"I don't know, Diaz."

"What about Sanders and Robbie? Do you trust these guys?"

"I don't know," Davis repeated, trying not to snap at Diaz's barrage of questions.

Sergeant Sanders and PFC Robbie were sitting in the bed of the truck, weapons cradled across their chests. Neither of the men wore CBRN suits, but they did have NVGs. They both appeared exhausted, and judging by their wild shooting back at OP119, they weren't going to be much help. They had come through with the C4, though. Davis had enough to effectively scuttle the *GW* and destroy the 140s if charges were placed in the right spots.

But she was too late to prevent the first of the attacks, and she wouldn't forgive herself for that. She could still picture the twin exhaust trails as the missiles launched. Their trajectories were tattooed on her mind's eye. Davis couldn't be certain of their targets, but she would make damn sure Wood didn't get the chance to launch any more missiles from her ship.

"I'm surprised Black didn't beat the shit out of them," Diaz said, jerking her chin at the rearview mirror. "The bastards *shot* him."

In the back of the truck, Sanders pulled off his Dolphins hat and ran a hand over his head, then put the cap back on and bent the bill. Robbie raised his rifle to scope the side of the road.

"Black is lucky to be alive. He realizes that, and he also realizes we need Sanders and Robbie's help."

Diaz just nodded, her NVGs wobbling over her eyes. They were way too big for her. She still hadn't asked Davis what her plan was. That was good, because Davis wasn't exactly sure herself. First they had to find Marks and his men, assuming they were still alive. Then they would figure out how to board the *GW*—assuming the ship was even there.

Davis stroked her M4 and concentrated on taking deep breaths. She could almost feel her blood quickening in her veins as they neared Fort Pickens.

"Where should I pull off?" Diaz asked.

"How far out are we?"

"We just passed the intersection where we got this ride."

Davis looked out of the broken passenger window and cursed. She hadn't been paying attention. She was losing her edge.

"Pull over by that sign." She pointed at a billboard advertising deep-sea fishing excursions.

A salty breeze filled the truck as Diaz drove onto the shoulder and rolled to a stop. Davis jumped out and made her way to the bed. Sanders and Robbie were already sweeping the terrain for contacts. Black grabbed the bags of C4 and threw them over his shoulders.

"Black, you're on rear guard." She didn't need to tell him to keep an eye on the two new unofficial members of Team Scorpion. "Everyone else, on me."

The team followed her into the woods. The canopy of tropical trees swayed in the wind. Davis had to dodge branches as she worked her way through the jungle. She used the muzzle of her M4 to knock some out of the way while Diaz held others up so they could both pass.

The lance corporal raised her M4 and swept it over the foliage from nine o'clock to twelve o'clock, while Davis covered twelve to three o'clock. There were several blind spots, and it was difficult to hear over the buzzing chorus of insects.

The rally point she'd given Marks was a quarter mile away. She pushed on, moving faster despite the ache of her injuries and the ever-present fear that a juvenile would leap on her at any second.

Fort Pickens loomed like a shadow beyond the trees up ahead. She was working her way around a tree choked with vines when the all-too-familiar scent of rotting fruit made her freeze. She balled her right hand into a fist, her feet sinking into the mud with a gurgle when she stopped moving. A nickel-sized spider crawled up her arm. Davis fucking hated spiders, but she didn't dare move.

Once you'd smelled a Variant, you never forgot that stench.

Sweat dripped down her forehead as she listened for the monsters. The stink of moldy lemons faded away, and she shook the spider off. Another sweep for contacts revealed nothing but more bushes and tropical plants.

Davis flashed an advance signal and continued on. Sanders and Robbie moved quietly in the middle of their group, and Black kept a few paces behind them as they moved through the woods.

The slap of waves grew louder as they approached the rally point. Davis scoped a clearing ahead, cautiously moved into the center of the small break in the trees, and centered her crosshairs on the walls of Fort Pickens.

Nothing moved.

No one was here.

Davis searched the trees for any sign of Marks and his men. But she already knew, deep down, that they wouldn't be making the rendezvous.

"Isn't this the rally point?" Davis whispered, just to be sure.

Diaz nodded grimly.

Davis pointed at Sanders and Robbie. "Stay out of sight for now. Diaz, you stay here with them. Black, leave the C-Four here and follow me."

Diaz opened her mouth to protest, but Davis shook her head. She trusted her bodyguard to keep an eye on the men from the outpost—and frankly she wasn't sure Black could resist throwing a punch if she left him alone with them.

"Let's go." Davis jogged toward the clearing. Black gave Diaz the C4 and then ran to catch up. He kept his SAW at eye level with the muzzle roving back and forth.

They stopped at the edge of the foliage to push their gas masks into position before exchanging a nod. Beyond the trees rose a grassy embankment. On the other side stood the brick walls of Fort Pickens. Her heartbeat climbed toward her throat when she saw the *GW* was still in the harbor.

Ringgold hadn't sunk the ship, which meant Davis still had a chance to make things right. She flattened her body against the dirt and zoomed in on a ROT soldier moving on top of one of the fort walls. The crosshairs covered his torso. She moved them to his head as her finger tightened on the trigger.

Almost, Rachel. You'll get your chance.

She lowered her rifle and moved in a stealth crouch up the embankment. Every muscle in her body screamed at her. Black followed, and they hit the ground on the other side of the embankment together just as beams from a flashlight shot overhead. She heard footsteps in the dirt and the rustling of the tall grass on the hill as someone walked past.

Davis rolled to her back and angled her rifle up. Black held up two fingers toward her to signal two ROT soldiers. Taking them down would be easy, but she didn't want to draw attention to their position if they could avoid it.

The crunch of boots drew closer.

Shit…

She had to act.

Davis made sure her mask covered her face. Then she turned to Black and held her finger up to her lips. He shook his head in protest when she reached for her knife.

"Watch my six," Davis whispered.

She sprang up from the knee-high grass like a jack-in-the-box. The ROT men reared back in shock, then centered their SCARs on her.

"Woah, woah, friendly," Davis said. She scrutinized the men she was about to kill. The one on the right was middle-aged without any remarkable features. His partner, however, reminded her of Big Horn. He had the build of an athlete and the cauliflower ears of a wrestler.

"Hey man, what you doin' out here?" said the larger of the two men.

"Taking a shit…" Davis said, trailing off as something caught her eye farther along the beach. Three posts had been driven into the ground, and hanging from them was a trio of corpses. Their skin had been ripped away, leaving nothing but muscles and tendons.

The big man followed her gaze. "Those assholes thought they could take us with just three guys. I mean, what's the point? We already killed that black bitch who claimed she was the president. The fight's already over, man." He shook his head. "Idiots."

Davis let out a weak laugh, but her heart rate was racing as anger-fueled adrenaline dumped into her veins. "Yeah, idiots."

The smaller man was looking at her now—no, he was looking at her M4.

Shit. She had forgotten the ROT soldiers all carried SCARS.

Davis took a step toward the smaller man, keeping her center of gravity low, the blade of her knife reversed along her arm.

"Hey man," the other one said again.

She reached up and pulled off her helmet and gas mask, then shook her hair so it fell to her shoulders.

"I'm not a man," Davis said.

Both of the soldiers exchanged a laugh and the wrestler licked his lips.

"We're going to have some fun," the other man said.

She thrust the hidden knife into the soft spot under the smaller soldier's chin with a crunch as he reached out for her. A flash of motion came into her peripheral as Black tackled the larger ROT soldier into the dirt.

Davis yanked on her blade. It caught on his jawbone, and he stumbled forward, his mouth opening and closing. She lost her footing and fell on her back. The soldier crashed on top of her, but he was light and she easily rolled him off.

He lay there choking, his fingers grasping at the blade lodged into the bottom of his skull. Davis kicked him in the side of the head, then hurried over to Black. He was rolling in the grass with the other soldier, both of them grunting like wild animals.

The big guy had twenty or thirty pounds of muscle on Black. This ROT soldier wasn't going to be easy to kill. But that didn't mean she wouldn't enjoy it. She went back to the other one, who had finally fallen still, to retrieve her knife. She put her left boot on his shoulder and her right on his face, then yanked the blade free, stumbling backward in the process.

She walked back over to Black, who was kneeling on top of the ROT soldier. He had his hands around the bigger man's thick neck. Davis crouched down beside them. The soldier's eyes flitted from Black to Davis.

"Please," he choked. "Please."

Davis looked at the bodies on the beach, then back down at the ROT soldier.

"You stole my ship, executed my men, and launched a terrorist attack on the United States of America," she said. "Black, take your hands off him."

"Captain, what . . . ?"

"That's an order, Black."

He let go and backed off, staring at Davis like she'd gone crazy.

"Thank you," the soldier wheezed. He started to sit up, but Davis pushed him back down and planted a knee in his groin. She pressed with her entire body weight, and the man cried out in pain.

She leaned down over the soldier and said softly, "I'm in a hurry, so I'll have to make this quick."

Clamping one hand over the man's mouth, she used the other to plunge the knife into his right eye. She felt a slight resistance and then a pop as the blade went in. He bucked and screamed, but the noise was muffled by her gloved palm.

"That's for Humphrey," she said. Davis didn't recognize her own voice. It was low and cold, completely devoid of mercy.

She yanked the knife free, then blinded his other eye.

"And that's for Marks and his men."

Waves of bloodred anger rolled across her vision. She had never felt like this before, not even when she'd taken the bullet for President Ringgold during Kramer's mutiny. Not even when she'd found out that her husband and nephew had died during the outbreak. She'd kept the pain and fear bottled up inside for so long.

Captain Rachel Davis had reached her breaking point. She was sick of living in a world where the evil just kept coming no matter how many times you beat it down. She was done playing by the rules. If she had to destroy her own goddamn ship to stop Wood from dropping the hemorrhage virus on more innocents, then that's what she'd do.

And if she had to become a monster to save the world, then that was okay too.

The ROT soldier was still trying to scream as she slit his throat.

She looked down at her handiwork and felt...nothing. It was an easier death than he'd deserved.

When Davis looked up, Team Scorpion was gathered around, staring at her. Diaz looked like she might throw up, but Black wore an expression of grim satisfaction. Sanders and Robbie just looked terrified.

"Got you some uniforms, boys," she said to the newcomers. "Put them on. We're moving out."

Three candles burned on the altar in the crypt under the Basilica of Saint Thérèse. The putrid scent of body odor hung in the stagnant air. Team Ghost waited by the barricaded door with Michel. The other children huddled around Mira in the center of the room. The weak glow of the candlelight illuminated their frightened gazes.

"Don't worry," Michel whispered to Fitz. "They don't look so tough now, but the Ombres will fight when the time comes. How do you think we survived so long against the monsters?"

Fitz looked back at the Ombres. He no longer saw children carrying weapons too big for them or kids in filthy clothing. He saw survivors who had been forced to grow up too early. Their parents had probably told them the same thing Fitz's parents told him when he was young: Monsters weren't real. But these kids knew the truth.

Whatever doubts he'd had before, Fitz knew that when the time came, Michel would be right.

The Ombres would fight.

"All of the barricades are secured, and the escape route outside to the MATV is ready if we need it," Dohi whispered.

Fitz nodded. They were all set, but he wasn't exactly confident in his plan. He wasn't even sure he was doing the right thing.

What would Beckham do?

It was the third time Fitz had asked himself that question today. But Beckham wasn't here. All the choices were up to Fitz, and there weren't any good ones. If Fitz made a run for the MATV now, he risked losing everything. Then again, if the Variants found them down here, they wouldn't stand a chance. In the end, Fitz had decided to hunker down and wait, like Bradley had ordered, hoping the monsters passed over the basilica and that Command would send evac before Operation Reach started.

All around them, the walls groaned like a hungry stomach. Now he knew what Jonah felt like when the whale swallowed him.

Some of the children whimpered as dust fell from the ceiling. Mira shushed them with a finger to her mouth.

"Can those things get through stone?" Rico asked.

Michel nodded. "Mira said that's how they got my dad and his men. He was at Versailles. They broke right through the walls."

"They might pass us by," she whispered. "We need to keep quiet."

Tanaka didn't look convinced. He shouldered his rifle and pointed the muzzle at the barricade. It was pretty impressive for such a makeshift structure, built with pews, bookshelves, and tables made of heavy wood. But it wouldn't hold the monsters for long.

Stevenson and Dohi flanked the barricade, weapons raised. Rico lifted her shotgun with deliberate care, but the stock banged against her ammo pouch. The sudden breach of silence made Fitz cringe.

Creaking rafters overhead seemed to answer the sound. More dust rained down. Apollo stood, hackles raised and a low growl rumbling in his throat. Fitz put a hand on the dog's flank, and Apollo settled back onto his haunches.

Silence reigned again. Fitz's mind drifted to Plum Island. He'd promised he would be back in time to see Kate and Beckham's child born, but now it looked like it would be a miracle if he made it home at all.

Don't think like that, Marine.

Fitz had survived worse odds back in New York when it was just him and Apollo. He had Team Ghost and the Ombres with him this time.

Dohi shifted his rifle toward the ceiling as yet more dust rained down. The barricade creaked behind them, and he whipped his gun toward the sound.

Silence filled the space again.

Fitz moved a sweaty finger to the trigger of his rifle and balled his other hand into a fist. His eyes flitted from face to face. The candle flames were the only motion in the entire room, swaying back and forth in an unseen breeze.

Apollo stood abruptly, and his tail dropped between his legs. That was his tell, a warning of what was about to happen.

The Variants were coming.

Cracks webbed across the center of the ceiling. A crunching came from the opposite side of the room near the altar. The ground broke open, chunks of ancient stone pushing up. One of the flames went out, and darkness shifted across the room.

A guttural thud echoed through the basilica above. Something massive was at the main entrance. The sounds of splintering and snapping wood followed as the monster broke through.

A sound like a cross between a snake and an insect rose into a piercing wail. Several of the kids dropped their weapons and cupped their hands over their ears. The blond girl from the tower took off running for the corner, only to trip over a crack in the ground. She fell to her knees, but Michel ran to pick her up. He moved quickly like a football player weaving between obstacles to get to her. Her knee was bleeding, and tears traced tracks down her dirty cheeks.

Something inside Fitz snapped at the sight. He took in everything like a machine, processing it quickly and efficiently. The fear of failure vanished, replaced by the confidence Beckham had worked to instill in him as they trained and fought together.

"Ghost, watch your zones of fire!" Fitz roared. "Mira, get the kids out of here!" He flashed signals to his team. Stevenson, Tanaka, and Dohi remained at the barricade while Fitz, Apollo, and Rico ran toward the altar.

A three-foot-wide section of stone floor broke apart. Dirt exploded out of the opening, and with it came something that made Fitz slow his pace. Tentacles wormed their way up through the earth, reaching blindly for their prey.

Rico shouted at the kids who had run in that direction to get back.

Fitz grabbed a boy wearing a scarf around his face and pointed at the staircase across the room. "Follow Mira!"

The kid might not have understood the English

command, but he got the gist of it. He took off running, guided only by the light of the two remaining candles. By the time Fitz had turned back to the altar, the monster squirming in the dirt was almost free.

The tentacles worked to heave the creature free of the earth. Its arms and legs were shriveled, almost vestigial, and hung limp from its soft, pale underbelly. Armored fins lined its back, and two horns protruded from the beast's forehead. A pair of sunken, ghostly white eyes gazed around the room, blinking rapidly as if even the dim candlelight hurt them.

It was difficult to imagine that this creature had once been a man, but a glance between its legs showed that the thing was male.

One of the tentacles reached out for Fitz, and he finally shook off his shock and opened fire. Gunshots broke out all around him, joining the fray. Stone cracked, and whole blocks fell from the ceiling. The chorus of destruction was joined by the frightened screams of the children and Apollo's frantic barking.

. In the sacred crypts beneath the Basilica of Saint Thérèse, all hell was breaking loose.

The final candles went out, plunging them into darkness.

Fitz flipped his NVGs into position, then shot the Wormer with a three-round burst. Blood poured from the wounds, but it didn't die. It moved toward them like an octopus, pulling itself along with its tentacles.

Rico fired into its open mouth, blowing away spiky teeth and sending the thing flipping from side to side on the ground, screeching in agony.

Apollo snapped at one of the tentacles as the dying monster flailed in his direction. Fitz whirled to fire on a second Wormer that had punched through the floor behind him. Tanaka sliced through the whipping tentacles with his long sword. One of them wrapped around his blade and pulled it out of Tanaka's grip, but he stabbed at the tentacle repeatedly with his shorter blade until it let go.

Across the room, Mira and the kids stopped. She herded them toward the staircase, but a Wormer broke through the ground in front of their exit, cutting them off. She fired her AK-47 at it, shouting French words that Fitz only half understood.

Michel and two of the other kids fired their rifles, and dozens of rounds punched through the monster's flesh. It slumped to the ground, half its body still inside its tunnel.

The Wormers were surprisingly easy to kill compared to other Variants, but if they'd compromised the foundation of the basilica, they could bring the entire building down. Especially with the weight of the beast thundering about in the main worship area above them. Fitz heard the thing's feet hitting the tiles, the *thud-thud* even louder than the gunfire.

Muzzle bursts lit the room with their brilliant flashes, giving Fitz a glimpse of the battle. Six Wormers had broken through the floor, and another worked its way through the wall above the altar. A kid in his teens crumpled to the floor, blood pooling around him from multiple gunshot wounds.

Shit, shit, shit. Was that us? It couldn't have been us.

He looked around the room at the other kids. Michel and the two kids with him were firing in disciplined bursts, but some others were shooting in random directions. A bullet whipped past Fitz's helmet.

"Watch your fire! Dammit!"

"We have to get out of here!" Rico shouted.

"Get to the exit!" Fitz yelled back. "And watch your fucking zones of fire!"

Mira was already helping the children climb over the

dead Wormer to get to the staircase. In the back of the room near the barricade, Stevenson and Dohi were firing at three more monsters that had burst through the ground, pinning them in a corner.

The pounding footsteps above them suddenly changed direction. Fitz raised his rifle upward as another network of cracks raced across the ceiling near the trapped members of Team Ghost.

"Get away from the barricade!" Fitz yelled.

The men either couldn't hear him or were too busy to answer. They continued cutting down Wormers as more broke through the walls and floor.

Fitz put a burst into the wrinkled face of a monster that wriggled through an opening to his right. The stone floor rose to his left, and the fins of another Wormer broke through like a shark under the surface. He fired the rest of his magazine at the raised dirt. The floor stopped moving.

An impact like a battering ram shook the barricade. One of the pews fell away.

That was the only warning they got.

Stevenson and Dohi were still turning around when the beast smashed into the doors with a force unlike any Fitz had witnessed before. The barricade blew apart, sending the heavy wooden furniture flying. A pew hit Stevenson in the side, knocking him to the ground. He pushed himself to his feet and raised his SAW. Dohi flanked him, while Tanaka continued to slice through the Wormers.

"Move, Ghost!" Fitz shouted. "To the MATV!" He searched for a target, but his men were in the way. Gunfire lanced into the door as the beast smashed its way through. A piercing hiss answered the shots.

Fitz cut down another Wormer emerging from the floor, then ran toward his men. Apollo and Rico were right behind him, and at the exit, Mira and Michel ushered the last of the kids into the stairwell.

A high-pitched scream pierced the air. Fitz turned just in time to see a Wormer wrap its tentacles around the girl with the blond braid.

Michel grabbed her other arm, but the creature was stronger and he lost his grip. She vanished inside the cavernous tunnel, her shoe falling off her foot and hitting the floor as she struggled in vain to get free.

"No!" Michel yelled. "Leila!"

Fitz gritted his teeth and turned to Rico. "Make sure they get to the MATV. Apollo, go with Rico."

The dog hesitated and then ran back to the Ombres on Rico's heels. Fitz changed magazines as he hustled toward the destroyed barricade. Tanaka, Stevenson, and Dohi held their own against the Wormers, but the monstrous creatures weren't the only threat.

The Black Beetle tore away the last of the barricade. It moved like a sumo wrestler, low to the ground and deceptively fast. The sheer size of it was intimidating enough, but Fitz had no doubt the serrated mandibles framing its jaw, as well as the jagged spikes lining its limbs, would tear Team Ghost apart in seconds.

Fitz fired half his magazine into the monster. The rounds pecked at the creature's armored shell but didn't draw blood. It turned slowly, its bulbous, multifaceted eyes flitting back and forth to see where the shots had come from.

"Retreat!" Fitz yelled. "Fucking retreat!"

The Beetle let out a guttural hiss that was followed by a loud crunch. The sound made Fitz turn to see the beast biting the head off an emaciated Variant that must have come through one of the Wormer tunnels. The snack kept it distracted long enough for Tanaka, Stevenson, and Dohi to escape. With a final swipe of his sword,

Tanaka took down the last of the Wormers, and the trio ran for the stairs with Fitz.

For a moment, he thought they were all going to make it, but that fleeting second of hope was ripped away by a loud crack and a human scream.

The Beetle had finished feeding. It picked up one of the fallen pews and threw it at Dohi. The wood hit him in the back and he tumbled into a mound of broken stone around one of the Wormer holes.

"Dohi!" Fitz yelled.

Stevenson fired his SAW into the Beetle's face, making it crouch down and retract its beady head into the cover of its shell.

Fitz ran toward Dohi's limp body. He was curled up in a fetal position. Halfway there, a pair of talons gripped the lip of stone surrounding the Wormer tunnel, and a Variant peeked through the opening into the room. Fitz squeezed off a shot that hit the monster between its reptilian eyes.

"Cover us!" Fitz yelled to Stevenson and Tanaka. They opened up on the Beetle again while Fitz checked Dohi's pulse. It was strong, but he was unconscious, and he had a head and back injury.

"Get Dohi out of here," Fitz yelled.

Stevenson let his SAW hang on its sling and bent down to scoop Dohi up. With a grunt, Stevenson hefted his comrade over his shoulders. Fitz grabbed Dohi's M4 and loaded the grenade launcher.

The Wormer holes continued to disgorge starving Variants. They scattered and came together to attack the Beetle, but the frail adults were no match for the beast. It tore through the Variants with spiky arms and claws.

"Tanaka, Stevenson, get Dohi to the truck!" Fitz shouted.

"What about you, sir?" Tanaka yelled back. He fired

off a burst that hit the Beetle in the head. It swung at the air with a skeletal arm and bellowed in anger, but the beast still didn't go down.

"I got this!" Fitz screamed. "Make sure the kids get into the MATV safely!"

Stevenson carried Dohi up the staircase, and Tanaka followed after a second of hesitation. A streak of black-and-tan fur raced down the stairs in the wrong direction, and a moment later Apollo bounded to Fitz's side.

"Get out of here, boy," Fitz said. The dog bared his teeth at the monsters and growled, clearly determined to fight by Fitz's side. If they got out of this, he and the German shepherd were going to have a long talk about obeying orders.

Fitz shouldered Dohi's rifle and aimed the launcher at the beast. It shook a Variant off its shell and ripped the head off another monster. Holding a breath in his chest, Fitz waited for the right moment. He couldn't let the creatures follow them outside, or they would never make it to the truck.

The Beetle barreled into another pack of Variants, crushing them flat with its massive shell. The smaller monsters fanned out across the room in retreat, leaving Fitz and Apollo to face the abomination.

Tilting its head from side to side, it scanned the room and then locked onto Fitz with its compound eyes. Instead of shooting the Beetle directly, Fitz fired a grenade into a Wormer hole in the center of the room. Earth, stone, and splinters of wood mushroomed in front of the Beetle, pelting its face and shell. The creature swatted at the debris raining down around it.

Fitz reloaded and aimed just above the creature's head.

"Die, you ugly piece of shit!" He pulled the trigger and turned away from the monster.

The explosion thumped behind him, heavy and loud, as Fitz ran for the exit, dragging Apollo with him by the collar. At the bottom of the stairs, he turned to watch the ceiling cave in on top of the Beetle, the stones crushing its shell and splattering the ground with green blood.

Fitz and Apollo loped up the steps, emerging through a door at the side of the Basilica of Saint Thérèse.

The Ombres and Team Ghost were huddled in the gardens not two hundred feet from the MATV. They had their weapons out, but they weren't firing. Dozens of Black Beetles and Wormers, full-grown juveniles, and ravening adult Variants waited for them. Reavers circled overhead like vultures waiting for a meal. The army of mutated monsters closed in, and Fitz felt the last tendrils of hope trailing away like smoke into the night.

21

President Ringgold had taken one hell of a risk coming to Plum Island, but leaders were only as smart as the men and women they chose to surround themselves with. She had chosen refuge with some of the most brilliant minds and courageous hearts left in the world.

She sat beside Kate at a kitchen table covered in bullets and stacks of magazines, listening to Nelson and Soprano argue with Beckham and Horn about the best way to protect her.

In the other room, Tasha, Jenny, and Bo were playing quietly with a few toys in front of the fireplace. Ellis and Donna sat on the couch supervising the children. Every few minutes, Ellis looked up as if to check on what was being said in the kitchen.

Sick of listening to their endless argument, Ringgold spoke up. "Enough. How did it even come to this? I'm the president of the United States, and I'm on the run."

Kate put her hand over Ringgold's and offered a warm smile. "You came to the right place."

"We'll protect you," Beckham said. His tone was confident and reassuring. "That's what we do, ma'am."

She trusted his word, knowing he would never dishonor himself by breaking it. But still, something tugged at her insides. She couldn't ignore her fear that her precarious rebuilding efforts would all come crashing down around them.

Then Beckham said something that made her pulse quicken.

"But we can only protect you if we disappear. I don't trust Walker or Rayburn. We can't go to them for anything. If word leaks that you're on Plum Island, Wood will kill everyone here. Rayburn and Walker have to know that. I'm not willing to risk them selling you out, so we have to get out of here."

"He's right. They'll try to use you as a bargaining chip," Nelson said.

"It will be okay. We'll figure this out. For your sake and ours." Kate looked down and rubbed a hand over the swell of her stomach.

"What about Fitz and the other forces in Europe?" Horn asked. "Wouldn't they rally against Wood? Let's call some of our boys and girls back to the home front."

"I didn't want to, but I have to contact General Nixon and request reinforcements," Ringgold said. "Meanwhile, I need to be able to talk to the mayors of the SZTs—and I need to do it from a safe location."

Horn crossed his tattooed arms over his chest. "Not sure we got any 'safe locations' left, ma'am. No disrespect."

"That's why I came here," Ringgold said. "Because I can't trust anyone else." She let the words sink in before continuing. "I wasn't going to sit in that bunker like I did at Raven Rock, waiting to die from the virus or at the hands of our own military."

"I also have to get an urgent message to General Nixon and the EUF," Kate said. "And not just because we need their help here. Ellis and I found something—"

"Something that could change the tide of this war."

The voice came from the family room. Ellis stood and

shoved his hands into his lab-coat pockets as he crossed into the kitchen.

"We have to tell them to halt Operation Reach," he said. "The radiation won't kill the Variants in Europe. It will only make things worse."

Ringgold narrowed her eyes. "What do you mean?"

"The Variants over there have evolved differently. The radiation causes a variety of mutations including—"

"Shhh," Horn said. "I don't want my girls to hear that shit."

Ellis lowered his voice. "Instead of killing them, the radiation mutates them. They have had more time to develop there, relatively unchecked. We're not exactly sure what differences in their genetic makeup have caused it to happen, but... you've heard of the monsters with wings, right? The Reavers?"

Ringgold nodded, and Kate picked up the explanation.

"We've also identified Variants with chitinous shells like beetles. Who knows how many others there are out there, or how much worse things would get if we irradiate them further?"

"We're looking at a disaster a hundred times worse than Operation Liberty," said Ellis.

Ringgold reached up to put her palm over her face, hiding her expression. The scar tissue on her shoulder burned. She wasn't sure if it was a phantom feeling this time, but it sure felt real.

Beckham scanned the room, his gaze falling on Kate last. They shared a worried look that made Ringgold wonder if she'd made the right decision. Coming here put their lives in jeopardy.

Nelson looked at his watch. "Operation Reach is scheduled to start in a few hours."

"Is there a way to get a message over there without giving away our location?" Ringgold asked.

Beckham cracked his head from side to side. "Not if it comes from you, Madam President. Who's going to believe you if Wood is on the radio waves saying you're destroying your own SZTs?"

"I'll do it."

Every face shifted toward Ellis.

He stepped forward. "I'll get a message to General Nixon and the EUF, but I'll need an escort."

The hushed voices of the children and the crackle of burning logs in the fireplace filled the silence that followed his statement. Outside, the air raid sirens had stopped wailing. For a moment Ringgold forgot where she was and enjoyed the quiet.

"Alright," Beckham finally said. "Here's what I think we should do. But we got to do it quick. If I don't report to Command soon, they are going to come looking for me."

"I bought us about thirty minutes," Horn said. "Told Rayburn that Kate isn't feeling well but that you'll be there as soon as you can."

Beckham nodded and pushed down on the edge of a map with his prosthetic hand. "I'll take our pickup and drive Ellis to this radio tower. It's not heavily guarded, and he should be able to get a message through once we clear the building."

"No," Kate said. "We're staying together."

"We will, but first we have to get this message off." Beckham turned to her, his jaw set. "Kate, you know someone has to—"

She held up a hand. "I know…but Pat can't go out there dressed in a white lab coat. He'll show up from a mile away."

Ellis looked down at his coat, frowned, then peeled it off. Kate walked over to the hall closet and found a dark hoodie of Beckham's and her navy-blue NASA ball cap.

"Be careful, Pat," she said, folding his coat over her arm. "I'll hang on to this for you until you get back."

"Thanks," Ellis replied. "You be careful too."

"Big Horn, you take Kate, Donna, and the kids in the jeep," Beckham said. "President Ringgold, your agents and staff will have to squeeze in somehow, unless we can find another vehicle."

"We have our own transportation," Soprano said.

"What? I thought you came in a chopper," Horn said.

"I...hot-wired a truck," Nelson said. "It's a Range Rover. Somebody left it parked at the edge of town, and there was nobody around, so..."

"Okay," Beckham said. "That's good. You take the Rover. Follow Horn to the Animal Disease Center buildings. Your chopper is close, right? There's also a boat there that we can take if we have to leave the island by sea."

"And go where?" Horn said.

Beckham hesitated. "I'm not sure."

"So you don't have a plan?" Soprano asked.

Horn snorted. "You got a better one, big guy? Because you came to us, and as far as I can tell, you didn't bring much firepower."

Nelson removed his tie and folded it neatly into his pocket. "We still have the Black Hawk. And we didn't come alone."

"How many agents you got?" Horn asked.

"Three," Nelson said after a beat.

Horn laughed condescendingly. "Three, plus us, against God knows how many of Wood's people. I'm sorry, but this is all crazy. Girls, come here. We need to get ready to go."

Ringgold studied Beckham as he rose from his seat. There were deep bags under his eyes, and his movements were slower than they had been before his injuries in Washington, DC. He wasn't the same man she had met at Raven Rock.

"We move in five," he said.

The front door creaked open and Barnes looked in. "There are two bogies incoming from the east. Look like Little Birds."

Beckham snatched the map off the table. "Everyone grab your gear. We're moving now!"

Beckham and Horn led the group outside. They threw their bags into the jeep while Barnes and the other two agents loaded the black Range Rover. Beckham arranged to drive Ellis to the radio tower in Donna's pickup truck.

Ringgold watched the two Little Birds sweep over the west side of the island. Their spotlights flickered over the terrain. They were searching for someone, and it wasn't hard to guess who.

Kate's voice pulled Ringgold's attention back to the driveway.

"I don't know about this, Reed. I still don't think we should split up."

Beckham unslung a rifle from his back. "I won't be any good if I'm worried about you. And if what you said is true, then our friends overseas are about to march into hell. I can't let that happen."

Kate put her arms around him, kissed his lips, and then whispered something in his ear that Ringgold couldn't hear. Everything was happening so fast she almost missed the sound of footfalls across the street. Beckham pulled his revolver and pointed it at a bearded man. He was holding the hand of a young boy about the same age as Bo.

"Jesus, Jake, you scared the shit out of me," Beckham said. He lowered his gun and holstered it. "What the hell are you doing out here?"

"Could ask you the same thing," Jake replied. "Where ya'll going? And what was with the sirens?"

"Ma'am, please get into the vehicle," Barnes said to Ringgold. She squeezed into the Range Rover between Soprano and another agent. Barnes took the wheel, and Nelson got into the passenger seat. The third agent got into the back and started loading shells into his shotgun.

Beckham tossed Jake a machine gun and gestured toward the jeep. The man led his boy over to the door, and Beckham approached the Range Rover to speak to Barnes. "Keep your lights off. Curfew is in effect, but patrols will be active. If you're spotted, you haul ass to the rally point."

"Got it," Barnes said. "And thanks."

Beckham patted the driver door and hurried back to the pickup. The three vehicles backed out one by one. Barnes reversed over the fresh sod, kicking up grass and dirt. The jeep was the first to pull out, and as they peeled away, Kate held up a hand and waved to Ringgold. She returned the gesture.

The convoy rolled through the residential neighborhood at a low speed. There wasn't a single vehicle on the road. Streetlamps illuminated the prefab houses from an actual power source and not generators like many of the safe-zone territories. She'd visited dozens of them across the United States, and very few looked like the one on Plum Island. Most were walled off with concrete barriers topped with razor wire and machine-gun nests. What she saw here, on the island, was the America she had fought to bring back from the brink of destruction. Mailboxes in front yards. A barking dog. The scent of freshly cut grass. Families eating dinner together.

Beckham took a right at the next street, and she watched the silhouette of the truck vanish into the darkness.

"Good luck, Captain," Ringgold whispered. She looked back out the window at the last block of houses. When she was a kid, she had ridden her bike to rich neighborhoods at night to look in windows from the sidewalk and see what other families had. Sometimes she would pretend she lived in one of those nice houses.

Growing up in the projects hadn't been easy, but seeing what was possible had motivated Ringgold to fight her way out of the poverty and violence. Looking in from the outside had always filled her with hope.

She clung to that hope now. It was the only thing keeping her going.

Beckham drove the truck into a cornfield for cover. He hadn't seen a single headlight on the road, but he didn't want to leave the pickup in plain sight.

He killed the engine and scanned the woods across the road. A tower jutted out of the canopy in the distance. That was their target.

"Coast looks clear," Ellis said.

"Can't always believe your eyes."

Beckham picked up his rifle and used the scope to scan the area. Beside him, Ellis cleared his throat.

"I'd like a gun, please. I know you have plenty to spare."

Beckham lowered his rifle to study the man. When

they'd first met, Ellis had been a timid, annoying scientist Beckham had to babysit. He was still annoying, of course, but he had also earned Beckham's respect. Ellis had stepped up, time and again, to save lives. Now he might just be a key player in saving their forces in Europe.

Beckham wasn't the same man he'd been back then, either. In his current state, he might actually be less of a threat than Ellis. He handed over an M9 pistol, and to Beckham's surprise, the doctor pulled back the slide to chamber a round.

"I've been practicing," he said with a shrug.

"Okay, Doc, listen very closely. We get in, you send your messages, and then we book it."

"Got it."

"Stay behind me at all times."

"Okay."

"And don't shoot anyone unless I give the order."

Ellis raised an eyebrow. "Reed, believe it or not, I can handle myself. Can we get moving?"

Beckham reached into his vest pocket where he kept the two most precious things he owned. The first was a picture of his mom. He pulled it out, kissed the plastic sleeve, and replaced it. The other was the ring Horn had given him. He was beginning to think that the perfect moment to propose would never come.

A breeze whipped through his hair as he quietly shut the truck door. The black fleece jacket and the bulletproof vest he wore over the top kept out most of the chill, but the temperature was plummeting. It wouldn't be long before winter hit Plum Island.

"Behind me. Back-to-back. Eyes out to either side and on our six," Beckham reminded him.

"Six is behind us, right?" When Beckham looked

back at him in dismay, Ellis just grinned. He raised the M9, and together they moved out.

Beckham crossed to the other side of the road. The tower was supposed to be guarded by a sentry, but most of the men had been reassigned to more vulnerable areas. He couldn't see any vehicles or soldiers outside.

After flashing an advance signal, Beckham tucked the butt of his gun under his left shoulder and gripped the trigger guard with his index finger. He propped the rifle up on his prosthetic hand.

Don't think of Kate. Don't think of Fitz. Don't think of Horn or his girls. Don't think of President Ringgold. Don't think of anything but completing this mission.

Tonight the aches and pains of his many injuries were buried by a rush of adrenaline. Beckham was back from retirement. He still didn't feel a hundred percent—not even fifty percent—but he was back in his element, a soldier on a mission.

He stopped to scope the road, then moved at a hunch and raked the crosshairs in an arc from nine o'clock to three o'clock. The darkness, the chill of the air, the buzz of bugs, and the uncertainty of their mission transported him back to the night he'd led Team Ghost to Building 8. If he could have only known the monsters they would face beneath the research facility...

A crunch came from under his blade, snapping him back to the present. He stepped out of the bed of leaves, cleared the road one last time, then moved to the shoulder. Ellis's footsteps behind him indicated the doctor was moving as instructed. Beckham glanced back and had to smile when he saw Ellis roving the path behind them with his M9 at the ready. They moved down into the ditch and up into the fort of trees.

Beckham put his back up against the trunk of a tree

and leaned to the right to check for contacts through the wall of branches. He still saw no sign of a sentry around the fenced-in tower.

Pushing his scope to eye level, Beckham continued into the thick foliage. Snags pulled on his fleece, and his blade threatened to tangle in the weeds and vines as he made his way forward. He hugged the trunks for protection, moving from base to base and staying out of the open as much as possible.

When he reached the clearing, he crouched and zoomed in on the concrete box of a building. It was small, with only a single control room. A lawn of overgrown grass separated the woods and the gate outside the tower.

Ellis knelt behind him, keeping low. Beckham let out an icy breath and went to signal an advance when he saw a puff of smoke. The scent of a cigarette hit his nose a moment later.

"Down," he whispered.

Ellis flattened his body on the ground next to Beckham.

"We got one contact," Beckham whispered. "You stay here."

He crawled through the grass—something he hadn't tried since losing his hand and part of his leg. It was a lot harder than it used to be. Another cloud of smoke swirled into the air, and Beckham got up and ran for the fence instead.

When he reached it, he slung the rifle over his back and grabbed the bolt cutters from his pack. The cutters slipped off the lock, and he had to try again to position them. Without the strength of both hands, he couldn't get the jaws to bite down hard enough.

Beckham closed his eyes for a moment, trying to

control his frustration. Exhaling, he waved to Ellis for help. The doctor ran across the field and took over with the cutters while Beckham grabbed his M4 and centered the muzzle on the corner where he'd seen the smoke.

Ellis broke through the lock and held out a hand to prevent the chain from clanking. Beckham squeezed past him. He angled his M4 up a ladder leading to the tower and then approached the side of the building. Hugging the wall, he raised his rifle. The smoke was gone, but there was a zipping sound coming from around the corner.

Beckham moved into position and centered his gun at the sentry, who was standing with his back turned to the building. An arc of steaming liquid hit the ground a few feet away.

"Pull up your pants and put your hands on your head," Beckham said.

The guard looked over his shoulder, then stumbled as he tried to run.

"Take it easy," Beckham said.

The moonlight illuminated the familiar face of an older marine with crow's feet and graying facial hair. Beckham remembered him from the embassy building the day of the town hall meeting. The respect he had shown then made it very difficult to do what Beckham needed to do.

"You the only one here?"

"Yes. What is this?" the marine asked, pulling his trousers up and doing his belt.

"Don't ask questions, just do as I say. Put your hands on your head and don't move. You have a key to the building?"

The marine nodded.

"Good. Hand it over."

"Captain, I—"

"Just do it," Beckham said.

The marine raised his hands.

"What's your name?" Beckham asked.

"Huxley," the marine replied.

"Alright, Huxley. Keys. Now."

He locked eyes with Beckham and said, "There's something you should know, Captain."

Beckham didn't have time to chat. "I'm sorry," he said. In a swift motion, he stepped forward and butted the marine in the side of the head with his M4. Huxley crashed to the ground, unconscious.

"Ellis," Beckham whispered.

The doctor came around the corner and stared at the marine.

"Little help, please," Beckham said.

He handed Ellis a zip tie. Ellis grabbed the marine's hands and bound them together while Beckham worked on his feet. When they had finished, Beckham apologized a second time before he dug through Huxley's pockets for the keys. He gave them to Ellis.

He approached the door with his gun shouldered and glanced up at the tower that was going to get their message to Europe. Clouds rolled across the dark sky, but he saw no sign of the Little Birds or other aircraft. The road was still empty.

Beckham took a step back as Ellis unlocked the door. He nodded, and the doctor pushed the steel door open. Beckham burst into the dimly lit control room, raking his gun over the sparsely furnished space. A bank of lights overhead flickered on, spreading a glow over a comms station on the left wall and a table littered with magazines and empty coffee cups on the right. Two chairs faced a computer monitor in the center of the room.

There was no one else here. Huxley hadn't lied after all.

"Clear," Beckham said. "Move your ass, Ellis."

The doctor ran, not to the radio but to the computer station, and pulled something from his backpack. While Ellis typed at the keyboard, Beckham shut the door. The windowless room was humid despite the chill outside.

"What are you doing, Doc?"

Ellis inserted a flash drive into the computer. "Uploading a report and relaying a message to my European counterparts. They're working with the EUF. I'll record the video for General Nixon, too."

"Maybe I should do the talking when it comes to General Nixon."

"What, you don't think he'll take me seriously? I've got a science hat." He turned slightly with a smug grin and pointed at his NASA cap. Then he reached up to reposition the webcam so it centered on him.

"This is an urgent message from Doctor Pat Ellis of Plum Island, asking you to abort Operation Reach. My partner, Doctor Kate Lovato, and I have discovered that the juvenile Variants in Europe respond to radioactive isotopes differently than those in the US. Instead of compromising their flesh, it mutates them ..."

Beckham crossed the room and left Ellis to continue his report. He put his ear against the door to listen, but it was difficult to hear over Ellis spewing rapid-fire jargon in the background. He unlocked the door and slowly opened it, raising his weapon.

Nothing stirred in the lawn or the road beyond. Beckham walked outside and checked on Huxley. The man was still lying in the dirt, unconscious.

"Sorry, brother," Beckham whispered. He lowered his rifle and walked back around the corner. A faint crunching noise made him pause. His eyes flitted from the sky to the road and finally to the cornfield. He couldn't see them, but he could hear the hum of vehicles on the gravel road on the other side of the crops.

"Shit." Beckham hurried back into the building. "Ellis, hurry the hell up. We got company."

"Just about done."

Ellis had finished recording his video but was now busy typing.

"What are you doing?"

"Uploading the data! Get over here if you're going to record the video to General Nixon."

Beckham looked back outside when he heard diesel engines. He scanned the road from left to right.

Ellis turned from the station. "What the hell is that?"

"Trouble!" Beckham yelled back. He ducked down into a crouch and directed his gun toward the field of cornstalks.

"On second thought, you go ahead and record that video to General Nixon," Beckham said. "And do it fast!"

He slowly backpedaled into the room with his weapon covering the road and the crops. The blurred vision in his right eye made it hard to judge distances. He blinked, trying to focus, and all at once three Humvees exploded out of the field and tore onto the gravel road. A chunk of ice formed in Beckham's guts. They were cut off from their truck.

Ellis continued talking into the cam, turning to look over his shoulder every few seconds.

"We're out of time!" Beckham shouted.

"Done. The videos and the report are uploading. They'll send as soon as they finish."

Beckham grabbed the doctor by his arm and pulled him outside. They couldn't stay here to make sure the videos were sent. They had to run for the woods and find a way to the Animal Disease Center buildings on foot. And with no way to radio Horn, they were on their own.

A bullet hit the door as they bolted out of the building. "Stay down!" Beckham said. He stopped to fire at the lead Humvee. His gun slipped on his prosthetic hand, but he recovered and squeezed off a burst. The bullets punched through the hood and windshield, making the driver swerve before the gunner in the turret could fire.

Ellis raised his pistol, but Beckham yanked him out of the line of fire. They made it another couple of yards before a pair of Little Birds swooped over the trees to the east. He turned back to the control room, but a stream of gunfire was chewing up the door and concrete walls, forcing Beckham and Ellis to their stomachs. The rounds came from all directions. They were completely surrounded.

Beckham gasped for air. His vision seemed to be getting worse, and his aching muscles tightened around his chest.

He spat out a curse. This was not the way Reed Beckham—Delta Force operator, former leader of Team Ghost, and, God willing, future husband and father— would die. He heaved himself to his knees and then stood, rifle raised.

"Get back inside!" Beckham yelled. He squeezed off a shot that hit the gunner in the turret of the lead Humvee. With a pang of guilt, he watched the man slump into the vehicle. The other two turrets opened up with the 240s, rounds kicking up dirt in a wide circle around Beckham and Ellis.

These guys were either terrible shots or else their orders were to capture and not kill. That told Beckham someone wanted them alive. He would use that to his advantage. He shifted his muzzle to the sky to fire on the Little Birds as they came around for another pass. The bullets pinged off the side of the closest chopper, forcing the pilots to pull away.

"You want some too?" Beckham shouted. He fired off another shot that hit the second bird in the windshield. Then he pivoted and sent three more bursts at the closest Humvee. Rounds shattered the driver's windshield. The internal machine inside him flipped his senses to full alert, and his weapon became another appendage, like his prosthetics.

His aim was true.

He *was* a Delta operator again.

A flurry of shots answered his own, one of them hitting him in his blade. He bit his lip as he went down and hit the dirt.

Motherfuckers, Beckham thought. He spat and pushed himself up on his good knee.

"Come on!" he yelled as he fired on the Humvee to the left. Another gunner fell. Ellis joined in, the *pop-pop* of his pistol cracking next to Beckham.

"I said to get clear!"

"You need my help!"

Beckham gritted his teeth and swallowed a mixture of saliva and blood. He pulled out his empty magazine and palmed another into the gun.

The soldiers opened their doors and hid behind them.

Beckham couldn't tell if they were Rayburn's men or Wood's, but at this point it didn't matter. He would kill every last one of them.

Ellis hit one of the men in the boot. He crashed to the ground, and Beckham shot him in the torso as he attempted to crawl back to safety.

The helicopters flew back around the building. The

wind from their blades slammed into Beckham and Ellis. One of them descended toward the open field while the other laid down covering fire. Beckham raised his M4 at a sniper clipped to the side of the bird.

He squeezed off a shot the same second the sniper fired. The enemy round zipped into his prosthetic hand, blowing it to pieces and sending his M4 cartwheeling away.

A piece of shrapnel grazed his temple. He winced and reached for his Colt .45. Pulling it from the holster, he then struggled to cock the hammer and raise the gun.

"Fuck you!" Beckham yelled. He fired a shot that streaked into the heavens. His next went wide, but Ellis managed a shot that hit the sniper in the chest. The man dropped his rifle and went limp in his straps.

Beckham trained his pistol on the windshield of the Little Bird, a much easier target. The pilot pulled away before he could fire, but the second bird hovered.

Rounds tore up the ground around Beckham. One whizzed past his ear.

"I'm out!" Ellis yelled.

"Then fucking run!"

Beckham squeezed off rounds three and four at the chopper. He aimed at the bird, then the Humvees. The soldiers were standing now, and they approached with their rifles shouldered.

"Give up, Captain!"

Beckham roved his gun toward the voice. It sounded familiar. He'd heard it taunting him in his dreams...but no, this wasn't Colonel Wood.

It was his little brother, the madman who planned to destroy the world.

Lieutenant Andrew Wood stepped out of a Humvee and approached the building within a fort of soldiers.

The toxins had all but ruined the vision in his right eye, but Beckham didn't need both of them to nail a head shot. He held in a breath, lined up the sights, and fired.

Wood jerked to the left when he saw the gun, and Beckham's bullet hit the ROT soldier behind him instead.

"You stupid fuck!" Wood yelled.

Beckham squeezed the trigger again just as something hard and sharp hit him in the back. He landed on his face in the dirt, his good eye pressed against the ground.

"I'm sorry, Captain," came a voice, "but I just saved your life."

Beckham squirmed and lifted his head to see Huxley. Ellis was still on his knees, but his hands were up now and his gun was on the ground.

Beckham tried to push himself up with his good hand and his stump of an arm, but a boot pressed on his back, holding him down.

"Damn it, stay down," Huxley growled.

"That will do, Marine," said Wood. "Step away from the traitor. I'll take it from here."

The boot relieved its pressure on his back, but before he could sit up, a kick to his side made him wheeze in pain. Another connected with his jaw, lighting up his skull with stars and knocking loose a tooth. A third kick felt like it broke a rib.

"Don't kill him," Ellis said, his voice trembling.

"Who the hell are you?" asked Wood.

"My name is Doctor Pat Ellis. We were sending a message to Europe to warn them—"

"Fuck Europe," Wood snarled. "And I highly doubt that's all you were doing, Doctor. I hate to disappoint you, but there's nobody left out there to call for help. I've already won."

Beckham spat out the broken tooth and gasped for air. Two ROT soldiers rolled him to his back and pinned his arms down with their boots. He blinked away the blood and tried to focus.

"So you're the great Captain Reed Beckham," Wood said. His eyes flitted up and down Beckham's body. "You don't look like much."

Beckham struggled, but the boots pressed down harder.

Wood leaned down, sniffing the air.

"You smell like a fucking dog. I'm not even sure the Variants are going to want you," he said. His thin lips curled into a mocking smile.

Beckham tried to speak, but all he managed was a grunt.

Wood looked to one of his men, who was striding out of the control room. "Did their transmissions go through?"

"No, sir, we stopped them before the uploads were complete."

"What?" Ellis twisted in the grip of the soldier holding him. "You don't know what you've done!"

"You're the one who doesn't understand. Colonel Gibson and my brother dreamed of an America that didn't waste the lives of our soldiers in foreign shit holes like Saigon or Fallujah. Jan Ringgold just sent thousands of our boys to die in Europe, and for what? Not for America! The entire point of the hemorrhage virus was to *stop* that from happening."

Blood trickled into Beckham's eyes. He spat, coughed, and summoned his scratchy voice.

"So that's why you killed all those innocent people here and in Chicago and New Orleans? That's why you're *murdering* kids?"

A soldier in Beckham's peripheral went to kick him,

but Wood held up a hand. That's when Beckham saw the blood dripping down the side of his face. The man's ear was hanging on by threads of cartilage. Fuck. An inch to the left and the shot would have killed the bastard.

"Jan Ringgold killed those people by not stepping down for her war crimes," Wood said. "You've been on the wrong side of this the entire time, Beckham. It's quite sad. You could have done well with ROT."

"President Ringgold is the best thing to happen to America. She helped rebuild what your brother destroyed," Ellis said. He glanced up like he was afraid he was going to be hit. "And she will continue to rebuild our great nation once people learn the truth about you."

Beckham wanted to tell Ellis to shut up, but Wood quickly cut in.

"Jan is hiding in her underground tomb, and she isn't coming out."

"That's what you think," Ellis said.

Beckham glared at the doctor, silently trying to tell him to shut his mouth.

"What did you say?" Wood asked. He walked over to Ellis, brows raised over his wild eyes.

Ellis didn't reply, and Wood nodded at one of his men. The soldier shot Ellis in the leg. He screamed in pain.

Wood laughed and took a step closer to the struggling doctor while Beckham fought his captors.

"Let him go! You have me!" He squirmed to his left and right, but it was no use. The men had him secured with their boots.

Ellis whimpered as Wood loomed over him. "I'm going to ask you one more time. Where is Ringgold?"

"Go to hell," the doctor said, his voice a pained gasp.

The lieutenant signaled his man again.

"No!" Beckham shouted. "Take me in—"

Another shot silenced him. Ellis's screech sounded like a mouse caught in a trap.

"Tell me what you know and this all ends," Wood said.

Ellis didn't say anything else, but Beckham could hear his breath coming in short, shallow bursts. Even if the bullets had avoided his arteries, the shock might kill him.

"You bastard!" Beckham yelled. "You shoot him again and I'll fucking kill you with my bare hands."

Wood laughed again. "I'll tell you what. Let's make a deal. You tell me where Jan is, or I'll kill you both and put your heads on pikes outside my new office. Sound fair?"

"Fuck ROT and fuck you, you treasonous piece of shit," Beckham said. Darkness was closing in on the edges of his already blurred vision, and he knew unconsciousness wasn't far off for him or Ellis.

"I'm running out of patience. This is my final offer: one of you tells me where Ringgold is, and the other one gets to live."

Beckham looked at Ellis and shook his head.

Don't do it, Pat. Don't fucking do it.

There was a long pause, and then Ellis said, "She's here. Ringgold is on Plum Island. Kill me, but don't kill Beckham, okay? I told you what you want to know."

"Deal," Wood said.

The crack of a third gunshot came before Beckham could protest. He caught a blurry glimpse of a blood-stained brim of a blue baseball cap flying to the ground, and then a body. One of the soldiers kicked it so it rolled over. Ellis, a neat bullet hole in the center of his forehead, stared lifelessly back at Beckham.

"Thank you, Doctor," Wood said, brushing down

the front of his jacket. He turned to his men. "Find the bitch."

"No," Beckham whimpered. He glanced up at Wood, expecting a bullet of his own. His mind raced as he fought to stay conscious. Horn would come. Horn would come and mow these bastards down. He would rip them limb from limb and then beat their corpses with those limbs. His best friend would kill them all. Or maybe Fitz would show up and blow Wood's head off like he had his brother.

But deep down Beckham knew the truth.

No one was coming to save them this time.

22

Fitz raked his M4 back and forth over an army disgorged from the pits of hell. The shrieks, squawks, and hissing of the angry beasts filled the early-morning air in front of the sacred Basilica of Saint Thérèse.

This place was anything but sacred now.

Everywhere he looked, his sights fell on a different mutated creature. To one side, what looked like fifty adult Variants prowled the gardens, joints popping and lips smacking. Wormers dug through the earth to the other side. Three Black Beetles lumbered through the woods straight ahead. Fitz could barely bring himself to look over his shoulder. At least a dozen juveniles perched like gargoyles on the roof of the vestibule, and Reavers circled overhead. Another pack of juveniles guarded the MATV, tilting their heads as though waiting for someone or something to give them orders.

Fitz looked for an Alpha but saw nothing that indicated the monsters had any kind of leader like the ones he'd faced back in New York. Not that it mattered. There were enough hostiles here to overwhelm them even if they weren't directed by an intelligent general.

The *click-clack* of armor and joints was joined by another sound Fitz couldn't quite place. He looked to the gardens, where a monster emerged from the shadows. The sight of it caused Fitz to tense every muscle in his body.

A man-sized beast crawled out of the foliage on all fours. Its torso was covered in the veiny flesh of an adult Variant, but the lower half was armored like a juvenile. It pushed itself up onto its feet with two massive claws. Both were rimmed with teeth, as was the maw in its disfigured human head.

"Pinchers!" someone yelled.

The screams of children echoed all around Fitz. He forced himself to look away. His mind processed every possible move to get them to the truck, but each thought was shut down.

They had nowhere to run or hide. They had no escape.

I've failed Beckham. I've failed Team Ghost. I've failed the world.

He swallowed hard. They were already a man down. Dohi was still unconscious in the center of the group.

Over the raucous screams of humans and screeching monsters came an adolescent voice.

"My dad told me something, before he died."

Fitz looked over at Michel. The other kids were huddled together in a knot of raggedy clothes. Shaking hands struggled to hold guns aloft. These *weren't* adults. Fitz had been wrong back in the crypts. They were just kids, and they couldn't win against monsters.

They'd never had a chance...

"Dad told me it's a good death to go down fighting. It's a brave way to die." Michel went to slap a magazine into his AK-47. His trembling fingers knocked the mag against the receiver, and he dropped it in the dirt. He scooped down, grabbed it, and slammed it into the gun.

"Jesus, Michel," Fitz began.

"I'm afraid," Michel said, looking Fitz in the eye. "I'm afraid I won't die well like he did."

The words shattered Fitz's already broken heart. He couldn't find his voice to reply. All around them, Wormers speared through the earth, raising a wall of rock and dirt around the group. The monsters were closing in from all directions, including the sky. Two juveniles climbed on top of the MATV, and although Fitz knew it wasn't possible, he could swear they were grinning at him.

God, how he wished Beckham was here to bark orders. Even in the worst situations, Beckham had always kept his cool. He was half a world away now, probably eating dinner with Horn, Kate, and the kids.

"It's okay to be afraid," Fitz said, repeating something Beckham had told him once. He paused and looked back over the writhing mass of monsters. "You ready, kid?"

Michel nodded. Apollo bared his teeth, snarling. Fitz exchanged a meaningful glance with Rico. She had picked up an RPG launcher from one of the older kids and held it at the ready. Tanaka and Stevenson flanked her, jaws set and eyes steely. Team Ghost was ready.

And Fitz was ready to lead them in their final battle.

"Rico, focus on the Beetles," Fitz said. "Stevenson, you got the juveniles. Tanaka, take those Pinchers. Mira, you and your kids need to keep the adult Variants and the Reavers off us." Fitz locked eyes with the woman. She'd kept her ragtag band of orphans alive for months, and Fitz couldn't shake the thought that he was responsible for bringing this army to her door.

Dear Lord, he thought, bowing his head, *please find it in your mercy to protect these children. I don't care much what happens to me, but get these kids out of here alive.*

Fitz opened his eyes and straightened his back. "Fight to the truck!" he called. "And hold the line!"

An RPG streaked away from the launcher as soon as the words left his mouth. It hissed across the gardens and smashed into the shell of a Black Beetle, blowing it in half. Stevenson leveled his SAW and fired on the juveniles that were leaping off the roof. They dropped to all fours, stampeding toward Team Ghost. Rounds broke through armor and splattered blood on the ash-covered pavement.

Fitz fired his grenade launcher. The projectile hit the dirt in front of the closest juvenile, and the explosion blew the monster to pieces. The shock wave slammed into the other creatures, knocking them aside, but they quickly rallied and continued their advance.

Mira fired her AK-47 at the adult Variants. The Ombres followed her lead and joined the fight. The frail beasts skittered across the dirt, plowing through the gunfire despite gaping holes in their translucent, veiny skin. Blood coated the ground outside the basilica, but the monsters still kept coming.

"Rico!" Fitz shouted.

The hiss of another rocket sounded. The Beetle bent down just as it zoomed overhead. An explosion bloomed in the canopy of trees ten feet behind it, fire raining down harmlessly on the shell. Three Pinchers waddled out of the smoke.

"Tanaka, more Pinchers!" Fitz shouted.

Rico fired again, blowing a hole in the enemy's line and cracking another Beetle in half. Tanaka and Stevenson worked together to mow down the smaller Pinchers in a desperate attempt to clear a path to the truck.

"Hurry!" Fitz shouted. "Michel, shoot the juveniles on the MATV!"

There was no answer, and Fitz spun to see the kid on the ground, clutching his leg. Acid bubbled on the surface of his skin. Another blast hissed toward the children, hitting a teenage boy on the side of his head. He dropped to his knees, his screams stifled by the toxins.

A wave of fire rushed through Fitz, a sickening cocktail of fear and guilt.

He ducked as a Reaver swooped down with claws extended. The spiked tail sliced through his left shoulder. Pain lanced along that arm, but Fitz was beyond caring. He raised his M4 and fired a burst that pierced the monster's wings. It fought for altitude, struggling to stay above the carnage.

Fitz swung his weapon to the juveniles perched on the MATV. They were both burping up more acid, building up enough of the toxic spit to spray again.

He dropped his M4 and unslung his MK11. He hefted the big gun up, held a breath in, and fired. The first shot punched through the forehead of the juvenile on top of the truck's roof. It fell limply onto the dirt. The second hit the creature on the hood in the right eye. That one skidded off the side, jerking violently before falling still.

He raced to where Michel was lying on the ground. Fitz reached down to grab the boy's hand. It felt small. So goddamn small.

He caught a glimpse of Dohi as he dragged the kid across the dirt. The man was stirring on the ground in the center of the group. He had a hand on his head and shook it from side to side.

"Dohi, we need you!" Fitz shouted.

Another RPG slashed overhead. This time Rico's aim was true. It hit the third Black Beetle in the right leg. The blast lifted the beast into the air in a shower of sparks and body parts.

"Keep fighting to the truck!" Fitz yelled.

The group slowly moved toward the MATV. He risked a glance over his shoulder to check for casualties. Three more of the older Ombres were dead, and some of the kids were injured, but Mira had kept the younger ones close to her, protecting them with her life.

Tanaka slung his M4 over his shoulder and pulled his swords just in time to engage a Pincher that had broken through the line of fire and was heading toward the brave Frenchwoman. The creature brought up a claw to meet his sword. The steel broke through the armor. He decapitated the monster with a swift slice and then stabbed an onrushing adult Variant through its sucker mouth.

Fitz had to let go of Michel's hand to fire a shot at an adult that was charging toward them. His first shot kicked up dirt in the monster's face. Before he could get off a second, the beast's head vanished in an explosion of gore.

Michel groaned and lowered the pistol he had used to blow off the Variant's face. His eyes rolled back in his head, the pain finally overwhelming him.

"Hang on, kid!" Fitz reached for Meg's hatchet. He was going to have to amputate Michel's leg to stop the toxins from spreading. A high-pitched wail from above made Fitz duck and raise his MK11. He fired at a Reaver dropping in a nosedive for their position.

Crack!

The first shot punched through a wing.

Crack!

The second hit an armored shoulder.

Crack!

The final shot hit the monster in the neck. It landed on the field between Fitz and the MATV with a thump. Their path was littered with corpses, but it was momentarily clear. He grabbed another magazine and palmed it into the weapon.

"To the truck! Everyone, go!" Fitz shouted.

As he reloaded, a pair of Wormers broke through the

dirt in front of him and to his side. Tentacles grabbed a girl from the line and dragged her toward the hole. From behind came another crack of breaking ground. Another Wormer smashed through the earth in the center of the group. Fitz turned to watch Dohi bring his combat knife down on the creature's skull.

"Come on!" Fitz yelled. He centered his rifle on the Wormer that had the girl, but he jerked the muzzle up when a human figure ran through his crosshairs.

The kids were sprinting toward the truck, urged on by their protector's stern French commands. Mira fired her weapon at a Wormer attempting to pull a girl into its tunnel. The shot tore through the soft flesh of the monster, drenching the girl in blood. She let out a wail and reached toward Mira, who pulled her free of the limp tentacles.

With her arm around the girl, Mira guided her back to the cluster of children. Tanaka was a few feet away, hacking a thin Variant to pieces. A second beast climbed out of a Wormer hole and bounded for Mira.

Fitz only had enough time for one shot. He lined up his MK11 and pulled the trigger, blowing off a piece of the monster's back. It crashed to the ground, flopping and gushing blood.

Mira glanced at the dying creature and held up a hand to Fitz when a shadow suddenly passed over her.

"Watch out!" Fitz yelled a moment too late.

A Reaver swooped from above, grabbed Mira with its talons, and pulled her away from the girl she had just saved. Fitz raised his gun at the beast, trying to get a clear shot. The wings and armored torso flickered in front of his crosshairs. He prepared to fire, but the woman's face suddenly emerged. He pushed the scope away for a split second. Mira's sharp green eyes were fixated on the kids below.

"Protect them!" she yelled as it pulled her toward the basilica.

Fitz pushed the scope back to his eye for a clear shot.

Come on, come on. I just need one clean...

A wing flashed across his sight and he squeezed off a round that punched through the armor, sending the creature sailing toward the steeple. It pulled up at the last second and flapped around the back of the basilica. Watching Mira vanish felt like a scab being ripped from his heart. She had done everything to save these kids.

Now it was his job to make sure she didn't die in vain.

Team Ghost lobbed grenades into the gardens and surrounding woods, trying to disorient the beasts long enough for the kids to reach the truck. Geysers of dirt and diseased flesh blew into the air. At this rate they'd run out of ammo soon. Reavers swooped down, one of them grabbing a boy and pulling him into the sky.

Fitz shot the monster in the spine, and it released the kid from its grip, dropping him back into the cluster of survivors. He couldn't see if the boy was still alive.

"Keep moving!" Fitz yelled. They were fifty feet from the vehicle, but it could have been fifty miles.

He saw they weren't going to make it.

A flicker of light suddenly peeked over the horizon, slowly spreading a wall of crimson over the French countryside. It was something Fitz hadn't thought he would see again.

They had survived the night, but they were out of time.

Apollo nudged up against him, whining softly. The dog had a slash on his right leg. It wasn't the first time he'd bled with the dog, but this would be the last.

"I love you, boy," Fitz said. They had endured much and succeeded against incredible odds, but Fitz knew that no matter how hard you fought, some battles couldn't be won. All it takes is all you got…but sometimes you just didn't have enough.

He hefted his gun back up with his injured arm and fired on a Reaver. There were three more of the winged monsters, but they abruptly changed direction. Fitz followed them to the west, where a black dot had emerged over the horizon. Whatever it was, it was leading the monsters away. He pivoted back to the MATV and blew the head off a Variant that had climbed on top.

Over the gunfire and screams, there was a faint sound that made Fitz's heart skip a beat.

Is that…?

Yes!

A transmission crackled in his ear.

"Ghost One, do you copy?"

"This is Ghost One!" Fitz shouted into the comms.

"I got you, brother! Hang on. One big-ass King Stallion, coming in hot over the city."

Fitz started laughing in sheer relief. He recognized that voice. It was Tito, Corporal Ryan "Tank" Talon's cousin, the chopper pilot who had saved their asses back in DC. The massive chopper closed in on the church and unleashed a salvo of gunfire that cut the remaining Reavers from the air.

A second line of machine-gun fire hit the wave of adult Variants. Tito made a quick pass over the group and then banked hard to the right to swing around for another run.

"Bradley's going to have my head!" Tito said, laughing like a madman. "I swear to God, this is the last time I steal a chopper for Team Ghost."

Rico ran ahead and jumped onto the hood of the MATV as the King Stallion swooped in with cables unfurled to connect to the truck. Gunfire came from all directions, holding back the monsters as they squawked, screeching in an evil discord that hurt Fitz's ears. They fanned back out into the gardens, retreating to the shadows as the morning sun rose in the sky.

He looked down at Michel, who was curled up on his side at Fitz's feet. Fitz wasn't sure how to pick the kid up without getting acid all over himself too. He glanced around for something to wrap him in.

"Kid, hang on. We're getting you out of here."

Michel's lips trembled and parted. He coughed, his lungs rattling. He rolled over, and Fitz's heart sank. It was too late for the boy. He'd been hit worse than Fitz had thought, or else the toxins had simply spread like wildfire.

"Would my dad be proud?" Michel's voice trailed off, barely more than a whisper. He coughed again.

Apollo licked the boy's face. A tear fell from Fitz's eye as he leaned down, grabbed the boy's clammy hand, and squeezed. "Your dad would be very proud."

Michel's hand went limp. He placed it gently on the boy's chest and tucked his Superman cape around him like a shroud. Fitz squeezed his eyes shut, gasping for air as sobs tore from his throat. A pair of gloved hands clapped him on the shoulder. He looked up to see Rico. Behind her were the survivors of the battle, bloody and wide-eyed, clinging to one another. They were all staring at him, tears streaking down their filthy faces.

"Where is *Maman*?" a young girl asked.

"Everyone inside of the truck!" Stevenson shouted.

The kids filed into the troop hold as ordered. Dohi stumbled along, disoriented from his concussion. Rico got a shoulder under his arm with Tanaka on his other side. They half carried the injured member of Ghost to the MATV just as the cables tightened. Fitz glanced down at Michel one last time, knowing he couldn't bring the boy with them due to the toxins.

"Good-bye, kid," Fitz said. He bent down to pick Apollo up and help him into the back of the truck. They were the last two in. Securely inside, Fitz let himself collapse on the smooth metal floor, his chest heaving.

"You did it, Fitzie, you got us out of there," Rico said.

Not everyone…

He sat up and counted twelve filthy faces. Fitz had gotten Team Ghost out, but they had lost seven of the kids—and Mira.

"She had just saved one of the little ones," he explained. "The Reaver came down, and then…Jesus, I'm so sorry. I only got off one shot. I just couldn't save her."

Rico stared at him, her swollen nose and eyes red, the color clashing with her blue hair. She sniffed and rubbed her hand over her cheeks, roughly wiping the tears away.

"It's okay," she said. "It wasn't your fault."

It is my fault.

Apollo laid down beside him, but he gestured for the dog to get up. He didn't deserve to be comforted.

"Go see the kids, boy," Fitz said. Apollo trotted over to the Ombres and sat on his hind legs in front of them. The young girl who had asked for Mira stroked his head. They were talking amongst themselves, and Fitz understood just enough French to know that they were scared and confused. More than one of them was still asking where Mira and Michel were.

"We're taking you all somewhere safe," Fitz said. One of the older kids, a girl with a vicious scratch running down the side of her face, translated his words into French for the others.

Fitz paused and took a deep breath. "Your *Maman* and Captain Michel aren't coming with us. They had to stay behind to…to watch over the basilica."

The Ombres looked back at Fitz—some of them old

enough to know the truth, others believing him. He wiped the sweat and blood from his face.

"Better look out your window, Ghost," Tito said over the channel.

Fitz turned to the window in the side of the MATV. At first he didn't see anything but whiteness, as if the ground were covered in a blanket of snow.

But snow didn't move.

"My God," Rico said. "There have to be thousands of them down there."

The roar of jets broke in the distance.

"Operation Reach is under way," Tito said. "Got you guys out right in time, too, because we're about to sizzle those bastards."

Fitz couldn't pull his eyes away from the sea of mutated flesh below. *This* was the Variant army Mira had spoken about. The force they had fought at the basilica had just been a recon party.

He turned his back to the window and relaxed against the bulkhead as the sound of the jets grew louder. Team Ghost had completed their mission. They had given Nixon and Bradley the intel they needed to fight their way to Paris and carry out Operation Reach.

Fitz had done his duty . . . so why did he feel like he'd utterly failed?

23

Piero finished tying a strip of his torn uniform around his wounded ankle. The makeshift tourniquet stopped the bleeding, but he had to find something to clean it. He could only imagine what kind of infection he might get from a demon. He tightened it one last time, then tested his weight on the ankle. It hurt, but he could still walk.

"You ready to see the world again, Ringo?" Piero whispered to his pocket.

The mouse peeked out, then ducked back down.

The mouse was scared of the light. Not that Piero blamed him. They couldn't hide in the sunlight. But he'd made up his mind. He wasn't returning to the tunnels. He wasn't hiding anymore.

Piero unlocked the door leading into Saint Peter's Basilica and eased it open. The staircase led out into one of the many chapels. Light from the windows circling the central dome revealed a layer of dried blood covering the marble floor like a red carpet.

Piero shouldered his rifle and walked out into the Chapel of the Presentation of the Virgin. He took a step toward one of the pews and slowly raked the muzzle across the other chapels in a clockwise motion. Skeletons littered the Choir Chapel and the Clementine Chapel.

He could not begin to count how many dead there were. All picked clean of flesh.

Another step forward. Something crunched under his boot.

He closed his eyes and winced as the sound echoed through the basilica.

Stupid. Stupid. Stupid.

Piero forced his eyes open, expecting a Varianti to jump from the shadows and gallop toward him. But nothing moved. He looked down and saw not a bone, as he had feared, but a crumpled clear-plastic cup. There were more cups fallen beneath the pews or dropped in the aisles.

He held the cup to his nose and sniffed. Piero couldn't be certain, but he thought he smelled wine. Something else too, bitter like rancid almonds.

Piero understood now what had happened here. This hadn't been communion. These people had come here for a different purpose.

Suicides.

All of them.

The church was where people flocked when things got bad. People came to the opulent basilica to pray. And, it seemed, to die. Catholics didn't believe in suicide, but he had no doubt that whoever had overseen these final moments had forgiven their sins. He looked around again, recalling that the massive space could hold sixty thousand people.

Piero wandered through the other chapels. Mangled bodies littered the marble floors. He roved his gun from left to right, overwhelmed by what he saw. The basilica was meant to be a place of wonder and awe, created by the finest artists, like Michelangelo, as a testament to God's glory, but now it was a charnel house.

It was when Piero made his way toward the central dome that he realized the true feat accomplished by man. Crepuscular rays shot through the windows. The golden sunlight rained down around him like the light of heaven itself.

Surrounded by something he never thought he would see again, Piero wept.

Lifting his hand to shield his blurred eyes, he squinted into the light. There was something else up there, some sort of black chandeliers hanging from the curved ceiling. He didn't remember those from the tour with his family over twenty years ago.

An object fell and clanked onto the marble floor to his right.

"What the hell?" Piero whispered. The thing came to a stop at the foot of a nearby pew. He slowly walked over to check it out.

It was a bone, stripped of all flesh.

Black tar plummeted from the dome and splattered the floor, more of the white bones sticking out of the pile.

The ceiling wasn't raining bones.

This was the excrement of something above him.

Piero watched in horror as one of the monsters woke up and spread its wings. The others moved restlessly. They were supposed to sleep during the day. They didn't like the light.

Ringo buried himself in his pocket as Piero limped away. He moved as fast as he could while still making as little noise as possible. Up ahead, five portals led out of the basilica to the piazza beyond. The largest of them, a massive bronze gateway, stood ajar.

He ran the last few yards, heedless of the noise he was making or the pain in his leg.

A brilliant sun blinded him as he half fell onto the

landing overlooking the piazza. His vision cleared to show him a battlefield. Tanks and armored vehicles filled the central courtyard. There were bones here, too, bleached white by the sun. He wasn't sure if he knew anyone in the units that had been deployed to defend the Vatican, but it didn't matter now. They were dead, like everyone else in the accursed world.

He looked out over the city he loved deeply. To the east, a bridge stretched across the Tiber River. An ancient castle rose to the north. Everywhere he looked, he saw visions of the best and worst of humanity.

And somehow, he was the last human standing.

The thought took the air from his chest, forcing him to take raspy breaths. A wave of nausea passed over him. He might have thrown up if he'd had anything in his stomach. Instead, he sat on the stairs listening to the screech of the beasts swooping through the basilica. He was too exhausted, mentally and physically, to push on. The mouse jumped onto his shoulder and looked out with him over the ruins of Rome.

For a moment they rested there together, a man and his mouse. Piero scanned the battlefield, looking for bodies that he might recognize. But all he saw were bones. There was a rucksack a few steps away. There could be food or supplies inside, but he was too fatigued to care.

What did it matter?

Part of him had still believed there would be people out here. Piero had hoped he wouldn't have to be alone anymore. He let out a long sigh, his weary heart pushing blood through his veins. Another screech from inside reminded him the clock was ticking.

"I'm sorry, Ringo. I...I can't go on. But at least we got to see the sun again."

Piero grabbed his rifle and positioned the muzzle under his chin. He squinted at the sun, basking in the rays one last time. Then he put his finger on the trigger and grabbed the mouse in his other hand.

"It's okay. It will be fast," Piero whispered to his friend. He tightened his grip around the mouse. He could feel its fragile ribs against his sweaty palm. It chirped and scratched at his fingers. Tiny black eyes centered on Piero, pleading for him to stop.

"It's okay, Ringo. We don't have to suffer anymore."

The creature bit his finger.

Ringo didn't want to die.

"Fuck," Piero said, loosening his grip.

He couldn't bring himself to kill his friend, even if it was out of mercy. Ringo jumped back to his shoulder and squeaked as if to say, *You asshole!*

It continued to talk in its high-pitched voice. Piero looked at the small creature, but the mouse was no longer looking at him. He followed Ringo's gaze toward the sky overhead.

The winged monsters were flapping away from the basilica.

Piero furrowed his brows and slowly rose to his feet.

They were definitely retreating, but what could frighten things like that?

He turned as a deep rumble sounded in the distance. On the horizon, a trio of black dots emerged in a V formation.

"It…it can't be," Piero whispered. His voice grew louder as he jumped into the air, pointing at the incoming planes. "They came for me! Look, Ringo, we're not alone!"

A smile split Piero's face. He felt like dancing.

"Down here! We're down here!"

He waved his hands as Ringo clung to his shoulder. The jets burst through clouds and shot over the western side of the city. At the foot of the steps, the radio inside one of the tanks squawked to life. Piero ran toward it just in time to hear the transmission repeat.

"Broadcasting on revolving frequencies. If you can hear this message, get underground now. Operation Reach is under way."

Piero grabbed the radio, but the voice on the other end of the comms was nothing more than a prerecorded message.

He'd never heard of Operation Reach. He looked to the sky again, and his face fell when he saw the bombs dropping from the bellies of the jets.

"No," he whispered.

The planes weren't looking for survivors. They were here to kill the monsters—and him, if he didn't move his ass.

Explosions bloomed in the distance, toxic flames bursting on the edge of the city as the bombs connected with their targets. The planes changed course. They were headed right in his direction.

Piero grabbed the rucksack on the stairs and stopped to pluck several magazines from the vest of a dead soldier. Then he turned and ran up the steps to the basilica, retreating back into the darkness, the sound of the jets growing ever louder.

Davis crawled through the mud with her M4 held across her arms. Salt water stung her eyes as the tide crashed against her body. She moved under the cover of the embankment on the west side of Fort Pickens. Black was on point, his Mohawk plastered to his skull like seaweed by the spray. Behind them came Diaz, Robbie, and Sanders. They had been moving like snails for an hour to get around the peninsula undetected. The second-hardest part—swimming out to sea and then back again—was over, but the hardest part was ahead. They still had to board the *GW*.

A wave hit the beach and slurped up under Davis. She closed her mouth and eyes as the water broke against the rocks around her. She pushed on. The routine was simple: wiggle, crawl a few feet, wiggle again, and keep crawling. It was painstakingly slow, but it gave her time to collect her thoughts.

The bloodlust from killing the ROT soldiers had faded. The anger hadn't gone away, but it hadn't gotten any worse, either. Mostly, she just felt numb.

Another wave crashed against her, pushing her over the sand and into a sharp rock. She winced but kept moving. They were almost to the other side of the peninsula. Davis was going to have a lot of bruises, but the aches were worth it when she saw her ship.

A transmission crackled on the headset she had pulled off one of the dead ROT soldiers. "Tiger Three, Tiger Four, do you copy, over?"

Static.

"Tiger Fifteen, get your boys out there and look for Tiger Three and Tiger Four. They were supposed to report back over an hour ago. And hurry the hell up, we're moving out in thirty minutes. Over."

ROT would never find their two missing men. Davis had made sure of that. Hopefully that would help delay the departure of the ship.

Black stopped ahead to scope the ship through the torpedograss. Davis used her gun to fight through the thick grass and crawl up to Black. Her body sank in the mud, and she had to push herself up with the butt of her M4 to see.

"What have you got, Black?"

"I don't know. They could be preparing to fire again. Who do you think they're targeting?"

"SZTs still loyal to President Ringgold," Davis whispered back. "Wood is going to hit them all."

Davis raised her M4 and zoomed in. Black was right. The ATACMS delivery launch vehicles had been moved to the starboard side of the aircraft carrier. There was motion on the deck, and she moved her crosshairs toward a crew of ROT soldiers loading missiles onto the helicopters and jets. An entire team was helping unload another crate.

Any further conflict in her mind about sinking her own ship vanished. She had to stop them. She couldn't let this go any further. Even if some of her crew were still alive, they had to be sacrificed for the greater good. Davis was ready to give hers for the same cause.

The clank of metal sounded as the anchor began to retract.

"Black, I need your eyes up there. See how many soldiers are left at Pickens."

He nodded and ran into the darkness. Within moments he was gone, vanishing over the hill. Davis waited in tense silence, her muscles aching as she held herself perfectly still. Black returned a few minutes later, breathing heavily.

"Looks like all but one squad have boarded the ship, Captain. There's just one Zodiac and five men left on shore."

"Perfect. We're going to kill those ROT soldiers, take their boat, and board the ship, pretending to be them. Black will plant the C-Four on the One-Forties with Robbie and Sanders. Diaz and I will take a batch to scuttle the ship."

Robbie and Sanders exchanged a glance, but Black and Diaz nodded back.

"Does anyone have a problem with that plan?" Davis asked.

Sanders slowly raised his hand.

"Let me make something clear," Davis said. "You are either with us or against us on this mission. Are you with us, Sanders?"

"Ah hell. If I'm going to die, might as well get blown up. Nearly did it to myself when I was a boy playing around with my daddy's fireworks."

He cracked a yellow grin. Davis didn't return it. This was no time for jokes.

"We have two suppressed M-Nines, so we make this quiet and quick. Black, you're with me. Diaz, secure our ride and hold on to the C-Four for us."

"Captain, please let me come with you," Diaz said.

"We can swap," Black said. "I'll make sure that C-Four gets to the ship if you don't come back."

After a moment of hesitation, Davis nodded. Black handed Diaz his M9.

She and Diaz trudged up the slope. They pushed their NVGs into position and fanned out across the field near the fort.

"High and low, keep quiet from here on out," Davis ordered.

Diaz was already scanning battlements of the fort and the weeds around them with her pistol. They followed the wildly swinging flashlight beams straight to the ROT soldiers. These guys weren't professionals. Davis was banking on most of the men on the ship being amateurs. She still held on to a sliver of hope that they might retake the ship instead of scuttling her.

A flash of motion froze Davis. Diaz dropped to a knee

and pointed across the open field. The ROT squad was about three hundred feet away. Davis moved toward the cover of a retaining wall. They put their backs against the brick, and Davis raised her M9, waiting as the soldiers approached.

"You take the two on the right. I'll take the left," Davis whispered. "We can shoot the middle one together."

"Aye-aye, ma'am."

"Wonder what the fuck happened to Belt and Herc," one of the ROT men said. "Think they got nabbed by some juveniles while they were taking a piss?"

There was a snort as someone hocked up a wad of phlegm. "That, or they abandoned their post. If they deserted, I'd string 'em up and skin 'em like them stupid marines."

Several laughs followed.

Davis bit her lip so hard she drew blood. She sucked in a breath, then looked at Diaz and nodded. They jumped around the wall at the same time.

In the moonlight, Davis saw the expression of shock and fear on the first man's face—right before she blew it off. She moved onto the next bastard, firing two bullets before he could even raise his weapon. Diaz took hers down with ease, and they came together to kill the fifth man with well-aimed shots to the chest. He dropped like a statue being tipped over, slowly and with a thud.

"Nice shooting," Davis said, lowering her weapon. She hurried over to the bodies and fired a bullet into each of their skulls, then stripped them of the Velcro name tags on their vests. When she was finished, she disarmed them and slung a pair of SCARs over her shoulder. She picked up a third while Diaz grabbed the other two.

"Okay, let's move," Davis said.

Diaz hesitated as she stared at the corpses.

"I...I can't..."

"It'll pass," Davis replied. Two months ago she would have had the same reaction after ambushing these men. But these soldiers weren't just following orders. They were monsters, like Wood.

"Let's go, Diaz."

She dipped her chin and cradled her SCAR across her chest. They ran back to the shoreline side by side.

Black stepped out from behind a tree when they approached. Sanders and Robbie emerged from a broken brick wall. She handed them the SCARs and the name tags.

"Put these on. We're going to try to sneak aboard."

"Billy?" Black said skeptically, looking at the name tag.

"Not sure I'll pass for a Colin," Diaz said.

Davis looked at her brown shoulder-length hair. The younger woman would never pass for a man, not even at a casual glance.

"Hold still," Davis said. She pulled her knife. Diaz reared back at the sight of the blade.

"Come on, we don't have time for this," Davis said. She grabbed her own ponytail and sheared it off with the blade, sawing until the last of the strands parted. She gestured at Diaz impatiently. Diaz squeezed her eyes shut and turned around.

Three minutes later, Davis and Diaz had haircuts that made them look like high school boys. Five minutes after that they were all in the Zodiac, coasting over the waves toward the *GW*.

Davis kept her SCAR at the ready.

On the deck, the silhouettes of three ROT soldiers waited for them.

"Tiger Fifteen, you copy, over?"

Black looked to Davis and she nodded to give her approval.

"Copy, we're on our way back. Didn't find all of Tiger

Three or Four, but we did find part of a leg. Juveniles must have got 'em."

"Roger that. Get your asses aboard, boys. It's time to go."

Davis swallowed hard. Everything she had been through in the past seven months had led up to this moment. If she failed, America would fall.

24

"Where are they?" Kate said. She paced back and forth on the edge of the forest nearest the Animal Disease Center buildings. She'd been pacing since they arrived over an hour ago.

Horn was as still as a statue, his rifle aimed out over the field and road that led to the buildings just over the hill. The Black Hawk that President Ringgold had arrived in was nearby, covered with a camouflage tarp. Two marine pilots awaited their orders. Somehow they'd managed to keep the helicopter hidden from Rayburn and Walker and everyone else on the island.

Kate looked at her watch. It had now been an hour and a half since Reed took Ellis to the radio tower.

"They should be back by now. Something's happened. We have to find them, Horn." When the big man gestured for her to be quiet, she said, "Damn it, give me the keys. I'll go myself."

Ringgold walked through the leaves to stand next to Kate. She had her shawl over her head again. She crossed her arms over her chest in the chilly night air.

"I have bad news," Ringgold said. "Barnes says we can only give Reed and Ellis another five. Then we have to leave. I'm sorry, Kate, but ROT is *here* on the island, and somehow they know that I escaped the PEOC."

Kate couldn't breathe. She couldn't leave Reed. She *wouldn't* leave him.

"You go," she said. "Horn, take the kids and go with them. Get somewhere safe."

"Nah," Horn said, shaking his head. "I ain't leaving either."

The baby kicked, and Kate wondered if he could feel how scared she was.

"I'm not leaving Reed," she said firmly.

"We wait five more minutes, then we get into the air with or without you," Barnes said. "We can't stay here any longer. I'm sorry."

Horn directed his gaze at Barnes and then Nelson. "Take us to the radio tower on the way out of here. If we see any sign of Beckham on the flyover, we drop down and search. You got it?"

Ringgold answered for the two men when they hesitated. "I'm good with that. It's the least we can do for them."

"Madam President," Barnes began to say. "I'd highly recommend—"

"That's an order, Barnes."

He nodded back.

Horn snorted, heaved his SAW onto his shoulder, and walked back into the woods to gather the kids. Jake emerged first with Donna, Bo, and his own son, Timothy. Tasha and Jenny were holding Horn's hands. The marine pilots pulled off the tarp, and they all piled into the chopper.

Five minutes later they lifted into the air.

In the cockpit, the pilots pushed their NVGs into position and pulled the bird toward a partially flattened cornfield. They flew low over the crops. The radio tower rose over the trees just ahead, and Kate's heart pounded harder as they got closer.

"There!" Horn shouted. He pointed toward a truck parked below. They came back in for a second pass, but Kate didn't see anyone in the pickup.

The next circle brought them over the front of the radio tower.

"Looks like a body," Nelson said.

A man was sprawled in front of the radio station, blood pooling around his head. Kate screamed and lunged toward the open door when she saw the blue baseball cap lying on the ground nearby, but Horn and Barnes held her back.

"Let me go! Let me go!" She kicked and shouted. The kids were bawling, and Kate felt her own hot tears. "We have to go down there! We have to help Pat!"

"He's gone, ma'am," Barnes said. "I'm sorry."

Horn stared out the door in shock as the pilots hovered, waiting for orders.

"I don't see Beckham," Horn said. He looked at Barnes. "Let me go look for him. Three minutes."

Barnes and Nelson exchanged a glance. "We can't—"

"We can't abandon Reed," Kate said, gathering the shreds of her composure. Ellis had been her closest ally and partner. They'd worked side by side for countless hours in the lab and debated over countless meals together. The thought that he was gone left a hole in her heart. But if she lost Reed too...that would break her.

"I'm going down there, Kate. I'll find him," Horn said. He turned to the secret service agents. "You ain't stoppin' me!"

Barnes moved to block his way. "We can't let you do that!"

Horn raised a fist, and Jake stepped up to support him.

"Captain Beckham risked everything for me and my son in New York. We can't abandon him now."

"I'm picking up a message over the comms!" one of the pilots yelled. "It's for President Ringgold."

A moment later, a calm, self-assured voice filled the troop hold. "You've proven to be harder to kill than I thought, Jan. I don't know how you escaped from the PEOC, but I will find you. It'll be fun, actually. By the way, I have your knight in shining armor right here. Say hello, Reed."

Kate grabbed Ringgold's arm, trying to steady herself.

"Don't give him what he wants," Reed growled. His voice sounded thick and muffled, as if he was talking through a fat lip.

"Reed," Kate called out. "Reed, hang on!"

"The comms are only one-way. He can't hear you," Nelson said.

Wood was speaking again, taunting them. "Go ahead and keep running, Jan. I will find you. In the meantime, Reed and I are going on a little trip. See you soon, Jan. It's been fun."

The transmission ended with a squawk of static.

"We have to leave the island, now!" Nelson shouted.

The pilots were already pulling away from the tower.

Kate clutched her chest, hyperventilating. This wasn't happening...She couldn't...

Horn locked eyes with her. "I *will* find him and bring him back."

"We got company!" Nelson yelled at the same moment.

He raised his gun at two Little Birds searching the forest to the west. They dipped low, then raced toward the Black Hawk.

Horn called out over his shoulder, "Can any of you secret service assholes shoot?"

Barnes and one of his agents stepped up to Horn's side with their rifles. Jake slammed a magazine into his gun and waited for a clear shot. The other agent covered Ringgold with his body.

"Take 'em down!" Horn shouted.

Rounds lanced away from the Black Hawk. The return fire was instant, and a bullet hit one of the agents in the chest. He dropped to the floor, clawing at the wound.

Kate crawled over to help him. The man looked up at her, his face a mask of pain. Screams from the children filled the troop hold as she placed her hand over his wound and applied pressure.

Another bullet punched into the floor beside her. Someone cried out, and she turned just in time to see Barnes slump over, blood blossoming over the back of his jacket. She watched helplessly as he tumbled out the open door.

The chopper rolled hard to the right, throwing off Horn's aim. He steadied his gun and continued to fire as the pilots wheeled away from the island.

Kate kept her hand pressed against the injured agent's chest, but her eyes were fixed on the radio tower they were leaving behind. She could still see Ellis lying there, surrounded by his own blood.

She glanced back at the skyline as Horn hit one of the Little Birds in the rotors. It spun away, smoking, and plowed onto the beach. An explosion lit up the night a moment later. The pilots pulled the Black Hawk over the ocean, heading east with the second Little Bird still in pursuit.

Horn fired off another volley of rounds that punched through the windshield of the other chopper. It went into a nosedive and hit the water with such force it snapped the rotors off.

He kept his weapon on the sinking helicopter.

"Turn this bird around!" Kate yelled. "We have to find Reed!"

Nelson shook his head. "It's too late. We go back and we're dead."

"I will find him. I promise, Kate. But Nelson's right. We have to get out of here," Horn said, his lips trembling.

Lowering his smoking weapon, he turned and looked at Kate with tears welling in his eyes. He slowly walked back to comfort his girls. They wrapped their arms around him.

Kate looked down at the agent she was trying to save. The man's blank eyes were focused on the bulkhead. She felt for a pulse.

He was gone.

She hadn't even learned his name.

"Where are we going?" Soprano asked.

Nelson shook his head. "I have no idea."

"There has to be someplace we can go," Horn said. "We can't just fly forever."

Kate shivered, shock setting in. Her home, the place where she was supposed to raise a family with Reed, was compromised, and the man she loved was missing.

A pair of hands grasped hers, and she found herself looking into Ringgold's eyes. The president was crying. The two women embraced, each holding the other up, as the Black Hawk carried them into the night sky.

Beckham tried to force his eyes open, but his right eyelid was too swollen from the beating he'd taken. The bright sunlight nearly blinded his good eye, and he squeezed it shut again. There was a distant humming beyond the rush of blood in his ears, and the floor beneath him vibrated. He heard faint voices nearby, but couldn't make out what they were saying.

His memories were all jumbled up, and he struggled to make sense of them.

A splash of water suddenly hit his face. He coughed and spluttered, trying to sit up.

"Wake up, Captain," someone said.

Another blast of freezing water hit his face. He blinked over and over until a blurred face came into focus. Wood looked down at him, wearing a smug expression.

"Ah, you're still alive. I thought we were going to lose you for a few minutes back when we stopped to refuel. You're tougher than I thought, but not as tough as I was told."

Beckham sat up and swung a right hook at Wood before he remembered that he'd lost that hand. A cord around his neck jerked him back to the floor. He choked, coughed, and tried to speak, but only ended up spitting out more blood.

"You aren't that bright, are you?" Wood said. "Seriously, I feel cheated. I'd hoped you'd be more of a challenge."

Wood crouched down in front of him, and for the first time Beckham saw where he was being held. He'd expected a prison cell, but they were in a helicopter. Outside the open door of the troop hold, the jagged skyscrapers of a large city came into focus. Skeletons of what had been great buildings were all that remained. Scars from bombs and missiles marred the structures.

"Chicago, if you're wondering," Wood said. He leaned closer to Beckham, so close Beckham could smell a trace of cigar smoke on his breath. "It's become something like a private game preserve. It's crawling with infected."

"You sick bastard," Beckham said.

Wood shrugged. "Maybe, but not as sick as they are. I'm going to drop you into the middle of the hot zone.

Once I find your friends, and Jan, they're coming here too." He glanced up as if in deep thought, then looked back down at Beckham. "I've read your file. I've read *all* the files. I know all about the people you love. Still haven't decided what I'm going to do with that dog yet. I've always wanted one myself. There's also that lady scientist of yours..."

"I'll fucking kill you!" Beckham spat in Wood's face and squirmed under the pressure of the boots holding him down.

"Yes, you keep saying that." Wood wiped the spit away, looked at his hand, then punched Beckham in the nose. Stars broke across his vision as pain spread into his skull. His left hand moved to his vest pocket, fumbling for Kate's ring. He wanted to hold it one last time.

I'm sorry, sweetheart, he thought. *I let you down. I let you all down.*

Ellis was dead. They'd never gotten their message to Europe. Operation Reach would turn the continent into a wasteland of radioactive monsters.

Beckham had never felt lower in his life.

Wood nodded at two of his men. The soldiers leaned down and grabbed Beckham under his arms. They walked him toward the open Black Hawk door. He squinted at the moving shapes below.

Infected.

Hundreds of them.

He brought the ring to his lips and kissed it.

"What's that you've got, Captain?" Wood yanked the ring away and held it to the light to examine it. He chuckled and shook his head. The diamond glittered as Wood tossed the ring out of the chopper.

"No!" Beckham yelled. He headbutted the soldier on his left, and used his shoulder to push the one on the right, nearly breaking free, only to have another soldier pull back on the leash around his neck. The chopper descended over a green park, the skids nearly brushing the tops of the trees.

Wood looked at his watch. "Looks like we're about out of time. Wish I could stick around, but I have more work to do. Then it'll be a quick trip down Inauguration Alley. President Andrew Wood has a nice ring to it, doesn't it?"

Beckham's eyes bulged as he pulled against the men holding him back. Veins popped out of his neck, and he could hear his heartbeat thundering in his ears.

"Good luck, Captain!" Wood said cheerfully. "If you see Jan's cousin, Emilia, down there, say hi for me!"

A swift kick to his back sent Beckham flying out the open door. He tumbled head over feet. The drop felt like it lasted an eternity, but he hit the grass only a few seconds later.

There wasn't much pain. Just numbness.

He rolled onto his back as the Black Hawk traversed the skyline. Wood stood in the door, waving.

Beckham tried to get up, but that earned him a jolt of paralyzing pain.

Motion flashed by his right, and then his left. He was in the middle of a park surrounded by benches, statues, and mature trees. There was movement in the branches. His body might not be working, but his mind was. There was no way out of his situation. His fight was over. There was only so much an old soldier could go through before he fell apart.

His body had given up on him.

But at least Wood hadn't found his friends yet. Horn would protect them. He would take care of Kate and little Javier Riley when Beckham was gone.

All around, he heard the sounds of monsters closing in. Creaking joints, popping lips, and high-pitched shrieks no longer scared him.

He didn't want to die, but he was ready to face his fate.

A creature moving on all fours skidded forward, the snap of joints like breaking tree branches. This beast had been a woman, maybe forty years of age, with pale skin and wispy brown hair. Her shredded shirt hung loosely from her body, and slashes marked her exposed flesh. She opened her sucker mouth, revealing broken teeth and bloody gums.

The strangled sound that came from her voice box was a wordless cackle, but Beckham wondered if she was trying to talk. She tilted her head to examine him, blinking yellow slotted eyes.

He wondered what her name had been, whether she'd had a family. If this was to be the final enemy that took him down, he wanted to meet her on his feet. He struggled upright, his bent blade groaning as it took his weight.

The guttural cackle rose into a high-pitched shriek.

He watched the creature break into a gallop toward him.

Good-bye, Kate.

A gunshot snapped the beast's head back. Three more shots sounded to his left. He turned to see three more of the monsters twitching on the ground, each one dropped by calculated shots to their heads and vital organs.

"Don't get any blood on you!" someone shouted. "They're contagious!"

Beckham followed the voice to a man running across the field wearing a blue baseball cap.

Ellis?

No. He shook his head. He had watched Ellis die at Plum Island.

Another screech rose above the gunshots. The infected

jumped back into the trees, swinging away to safety. For some reason, most of the monsters were afraid of the man in the blue hat.

He stopped to fire at two of the infected that weren't retreating. A half-naked male was making a run for Beckham. A bullet clipped it in the neck, arterial blood spraying toward the sky.

The man fired off the rest of his magazine, paused to change, and then jogged over to Beckham.

"You just going to stand there or what?"

Beckham limped a few steps, nearly stumbling.

The soldier gave him the elevator-eyes treatment. "Damn, brother. You look like *shit*. Can you fight?"

Beckham nodded. "Give me a gun."

The man handed him an M9.

"Name's Lieutenant Jim Flathman," he said, tipping the brim of his cap.

Beckham remembered hearing stories about Flathman. The guy was a drunk and a nutcase, according to Captain Davis, but he'd also managed to hold his post with nothing but a skeleton crew.

"What the hell are you doing here?"

"What am I doing? I'm saving your ass."

Flathman roved his rifle over the trees and the buildings. Faces peeked out of the shadows. The creatures continued to circle them, but they were cagey, staying back as Flathman and Beckham angled their weapons toward the beasts.

"Why aren't they attacking?" Beckham asked.

"I don't know, why don't you ask them?"

Together, the two men crept out of the park toward an empty storefront across the street. The beasts watched them, but none attacked. He followed Flathman into an apartment building and down to the basement. They shut the steel door behind them.

"Don't worry, they won't follow us down here, and they can't get through that door," Flathman said. He jerked his chin toward a table loaded with supplies, and Beckham gratefully grabbed a bottle of water and energy bar from the stash.

Flathman skipped the water and cracked open a bottle of whiskey. He took a long swig, sighed, and then wiped his mouth with the back of his hand. "What's your name, soldier?"

"Captain Reed Beckham."

Flathman raised a brow. "*The* Captain Reed Beckham of Delta Force Team Ghost?"

Beckham nodded.

"Damn! I've heard of you. So, who'd you piss off enough to get thrown out of a chopper into a wildlife preserve of monsters?"

"That was Lieutenant Andrew Wood. He's the bastard behind the attack on this safe zone."

Flathman took another swig. "The same prick that killed my men. I have a special bullet saved for that son of a bitch."

Beckham took a seat on a wood chair. He hurt all over, especially his heart. Kate was out there somewhere with Horn, Ringgold, and the kids. None of them would be safe until Wood was dead.

"Thanks for your help out there, but I have to get moving."

"Slow down, Captain. Don't take this the wrong way, but you look like a Variant ate you and then crapped you out again."

Beckham massaged his forehead with his left hand. "I have to get back to Plum Island. I have to get back to Kate and the president..."

"Pretty long walk, Captain," Flathman said.

"Look, I don't know how long you've been hunkered

down here, but the situation out there...it's bad. Really fucking bad. Our forces in Europe are about to face an army of mutated monsters, and Wood is going to drop the hemorrhage virus on more SZTs. He'll kill *everyone*."

For a long moment, it seemed like Flathman wouldn't answer. Tipping back the bottle, he drained the last of the whiskey, tossed the bottle into the corner with half a dozen other empties, and then stood up. "Okay, then." He looked at his supplies. "I'm about out of whiskey anyways. So what's your plan?"

Beckham paused to think. He had to find a way to get to Plum Island, but first they needed a ride and some firepower.

"Do you have a way out of the city?" he asked.

"We got a Black Hawk at my post, but it's a ways from here. There's a shit ton of infected between here and there."

Beckham nodded. It was a start. He would figure out the rest if they made it out of Chicago. "What about weapons?"

"Follow me."

Beckham limped after Flathman into another room. The crazy lieutenant had managed to amass an impressive arsenal in addition to the supplies he'd scavenged from the city above. Beckham grabbed an M4 and a knife.

They each loaded up as much as they could carry into rucksacks. Beckham still hurt all over, but he shouldered his pack and heaved another bag onto his right shoulder. His blade groaned under the extra weight, but it held. He would have to figure out something for his missing right prosthetic, but for now, he would get along without it.

Captain Reed Beckham was broken and battered—but he wasn't done yet.

Hang on, Kate, he thought as he followed Flathman up the stairs. *I'm coming.*

If you want to hear more about Nicholas Sansbury Smith's upcoming books, join his newsletter or follow him on social media. He just might keep you from the brink of extinction!

Newsletter: www.eepurl.com/bggNg9

Twitter: www.twitter.com/greatwaveink

Facebook: www.facebook.com /Nicholas-Sansbury-Smith-124009881117534

Website: www.nicholassansbury.com

For those who'd like to personally contact Nicholas, he would love to hear from you.

Greatwaveink@gmail.com

Acknowledgments

It's always hard for me to write this section for fear of leaving someone out. My books would not be worth reading if I didn't have the overwhelming support of family, friends, and readers.

I also owe a great deal of gratitude to my primary editors Aaron Sikes and Erin Elizabeth Long. They have spent countless hours on the Extinction Cycle books. Without them these stories would not be what they are. Erin also helped edit Orbs when it was still self-published. She's been with me pretty much since day one, and I appreciate her more than she knows. So thanks, Erin and Aaron.

A special thanks goes to David, my agent, who provided valuable feedback on the early version of *Extinction Horizon* and throughout the Extinction Cycle. I'm grateful for his support and guidance.

I would be remiss if I didn't also thank the people for whom I write: the readers. I've been blessed to have my work read in countries around the world by wonderful people I will probably never meet. If you are reading this, know that I truly appreciate you for trying my stories.

To my family, friends, and everyone else that has supported me on this journey, I thank you.

extras

orbit

meet the author

Maria Diaz

NICHOLAS SANSBURY SMITH is the *USA Today* best-selling author of *Hell Divers*, the Orbs trilogy, and the Extinction Cycle. He worked for Iowa Homeland Security and Emergency Management in disaster mitigation before switching careers to focus on his one true passion: writing. When he isn't writing or daydreaming about the apocalypse, he enjoys running, biking, spending time with his family, and traveling the world. He is an Ironman triathlete and lives in Iowa with his fiancée, their dogs, and a houseful of books.

if you enjoyed

EXTINCTION AFTERMATH

look out for

EXTINCTION WAR

THE EXTINCTION CYCLE

by

Nicholas Sansbury Smith

An army advances....

In Europe, Master Sergeant Joe Fitzpatrick and Team Ghost return from a mission deep into enemy territory only to find that the Variant army has grown stronger, and they are advancing toward the EUF's stronghold in Paris.

On the brink of Civil War...

Back in the United States, President Ringgold and Dr. Kate Lovato are on the run. The Safe-Zone Territories continue to rally behind the ROT flag, leaving Ringgold more enemies than allies. But there are still those who will stand and fight for America. Captain Rachel Davis and Captain Reed Beckham will risk everything to defeat ROT and save the country from collapsing into Civil War.

Humanity may be its own worst enemy....

1

`Three days later...`

Hatteras Island didn't have any of the comforts of the White House, but the view of the ocean under the stars was breathtaking—and, even better, it was quiet here.

President Jan Ringgold sat on the fallen trunk of a palm tree with her bare feet dug into the sand, listening to the waves lap the shoreline. This was the second time in her brief tenure as president that her White House had been relocated. The most recent command center, at the Greenbrier in West Virginia, was gone now, the grounds poisoned and her staff likely infected with the hemorrhage virus. She still didn't know the fate of Vice President George Johnson or anyone else who had been in the Presidential Emergency Operations Center, but each passing hour of radio silence told her with more certainty they were dead or infected. Her entourage, or what remained of it, was in the stealth Black Hawk behind her, combing the radio frequencies for information.

I told you there's always hope. Together, we will persevere. The war will be over soon, Ringgold had said to Doctor Kate Lovato not long ago.

The doctor stood ankle deep in the surf, hand on her swollen stomach, staring up at the stars. Ringgold wasn't the type of person to regret her words, but the line seemed hopelessly naive now.

How could she have known then that a madman like Lieutenant Andrew Wood was waiting in the shadows for a chance to strike? How could she have predicted that he would deploy the very virus that they had worked so hard to eradicate?

Ringgold shook her head and stood. The only remaining Secret Service officer in her detail, Tom King, followed her down the beach, keeping his distance.

She checked the silhouetted figures of her team above the beach. Most of them were clustered under the canopy of trees set on a grassy bluff overlooking the ocean. The Black Hawk was positioned to the right, a camouflage tarp thrown over everything but the troop hold. They had taken refuge at the southern tip of Cape Point, away from the roads and the Woods Coastal Reserve.

Ringgold joined Kate at the water's edge. She remained silent, not wanting to disturb the doctor but still trying to show she was here if Kate needed support. It had been three days since Dr. Ellis was killed and Kate's partner, Captain Reed Beckham, kidnapped.

Three days of hiding and listening to the communications channels as the country slowly collapsed into civil war. Three days of waiting helplessly as SZTs joined forces with ROT, and three days of hearing about the losses of American and European Unified Forces in Europe.

The human race wasn't just back on course for extinction—it was barreling right toward the black hole that would end them forever.

"He's out there," Kate said, turning away from the ocean to look at Ringgold. "Reed is out there looking up at this same sky. I know it."

Ringgold had figured that was what Kate was thinking about, and as much as she wanted to believe Kate was right, Ringgold was losing faith. There was chaos in every direction. She had thought they'd seen the worst possible threat in the Variants, but Wood was more evil than the monsters. At least the beasts didn't have access to weapons of mass destruction.

"I better get back to Tasha and Jenny," Kate said. She walked past Ringgold, feet slurping in the wet sand, but Ringgold reached out to stop her. "Madam President?" Kate asked.

Ringgold struggled to find the right words. After a moment, she let her hand drop. "It's nothing. Come on, let's go."

Side by side, they walked up the beach toward the Black Hawk.

Master Sergeant Parker Horn greeted them at the edge of the forest, his machine gun cradled across his broad chest, his strawberry-blond hair rustled by the wind.

"All clear up here," he said, voice gruff. He offered a brief nod, then strode out into the grass and took a knee to scan for hostiles.

Ringgold was used to having a dozen men protecting her, but now they were down to just Secret Service agent Tom King, Horn, former NYPD officer Jake Temper, and the two Black Hawk pilots, Captain Ivan Larson and Captain Frank Spade. Both of the pilots were holding security just to the north, watching for any possible juvenile Variants that might have fled Kryptonite by jumping into the ocean.

National Security Advisor Ben Nelson and Chief of Staff James Soprano were both armed, but she didn't trust them to do much in a fight. They were ideas men— men of strategy, not violence. Both sat on stumps listening to the radio.

Ringgold found her shoes and shoved her feet inside. A crunching sounded, and she looked over as Jake tried to fasten the tarp over the troop hold of the Black Hawk. She could see several sleeping figures inside. Jenny and Tasha were nestled up next to Bo and his mother, Donna. Timothy, Jake's son, was sitting up, wide awake. He waved at Ringgold, and she waved back.

She finished securing her shoes and checked the cluster of backpacks neatly arranged at the foot of the trees. Even in the moonlight she could see their contents had dwindled. They would have to find water and food soon.

"Have you heard anything from the PEOC?" Ringgold asked, joining Kate and the men by the radio.

Nelson and Soprano shook their heads.

"Whatever ROT did, they completely cut off the PEOC," Nelson said. "I'm guessing they used some sort of electromagnetic pulse."

"SZT Forty-Nine just declared loyalty to them," Soprano added. "That pretty much evens the playing field. Once we lose half of them, I'm sure the other mayors will quickly fall into line behind Wood."

"We need support from our forces in Europe," Nelson said. He removed his suit coat and rolled up his shirtsleeves. "I say we try to reach General Nixon and recall our troops."

"We don't know what side he's on," Soprano replied. "For all we know, he believes we're behind the missile attacks on the SZTs." He paused and wagged a chubby finger. "We're better off trying to find help Stateside."

"The moment we send out an SOS, we're toast," King said. It was the first time Ringgold had heard the Secret Service officer voice his opinion. It was good, though; she needed all of the opinions she could get right now.

Kate remained silent, her arms still folded over her stomach. She was shaking, but it wasn't from the chilly breeze. Ringgold could tell her friend was near her breaking point, and all of that stress was terrible for the baby.

"Kate, why don't you go get some rest?" Ringgold said.

"I'm fine."

Horn walked over and whispered something in Kate's ear. She huffed and walked away to the chopper. The bulky Delta Force operator hurried after her.

"Kate, wait up. I'm sorry," he said.

Ringgold watched them move toward the helicopter. The children stirred inside the dark troop hold as Horn and Kate spoke outside. When they had finished talking, Horn bent down to kiss his daughters.

All of their lives were in Ringgold's hands. They couldn't stay here forever. They were running out of food, and there was a risk of Variant juveniles in the area. It was either take a chance on finding help or wait to die.

"Send out the SOS to our forces here in the States," she ordered.

Soprano nodded in agreement, but Nelson raised a hand.

"Ma'am, there are several commanders who know our call sign," he stated. "If any of them are compromised, then we're giving up our position. We can't trust—"

Ringgold glared at her advisor. "Ben, I've made my decision." She wasn't sure if it was the right one, but she also knew General Nixon needed to focus on winning the war in Europe. Besides, he was too far away to help her right now anyway. America had started this nightmare, and they would help finish it, one way or another.

Soprano picked up the radio and scanned through the frequencies. Nelson sighed and neatly folded his suit coat. Then he gently set it over the stump and held out his hand for the radio receiver.

Nelson met Ringgold's gaze, and she nodded firmly.

"This is Black Cat calling all Eagles in the area, requesting assistance at the following coordinates..."

Ringgold walked away. The deed was done; now they just had to wait. She strode to the chopper with her hands tucked into her pockets. If ROT was going to come, she wanted to be with her friends when they did.

She sat at the edge of the troop hold between Kate and Horn.

"I keep thinking Fitz is going to drop in and save the day," Kate said with a sad smile. "Or that Reed will show up with a tank and whisk us all to safety. Kind of stupid, right?"

"Don't say that, Kate," Horn said quietly. "Fitz, Beckham, Apollo, and our other friends are still out there. We'll get through this, and we'll see them again."

Kate wiped her eyes but didn't reply.

An hour later, Ringgold began to feel the tug of sleep. It was late, probably after midnight. Horn had returned to the beach with King to hold security. Storm clouds drifted in from the west, crossing the moon and carpeting the island in darkness.

Ringgold felt a prick of water on her leg. The adrenaline had worn off, and her eyelids drooped, but she stood with Kate as Soprano and Nelson walked over.

"Well?" Ringgold asked.

Soprano frowned. "Not a single reply."

"My guess is that any friendlies who are listening are too afraid to show up here," Nelson said. "I think we should fire up the Black Hawk and be ready to move."

"And go where?" Kate whispered.

The president of the United States and her few remaining allies had nowhere to go.

"We don't have enough fuel to get far," Horn said, coming in from his rounds. He leaned back into the troop hold to check on Tasha and Jenny. "You should try and get some sleep, Madam President—and you too, Kate."

Ringgold sat back down and sighed inwardly, desperate for sleep but too afraid to close her eyes. The pain of her bullet wound was flaring up again.

"He's right," Kate said quietly. "We should get some rest."

Ringgold balled up her coat for a pillow and set it beside her on the floor of the troop hold. She had slept in worse places than this during the nights she had hidden from the Variants in Raven Rock. Each time she had closed her eyes while hiding there, she had wondered if she would wake up to the deformed face of a monster. Now she wondered if she would wake up staring down the barrel of a ROT gun.

The nightmares were bad tonight. She saw her cousin transforming into a raging beast. In her dream, Emilia contorted, her body cracking and jerking as the hemorrhage virus pulsed through her veins. Then came the blood oozing from her frightened, enraged eyes, then the pained shrieks, and finally the cracking of joints.

Ringgold's eyes snapped open. Wrapping her arms across her chest, she leaned back against the bulkhead and waited for the rain to stop. Waves slapped against the beach, then receded back to sea. It was almost pitch black now that the storm had moved over the island.

She had nearly nodded off again when movement in the darkness caught her eye. Six figures clad in black armor moved up the beach. Ringgold blinked, her heart kicking.

"Kate," she whispered. "Kate, wake up."

King, silhouetted out on the beach, suddenly crashed to the ground, two men in black tackling him from behind. A muffled shout came from the other side of the bird—from Jake or the pilots, Ringgold wasn't sure.

Horn ran over to the helicopter, his eyes wide. "We have to go, *now.*"

The kids stirred awake, sleepily calling out for their parents. Ringgold kept her focus on the men in black. They were all carrying machine guns.

Horn turned and raised his rifle, the muzzle shifting from target to target. He cursed. Even Ringgold, who was no soldier, could see that they weren't going to win this fight.

One of the men stepped out in front of the others and shouted, "We have you surrounded. Drop your weapons and identify yourselves!"

"You first!" Horn yelled back.

The leader of the team continued to advance. "Drop your weapons and give up the president."

The moon spilled across the ocean, its light parting the waves like a highway running through an endless desert. Ringgold didn't see any sign of a ship out there— so where had these men came from?

"I'm not going to ask you again," the leader said, his voice rising. The other men all fanned out to surround the Black Hawk. Two more showed up around the front of the chopper, shoving the marine pilots and Jake into the sand, their hands already bound.

Horn shifted from target to target. Nelson was standing to his left with a pistol raised. Ringgold couldn't see Soprano.

"Last chance," the leader said. He balled his fist, and the other men stopped, all of them directing their guns at Horn. He blocked the front of the troop hold with his body, the only person standing between Ringgold and these men.

Tasha called out for Horn.

"Stay where you are, kiddo!" he yelled back.

Ringgold would not allow Horn to be slaughtered in front of his own children. Not if she could do anything about it. ROT wanted her, and only her.

"Put down your weapons," she ordered as she scooted out of the chopper.

Nelson moved in front of her. "Get back, ma'am. I'm not letting them take you."

"Me either," Horn said with a snort. "Just give me the word, Madam President, and I will light these bozos up."

"Get away from her," the leader said. She could see his features now. The whites of his eyes stood out against his dark skin. She wondered what was going through his mind.

Nelson took a step forward and aimed the gun at the man speaking.

"Put your gun down!" he yelled at Nelson.

Ringgold reached over and put her hand on the barrel of Nelson's gun, slowly pushing it to the ground.

"I'll go with you. Just let everyone else go," she said to the leader.

She strode past Horn and Nelson and prepared herself to be riddled with bullets, or at the very least to be whisked away to a dark prison cell to await execution later. If it was the latter, she hoped she would get to look Wood in the eyes before she was killed.

"Ma'am," Horn pleaded. He tried to move in front of her, but she turned and faced him. "It's okay. You did your job protecting me, but you have to look after your daughters now, and Kate."

Horn snorted like a bull, his gun moving from face to face. The men in black all watched her as she strolled from the chopper toward them.

"Stand down," the leader said, balling his fist.

One by one the rifles were lowered. All but Horn's.

The leader approached slowly, his eyes flitting from Ringgold to Horn. "These men are with you, President Ringgold?" he said.

Horn finally pushed his rifle's barrel toward the sand.

She straightened her back. "Yes, they are."

"You could have just said so earlier," the man said in a gruff voice. "I'm Senior Chief Petty Officer Randall Blade with SEAL Team Four. We're here to evacuate you to the USS *Florida*."

Ringgold narrowed her brows. "You're SEALs? Why the hell didn't *you* say so earlier?"

Blade flashed a white grin. "We thought this could be a trap. ROT was on the airwaves warning of something like this. We took a risk by coming here—a pretty damn big risk, if you ask me, but someone above my pay grade thought it was worth it, and they were right. You still have some friends out there, President Ringgold."

Horn and Kate stepped up to flank Ringgold on both sides. "I'm Doctor Kate Lovato," Kate said. "Please, have you heard anything about Captain Reed Beckham?"

Shaking his head, Blade said, "I'm sorry, ma'am. Get your things. We don't have long." Blade nodded at one of his men, who pulled out a radio. He called in a ride over the channel.

The other SEALs unbound the hands of the marine pilots, Jake, King, and Soprano, who had also managed to get himself captured. The men took up positions along the beach while Ringgold and her friends gathered their belongings.

"Where exactly are you taking us?" Kate asked Blade.

"To the USS *Florida* and then to a small fleet of warships, boats, and a French research vessel two hundred miles to the east," he said.

"French?" Ringgold cut in.

"Yes, ma'am. Those friends I was talking about, they aren't just Americans." Blade paused and looked at Kate. "They're also looking for help. Apparently, there's some new kind of monster in Europe."

Andrew Wood stroked his scarred chin as he watched his fortress come into view from the plush leather seat of his newly acquired Boeing VC-25. The military version of the 747 was nicer than he had expected. Although he had been hoping for better in-flight meals.

"An MRE?" he said, staring at the package set in front of him by a female soldier who was doubling in duty as a glorified flight attendant. She stuttered and batted long eyelashes over a pair of blue eyes.

"I-I'm sorry, sir," she replied. "That's all we have."

"No fresh fruit or grilled salmon? What is this world coming to?"

She shook her head ruefully, and Wood chuckled. With their ranks swelling, he hardly knew anyone outside his inner circle.

"What's your first name?"

"It's, um, it's Yolanda, sir."

"Yolanda—what a sweet name."

"Uh, thank you, sir."

She swallowed and took a step back. Wood loved making people nervous and paused for dramatic effect. Then he raised a hand and laughed again.

"I'm just messin' with you, sweetie, but I would like an alcoholic beverage. I'm assuming we have something on board. I'd like something stiff—stiff and cold."

"Yes . . . Yes, I can do that, sir."

Yolanda hesitated again and then backed up as he shooed her away like an insignificant fly.

He took a bite of dry beef and turned back to the view. Snow-brushed forests peppered the terrain below, and crystal-clear rivers meandered through the frozen tundra. At night, the temperature dropped far below freezing. It was one reason the hemorrhage virus had never made it here, and if Wood had to guess, it was for that reason Jan Ringgold and her staff had evacuated survivors from Anchorage and other cities to SZT 19, which was only about twenty miles to the west.

But this time Wood wasn't heading off to take over an SZT. His growing army was doing that for him. He was going home to the place where he had spent the majority of his career in the military.

Xerxes, the code name for the Resistance of Tyranny military base near the Knik Glacier, was one of the most secure places in the United States. That was obvious even from the sky. The five-cornered former military facility was nestled along the blue wall of a glacier.

The men and women living there now had spent the past seven months beneath the ice. It was one of the most inhospitable places in the world, too cold and isolated even for the Variants. That was why Wood had picked the base to be the ROT headquarters.

He continued stroking his scarred face and leaned closer to the window for a better view of the blue glacier in the distance. Tucked against the bottom were five circular structures peeking above the snow. Most of the base, however, was hidden beneath the ground. He had renamed the top secret facility after the great Persian king who had sought to take over the Greek empire— and much of the rest of the world. The story had always fascinated Wood, but where Xerxes had ultimately failed, he would succeed.

Before he did that, he needed to get General Nixon on the ROT team, and the general wasn't the easiest man to coerce. It was going to take some major convincing to get the United States military in Europe to ally itself with him. Luckily, Wood had the perfect plan to make it happen.

Yolanda returned with a vodka on the rocks. For a moment, he wondered what her story was. You didn't survive the apocalypse and get a job working for Wood by being a loser.

"Prepare for landing," one of the pilots said over the PA system.

Wood sipped the vodka and looked away from Yolanda, no longer interested in the young woman. He glanced down at the graveyard of armored vehicles on the southern edge of the base, recalling the cold nights he had spent on patrol down there thirty years ago, waiting for the Soviets to invade. That experience—and working for a paranoid, borderline schizophrenic commander—had prepared Wood for a different type of invasion.

Wood didn't see the monsters populating the earth as the end of humanity. He saw them as an opportunity—an opportunity to finish what his late brother, Colonel Zach Wood, had started while working with the Medical Corps.

Before he could finish their work, he had to take down the most dangerous enemy of all—Jan Ringgold. The former president was an outlaw who had escaped his attack on the PEOC. He had been chipping away at her power and credibility with an intricate web of lies for the past few weeks, but the time for playing games was over.

His masterstroke had been attacking SZT 15, in what was once Chicago, and blaming the hemorrhage virus outbreak there on Ringgold. Once he'd discovered that Ringgold's nearest living relative, a cousin, was sheltering there, SZT 15's fate had been sealed. After all, who in their right mind would support a woman who had knowingly turned her own family member into a monster?

Wood resisted the urge to chuckle, fearing it would make the wrong impression on his inner circle. He was to be supreme ruler of the new world order, but he didn't want to be seen as an eccentric despot. If there was one thing Wood hated—other than Reed Beckham and his band of tyrants, of course—it was a stereotype.

The men who made up Wood's team sat in front of him. Three days earlier there had been four advisors, but Wood had lost Jack Johnson when he'd sent the man to check on the USS *George Washington*.

Someone had gotten to the aircraft carrier, blowing a gaping hole in the ship and destroying several of the hemorrhage-virus missiles. Wood wasn't sure who, but it didn't matter now. The bastards were undoubtedly all dead or infected.

The VC-25's pilots circled the base, providing an aerial view of a lake and the glacier below. Wood could even see SZT 19 in the distance, although it was hardly anything to look at—basically just a run-down fort built to house a couple thousand survivors. It had only taken one visit to get them to align with ROT. Most of the mayors of the SZTs were spineless cowards. And those who weren't, Wood would dispose of when the time came.

"Sir, sorry to interrupt, but I have news," said the rough voice of Michael Kufman.

Wood looked up at a pair of ruthless black eyes. The former Delta Force operator stood six feet, three inches tall, with linebacker shoulders and the massive biceps of an Olympic arm wrestler.

"Well?" Wood said. "What's your news?"

"I just got word that Coyote has been captured at the SZT in Los Angeles." Kufman didn't smile or show any hint of emotion as he gave the news.

"That's excellent," Wood said. He smiled, and Kufman returned the gesture with something that looked more like a scowl, his thin lips parting to show the gap between his two front teeth. Wood wasn't sure the soldier was capable of smiling.

"Have you ever cracked a joke, Kufman?" Wood asked.

"Your brother wasn't one for jokes, sir," Kufman said stiffly.

Wood took another sip of vodka, welcoming the burn. His older brother and Kufman had been good friends. The best of friends, in fact—there wasn't any other man Zach would have wanted at Andrew's side to see him through to the end.

"Tell the pilots to keep the plane hot. It seems I'm headed for La La Land shortly," Wood said. His smile was gone, and he turned back to the window to watch the tarmac rise up to meet the plane. The wheels hit the snowy asphalt with a jolt.

He finished off the vodka and waited for the plane to come to a stop. In moments like this, when he had nothing to do but wait, he would contemplate his revenge. Beckham was dead, but he was still looking for Master Sergeant Joe Fitzpatrick, the cripple who had blown his brother's head off at Plum Island.

At first, Wood had thought Beckham was his King Leonidas, but the Spartan king who had stood with three hundred of his warriors against the Persian masses was not Beckham after all. He had been far too easy to kill. In Wood's eyes, his great nemesis was Fitzpatrick, and Wood would have his revenge soon.

He walked through the plane's open door and stood at the top of a ladder overlooking the icy terrain. Gathered on the tarmac were a hundred men dressed in black parkas, automatic rifles slung over their backs and helmets with goggles atop their heads.

Sure, they weren't a million-strong Persian army, but they would have to do.

Despite the rage swirling through his veins, he forced a smile and waved at his men, imagining what Xerxes, the King of Kings, must have felt when he walked off his ships before the invasion of the Hellespont.

"You ready, sir?" said Kufman.

Wood nodded, but he knew the swearing-in bullshit was just words. Actions were more important than petty titles like "President Wood" or "King Whoever." He would never feel truly in control until he had taken revenge on the man who killed his brother. He was ready to lead the world into a new age—but first, he had a score to settle.

if you enjoyed
EXTINCTION AFTERMATH

look out for

SIX WAKES

by

Mur Lafferty

On a space ship far from earth, someone is murdering the crew. And the crew's newly awakened clones will have to find their killer—before he strikes again!

Maria Arena awakens in a cloning vat streaked with drying blood. She has no memory of how she died. This is new; before, when she had awakened as a new clone, her first memory was of how she died.

Maria's vat is one of seven, each one holding the clone of a crew member of the starship Dormire, *each clone waiting for its previous incarnation to die so it can awaken. And Maria isn't the only one to die recently....*

THIS IS NOT A PIPE

DAY 1
JULY 25, 2493

Sound struggled to make its way through the thick synth-amneo fluid. Once it reached Maria Arena's ears, it sounded like a chain saw: loud, insistent, and unending. She couldn't make out the words, but it didn't sound like a situation she wanted to be involved in.

Her reluctance at her own rebirth reminded her where she was, and who she was. She grasped for her last backup. The crew had just moved into their quarters on the *Dormire*, and the cloning bay had been the last room they'd visited on their tour. There they had done their first backup on the ship.

Maria must have been in an accident or something soon after, killing her and requiring her next clone to wake. Sloppy use of a life wouldn't make a good impression on the captain, who likely was the source of the angry chain-saw noise.

Maria finally opened her eyes. She tried to make sense of the dark round globules floating in front of her vat, but it was difficult with the freshly cloned brain being put to work for the first time. There were too many things wrong with such a mess.

With the smears on the outside of the vat and the purple color through the bluish fluid Maria floated in, she figured the orbs were blood drops. Blood shouldn't float. That was the first problem. If blood was floating, that meant the grav drive that spun the ship had failed. That was probably another reason someone was yelling. The blood and the grav drive.

Blood in a cloning bay, that was different too. Cloning bays were pristine, clean places, where humans were downloaded into newly cloned bodies when the previous ones had died. It was much cleaner and less painful than human birth, with all its screaming and blood.

Again with the blood.

The cloning bay had six vats in two neat rows, filled with blue-tinted synth-amneo fluid and the waiting clones of the rest of the crew. Blood belonged in the medbay, down the hall. The unlikely occurrence of a drop of blood originating in the medbay, floating down the hall, and entering the cloning bay to float in front of Maria's vat would be extraordinary. But that's not what happened; a body floated above the blood drops. A number of bodies, actually.

Finally, if the grav drive *had* failed, and if someone *had* been injured in the cloning bay, another member of the crew would have cleaned up the blood. Someone was always on call to ensure a new clone made the transition from death into their new body smoothly.

No. A perfect purple sphere of blood shouldn't be floating in front of her face.

Maria had now been awake for a good minute or so. No one worked the computer to drain the synth-amneo fluid to free her.

A small part of her brain began to scream at her that she should be more concerned about the bodies, but only a small part.

She'd never had occasion to use the emergency release valve inside the cloning vats. Scientists had implemented them after some techs had decided to play a prank on a clone, and woke her up only to leave her in the vat alone for hours. When she had gotten free, stories said, the result was messy and violent, resulting in the fresh cloning of some of the techs. After that, engineers added an interior release switch for clones to let themselves out of the tank if they were trapped for whatever reason.

Maria pushed the button and heard a *clunk* as the release triggered, but the synth-amneo fluid stayed where it was.

A drain relied on gravity to help the fluid along its way. Plumbing 101 there. The valve was opened but the fluid remained a stubborn womb around Maria.

She tried to find the source of the yelling. One of the crew floated near the computer bank, naked, with wet hair stuck out in a frightening, spiky corona. Another clone woke. Two of them had died?

Behind her, crewmates floated in four vats. All of their eyes were open, and each was searching for the emergency release. Three *clunk*s sounded, but they remained in the same position Maria was in.

Maria used the other emergency switch to open the vat door. Ideally it would have been used after the fluid had drained away, but there was little ideal about this situation. She and a good quantity of the synth-amneo fluid floated out of her vat, only to collide gently with the orb of blood floating in front of her. The surface tension of both fluids held, and the drop bounced away.

Maria hadn't encountered the problem of how to get out of a liquid prison in zero-grav. She experimented by flailing about, but only made some fluid break off the main bubble and go floating away. In her many lives, she'd been in more than one undignified situation, but this was new.

Action and reaction, she thought, and inhaled as much of the oxygen-rich fluid as she could, then forced everything out of her lungs as if she were sneezing. She didn't go as fast as she would have if it had been air, because she was still inside viscous fluid, but it helped push her backward and out of the bubble. She inhaled air and then coughed and vomited the rest of the fluid in a spray in front of her, banging her head on the computer console as her body's involuntary movements propelled her farther.

Finally out of the fluid, and gasping for air, she looked up.

"Oh shit."

Three dead crewmates floated around the room amid the blood and other fluids. Two corpses sprouted a number of gory tentacles, bloody bubbles that refused to break away from the deadly wounds. A fourth was strapped to a chair at the terminal.

Gallons of synth-amneo fluid joined the gory detritus as the newly cloned crew fought to exit their vats. They looked with as much shock as she felt at their surroundings.

Captain Katrina de la Cruz moved to float beside her, still focused on the computer. "Maria, stop staring and make yourself useful. Check on the others."

Maria scrambled for a handhold on the wall to pull herself away from the captain's attempt to access the terminal.

Katrina pounded on a keyboard and poked at the console screen. "IAN, what the hell happened?"

"My speech functions are inaccessible," the computer's male, slightly robotic voice said.

"Ceci n'est pas une pipe," muttered a voice above Maria. It broke her shock and reminded her of the captain's order to check on the crew.

The speaker was Akihiro Sato, pilot and navigator. She had met him a few hours ago at the cocktail party before the launch of the *Dormire*.

"Hiro, why are you speaking French?" Maria said, confused. "Are you all right?"

"Someone saying aloud that they can't talk is like that old picture of a pipe that says, 'This is not a pipe.' It's supposed to give art students deep thoughts. Never mind." He waved his hand around the cloning bay. "What happened, anyway?"

"I have no idea," she said. "But—God, what a mess. I have to go check on the others."

"Goddammit, you just spoke," the captain said to the computer, dragging some icons around the screen. "Something's working inside there. Talk to me, IAN."

"My speech functions are inaccessible," the AI said again, and de la Cruz slammed her hand down on the keyboard, grabbing it to keep herself from floating away from it.

Hiro followed Maria as she maneuvered around the room using the handholds on the wall. Maria found herself face-to-face with the gruesome body of Wolfgang, their second in command. She gently pushed him aside, trying not to dislodge the gory bloody tentacles sprouting from punctures on his body.

She and Hiro floated toward the living Wolfgang, who was doubled over coughing the synth-amneo out of his lungs. "What the hell is going on?" he asked in a ragged voice.

"You know as much as we do," Maria said. "Are you all right?"

He nodded and waved her off. He straightened his back, gaining at least another foot on his tall frame. Wolfgang was born on the moon colony, Luna, several generations of his family developing the long bones of living their whole lives in low gravity. He took a handhold and propelled himself toward the captain.

"What do you remember?" Maria asked Hiro as they approached another crewmember.

"My last backup was right after we boarded the ship. We haven't even left yet," Hiro said.

Maria nodded. "Same for me. We should still be docked, or only a few weeks from Earth."

"I think we have more immediate problems, like our current status," Hiro said.

"True. Our current status is four of us are dead," Maria said, pointing at the bodies. "And I'm guessing the other two are as well."

"What could kill us all?" Hiro asked, looking a bit green as he dodged a bit of bloody skin. "And what happened to me and the captain?"

He referred to the "other two" bodies that were not floating in the cloning bay. Wolfgang, their engineer, Paul Seurat, and Dr. Joanna Glass all were dead, floating around the room, gently bumping off vats or one another.

Another cough sounded from the last row of vats, then a soft voice. "Something rather violent, I'd say."

"Welcome back, Doctor, you all right?" Maria asked, pulling herself toward the woman.

The new clone of Joanna nodded, her tight curls glistening with the synth-amneo. Her upper body was thin and strong, like all new clones, but her legs were small and twisted. She glanced up at the bodies and pursed her lips. "What happened?" She didn't wait for them to answer, but grasped a handhold and pulled herself toward the ceiling where a body floated.

"Check on Paul," Maria said to Hiro, and followed Joanna.

The doctor turned her own corpse to where she could see it, and her eyes grew wide. She swore quietly. Maria came up behind her and swore much louder.

Her throat had a stab wound, with great waving gouts of blood reaching from her neck. If the doctor's advanced age was any indication, they were well past the beginning of the mission. Maria remembered her as a woman who looked to be in her thirties, with smooth dark skin and black hair. Now wrinkles lined the skin around her eyes and the corners of her mouth, and gray shot through her tightly braided hair. Maria looked at the other bodies; from her vantage point she could now see each also showed their age.

"I didn't even notice," she said, breathless. "I-I only noticed the blood and gore. We've been on this ship for *decades*. Do you remember anything?"

"No." Joanna's voice was flat and grim. "We need to tell the captain."

"No one touch anything! This whole room is a crime scene!" Wolfgang shouted up to them. "Get away from that body!"

"Wolfgang, the crime scene, if this is a crime scene, is already contaminated by about twenty-five hundred gallons of synth-amneo," Hiro said from outside Paul's vat. "With blood spattering everywhere."

"What do you mean *if* it's a crime scene?" Maria asked. "Do you think that the grav drive died and stopped the ship from spinning and then knives just floated into us?"

Speaking of the knife, it drifted near the ceiling. Maria propelled herself toward it and snatched it before it got pulled against the air intake filter, which was already getting clogged with bodily fluids she didn't even want to think about.

The doctor did as Wolfgang had commanded, moving away from her old body to join him and the captain. "This is murder," she said. "But Hiro's right, Wolfgang, there is a reason zero-g forensics never took off as a science. The air filters are sucking up the evidence as we speak. By now everyone is covered in everyone else's blood. And now we have six new people and vats of synth-amneo floating around the bay messing up whatever's left."

Wolfgang set his jaw and glared at her. His tall, thin frame shone with the bluish amneo fluid. He opened his mouth to counter the doctor, but Hiro interrupted them.

"Five," interrupted Hiro. He coughed and expelled more synth-amneo, which Maria narrowly dodged. He grimaced in apology. "Five new people. Paul's still inside." He pointed to their engineer, who remained in his vat, eyes closed.

Maria remembered seeing his eyes open when she was in her own vat. But now Paul floated, eyes closed, hands covering his genitals, looking like a child who was playing hide-and-seek and whoever was "It" was going to devour him. He too was pale, naturally stocky, lightly muscled instead of the heavier man Maria remembered.

"Get him out of there," Katrina said. Wolfgang obliged, going to another terminal and pressing the button to open the vat.

Hiro reached in and grabbed Paul by the wrist and pulled him and his fluid cage free.

"Okay, only five of us were out," Maria said, floating down. "That cuts the synth-amneo down by around four hundred gallons. Not a huge improvement. There's still a lot of crap flying around. You're not likely to get evidence from anything except the bodies themselves." She held the knife out to Wolfgang, gripping the edge of the handle with her thumb and forefinger. "And possibly the murder weapon."

He looked around, and Maria realized he was searching for something with which to take the knife. "I've already contaminated it with my hands, Wolfgang. It's been floating among blood and dead bodies. The only thing we'll get out of it is that it probably killed us all."

"We need to get IAN back online," Katrina said. "Get the grav drive back on. Find the other two bodies. Check on the cargo. Then we will fully know our situation."

Hiro whacked Paul smartly on the back, and the man doubled over and retched, sobbing. Wolfgang watched with disdain as Paul bounced off the wall with no obvious awareness of his surroundings.

"Once we get IAN back online, we'll have him secure a channel to Earth," Katrina said.

"My speech functions are inaccessible," the computer repeated. The captain gritted her teeth.

"That's going to be tough, Captain," Joanna said. "These bodies show considerable age, indicating we've been in space for much longer than our mindmaps are telling us."

Katrina rubbed her forehead, closing her eyes. She was silent, then opened her eyes and began typing things into the terminal. "Get Paul moving, we need him."

Hiro stared helplessly as Paul continued to sob, curled into a little drifting ball, still trying to hide his privates.

A ball of vomit—not the synth-amneo expelled from the bodies, but actual stomach contents—floated toward the air intake vent and was sucked into the filter. Maria knew that after they took care of all of the captain's priorities, she would still be stuck with the job of changing the air filters, and probably crawling through the ship's vents to clean all of the bodily fluids out before they started to become a biohazard. Suddenly a maintenance-slash-junior-engineer position on an important starship didn't seem so glamorous.

"I think Paul will feel better with some clothes," Joanna said, looking at him with pity.

"Yeah, clothes sound good," Hiro said. They were all naked, their skin rising in goose bumps. "Possibly a shower while we're at it."

"I will need my crutches or a chair," Joanna said. "Unless we want to keep the grav drive off."

"Stop it," Katrina said. "The murderer could still be on the ship and you're talking about clothes and showers?"

Wolfgang waved a hand to dismiss her concern. "No, clearly the murderer died in the fight. We are the only six aboard the ship."

"You can't know that," de la Cruz said. "What's happened in the past several decades? We need to be cautious. No one goes anywhere alone. Everyone in twos. Maria, you and Hiro get the doctor's crutches from the medbay. She'll want them when the grav drive gets turned back on."

"I can just take the prosthetics off that body," Joanna said, pointing upward. "It won't need them anymore."

"That's evidence," Wolfgang said, steadying his own floating corpse to study the stab wounds. He fixated on the bubbles of gore still attached to his chest. "Captain?"

"Fine, get jumpsuits, get the doctor a chair or something, and check on the grav drive," Katrina said. "The rest of us will work. Wolfgang, you and I will get the bodies tethered together. We don't want them to sustain more damage when the grav drive comes back online."

On the way out, Maria paused to check on her own body, which she hadn't really examined before. It seemed too gruesome to look into your own dead face. The body was strapped to a seat at one of the terminals, drifting gently against the tether. A large bubble of blood drifted from the back of her neck, where she had clearly been stabbed. Her lips were white and her skin was a sickly shade of green. She now knew where the floating vomit had come from.

"It looks like I was the one who hit the resurrection switch," she said to Hiro, pointing to her body.

"Good thing too," Hiro said. He looked at the captain, conversing closely with Wolfgang. "I wouldn't expect a medal anytime soon, though. She's not looking like she's in the mood."

The resurrection switch was a fail-safe button. If all of the clones on the ship died at once, a statistical improbability, then the AI should have been able to wake up the next clones. If the ship failed to do so, an even higher statistical improbability, then a physical switch in the cloning bay could carry out the job, provided there was someone alive enough to push it.

Like the others, Maria's body showed age. Her middle had softened and her hands floating above the terminal were thin and spotted. She had been the physical age of thirty-nine when they had boarded.

"I gave you an order," Katrina said. "And Dr. Glass, it looks like talking our engineer down will fall to you. Do it quickly, or else he's going to need another new body when I'm through with him."

Hiro and Maria got moving before the captain could detail what she was going to do to them. Although, Maria reflected, it would be hard to top what they had just apparently been through.

Maria remembered the ship as shinier and brighter: metallic and smooth, with handholds along the wall for low-gravity situations and thin metal grates making up the floor, revealing a subfloor of storage compartments and vents. Now it was duller, another indication that decades of spaceflight had changed the ship as it had changed the crew. It was darker, a few lights missing, illuminated by the yellow lights of an alert. Someone—probably the captain—had commanded an alert.

Some of the previous times, Maria had died in a controlled environment. She had been in bed after illness, age, or, once, injury. The helpful techs had created a final mindmap of her brain, and she had been euthanized after signing a form permitting it. A doctor had approved it, the body was disposed of neatly, and she had woken up young, pain-free, with all her memories of all her lives thus far.

Some other times hadn't been as gentle, but still were a better experience than this.

Having her body still hanging around, blood and vomit everywhere, offended her on a level she hadn't thought possible. Once you were gone, the body meant nothing, had no sentimental value. The future body was all that mattered. The past shouldn't be there, staring you in the face with dead eyes. She shuddered.

"When the engines get running again, it'll warm up," Hiro said helpfully, mistaking the reason for her shiver.

They reached a junction, and she led the way left. "Decades, Hiro. We've been out here for decades. What happened to our mindmaps?"

"What's the last thing you remember?" he asked.

"We had the cocktail party in Luna station as the final passengers were entering cryo and getting loaded. We came aboard. We were given some hours to move into our quarters. Then we had the tour, which ended in the cloning bay, getting our updated mindmaps."

"Same here," he said.

"Are you scared?" Maria said, stopping and looking at him.

She hadn't scrutinized him since waking up in the cloning bay. She was used to the way that clones with the experience of hundreds of years could look like they had just stepped out of university. Their bodies woke up at peak age, twenty years old, designed to be built with muscle. What the clones did with that muscle once they woke up was their challenge.

Akihiro Sato was a thin Pan Pacific United man of Japanese descent with short black hair that was drying in stiff cowlicks. He had lean muscles, and high cheekbones. His eyes were black, and they met hers with a level gaze. She didn't look too closely at the rest of him; she wasn't rude.

He pulled at a cowlick, then tried to smooth it down. "I've woken up in worse places."

"Like where?" she asked, pointing down the hall from where they had come. "What's worse than that horror movie scene?"

He raised his hands in supplication. "I don't mean literally. I mean I've lost time before. You have to learn to adapt sometimes. Fast. I wake up. I assess the immediate threat. I try to figure out where I was last time I uploaded a mindmap. This time I woke up in the middle of a bunch of dead bodies, but there was no threat that I could tell." He cocked his head, curious. "Haven't you ever lost time before? Not even a week? Surely you've died between backups."

"Yes," she admitted. "But I've never woken up in danger, or in the wake of danger."

"You're still not in danger," he said. "That we know of."

She stared at him.

"*Immediate* danger," he amended. "I'm not going to stab you right here in the hall. All of our danger right now consists of problems that we can likely fix. Lost memories, broken computer, finding a murderer. Just a little work and we'll be back on track."

"You are the strangest kind of optimist," she said. "All the same, I'd like to continue to freak out if you don't mind."

"Try to keep it together. You don't want to devolve into whatever Paul has become," he suggested as he continued down the hall.

Maria followed, glad that he wasn't behind her. "I'm keeping it together. I'm here, aren't I?"

"You'll probably feel better when you've had a shower and some food," he said. "Not to mention clothes."

They were both covered only in the tacky, drying synth-amneo fluid. Maria had never wanted a shower more in her life. "Aren't you a little worried about what we're going to find when we find your body?" she asked.

Hiro looked back at her. "I learned a while back not to mourn the old shells. If we did, we'd get more and more dour with each life. In fact, I think that may be Wolfgang's problem." He frowned. "Have you ever had to clean up the old body by yourself?"

Maria shook her head. "No. It was disorienting; she was looking at me, like she was blaming me. It's still not as bad as not knowing what happened, though."

"Or who happened," said Hiro. "It did have a knife."

"And it was violent," Maria said. "It could be one of us."

"Probably was, or else we should get excited about a first-contact situation. Or second contact, if the first one went so poorly…" Hiro said, then sobered. "But truly anything could have gone wrong. Someone could have woken up from cryo and gone mad, even. Computer glitch messed with the mindmap. But it's probably easily explained, like someone got caught cheating at poker. Heat of the moment, someone hid an ace, the doctor flipped the table—"

"It's not funny," Maria said softly. "It wasn't madness and it wasn't an off-the-cuff crime. If that had happened, we wouldn't have the grav drive offline. We wouldn't be missing decades of memories. IAN would be able to tell us what's going on. But someone—one of us—wanted us dead, and they also messed with the personality backups. Why?"

"Is that rhetorical? Or do you really expect me to know?" he asked.

"Rhetorical," grumbled Maria. She shook her head to clear it. A strand of stiff black hair smacked her in the face, and she winced. "It could have been two people. One killed us, one messed with the memories."

"True," he said. "We can probably be sure it was premeditated. Anyway, the captain was right. Let's be cautious. And let's make a pact. I'll promise not to kill you and you promise not to kill me. Deal?"

Maria smiled in spite of herself. She shook his hand. "I promise. Let's get going before the captain sends someone after us."

The door to medbay was rimmed in red lights, making it easy to find if ill or injured. With the alert, the lights were blinking, alternating between red and yellow. Hiro stopped abruptly at the entrance. Maria smacked into the back of him in a collision that sent them spinning gently like gears in a clock, making him turn to face the hall while she swung around to see what had stopped him so suddenly.

The contact could have been awkward except for the shock of the scene before them.

In the medbay, a battered, older version of Captain Katrina de la Cruz lay in a bed. She was unconscious but very much alive, hooked up to life support, complete with IV, breathing tubes, and monitors. Her face was a mess of bruises, and her right arm was in a cast. She was strapped to the bed, which was held to the floor magnetically.

"I thought we all died," Hiro said, his voice soft with wonder.

"For us all to wake up, we should have. I guess I hit the emergency resurrection switch anyway," Maria said, pushing herself off the doorjamb to float into the room closer to the captain.

"Too bad you can't ask yourself," Hiro said drily.

Penalties for creating a duplicate clone were stiff, usually resulting in the extermination of the older clone. Although with several murders to investigate, and now an assault, Wolfgang would probably not consider this particular crime a priority to punish.

"No one is going to be happy about this," Hiro said, pointing at the unconscious body of the captain. "Least of all Katrina. What are we going to do with two captains?"

"But this could be good," Maria said. "If we can wake her up, we might find out what happened."

"I can't see her agreeing with you," he said.

A silver sheet covered the body and drifted lazily where the straps weren't holding it down. The captain's clone was still, the breathing tube the only sound.

Maria floated to the closet on the far side of the room. She grabbed a handful of large jumpsuits—they would be too short for Wolfgang, too tight for the doctor, and too voluminous for Maria, but they would do for the time being—and pulled a folded wheelchair from where it drifted in the dim light filtering into the closet.

She handed a jumpsuit to Hiro and donned hers, unself-consciously not turning away. When humans reach midlife, they may reach a level of maturity where they cease to give a damn what someone thinks about their bodies. Multiply that a few times and you have the modesty (or lack thereof) of the average clone. The first time Maria had felt the self-conscious attitude lifting, it had been freeing. The mind-set remained with many clones even as their bodies reverted to youth, knowing that a computer-built body was closer to a strong ideal than they could have ever created with diet and exercise.

The sobbing engineer, Paul, had been the most ashamed clone Maria had ever seen.

The jumpsuit fabric wasn't as soft as Maria's purple engineering jumpsuits back in her quarters, but she was at least warmer. She wondered when they would finally be allowed to eat and go back to their quarters for a shower and some sleep. Waking up took a lot out of a clone.

Hiro was already clothed and back over by the captain's body, peering at her face. Maria maneuvered her way over to him using the wall handles. He looked grim, his usually friendly face now reflecting the seriousness of the situation.

"I don't suppose we can just hide this body?" he asked. "Recycle it before anyone finds out? Might save us a lot of headache in the future."

Maria checked the vital-signs readout on the computer. "I don't think she's a body yet. Calling her a body and disposing of it is something for the courts, not us."

"What courts?" he asked as Maria took the wheelchair by the handles and headed for the door. "There are six of us!"

"Seven," Maria reminded, jerking her head backward to indicate the person in the medbay. "Eight if we can get IAN online. Even so it's a matter for the captain and IAN to decide, not us."

"Well, then you get to go spread the latest bad news."

"I'm not ready to deal with Wolfgang right now," Maria said. "Or hear the captain tear Paul a new asshole. Besides, we have to check the grav drive."

"Avoiding Wolfgang sounds like a good number one priority," said Hiro. "In fact, if I could interview my last clone, he probably avoided Wolfgang a lot too."

The bridge of the starship *Dormire* was an impressive affair, with a seat for the captain and one for the pilot at the computer terminals that sat on the floor, but a ladder ran up the wall right beside the room entrance to lead to a few comfortable benches bolted to the wall, making it the perfect place to observe the universe as the ship crept toward light speed. The room itself comprised a dome constructed from diamond, so that you could see in a 270-degree arc. The helm looked like a great glass wart sitting on the end of the ship, but it did allow a lovely view of the universe swinging around you as the grav drive rotated the ship. Now, with the drive off, space seemed static, even though they were moving at a fraction of the speed of light through space.

It could make someone ill, honestly. Deep space all around, even the floor being clear. Maria remembered seeing it on the tour of the ship, but this was the first time she had seen it away from Luna. The first time in this clone's memory, anyway.

Drawing the eye away from the view, the terminals, and the pilot's station and benches, Hiro's old body floated near the top of the dome, tethered by a noose to the bottom of one of the benches. His face was red and his open eyes bulged.

"Oh. There—" He paused to swallow, then continued. "—there I am." He turned away, looking green.

"I don't know what I expected, but suicide wasn't it," Maria said softly, looking into the swollen, anguished face. "I was actually wondering if you survived too."

"I didn't expect hanging," he said. "I don't think I expected anything. It's all real to me now." He covered his mouth with his hand.

Maria knew too much sympathy could make a person on the edge lose control, so she turned firm. "Do not puke in here. I already have to clean up the cloning bay, and you've seen what a nightmare that is. Don't give me more to clean up."

He glared at her, but some color returned to his face. He did not look up again.

Something drifted gently into the back of Maria's head. She grabbed at it and found a brown leather boot. The hanged corpse wore its mate.

"This starts to build a time line," Maria said. "You had to be hanged when we still had gravity. I guess that's good."

Hiro still had his back to the bridge, face toward the hallway. His eyes were closed and he breathed deeply. She put her hand on his shoulder. "Come on. We need to get the drive back on."

Hiro turned and focused on the terminal, which was blinking red.

"Are you able to turn it on without IAN?" Maria asked.

"I should be. IAN could control everything, but if he goes offline, we're not dead in the water. Was that my shoe?" The last question was offhand, as if it meant nothing.

"Yes." Maria drifted toward the top of the helm and took a closer look at the body. It was hard to tell since the face was so distorted by the hanging, but Hiro looked different from the rest of the crew. They all looked as if decades had passed since they had launched from Luna station. But Hiro looked exactly as he did now, as if freshly vatted.

"Hey, Hiro, I think you must have died at least once during the trip. Probably recently. This is a newer clone than the others," she said. "I think we're going to have to start writing the weird stuff down."

Hiro made a sound like an animal caught in a trap. All humor had left him. His eyes were hard as he finally glanced up at her and the clone. "All right. That's it."

"That's what?"

"The last straw. I'm officially scared now."

"Now? It took you this long to get scared?" Maria asked, pulling herself to the floor. "With everything else we're dealing with, *now* you're scared?"

Hiro punched at the terminal, harder than Maria thought was necessary. Nothing happened. He crossed his arms, and then uncrossed them, looking as if arms were some kind of new limb he wasn't sure what to do with. He took the boot from Maria and slid it over his own foot.

"I was just managing to cope with the rest," he said. "That was something happening to all of you. I wasn't involved. I wasn't a Saturday Night Gorefest. I was here as a supporting, friendly face. I was here to make you laugh. *Hey, Hiro will always cheer us up.*"

Maria put her hand on his shoulder and looked him in the eyes. "Welcome to the panic room, Hiro. We have to support each other. Take a deep breath. Now we need to get the drive on and then tell the captain and Wolfgang."

"You gotta be desperate if you want to tell Wolfgang," he said, looking as if he was trying and failing to force a smile.

"And when you get the drive on, can you find out what year it is, check on the cargo, maybe reach IAN from here?" Maria asked. "With everything else that's happened, it might be nice to come back with a little bit of good news. Or improved news."

Hiro nodded, his mouth closed as if trying to hold in something he would regret saying. Or perhaps a scream. He floated over to his pilot's chair and strapped himself in. The console screen continued to blink bright red at him. "Thanks for that warning, IAN, we hadn't noticed the drive was gone."

He typed some commands and poked at the touch screen. A warning siren began to bleat through the ship, telling everyone floating in zero-g that gravity was incoming. Hiro poked at the screen a few more times, and then typed at a terminal, his face growing darker as he did so. He made some calculations and then sighed loudly, sitting back in the chair and putting his hands over his face.

"Well," he said. "Things just got worse."

Maria heard the grav drive come online, and the ship shuddered as the engines started rotating the five-hundred-thousand-GRT ship. She took hold of the ladder along the back wall to guide her way to the bench so she wouldn't fall once the gravity came back.

"What now?" she said. "Are we off course?"

"We've apparently been in space for twenty-four years and seven months." He paused. "And nine days."

Maria did the math. "So it's 2493."

"By now we should be a little more than three light-years away from home. Far outside the event horizon of realistic communication with Earth. And we are. But we're also twelve degrees off course."

"That... sorry, I don't get where the hell that is. Can you say it in maintenance-officer language?"

"We are slowing down and turning. I'm not looking forward to telling the captain," he said, unstrapping himself from the seat. He glanced up at his own body drifting at the end of the noose like a grisly kite. "We can cut that down later."

"What were we thinking? Why would we go off course?" Maria thought aloud as they made their way through the hallway, staying low to prepare for gravity as the ship's rotation picked up.

"Why murder the crew, why turn off the grav drive, why spare the captain, why did I kill myself, and why did I apparently feel the need to take off one shoe before doing it?" Hiro said. "Just add it to your list, Maria. I'm pretty sure we are officially fucked, no matter what the answers are."